An author of more than ~~adults (more than seventy~~ **Kay Johnson** writes a~~books of gripping romantic~~ bestselling author and an eight-time finalist for the Romance Writers of America RITA® Award, she won a RITA® Award in 2008. A former librarian, Janice raised two daughters in a small town north of Seattle, Washington.

Michele Hauf is a *USA TODAY* bestselling author who has been writing romance, action-adventure and fantasy stories for more than twenty years. France, musketeers, vampires and faeries usually feature in her stories. And if Michele followed the adage "write what you know," all her stories would have snow in them. Fortunately, she steps beyond her comfort zone and writes about countries and creatures she has never seen. Find her on Facebook, Twitter and at michelehauf.com.

Also by Janice Kay Johnson

Hide the Child
A Hometown Boy
Anything for Her
Where It May Lead
From This Day
On One Frosty Night
More Than Neighbours
Because of a Girl
A Mother's Claim
Plain Refuge

Also by Michele Hauf

The Witch's Quest
The Witch and the Werewolf
An American Witch in Paris
The Billionaire Werewolf's Princess
Tempting the Dark
This Strange Witchery
Ghost Wolf
Moonlight and Diamonds
The Vampire's Fall
Enchanted by the Wolf

Discover more at millsandboon.co.uk

TRUSTING
THE SHERIFF

JANICE KAY JOHNSON

STORM
WARNING

MICHELE HAUF

MILLS & BOON

First Published in Great Britain 2019
by Mills & Boon, an imprint of HarperCollins*Publishers*
1 London Bridge Street, London, SE1 9GF

Trusting the Sheriff © 2019 Janice Kay Johnson
Storm Warning © 2019 Michele Hauf

ISBN: 978-0-263-27406-6

0319

MIX
Paper from
responsible sources
FSC **FSC® C007454**
www.fsc.org

TRUSTING
THE SHERIFF

JANICE KAY JOHNSON

My thanks to Victoria Curran for persuading me to try to write an Amish story! Here I am on my third, still having fun.

Prologue

Footsteps. Night made murky by filtered light. A stench. Agony in her head.

"Why? Why would you do this?" Angry male voice. She knew it, but her mind wouldn't quite supply a face or name. "Tell me before—"

Gunfire blasted. Once, twice.

She managed to fumble a hand toward her unsnapped holster. Empty. Why was it empty? She could see booted feet move, the back of someone crouching over—she couldn't remember who lay still now.

Darkness beckoned and she moaned. When the footsteps approached, it took everything she had to open her eyes a slit. The toes of the boots were inches away. He must be looking down at her.

From somewhere, a voice yelled, "Hey! I called 9-1-1."

Crack. The impact of the bullet bounced her body on the pavement. Pain blossomed like hot red lava.

I'm dead.

Crack.

Chapter One

A hammer pounded Abigail Baker's head. Again. Again. Wasn't the nail in yet?

Pain washed her body, but with her eyes still closed, she homed in on the hot points. Shoulder. Middle of her chest beneath her breasts. Spike through her head.

Someone had applied super glue to her eyelids, but she succeeded in prying them open. She stared blankly upward at an unfamiliar ceiling, then rolled her eyes to see to each side. Her head let her know that she really shouldn't move it.

Curtains surrounded the bed. Abby could just see an IV pole out of the corner of her eye. White, waffle-weave blankets covered her.

Hospital.

The curtain rings rattled and a sturdily built middle-aged woman appeared at the side of her bed. Beaming, she said, "You're awake! Oh, my. How do you feel, dear?"

Abby worked her bone-dry mouth and finally moaned, "Hurt."

"You're with us. Excellent. I need you to wait just a few minutes for the pain relief. The doctor will want to talk to you first."

A hint of temper increased the force of the hammer blows. Note to self: *Don't get mad.* She sank into a near doze, feeling every beat of her heart, conscious of her shallow breaths, floating on the sea of pain.

"Abigail?" A man's voice.

It was a fraction easier to open her eyes this time.

"I'm told you hurt."

"Yes."

"Can you tell me where? Or show me?"

She tried to move her mouth.

"Let me give you some ice chips."

He gently tipped some into her mouth. The cool moisture was nirvana. While she sucked on them, she lifted her right hand, seeing that the IV was in it. She studied it for a minute, then touched her head, her shoulder—feeling a thick dressing—and her breastbone—no padding. Why not, when it hurt, too?

"Good," he said with obvious satisfaction.

She had to work to focus on his face. He was lean, blond with grey hair at his temples. Lived-in face.

"Why am I here?"

Hazel eyes narrowed a flicker. "Do you remember what happened?"

Impatient, Abby made the mistake of starting to shake her head. Pain exploded, and she groaned.

He was suddenly closer. "There's a button here you can push when you need pain relief." He said some more things, but she didn't listen, because he'd put the button in her hand. She squeezed it, and felt relief flooding from her neck to her fingers and toes. Another squeeze, and her headache receded enough for her to think about what he'd asked—and what she'd asked.

"No."

"What's the last thing you do remember?"

That took some concentration. "Laundry. Basement of my building. Someone dumped my clothes and stole the dryer cycle."

He grinned. "I'd remember that, too."

"Partner—Neal—worried about something." After being promoted almost a year ago from patrol to detective in the Major Crimes division of the Kansas City, Missouri, police department, she'd been paired with Neal Walker. His previous partner had just retired. The two of them hit it off, even socializing. Abby and his new wife had become friends. "Wouldn't say." She recalled telling him she'd help, his crooked grin. His voice, tenser than usual. *Let me make sure I'm not imagining things.* He'd dropped her off by her car. And then...

Abby stared into space. And then... There was nothing. Not a single thing. Panic soared and she struggled to sit up.

She and the doctor wrestled briefly. She was so ridiculously weak, he was able to ease her down.

"You need to stay calm," he said soothingly. "Don't worry. People often lose their memories of a period surrounding traumatic events. Right now, your body has to deal with the physical injuries. You've been in a coma, so it's not surprising that your brain isn't entirely booted up yet. Do you understand?"

"Yes." She didn't even blink as she stared at him, afraid to sink into that black void. "How long...?"

"You've been here for three days. We're really happy to see you regaining consciousness."

"What...happened?"

"Your injuries? You were shot twice. Fortunately,

you were wearing a Kevlar vest. It didn't stop the bullet in your shoulder, but the shot to your chest might well have killed you. Instead, you have only severe bruising and a cracked sternum. It also appears that when you fell, you struck your head against the corner of a dumpster. I understand you were found in an alley."

Dread supplanted the panic. "Neal?"

The doctor took a step back, his expression becoming guarded. "Your partner?"

"Yes."

"I think I'll let your Sergeant Donahue tell you about that. He's been haunting the place."

She knew. She *knew*.

She managed to turn her face away.

HER DOCTOR DIDN'T allow any visitors until the following day, after they'd moved her from intensive care to a room she currently had to herself. She could only imagine how frustrated Donahue was to be thwarted. Given the severity of her head injury and the length of time she'd spent in a coma, Dr. Sanderlin insisted she rest, use pain medication as needed and not worry.

Yes, he actually said that again. After patting her hand. "Don't worry."

Abby would have done nothing *but* worry if she hadn't felt so rotten. If she didn't push the little button, her head felt like a rocket right at blastoff, spewing fire. If she did use the stuff, she dozed. Quite honestly, she didn't feel much better the day after regaining consciousness, but when she was capable of thinking clearly, she chased herself in circles. What could possibly have happened? If Neal was alive, why wouldn't the doctor have told her so? Or said, *Gosh, I don't know who Neal is?*

And why couldn't she remember?

An orderly had just removed her breakfast tray when she heard a cleared throat and Sergeant Michael Donahue stepped into view. He supervised her unit of detectives, and they all felt lucky. He could be gruff, but never failed to support them against higher-ups or the public when needed. He was smart and capable of compassion, and his detectives very rarely encountered a difficulty he hadn't already met and overcome in his lengthy career.

He'd turned fifty-four back in February, when they threw him a surprise party. Donahue was still a good-looking man, his gray hair short but not buzz-cut. His wife liked to run her fingers through it, he'd tell them with a hidden smile. He dressed well, his suits appearing custom-made to fit his tall body and bulky shoulders, but within an hour or two at the station, he invariably looked rumpled. Abby had met his wife, Jennifer, who was known to roll her eyes on occasion when she dropped by the station and first set eyes on him.

"Abby," he said, his face creased with what she took for concern. "You scared us."

She managed a weak smile.

He pulled a chair close to the bed and lowered himself into it. "Shot twice."

"So they tell me."

The lines on his forehead deepened. "The doctor claims you have no memory of what happened."

"The doctor's right," she said huskily. "I have this huge blank." Her hand rose to touch her temple.

He studied her in silence for longer than she understood. Then he leaned back in the chair and said, "That's a problem for us. The...scene where you were found is puzzling, to put it mildly. I've been hoping you can tell us what occurred."

She gave her head a very careful shake. "I can't. All I know is that I was found in an alley."

"Neal was with you," Donahue said, "also shot twice. Unlike you, he didn't survive."

Yes, she'd known, but the news threw a punch anyway. Abby felt tears burn in her eyes. "How?"

His face hadn't softened at all. She didn't see the expected sympathy. Instead, he had the kind of stony expression suspects saw.

"It appears that you shot Neal with your service weapon and he shot you with his. You apparently struck your head on the dumpster as you fell. You need to tell me if you've been having issues with him, or if he had a problem with how you handled any investigation."

"How *I* handled...?" She gaped at him. "You think we quarreled?"

"How else can you explain the physical evidence?" he said implacably.

"I can't explain anything! Neal and Laura are— were—my best friends! We never disagreed."

"Then why would you have shot him?"

"Did you test for gunpowder residue on my hand?"

He hesitated. "We did, and didn't find any. But the only fingerprints found on your Glock were yours."

Something was very wrong.

"And Neal's?"

"The same."

"There had to have been someone else there," she

said, having trouble believing he'd suspect either of them. "You *know* both of us."

"I've seen cops go bad before. It stinks, but it happens. If Neal did, I need you to tell me."

She looked right into his eyes. "I'll never believe he would."

His graying eyebrows rose, obviating any need for him to say what she knew he was thinking: *Then you have to be the bad apple.*

SEVERAL OF ABBY'S fellow detectives came by to see her. Most of them had apparently gathered here at the hospital after she and Neal were found in that alley, holding vigil for her after they learned he was dead. She was told that Sergeant Donahue had worked the scene himself, along with an experienced detective, Sam Kirk. The CSI team had gathered trace evidence—too much of it. Alleys ranked right up there as the most impossible scenes. Employees from businesses along the block came out regularly to drop garbage into a dumpster or smoke a cigarette, grinding the butt out with a shoe and leaving it where it lay. Homeless people lurked, scrounging in the dumpsters, sleeping behind them, having sex and getting into fights. Cars cut through, passengers or drivers tossing litter out windows. Rats frequented the alley, as did stray cats.

The man who'd heard the gunshots and had the guts to run toward them rather than away would have left his own trace evidence. He claimed to have seen a dark shape standing over her, a man—he thought male—who ran away when he called out.

Sergeant Donahue was clearly not convinced the sole

witness hadn't conjured the sight of a villain to make himself appear more heroic.

Laura Walker never came. Abby called her a week after she'd regained consciousness.

"Laura? This is Abby. I wanted to tell you—" She was talking to dead air. A woman she'd considered a good friend had learned of Sergeant Donahue's suspicions and immediately bought into them. What other explanation was there?

That was the first time in a very long while that Abby let herself cry—but only after the lights had gone out and she was alone. Better than falling asleep. Nightmares grabbed her the minute she dropped off. They were lurid and felt important. She'd wake gasping with shock and fear, but couldn't remember any details.

Visits from her coworkers tailed off. They were busy; she understood that. But she wondered if they had any idea how isolated she felt when she trudged up and down the halls of the hospital, trying to regain enough strength to go home. Nurses and orderlies fussed over her, but that was their job. Why hadn't she made more friends? The kind who would stand by her?

But she knew. She'd never quite fit in, wherever she was. Not as a child, migrating between her grandparents' farm and a "normal" life with her silent, wounded father. Certainly not in college, where the sense of morality she'd absorbed from the deeply religious Amish part of her family separated her from other students. And then she became a cop, joining a small minority who were women.

Maybe she hadn't really tried. Was she more comfortable alone? she asked herself, troubled.

Five days after she'd woken from the coma, Dr. Sanderlin told her she was ready to leave the hospital.

"I'll have a social worker stop by to help you form a plan," he assured her. "If you live alone...?"

"Yes."

"You need to have someone around to help you. I'd rather not extend your hospital stay if we can come up with a solution, but I'm not willing to send you off to pass out or fall or have a traumatic flashback where nobody will see. If you don't have family you can go to, I recommend at least a week in a rehab facility."

Her father... No. They stayed in touch, but conversations were always stiff, awkward. She hadn't even let him know yet that she'd been shot. He'd grown up in foster care, and now had no family but her. Her mother's parents, who'd half raised her, were gone, too, but Aenti Nancy and Onkel Eli would take her in. She knew they would. The Amish were like that. They loved visitors, and they took care of the people they loved. Even people they didn't love. If their church community included an irascible old woman who was difficult to like, they took care of her anyway, with generosity, humor and no grumbling. She'd heard her grandfather—her *grossdaadi*—say, "How would we learn to forgive, if the Lord didn't give us cranky neighbors?" Then he'd grin. "And teenagers."

Of course, she wasn't one of them, never had been, really, even though she'd attended Amish schools for weeks or even, once, several months at a time. She dressed "plain" when she was with her Amish family, grew so accustomed to having no television, she'd never watched much even as an adult. Her grandparents might have hoped she'd choose to be baptized to join their faith, but weren't surprised when she didn't. Especially after what happened to—

No, the past had nothing to do with the here and now. She needed to focus on her next step. Physical recovery, Abby could already tell, was going to be slow. Plus, even if she bounced out of bed feeling great, going back to the job clearly wasn't an option until she could explain what had happened that night in the alley.

If she ever could. The doctor had explained that her memory of the missing week might return in its entirety, she might recall pieces of it…or it might never come back.

Her aunt and uncle would take her in without question, pamper her even as they set her to doing chores she could handle. The idea of sitting at the long table in that big farm kitchen, peeling potatoes or rolling out pie dough while the women chattered and the younger children helped to the extent they were able sounded heavenly to Abby right now.

Her smile felt rusty, but real. *Heavenly?* That might've been a pun, but it was also truth.

She'd call and leave a message on the machine in the phone shanty out by the road that passed her family's farm, and hope Onkel Eli checked it soon so that her arrival wasn't a complete surprise.

Unfortunately, she didn't think she was up to the meandering pace, clouds of exhaust and swaying ride of a bus. Now all she needed was to find a ride.

"LEFT UP AHEAD." All ten families who lived on this gravel road were Amish. Abby felt sure Aenti Nancy would have told her if someone had had to sell out. She wrote to Abby weekly, long, chatty missives that always made her feel as if she mattered.

Despite the bands of pain tightening around her head, excitement fizzed inside her. Abby leaned forward until the seat belt put uncomfortable pressure on her shoulder and chest. She hadn't been here since Thanksgiving, having volunteered to work over the Christmas holidays so that a detective who had children could take the time off. The farm felt like home, more so than her father's house had since her mother died. Why hadn't she visited in the spring? It had been nine, no, ten months since she'd made it to see her family here.

Sam Kirk, the detective working her case, had offered to drive her. She'd fully expected him to grill her during the two-hour drive, but had decided not to look a gift horse in the mouth. Besides, if he could ask the question that would unlock her memories, she'd be as glad as he would.

Sam was in his late thirties or early forties and tended to be quiet, but when he spoke, people listened. He had a presence, she'd long since decided, even though he was lean and not above average height. Abby had always felt shy around him, and hadn't yet had occasion to work closely with him.

When he'd first picked her up, he drove her to her apartment and helped her pack a duffel bag full of clothes. Without complaint, he also carried a tote bag of books she kept meaning to read out to the car.

Returning, he nodded at her laptop. "You'll want that."

"No electricity where I'm going." Seeing his puzzlement, she had to explain why the Amish refused to be on the grid, linked with people who didn't share their faith.

He looked stunned. "No TV? But…the Chiefs' first regular-season game is next weekend."

She laughed at him, relaxing for the first time.

When he offered to come back to dispose of any foods that would rot while she was away and empty the kitchen trash, Abby handed over her key. If he could figure out her laptop password, he was welcome to browse her emails and files. He'd probably search her apartment, but she didn't care. She had nothing to hide. In fact…she didn't have much at all.

The first fifteen minutes of the drive had passed in silence. Then he broke it. "The sergeant is doing his job, you know."

She stiffened. "I know."

"I go with my gut more than he does, and my gut tells me whatever happened in that alley was a setup."

Good cop, bad cop was her first thought. She knew she was right, but was still susceptible enough to kindness and a pretense of belief in her to give her a lump in her throat. "Thank you for saying that."

He nodded, and asked about physical therapy and whether her headaches were receding. Abby gave him the upbeat answers, refusing to admit that the vibration of the moving vehicle and the occasional bumps had her thinking about hammers again. Just sitting upright tired her.

But seeing the farm now made her forget her tiredness and every ache and pain. She exclaimed, "Oh, the corn looks almost ripe!"

White-painted board fencing separated the fields from the gravel road that showed the narrow tracks

made by the steel wheels of Amish buggies. The corn
stalks stood tall, topped with fluffy yellow silks surrounding the ears. Last year, corn crops throughout the
Midwest had dried up with the drought. Aenti Nancy
mentioned the weather in every one of her letters, although she would never complain if it were too dry or
wet. The Amish accepted God's purpose, whether they
understood it or not. That didn't mean they wouldn't
be rejoicing in what promised to be a bumper crop this
year.

"Do they grow anything else?" Sam asked, turning into the narrow lane leading up a gentle slope to
the house.

"Yes, of course," she said distractedly. "Raspberries,
strawberries, soybeans. They have a good-sized orchard
of fruit trees, and two black walnut trees. And a kitchen
garden, of course. Plus, my aunt and uncle raise a few
steers each year, and keep chickens. Most of their food
comes from the farm."

He shot her a look from dark eyes. "I'd never have
guessed you came from a background like this. You
actually wear that getup? Bonnet and all?"

"Yes, when I'm here. I didn't grow up Amish, you
know. I just…" There was no reason to explain. She
continued, "They wouldn't say anything if I came for a
short visit and wore jeans and T-shirts, but I don't." She
explained simply, "It wouldn't be respectful."

By the time the car rolled to a stop in front of the
white-painted farmhouse with a wraparound porch,
two women had rushed out of the front door and a man
strode toward them from the huge barn.

Abby scrabbled for the seat-belt release and the car
door handle at the same time, eager to leap out.

Sam's hand on her arm slowed her. "Take it easy, Detective. You don't want to collapse at their feet."

She didn't. She climbed out very carefully and, eyes stinging, fell into her aunt's arms. "Aenti Nancy."

"So glad we were to hear you were coming!" her aunt exclaimed. "Excited, we are."

Abby gently pulled free to greet first her cousin Rose, then her uncle, a tall, stern man who nonetheless hugged her and murmured, "You have stayed away too long."

She hugged him back, managing to knock his summer straw hat off. He laughed when he bent to pick it up. Abby transferred her gaze to Rose, who was pregnant. Very pregnant.

"Oh, my! Aenti Nancy told me, but I didn't know you were so far along."

Brown-haired, gray-eyed and tending to plumpness, Rose wrinkled her nose. "The midwife sent me to the doctor for an ultrasound. I'm having twins." She splayed her hands on her sizeable belly. "I still have three months to go, but the doctor said I won't make it that long."

"Girls or boys?"

"One of each, he thought." She beamed. "I drove myself over today even though Matthew doesn't like me going out now, but to have you home!"

Hearing her genuine delight, Abby felt her tears spilling over at last. She used the backs of her hands to swipe at her wet cheeks, introduced Sam to her family and allowed her aunt to usher them into the house.

"Sit, sit!" she told both Abby and Sam, who appeared bemused and a little uncomfortable. A cup of coffee and raspberry pie topped with fresh cream proved irresistible to him, however, and although he stood strong enough to repeat several times that he couldn't stay for dinner, he did accept containers of food that would probably feed him for several days.

His mouth quirked as he said goodbye to Abby. "Don't put on too much weight while you're here. Wouldn't want you to get slow on your feet."

She laughed and said, "Thank you. For bringing me home. It can't be what you wanted to do on your day off." Assuming, her cynical side reminded her, that this hadn't actually been a working day for him. Good cop, remember?

"I was glad to do it," he said, and left.

Abby sat at the kitchen table, inhaling the smell of good things cooking, very aware of Rose reaching out to clasp her hand, her aunt fussing at the stove and Onkel Eli smiling gently at her from his place at the head of the table.

Home.

Chapter Two

Phone to his ear, Caleb Tanner leaned back in his large desk chair and stacked his booted feet on his desk. He thought it unlikely Mike Donahue had called in the middle of a working day for no reason but to catch up, but so far, all they'd done was chitchat—his mother's description for meaningless talk. Fortunately, he was a patient man. He didn't have anywhere he needed to be.

He and Donahue had known each other as Kansas City PD officers, partnering together in the drug-enforcement unit for a couple of years. Undercover work was hell on marriage or having a family—or even meeting a girlfriend or buddies at a bar to watch football games. Caleb, for one, had decided he wasn't made for a high-adrenaline lifestyle. He didn't know what motivated Donahue, but both had ultimately made the move to Homicide, where they'd stayed friends of a sort despite the twenty-year difference between them. They hadn't been close enough to really stay in touch after Caleb left KCPD and took the job as sheriff of this rural northeast-Missouri county.

Which made today's phone call a puzzle.

"You're not bored out of your skull yet?" Donahue asked him.

Thinking of his last few wildly busy days, Caleb laughed. "Don't have time to get bored. Do you have any idea how shorthanded a department like mine is? When I'm not juggling too few officers to cover shifts, I'm riding patrol to fill a gap, or giving talks to community organizations. I respond to accidents. My two detectives need guidance. When we have anything halfway serious happen, I usually take lead. I give press conferences, deal with the county commissioners, unhappy citizens. Come to think of it, it's not all that different from heading a homicide squad, except you can keep out of the public eye."

"Good thing, considering my general lack of tact."

With a grin, Caleb said, "Won't disagree." When Donahue didn't make an immediate comeback, Caleb remarked, "Saw on the news that you had a couple of detectives shot a week or so ago. They yours?"

The sergeant gusted a sigh. "Yeah, and that's really why I called. I'm hoping you'll do something for me."

Caleb's eyebrows climbed. Now, this was unexpected. "And what would that be?" he asked, trying to hide his caution.

"Has to do with the shooting." Donahue gave him more detail about the ugly scene in the alley than news outlets had reported. Two young detectives—partners—who'd to all appearances shot each other. One dead, one badly injured but surviving.

"The survivor is a woman," Donahue said grimly. "She came up from patrol not quite a year ago. Seemed to be catching on fine. Detective Walker said he was happy with the pairing. Still, I had a lot of faith in him, and she's new. I think she's corrupt, and murdered him when he found out she was involved in something bad."

"You're thinking drugs?"

"We both know that's the likely answer. They were in the Prospect corridor, behind a bar where we've made more than a few arrests for drugs and prostitution. So far as I can determine, there was no reason they should have been there. I can't find a connection between the bar or nearby businesses and any of the investigations they were conducting."

Caleb frowned. The neighborhood surrounding the intersection of Prospect and Independence ranked as one of the most dangerous areas in Kansas City.

He asked questions; Donahue answered them with seeming frankness. No, he had no concrete evidence that Detective Baker had gone bad.

"I'm going with my gut here," he admitted.

"What's *she* say?"

"She claims amnesia. Can't remember a damn thing. I don't buy it."

"I've seen people with post-traumatic amnesia," Caleb said neutrally.

"This is just too convenient for me."

Inclined to agree with that assessment, Caleb still reserved judgment. It happened, in particular after a head injury, which he understood the woman detective had suffered. He had no trouble understanding Mike Donahue's frustration, though.

He took his feet off the desk so that he could rock forward and reach for his coffee cup. After a swallow, he asked, "So what's this favor?"

"Baker left the hospital yesterday to stay with family to recuperate. Aunt and uncle have a farm in your county. Sam Kirk drove her up there. You remember him, don't you?"

"Mostly by reputation," he said. The guy was a little older than Caleb, solid at his job so far as he knew.

"It's a strange setup, way I hear it. This family is Amish."

Stunned, he said, "What?"

"You heard me. I don't know how Baker is connected to these people. They don't usually want anything to do with law enforcement, from what I understood."

"You understand right. For the most part, they're law-abiding people. They keep to themselves and avoid mixing with government or police authority as much as possible. I've never heard of an Amishman—" and a woman was even more unlikely "—becoming a cop." Caleb shook his head in bemusement. There had to be a story here.

"Not sure she ever was Amish, just somehow related." Donahue cleared his throat. "I'm hoping you'd be willing to stop by, express concern and sympathy. Be good if you could get to know her, sound her out."

"Earn her trust."

"You got it."

The role sounded distasteful to Caleb, but if this woman had really shot her partner in cold blood because she'd taken payoffs to protect drug traffickers, he had no sympathy for her. He couldn't quite see her spilling to him, but people made mistakes. She might forget some detail of whatever story she'd given Donahue, tell Caleb something different. Anything was possible.

"I'll give it a shot," he said, then winced at his choice of words. "Email me everything you've got on the incident. Name and address of this aunt and uncle, too."

His day stayed busy. It wasn't until after dinner at home that he was able to open his laptop and read the police reports and autopsy report Donahue had sent, as promised. Crime scene photos were included. Caleb studied those carefully, but nothing jumped out at him.

Then he saw where Abigail Baker had taken refuge.

Caleb knew Eli and Nancy Kemp. They were good people, Eli a farmer who also worked in leather, making and repairing horse tack, essential to a people whose principal mode of transportation was horse and buggy. Frowning, Caleb tried to find an explanation of why this female cop would have been taken in by an Amishman who also happened to be a minister in his church district.

Nothing.

Abigail was a common name among the Amish, he reflected, but not as much these days among the Englisch, as the Amish labeled most Americans outside their faith.

Caleb sat thinking for a minute. Then he went online again and searched for news coverage of the shooting.

Nothing was materially different from what he'd seen covered on news channels at the time it happened, or what was contained in the information Donahue had sent him. There was a photo of the deceased, Detective Neal Walker. Good-looking fellow listed as thirty-five years old, newly married, a decorated cop.

Could he have been involved with his female partner, then dumped her to maintain his marriage? Say she stewed for a while, then they had it out?

It took him a little longer to find a decent picture of Detective Abigail Baker. Eventually, several popped up. The first was a posed image taken by a professional photographer, Baker dressed in her uniform, looking solemn. And, damn, she was a beautiful woman.

No, he decided after a minute, not exactly that; *pretty* might be a better word, or *cute*. She had a heart-shaped face with a high, wide forehead, a dainty, straight nose and a pretty mouth. Her hair, swept into a sleek arrangement of some kind on the back of her head, was the color of corn silk. Her eyes were sky blue.

Yeah, and he was descending to clichés to describe a lovely woman he didn't want to believe could be accepting payoffs from drug traffickers or the like.

He clicked on a couple of other photos, one taken at the scene of a four-car accident with fatalities, the other of her coming out of the courthouse after testifying in a trial. Both let him see that she had spectacular curves and was tall for a woman, likely five foot ten or so.

Caleb realized he could easily picture her in Amish dress and prayer *kapp*. Eli Kemp was blond and blue-eyed, in fact. Abigail's height would be unusual for an Amishwoman, however.

He went back to the first picture that only displayed her from the shoulders up, mesmerized by eyes he found…haunting. Her lips were shaped into a pleasant smile, but her eyes said something else altogether. She looked sad.

Caleb frowned at the photo for another minute and then closed his laptop. For Pete's sake, he knew better than to read so much into appearances, especially when that person had been caught at a particular moment by a camera. She might have felt queasy, or been worrying about a bill she hadn't paid…or a lover who'd dumped her.

Lucky that maintaining his cop's skepticism came naturally to him. Given his profession, it was a useful skill.

ABBY CLUTCHED THE handrail as she descended the stairs the following morning. She'd slept better than she had in the hospital, in part because of the blessed silence and the true darkness of countryside not brightened by electric lights, and with the moon at a quarter. The moment she'd sat up, dizziness had almost persuaded her to sink back onto her bed. But her aunt and uncle were early risers, and she didn't want to lounge in bed when she ought to be offering to help with daily chores. Still, donning a dress worn without a bra and fastened by straight pins rather than zippers and buttons felt like a huge effort. She managed, but gasped a few times when her healing wounds protested as she stretched too much. And her head… Would it *ever* stop pounding?

Dismayed by how weak she felt, she sat again on the edge of her bed to brush her hair, careful to avoid the still-painful lump, and bundle the mass into a bun she covered with the *kapp*. Of course, she couldn't check her appearance in a mirror; vanity was not encouraged by the Amish, probably why she'd never wasted much time worrying about her looks. In college she'd tried wearing makeup, but felt uncomfortable, not like herself at all, and had thrown it all away.

When she reached the first floor, Aenti Nancy popped out of the kitchen, exclaiming, "You should have stayed in bed! You have no color in your face." She shook her head. "Ah, well, you're this far. *Komm, komm.* You must have something to eat, feel better then, ain't so?"

Abby trailed her into the kitchen.

"Sit," her aunt ordered. "Tea?"

Abby actually had switched to coffee on an everyday basis, since it was nearly impossible to get a decent cup of tea at the station or a convenience store when she was patrolling, but she always reverted when home.

"Ja," she said in Deitsch, better known as Pennsylvania Dutch even though it was actually a Germanic dialect. *"Denke.* But I can get it..."

Aenti Nancy flapped her apron at her. "It's too soon. You must sit, let us take care of you. So good it is to have you home."

Abby felt her smile wobble. "It is good to be here. I can't thank you enough for taking me in. I didn't know where else to go."

"Always," her aunt said simply, good enough not to ask about Abby's father. "Did Rose tell you she plans to name her girl baby for you?"

"No. Oh, my." An unexpected emotional response sweeping over her, Abby imagined holding a baby girl, her namesake, blinking up at her, her cheeks rosy.

Aenti Nancy set a plate heaped with pancakes in front of her. Within moments, she added butter and syrup as well as a bowl of applesauce and a giant sweet roll, as if Abby could possibly eat so much.

Made-from-scratch pancakes were so much better than anything she got at chain restaurants, and the butter was real, the syrup made from blueberries grown here on the farm. The sweet roll, still warm from the oven, Abby could only call heavenly. Even so, the best she could do was a few bites, earning her a chiding from her aunt.

Sipping tea, she watched her aunt work, dashing between the pantry and the stove, occasionally trotting down to the cellar for jars of fruit or vegetables she'd preserved herself. Since her youngest daughter, Sarah, had married and moved out, Aenti Nancy was alone to cook and manage the house. Of the two sons still at home, one was only sixteen, the other, Isaac, in his early twenties, as yet unmarried.

She did allow Abby to string and snap green beans for the midday meal, and rinse marionberries before they went into a pie. Then she conceded that Abby could step out on the back porch and ring the bell to summon the men.

Onkel Eli, Isaac and lanky, shy Joshua came in the back door, hung their broad-brimmed hats on hooks just inside and went to the sink to wash their hands before sitting down at the long table. Aenti Nancy had what always seemed to Abby to be an enormous midday meal all ready. But Amish men and women alike did hard physical labor almost from the moment they rose in the morning, and needed the calories.

They all bowed their heads in silent prayer before beginning to dish up. Like a swarm of locusts, the men emptied serving dishes piled with mashed potatoes, gravy, green beans and applesauce, while the fried chicken and sourdough biscuits disappeared as fast. Still full from her abundant breakfast, Abby only nibbled. The marionberry pie met the same fate as the rest of the meal.

With a few words of thanks, the men went back to work. Her aunt rejected her offer to help clear the table or wash dishes, suggesting she ought to nap.

"I've been in bed for a week," she protested. "I might go sit out on the porch swing, or lie on the grass in the shade beneath the tree."

Aenti Nancy smiled. "*Ja*, that is a good idea. I remember as a girl seeing many things in the clouds as they floated in the sky. Castles and galloping horses and ships with full sails. All foolishness, but fun."

"Me, too. I haven't done that in a long time." Since she was a child, here at the farm.

Her aunt gave her a speaking look. "Then go."

This early September day had to be in the nineties, but a faint breeze stirred the leaves of the red maple tree rising close enough to the house to shade the front porch for a few hours of the day. Abby lowered herself slowly to the lawn right at the edge of the shade. The grass felt stiff beneath her hands. She brushed it back and forth, enjoying the texture. An apartment dweller now, when had she last sat on the grass? After a minute, she did lie back and gaze up at the canopy of leaves just starting to be tinged with autumn colors.

The sun blazed, and the sky was an arch of blue without a cloud for her to turn into a fantasy castle. Somehow, she didn't mind. Just lying here felt good. Except... her mind kept wanting to nudge at the dark wall separating her from important memories, like a tongue irresistibly drawn to poke at a loose tooth.

She pushed gently at the wall. It didn't so much as quiver. Ran at it and bounced painfully off, leaving her brain feeling bruised.

Wincing, she told herself to quit. The doctor had said her memories would come in their own time.

Aenti would have any number of biblical quotes to chide her for her impatience. In fact, one popped into her head.

This is the day which the Lord hath made; we will rejoice and be glad in it. Psalms 118. That couldn't be more fitting, she decided, relaxing.

The sun began to creep over her. She ought to move.

As fair-skinned as she was, she'd burn. But the heat had made her sleepy. She drifted, aware of distant voices, where her uncle and cousins worked, the bang of the screen on the back door closing once, the darting movement of a squirrel scuttling up the maple. Birds calling, and was that the buzz of a cicada? Her eyelids sank closed.

The sound of an approaching car, its throaty engine and the crunch of gravel beneath its tires, disrupted the utter peace of the afternoon. Abby pried open her eyes and rolled her head on the grass to see the long driveway. It wasn't as if cars didn't sometimes come down this road. Amish had Englisch friends, or at least acquaintances. Customers for their businesses. During their *rumspringa*, or running-around time, teenagers could take advantage of the freedom to ride in cars, and even use cell phones. This might be a friend of Joshua's.

It was actually a big, black SUV that turned into the Kemp driveway. Too large and expensive for any teenager to be driving, surely. Abby sat up, then wished she hadn't. She'd rather be unnoticed by this visitor. Left to her peace.

But instead of proceeding toward the huge, German-style barn, as the driver would have if he'd had business with her uncle, the SUV stopped closest to the house. A man got out on the far side of it and walked around to the front bumper.

A police officer, she saw with a jolt, tall, well built, his hair brown. He wore dark glasses, but she'd swear he was looking straight at her.

He turned, then, though, and she saw that Onkel Eli was coming from the barn to meet this man. The screen door rattled, and she suspected that her aunt was sneaking a peek out, too, to see who was here. Having a law-enforcement officer show up, that couldn't be a common occurrence. Well, besides her.

Her uncle and the stranger spoke briefly as she watched. Surely Onkel Eli would answer his questions and he'd go away.

But, no. They both turned to look at her now, then walked toward her. Inexplicably disturbed, Abby saw that the cop was a head taller than her uncle, broad shouldered, and moved with a confident, purposeful stride. The short sleeves of the moss green uniform shirt exposed strong brown forearms dusted with hair bleached almost blond. As he approached, she realized he had to be six foot four or taller. And she was a little bit embarrassed to notice what large hands he had, too.

She ought to get up, she realized, but knew the process would be awkward. She hated the idea of being on her hands and knees in front of this man. So she stayed put, squinting against the sun as she gazed up at them.

"Onkel?"

"*Ja*, niece, this is Sheriff Caleb Tanner. He has come to see you."

"To see me?" How strange.

"That's right." The sheriff crouched to be closer to her level, the fabric of his black uniform trousers pulling tight over powerful muscles. Resting an elbow on his thigh, he held out the other hand to her.

Feeling reluctant, she let him engulf and gently squeeze her hand.

"I'm sure Sheriff Tanner would like a cup of coffee and a slice of your *aenti*'s *schnitz* pie, *ja*?"

It almost sounded good, despite the nausea that returned unpredictably. Abby knew her aunt and uncle were dismayed by her scant appetite.

The sheriff smiled, momentarily brightening hazel eyes. He extended his hand again. "Let me help you up?"

She hesitated, but finally mumbled, "Thank you," and once again felt his grip close around her fingers. As he rose, he easily pulled her to her feet. She ended up disturbingly close to his big body and took a hasty step back. Her cheeks burned, and she tried to convince herself she'd gotten too much sun.

The three of them walked in together, using the front door because it was closest. Or perhaps because the sheriff was, if not a stranger to her aunt and uncle, an *auslander*, an outsider, for sure. Family and friends used the back door.

Abby would have hurried if she could, knowing what a mess she must be. *Strubly*, in Deitsch. *Disheveled*. Her apron was askew, hair tumbling out of the bun, and when she lifted a hand to her head, she realized her *kapp* had slid back. Then, of course, she must have bits of grass in her hair and on her skirts.

Once inside, she mumbled, "Excuse me for a minute," and hustled for the downstairs bathroom. A small mirror hung there, allowing members of the household to check to be sure their hair was smooth, or *kapps* and bonnets in the proper position. Indeed, she had to pick blades of grass out of her hair, which she finger-combed and reanchored before settling the filmy white *kapp* back on her head, leaving the ties dangling. She made a face at herself, dismayed by still pink cheeks.

By the time she reached the kitchen, Onkel Eli and the sheriff were both digging into huge pieces of *schnitz* pie, made from dried apples. The sheriff paused when he saw her, a forkful halfway to his mouth. His eyes narrowed slightly as his gaze swept over her, head to foot and back up again, bringing renewed warmth to her cheeks.

Her aunt spoke to her in Deitsch. "Sit, Abby. You must eat, too. Hot water I have on for tea. Eat yourself full, and no nonsense about you not being hungry. You hear me?" She slid a plate in front of Abby as she sat beside Onkel Eli.

"I hear you," Abby said meekly, in English.

Sheriff Tanner looked amused. Had he understood the Deitsch? Abby wondered.

"Your sergeant called me," he said. "Asked me to make sure you're doing okay. He was worried that they'd let you out of the hospital too soon."

"With family, she's better off," Aenti said fiercely.

"Yes, I have no doubt."

This smile for her aunt transformed an astonishingly handsome face that had first seemed grim to Abby. He had high cheekbones, a strong jaw already showing a hint of brown stubble, a thin nose that might have a tiny crook, as if it had been broken at some time, and a mouth Abby had trouble taking her eyes from.

"Who wouldn't rather lie in the sun than a hospital bed?" he added.

"It did feel good," Abby admitted. She took a small bite, seeing Aenti Nancy's nod of satisfaction. Once she'd chewed and swallowed, Abby met his eyes. "How did Sergeant Donahue choose you?" If he heard some sharpness, she didn't care.

"We knew each other years ago. I was with KCPD before I became sheriff here. Mike is sure I must be bored."

"Maybe he's right, if you had enough time on your hands to drive out here to see whether I was in dire straits or up and walking."

Her uncle's eyebrows rose, but he didn't say anything. The sheriff's twitched, too.

"I like to get out and drive around my county," he said mildly. "Say hello to people. Haven't spoken to Eli in a while."

That might all be true. Abby didn't even know why she was bristling. And being rude.

No, she knew, all right. She'd reacted to him instantly in a way she never had to any man. It made her uncomfortable. She didn't really know how to flirt, and shouldn't anyway in case he was married. Or, even more likely, not attracted to her. And then there was the idea that Sergeant Donahue had sent him. The sergeant she'd trusted, who'd stood at the foot of her hospital bed looking at her with suspicion and something stronger. Dislike? Anger? And suddenly now he'd become considerate, deeply concerned about her well-being? Abby didn't think so.

Caleb Tanner drained his coffee. She saw that he'd finished his pie, too.

So she said politely, "Thank you for coming. You can tell him I'm fine, but no, I haven't remembered anything."

He studied her with eyes that she decided were a very dark green flecked with gold and possibly whiskey brown. With a nod, he said, "I'll tell him."

He thanked Aenti Nancy for the pie, said a general goodbye and walked out, Onkel Eli accompanying him. Abby sagged and closed her eyes.

Chapter Three

Three days later, Caleb thought of an errand that would provide him with an adequate excuse to be in Eli Kemp's neighborhood so that he could reasonably stop by again. He felt certain Abigail Baker—Abby, her aunt had called her—would not be thrilled to see him again. Because she had secrets? Or suspected his motives?

One thing he knew: she wasn't fine. As he'd tugged her to her feet the other day and then when she walked to the house slowly, pain had tightened a face that was already drawn and too pale—except when she'd blushed. Caleb doubted the bruised circles beneath her eyes were usual for her, either. Was she having difficulty sleeping? Guilt could do that—but so could trauma. Even if she'd truly lost all memory of what happened, she *had* seen her partner go down. The subconscious was powerful. He'd bet money she was having nightmares when she did sleep. If he could get her to talk about the nightmares…

And what were the odds of that? She hadn't exactly been grateful he'd come by, or seen the possibility of a new friend in him. He grimaced. Apparently, he'd have to be more charming. Maybe steer away from asking about the shooting for now, unless she raised the subject.

He turned into the driveway, which was really two dirt ruts with a hillock of grass between them. At the sight of the big white farmhouse ahead, his stomach growled. It occurred to him that there'd be a substantial culinary benefit to courting Abby Baker's trust.

Once again, he parked close to the house. Eli stuck his head out of the barn, but Caleb waved him off and went to the front door. Nancy let him in with a big smile, expressing in her strongly accented English her delight at seeing him again.

Then she lowered her voice. "Good for Abby, seeing you will be." A hint of worry crossed her face. "Do you understand Deitsch?"

"Ja," he said, switching languages. "I had many Amish friends as a boy."

"Gut, gut!" Her smile didn't return, however, and she was almost whispering. "Abby is feeling low, I think. I tell her she must trust in God, and try, she does, but…" She shook her head sadly.

"She's depressed," he said in English, not sure of the word in Deitsch.

Nancy sounded out the word, looking uncertain.

"Where is she?"

She straightened and assumed the smile that he imagined was her usual expression. "The kitchen. Today, we bake."

Caleb hoped Abby wasn't helping too much. Even aside from the consequences of her concussion, she'd been seriously wounded less than two weeks ago.

He followed Nancy inside.

"Who's here?" Abby asked, then saw him when he stepped into the kitchen. Some emotion flared in her blue eyes before she shut the door on whatever she'd been thinking.

Caleb was reminded that she was a cop, not a sweet-natured Amish *maidal* who'd never learned to veil her thoughts.

"Abigail," he said with a nod. "Or do you prefer Abby?"

Her hesitation was brief. "Abby. I didn't expect to see you again so soon, Sheriff."

"Caleb."

Despite clear reluctance, she nodded acceptance. "Caleb."

At Nancy's urging, he sat across from Abby, who had been shaping dough into balls she set on cookie sheets and then gently flattened with the bottom of a canning jar. For a fleeting instant, he imagined her hand competently holding a nine-millimeter gun. Cookies and guns didn't go together.

Despite the photos of Abigail he'd seen online, here and now she looked Amish. An Amishwoman brandishing a handgun? Never.

Her aunt brought him a cup of coffee and an enormous wedge of marionberry pie topped with ice cream. He thanked her and dug in. For the first time, Caleb saw a spark of amusement on Abby's face.

"Now I know why you're here."

He grinned. "When I pulled in, I was thinking I'd better put in some extra time on the treadmill if I plan to stop. No way I'm turning down one of Nancy's desserts."

"Denke," her aunt said over her shoulder. "Abby helped with the pie, ain't so?"

Abby chuckled. "I rolled out the crust. I'll take credit for that much."

She continued with the cookies, her hands quick and sure. Every so often, she glanced at him, her expression one of perplexity, if he was reading her right. Finally, she asked, "Did you report to Sergeant Donahue that you'd done your duty?"

He took a long swallow of coffee. "I did. I assured him you seemed to be on the road to recovery but haven't remembered anything, just as you told me." He frowned. "A concussion that can cause partial amnesia is a bad one. Are you still having headaches?"

"Yes, unfortunately. *Headaches* plural isn't quite the right word. My headache doesn't come and go," she said wryly. "It just stays."

"Seriously?" He pushed his empty plate aside.

"Seriously. I have pills, but they make me sleepy and foggy. I don't like the feeling."

"You like having a chronic headache?"

She wrinkled her nose, for a second looking like a teenager. "You know the saying, 'Between the devil and the deep blue sea.'"

Out of the corner of his eye, Caleb saw her aunt watching them, crinkled lines of perturbation between her eyebrows.

"I understand," he said gently. "I was in a bad car accident a few years back." He'd been part of a vehicle pursuit, unaware the driver they were chasing had circled back until he burst from a side street and smashed into the driver's side of Caleb's patrol car at full speed. "Recovery and rehab took almost three months." His hip still hurt fiercely when he overdid it.

"Really?" Those astonishing blue eyes searched his,

as if she needed to know he was sincere, that he truly understood what she was going through.

"Really."

"I'm lucky I only have the one cracked bone," she said thoughtfully, likely not aware that she'd laid a hand over her chest. "They're slower to heal than soft tissue."

"I can speak to that." He rubbed his hip without thinking. "The trouble is, with broken bones you lose a lot of muscle tone before you can start physical therapy." Caleb frowned again. "Shouldn't you be having therapy?"

"I started in the hospital, and came with a long list of exercises. The therapist would like me to check in weekly with him, but I'd need to hire a car and driver or take the bus. He said I could find someone local instead."

"I'd drive you to Kansas City," Caleb heard himself say.

Nancy smiled at him. "What a kind suggestion!"

Abby was slower to respond, instead studying him again, as if trying to see a lot deeper than he'd like. "Why would you do that?" she said finally, but without the underlying hostility he'd heard at his last visit.

"This has been rough on you." And it would give him lots of time to earn her trust, encourage confidence. "I spent twelve years with KCPD, which means we ought to be able to rely on each other." That, he decided, was actually honest.

She nodded after a minute. She had a habit of taking her time before committing to anything, Caleb realized.

"If you can drive me this week, that would be good. Gerald, my physical therapist, can tell best if I'm progressing. If he thinks I'm doing well, it would make sense for me to find someone here after that."

"Make an appointment and let me know when. Ah... can you? Did you bring your phone or computer?"

"No," she said softly. "But I have the number and can call from the phone shanty."

"Or do you want to use my phone and do it now?"

"I'd rather finish this." She lifted flour-covered hands.

"You'll call me, too?"

"*Ja*, you, too." This sounded impish.

"Then let me give you my number." He pulled card and pen from his vest pocket and jotted down his mobile phone number, then slid it across the table to Abby. "I don't have any set appointments this week—" actually, he did, but would change them for this "—so any time is good."

"Thank you." She looked at him with an openness and warmth that hit him like a blow. "Aenti Nancy is right. Your offer is kind."

Leaving, he told himself he'd been smacked with guilt, that's all...but he knew better than to lie to himself. Abby Baker might not have the finely carved face of a model, but in his eyes she was beautiful. Especially at that moment.

After getting in his department SUV, he sat for a minute, unmoving, gazing toward the house.

He couldn't let himself get sucked in. Donahue wouldn't have asked him to do this if he hadn't had good reason for his suspicion. Caleb knew the man. Caleb didn't know Detective Abigail Baker, and wasn't fool enough to let a pretty face and bright blue eyes divert him from keeping his promise.

Besides, if he could confirm her innocence, he'd be doing *her* a favor.

He started the engine, lifted a hand toward a young man who was peering out from between open barn doors, and swung in a U-turn to go back to town, and the pile of work awaiting him.

A GUN BLASTED. Once, twice.

She managed to fumble a hand toward her un-snapped holster. Why was it empty? She was peering at the dark bulk of someone crouching over—puzzlement. She ought to know who lay there, not so far from her.

She hovered on the edge of darkness. When the foot-steps approached, it took everything she had to open her eyes a slit. The toe of the boots came to a stop inches from her. He must be looking down at her.

A voice calling from a distance.

Crack. She jerked, and pain exploded in her chest. I'm dead, she realized.

But she couldn't be, because hands were shaking her.

"Abby!" the woman exclaimed. "Abby? *Was is letz?*" *What is wrong?*

The nightmare faded out of sight, leaving only dread and shock. Abby forced her eyes open and pushed herself to a sitting position, her wounds protesting. "Aenti Nancy?"

"*Ja.* Oh, child." Warm, comforting arms came around her. "You cried out, as if—"

"It was a nightmare." She sagged. "Just a nightmare." Even if she'd been able to remember it, the mind twisted real events in a dreamscape. She couldn't rely on whatever she saw in a nightmare.

Aenti Nancy insisted on bringing her a cupful of warm milk to help her sleep. Weirdly, the idea was comforting. Grossmammi had warmed milk for her when she was a child with insomnia or after a nightmare. Abby didn't love the taste, but she would drink it anyway, and gratefully.

Once she had, and had persuaded her aunt that she could go back to sleep now, Abby lay gazing toward the uncovered window, where she could see a crescent moon.

This would be a big day. The sheriff was to pick her up at nine in the morning to drive her to her appointment in Kansas City. She had to squelch any sense of anticipation. He might have offered only so as to look good in her aunt's and uncle's eyes, and thereby the view of all the Amish in their church district. Abby imagined Aenti nodding firmly to her friends and saying, "The sheriff is Englisch, but a *gut* man." The others would take that in and decide that if they had to have dealings with authorities, he at least might be trustworthy.

Of course, there was also the distinct possibility that he intended to worm his way into her confidence so that she'd tell him everything that happened in that alley. If Sergeant Donahue hadn't believed in her memory loss, why would the sheriff? Testing her, that's what he was doing, she decided.

He might actually *be* a good man, but not one she could trust. Not yet. Not until she did remember.

Once in a while, she thought she did. Only shreds. Footsteps. The press of dirty asphalt on her cheek. She might think she smelled something rancid, but then it was gone. Abby had no intention of telling anyone that even such meaningless pieces seemed to float to the surface occasionally. The doctor had told her not to try to force memories, that it wouldn't do any good, that her mind needed to heal.

Onkel Eli had checked messages at the shanty this afternoon, too, and found three for her. Two were from other detectives, wanting to know how she was. The third had been left by Sergeant Donahue, who asked that she call.

She wished he hadn't given out her number to the others. They might be able to find where she was, with the phone number as a starting point.

No, wait. Sam Kirk had the address, too, so it wasn't exactly a secret. Anyway, she was here to recover, not to hide.

Except… Abby couldn't forget that *somebody* had tried to kill her, and she didn't believe for a minute that it had been Neal. Someone else had to have been there.

She concentrated, but not so much as a flicker of memory materialized out of the night.

She remained restless enough to be glad when the window framed the pearly gray of dawn. Abby watched as the sky slowly brightened, waiting until she heard footsteps in the hall, first soft ones, then firmer, booted steps. As tired as she was, her lips curved; Joshua would have a hard time dragging himself out of bed this morning. She'd heard him come in late last night, trying to be quiet, but he'd bumped the wall twice. He'd likely been drinking, which wouldn't make his parents happy, even if it was common with kids during *rumspringa*. One of Abby's cousins had done worse than that. Ruth had gotten pregnant. Of course her come-calling friend had married her, after both had gone through counseling with the bishop and sworn repentance before the congregation. Ruth and Aaron had four children now and were expecting another, according to Aenti Nancy. They had moved farther south for affordable land, but visited once or twice a year.

Abby got dressed, the motions practiced. With each passing day, she walked better, but still had to take the stairs with extra care. Isaac reached the kitchen only moments after she did, his relief obvious when he saw that the coffee was ready. Abby took over making the scrambled eggs while Aenti cut up and fried potatoes and toasted bread in the oven. Refrigerator and stove were powered by gas. Many of the smaller appliances, like Aenti's prized food processor, were hand cranked and did the job splendidly.

Onkel Eli sent Isaac back upstairs to wake his brother, who trailed down ten minutes later, eyelids heavy, hair poking every which way. His father scrutinized him, but said nothing. Breakfast was usually a quiet meal, the men eager to eat and get out to work. Abby felt a little queasy again, and had only eggs and a single piece of toast. She had to be losing weight, which wasn't a bad thing, whatever Aenti said to the contrary. Out in the world, slender figures were admired, not too-tall women with too-generous curves.

Despite her tiredness, she cleared the table and washed the dishes, too, while Aenti dried. Her indefatigable aunt planned to do some canning, but Abby admitted to needing to sit down. Shooed out onto the front porch, she settled on a rocker and set it into gentle motion.

CALEB GLANCED SIDELONG at Abby, who still looked befuddled. Or, as the Amish would say, *ferhoodled*. When he'd arrived, he had spotted her immediately, sound asleep in a rocking chair on the porch. Her head had hung at an awkward angle, and now she occasionally rubbed her neck, as if it was stiff. He knew she'd been embarrassed to be caught unawares.

Cop, he thought again. Of course she was disturbed to discover anyone at all could have walked right up to her while she dozed. For Abby, the bone-deep dislike of being vulnerable must be cranked up tenfold, given that she'd lost her partner and been shot herself so recently, with no idea who her enemy was.

Unless she knew exactly what had happened.

He cleared his throat. "Did you have trouble sleeping last night?"

She studied his profile in her serious way. "Yes," she said at last. "I had a nightmare and then couldn't get back to sleep."

"About the shooting?"

"I...don't know."

Hearing reservation in her voice, he gave her a sideways look. "It probably was. I deal with things I've seen and done on the job pretty well during the day, but corralling my sleeping mind is another story."

"That's true. As I wake up, I think I'll remember, but then it's just gone. It's really frustrating." She frowned, looking ahead through the windshield at the rolling, forested country they were passing through. "Although I can't trust that a nightmare was truthful."

"Probably not," Caleb agreed, "but there might be a nugget in there that would start a cascade of memories. In fact, if you *are* dreaming about the shooting, I'd guess it's probably because your memory is starting to break through. Did you have nightmares at first?"

The creases on her forehead deepened. "No. They had me pretty doped up, though."

"That doesn't do much for clarity of thinking, does it?"

She smiled wryly. "No."

Which was why she had a headache bad enough he could see it, like a dark aura.

"I wonder if massage would help your headaches. *Headache,*" he amended.

"Don't know. My neck, now..." Abby kneaded it again with her right hand.

He itched to take over the task, suspecting her skin would feel like pure silk beneath his fingertips.

"Why aren't you tanned?" he asked, probably too abruptly.

Obviously startled, she said after a pause, "I just don't. I use a lot of sunscreen, because otherwise I burn. I should probably move to the Pacific Northwest, where the skies are gray a good percent of the time."

He laughed. "Your nose is a little pink."

Abby sighed. "And I've been trying to stay in the shade."

Conversation wandered, with Caleb forgetting for stretches what his real purpose was here. Eventually, Abby asked about his decision to leave the Kansas City PD to become the sheriff of a rural county.

"Each promotion meant more time spent doing admin. As a lieutenant, I traded off getting out in the field with having more control over decisions that impacted the officers beneath me." He grimaced. "Or so I thought. After a while, I realized I felt as if I was being ground between two big rocks."

"The *mano* and the *metate*," Abby murmured.

"What?"

"That's what the Mayans and Aztecs and a lot of the Southwest Native Americans used to grind corn. When I was a kid, my parents took me to New Mexico, and I saw a Navajo woman using a *mano* and the *metate*." She mimed the action, then shrugged. "It was interesting."

Intrigued, he looked at her a little too long and had to jerk his attention back to the road.

"That was me. A kernel of corn. I heard the sheriff here in Hearn County had to step down because of health problems, and I liked the idea of complete control." His mouth curved. "Goes without saying that was a fantasy. I let myself forget the county commissioners, outraged citizens, news reporters…" He exaggerated his disgruntlement. "Somebody is always mad about something."

Her chuckle was a happy sound that had him stealing another too-long glance. "Not a lot of exciting investigations, either, I bet."

"In the sense of a puzzle, no." Until she'd come along. "I'm finding I like the challenges, though. Dealing with the Amish, not to mention the tourists, being a politician, improving training for my deputies, juggling to fill shifts and have people where they need to be." His shoulders moved. "And I'm home."

She asked about that, too, and he told a few stories about growing up in a rambling old house on acreage just outside Ruston with his brother and sister, being free to roam the woods up behind the house, ride his bike to friends', fish in the pond and creek. "I like the pace here," he finished.

"I do, too," she admitted, sounding subdued. Or was that sad?

"If you don't mind my asking, how'd you end up with Amish relatives?"

"My mother left the faith to marry my father." That much she said matter-of-factly. "She hadn't been baptized yet, so she was able to visit. I loved spending time on the farm, which belonged to my grandparents then. Onkel Eli took over after Grossdaadi died."

Since the Amish were a sect of the Anabaptists, they didn't believe in infant baptism. In their view, each individual was baptized upon accepting the faith—which was usually in the late teens or early twenties. Caleb nodded his understanding and asked, "Your grandmother?"

"She only lived two years after he was gone. I wasn't around much, which I regret, but when I saw her, I had the feeling she was tired. She missed him."

Caleb could see that happening to his parents, who had a spark and a friendship that he didn't often see in couples married as long as they'd been. Maybe he couldn't solely blame his job for the failure of his two or three more serious relationships. He had wanted what his parents had, and not found it.

"What about your parents?" he asked.

"My mother died when I was a child," she said calmly. "I spent a lot of time here after that. Oh," she said, in what he had no trouble recognizing as a diversion, "I didn't tell you what exit to take, did I?"

Interesting. Caleb felt sure a story lay behind her few words, but it wasn't one she was ready to tell him. He wondered if she ever talked about her childhood. Some instinct said no. Yeah, and while he was wondering, he was struck anew by her decision to become a cop despite what had to have been a serious dose of Amish values.

The Amish had been persecuted and even burned alive in the old country, and had determined in North America to stay apart, to avoid being influenced by the wider culture—and to submit as little as possible to government authority. They believed in forgiveness rather than vengeance. Among themselves, if a man repented, he was accepted wholeheartedly back into the fold. Conviction at trial and prison terms were measures they occasionally upheld only in the belief that a man who had stumbled from the path of goodness might be given time to regret his sins and do penance.

Amish did not become law-enforcement officers. So what had motivated Abby Baker?

One more answer he wouldn't get today.

They'd wandered into discussing the health-care system by the time he parked in the lot outside the medical building that housed her physical therapist. When she quit talking midsentence, Caleb followed her gaze to see an unmarked police car two slots away. Sergeant Michael Donahue climbed out, his eyes on Abby.

Irked, Caleb wondered why he was here, and without issuing a warning.

Chapter Four

Sergeant Donahue stood with his feet planted apart, blocking her way on the sidewalk in front of the clinic. His arms were crossed and his eyes lingered either on her face or the filmy white *kapp* covering her hair, she couldn't decide.

Abby was slow enough to move; Caleb had gotten all the way around to her side and opened the door. He helped her out of his car and kept a hand beneath her elbow. Whether he intended to support her physically or emotionally she had no idea. Or was any support at all only a pretense? She didn't shake him off, because her headache pulsed at the mere sight of the hard suspicion in Donahue's eyes.

"Sergeant," she said stiffly. Furious because she knew her cheeks were reddening, she dipped her head. "If you don't mind, I need to check in."

Donahue didn't bother with a greeting. "What in hell is that getup?"

Her chin tipped up. "I dress plain when I stay with my Amish family," she said, praying she could maintain her dignity. "I'm sure Detective Kirk told you about my aunt and uncle."

His lip curled. "He didn't say you'd be trying to blend in."

How could this man look at her with such dislike? He *knew* her. At least she'd believed he did. She was only grateful that Caleb hadn't leaped to defend her. Or, come to think of it, to greet his old friend.

Because they planned this confrontation, a voice murmured in her head. How else would the sergeant have known the date and time of her appointment?

She ordered herself to think about that later. She'd have plenty of time during the return drive to tell Sheriff Tanner what she thought of him.

"I spent a great deal of time with my mother's family growing up. This—" she plucked at her calf-length dress and apron "—feels as natural to me as my uniform. Now, if you'll excuse me…"

He still didn't back out of her way. "I'm waiting for answers, Detective Baker. Don't think you can hide from me."

Abby kept her chin up and refused to look away first. After a minute, his gaze flicked to the sheriff beyond her shoulder. Then he stepped aside and swept an arm out in a courtly gesture that mocked her. She walked past him and kept going, not so much as glancing back.

Caleb took a few steps with her, murmuring in her ear, "I'll be right in. Let me talk to him for a minute."

"Of course you want to talk to him," she said acidly, not looking to see how he reacted.

The receptionist inside appeared startled by her garb, but didn't remark. The Amish didn't like big cities, so the woman might never have seen an Amish person unless she'd spent a weekend sightseeing in Amish country, where most who visited would squeal with delight at spotting a horse-drawn black buggy on the road or a vegetable stand overseen by women in their distinctive dresses, aprons and *kapps*.

A part of Abby wished she'd brought her Englisch clothes and asked Caleb to stop at a service station so she could go into the restroom and change. Another part refused to feel embarrassed. Certainly, she wasn't ashamed. This was her, as much as the cop was.

And *that* was something Sergeant Donahue hadn't known about her.

CALEB GLARED AT DONAHUE. "What are you doing here?"

"Figured she was due for a little reminder."

"You've just undermined any progress I made with her. Now she thinks I set this up."

A dark eyebrow lifted. "Didn't you?"

"I gave you an update." Caleb's voice rose. "I thought you had the brains not to blow it!"

"Don't tell me that sweet face has gotten to you," the other man said contemptuously.

Caleb took a step forward, letting the jackass know how aggressive he felt. He reveled in the advantage his greater height gave him. "You're the one who set this up. You want me to drop her at home and forget about it?"

Donahue's jaw muscles knotted. "No."

"Then make an effort not to sabotage me."

A lot angrier than was probably justified, Caleb stalked toward the entrance of the physical-therapy clinic, much like Abby had.

A quick scan didn't find her in the waiting area, although several people were there slouching in chairs, either staring blankly at a big television screen tuned to a twenty-four-hour news station or flipping idly through magazines. When the receptionist asked brightly if she could help him, he shook his head.

"I'm waiting for Ms. Baker."

He took a seat where he could see everyone else in the room as well as the front entrance and the door that led to the back. He let his gaze flick to the television—and the latest political squabble—then back to the glass doors. There was no reason for him to feel so on edge. Abby wasn't in any danger at the moment, nor could he use this time to learn anything more about her. But he didn't relax well in the midst of strangers, and it took him a few minutes to understand that he'd been offended when that idiot Donahue looked at her the way he had only because of the clothes she wore.

To use Amish parlance, Caleb was a *modern*, through and through. Even if he'd shared their faith, he was incapable of what they called *gelassenheit*. The concept meant yielding oneself to the will of God and to the church in the form of the bishop and ministers. Caleb had never been good at yielding himself to anyone's authority, which explained his decision to take the job as sheriff. He'd seen for himself that the Amish acceptance of God's will gave them a peace he'd never find, any more than other moderns would. Most Americans were too competitive, their lives too taken up with striving for more success, more respect, more money.

And yet, he thought he'd learned from his Amish friends as a boy, if only a tolerance that they might call *forgiveness*. He admired much about the Leit—the people, as they called themselves—liked many of the individuals he'd gotten to know. Mike Donahue dropped a few notches in Caleb's esteem for his seeming disdain for a good people.

He frowned, wondering how much Abby had learned from her Amish family. She spoke Deitsch fluently, so she had to have spent substantial time with them. And yet, she'd become a cop.

Maybe on the way home, he could get her to open up to him.

THREE DAYS LATER, Abby was alone in the kitchen, shaping dough to go into greased bread pans, when she heard an unfamiliar engine out front. She groaned. Now who? And why had her fellow officers all taken it into their heads to visit at the same time?

The first she'd appreciated. Julie Luong and Abby had gone through the academy together and been lucky enough to be assigned as rookies to the same precinct. In an environment dominated by men, Abby had been grateful to have a friend she knew wouldn't betray her confidence and who was having a lot of the same experiences she was, good and bad.

Julie initially had looked startled when she saw Abby in Amish garb, and then Onkel Eli with his broad-brimmed hat, clean-shaven upper lip and long beard, but she'd been accepting enough to be warm and friendly when she joined the family for lunch. Before she left, she hugged Abby carefully and whispered, "Please come back. I miss you."

Abby had felt a little emotional.

In contrast, she didn't feel at all weepy after the next day's visitor, a detective from her unit who had laughed raucously when he saw her. Aenti Nancy had been excited that another friend had come to visit and started dishing up pie even before Abby answered the door, but ended up disappointed when she didn't even invite him in. Instead, she told him she didn't feel well and needed to lie down.

She could tell he didn't believe her, but he did leave.

Of course, the sheriff had stopped by daily, sometimes just to say hello, other times lingering for coffee, a piece of pie and conversation with whomever was willing to talk to him.

Which did not include her.

On the drive back from Kansas City the day of her appointment, he'd tried to grill her about her background. Well, he disguised it as conversation, but she knew what he really had in mind. Her aunt and uncle might like this man, but she didn't. She wouldn't relax her guard so quickly again.

That she responded to him on a physical level was something she did her best to hide. Abby didn't even like admitting to herself that her heart stumbled every time she saw him, then sped up. That when he smiled or touched her she felt an unfamiliar, honeyed warmth in her belly and lower.

She'd get over these feelings, she told herself every day after he left. How could she be attracted to a man who believed she was capable of killing her own partner? A man who was only being nice to her because he thought he could lull her into a full confession before he slapped on the cuffs?

The engine she heard now had the throaty roar of a pickup truck or SUV, but she felt sure it wasn't the sheriff's department vehicle.

She took a minute to set the bread pans in the oven to rise again, a cloth laid over them, before she went to peek out the window beside the front door.

Two more detectives from her unit walked toward

the porch. She ought to be glad to see them. Hadn't she thought of her fellow officers as family? Until this moment, she hadn't realized how much the sergeant had tainted her feelings. Yesterday's visitor hadn't helped, either.

She wished she weren't alone, but Onkel Eli and Aenti Nancy had left after lunch to visit Rose. Abby had been tempted to go along but was afraid the jolting ride in a buggy would be more than her perpetually aching head could bear. The pain in her sternum wasn't receding as fast as she'd hoped, either. Isaac and Joshua were working out in the field this afternoon and would assume she could handle visitors.

Annoyed with herself, she thought, *Of course I can.* Anyway, if they, too, were going to be jerks, she'd prefer none of her real family were present to see.

Of the two men, she liked Ron Caldwell the best. He'd always teased her as if she was a little sister, and had been helpful when she had questions. His partner, Jason McCarthy, was also big on jokes, but they were cruder, even sometimes seeming mean. He'd sized her up a few times in a way that made her uncomfortable, too, although he'd never asked her out or touched her inappropriately.

Resigning herself, she opened the front door before they'd gotten far enough to knock. "Ron. Jason. I'm surprised to see you."

Ron trailed, his foot on the first step, while Jason was ahead of him. Both stopped dead and stared at her. Of course, it was Jason who let out a whoop of laughter.

When he could control himself, he started to sing.

"Mary had a little lamb, little lamb, little lamb. Mary had a—"

She interrupted without compunction. Tersely. "Not funny."

Behind him, Ron was grinning.

"Yeah, it is." Jason turned to his partner and buddy. "Tell her it's funny."

"It's funny," Ron agreed.

Jason let out a hoot. "Man, I didn't believe Donahue, but he was right. This was worth the drive. You look like—I don't even know what. It's like a historical reenactment."

She heard footsteps behind her.

"Abby?" It was Joshua, sounding puzzled. In Deitsch, he said, "Who are these men? What's so funny?"

"These are men I work with in Kansas City. Police officers." She switched to English. "Detective Caldwell and Detective McCarthy, this is my cousin, Joshua Kemp."

Jason's grin widened.

Joshua's expression froze, even as the fiery red color of humiliation rose from beneath his shirt collar and spread to his face. He recognized that he was being mocked. It wouldn't be the first time. Amish had learned to hold up their heads and ignore the ignorant who made fun of them. Unfortunately, what teenager had real confidence?

She'd just never expected men she'd worked with and respected to be among those ignorant.

Jason smirked. "Do you go out in public dressed like this, Detective Baker? Maybe pin your badge to your apron?"

Ron, she knew with one part of her mind, was staying quiet. But he wasn't telling his partner to shut up, either.

A black SUV slammed to a stop behind the pickup the two detectives had driven. Wonderful. Would Sheriff Tanner appreciate the jokes?

At last, her temper sparked along with her headache. "Enough. You're an intolerant boor."

Jason's eyes narrowed. He took a step closer to her, his expression ugly. "You can't take a joke?"

Joshua remained silent behind her, but he was brave enough not to have fled.

"Or is the outfit supposed to convince all of us that you're an angel, that you couldn't possibly have gunned Neal down?"

His scathing tone stung, but she met his glare with her own. "You need to—"

A deep voice came from behind. "It's time for you to go. *Now.*"

Both men whipped around. Neither had noticed the new arrival until he spoke, which should have shocked them. Cops needed to stay aware.

"This isn't your business—" Belatedly, Jason took in the uniform and the star pinned to Caleb's chest pocket.

Caleb's gaze touched hers fleetingly, but long enough for her to see how angry he was.

Ron was smart enough to say, "Jason, get going."

"She didn't even let us in."

"You're invited to visit my jail." Now Caleb's eyes stayed on Jason. "I'm sure your sergeant would be pleased to come up to bail you out."

"I'm not breaking any law," the detective said sullenly. "I work with Abby, and all we did was come to see how she's doing."

"Is that what you were doing?" she asked. "Funny, your visit felt more like an assault than a friendly hello."

Caleb met her eyes again. "How about I arrest them for trespassing?"

She looked at Ron. "Just go, and don't come back."

His face was flushed now. "He really was just kidding around, Abby. But we're going." He turned, hesitated, then brushed by Caleb, who didn't step aside. "Come on, Jason."

Under Caleb's stony stare, Jason apparently lost his nerve and backed away from the doorway. She knew he was a dedicated weight lifter, but somehow his showy muscles didn't look all that impressive next to a man as large and solid as Caleb Tanner. He sidled past, then hurried across the grass toward the pickup truck.

No, he *scuttled*, she decided with satisfaction. Much better choice of words.

All three of them watched until the truck did a U-turn in front of the barn and disappeared down the driveway. Dust arose on the road a moment later.

"I was capable of getting rid of them without threats," she heard herself say.

Caleb's dark brows rose. "But I enjoyed threatening them."

A laugh burst out of her. She clapped her hand over her mouth but failed to hold back what were really giggles.

"Abby?" Joshua said anxiously. "Abby, are you all right?"

In contrast, Caleb didn't try to hide his amusement.

The skin beside his eyes crinkled, and his teeth flashed in a grin.

"Oh, my" were the first words she managed to get out.

Still smiling, Caleb came up on the porch. "What about me? Do I get to come in?"

"For sure," she said, before realizing how Amish that sounded. "I baked some butter cookies, probably not as good as Aenti Nancy's, but if you'd like—"

"I'd like," he said quietly.

For a minute, she couldn't look away from him. There was no amusement in his hazel eyes now, only a seriousness that set her pulse to bouncing.

It was her turn to flush. "I don't know what's wrong with me, standing here like...like..."

"Some kind of *doppick*?" he suggested, his mouth twitching.

Dummy.

"Thank you very much."

Joshua mumbled a shy greeting. As Abby led the way to the kitchen, the man and boy started talking about baseball. She knew Joshua and his friends were obsessed. He'd give a lot to see a real professional baseball game. Abby felt selfish because she'd never thought to take him to see the St. Louis Cardinals. Maybe, if she got to feeling well enough to drive...

The kitchen felt like a refuge to her. Here, she could stay busy instead of mooning over a man who was essentially a stranger. Since there was always coffee on, she was able to put mugs before both Caleb and Joshua, who drank as much of it as his *daad* and *brudder*, despite his youth. Abby put on a kettle to heat water for a cup of tea for herself, then piled cookies on a plate that she set in the middle of the table. By that time, the water was boiling, which gave her another excuse to keep her back to this caller.

Of course, once she turned with her cup of tea in hand, she found him watching her. He gestured toward the chair across from him. What could she do but sit down?

"Joshua," she said, "I never asked why you came in. Was there something you needed?"

He flushed again. "Just wanted coffee."

"I'm sure you've squeezed in a few cookies."

He grinned. "*Ja*, I will take a few for Isaac, too."

"*Sehr gutt.* Tell him to enjoy."

A sizeable pile of cookies clutched in his hand, he went out the back door.

Caleb laughed. "I wonder how many of those will make it to his brother?"

"He's always hungry."

Reaching for another cookie, he said, "I remember those days. I grew like a weed, and I could be starved ten minutes after eating dinner. Couldn't seem to fill up."

"You still seem plenty hungry." She was pretty sure he was on his third or fourth cookie, and they were huge.

"Ahh…" His hand stopped.

Abby chuckled. "As Aenti would say, eat yourself full. I'm used to it. The way Onkel Eli and the boys can sit down at the table and make heaps of food vanish in minutes still amazes me."

Caleb set the cookie on his plate. "You sound good. Are you feeling better?"

She had to think about that. "My shoulder does. My

chest—" she rested a hand over her sternum "—still hurts if I bend the wrong way or move too suddenly."

His intensity was entirely focused on her. He didn't reach for his coffee, scarcely blinked. "Your head?"

She wanted to believe he cared. Trusting him even this much felt risky. What she was actually risking... She'd think about that later.

"There are times it seems to be easing, and then pain hits me out of the blue. Well, sometimes it comes out of nowhere. If I get mad or upset," she admitted, "I can count on feeling as if I'd taken an axe to my head."

"When you try to remember?"

Looking away from him, Abby still said, "Yes. It's as if I'm being punished for trying." When he didn't say anything, she lifted her gaze to his face. With sudden hostility, she said, "I suppose, like Sergeant Donahue, you don't believe I've forgotten a thing."

Lines in his forehead deepened. "I've seen instances of temporary amnesia. Your version is more extreme than most, but it's not uncommon after a blow to the head."

"Thank you for saying that, even if you don't believe it," she said stiffly.

He shocked her by reaching across the table to cover her hand with his. Looking troubled, he said, "Abby, it is my fault that Donahue knew about your appointment. I mentioned it in passing, but I wouldn't have if I'd thought he'd show up. I just wanted him to know you were doing your part to recover."

Her hand balled into a fist as she withdrew it from beneath his, too warm, too strong, too disturbing. "Nobody cares how quickly I'm recovering. You must realize I'm not welcome back to work. Even if I fought for the right to do my job, nobody trusts me."

Caleb's frown deepened. "Donahue wants to get to the bottom of what happened. You can't blame him for that. Surely the detectives you work with believe in you."

Shoving back her chair so she could push to her feet, she laughed harshly. "Sure. Didn't you hear Detective McCarthy today?"

She saw that he had.

"The sergeant is making darn sure everyone thinks I gunned Neal down. I just don't understand—" Her voice broke. She shook her head and backed away. "Take your time, I need to—"

She fled, taking with her the memory of his expression, one she didn't understand at all.

Chapter Five

Abby knelt on the mulched ground, snipping off greens and dropping them into a bucket atop the broccoli and cabbage she'd already harvested. She had to remember to pick a few tomatoes, too. Only the ripe ones, Aenti Nancy had said firmly.

Lips curving, Abby paused to look around at the tidy garden, so carefully tended. Long rows of raspberry and blackberry vines were tied to wire strung between posts. The brightly colored squash and the ripening pumpkins would feed the family and be sold at weekend farmer's markets, too. Her aunt had made Joshua fetch a watermelon from the garden earlier—she'd decreed them to be too heavy for Abby to lift and carry yet. Nor would she allow her to pick apples, or dig potatoes or sweet potatoes. Abby hadn't argued; her chest ached constantly, and she still moved her shoulder cautiously. She wouldn't want to get up on a ladder and find herself dizzy, either.

But this—being here in the garden, seeing the quickness of the blue jay taking off from a branch in an apple tree, hearing the call of a whippoorwill, was a pleasure. In the city, she forgot what she was missing.

Tomorrow, she might walk into the deep Missouri

woods that backed the farm: huge old sycamores and pin oaks, dogwood and redbud. Birds, squirrels, rabbits were plentiful as, somewhere, were sleeping possums and raccoons.

Getting to her feet was still a challenge, but she'd perfected methods of rising without worsening any of her aches and pains. She always felt a tiny bit of triumph when she made it.

She bent to lift the bucket, but her eye caught a flash of light in the woods. Sun reflecting off glass or metal that shouldn't be there.

Abby's subconscious made a decision long before she could have reasoned out the wrongness of whatever that was she'd seen. She threw herself sideways, landing hard on the ground in the orchard that bordered the garden. Her sternum felt as if she'd split it in two, and lightning must have struck her head. The *crack* of a rifle being fired flooded her with remembered fear, even as she groped for a sidearm she didn't have. Operating on instinct, she tried to make herself small enough to hide behind the trunk of the closest apple tree.

Crack.

Bark peppered her face.

"Abby!" her uncle called urgently from the barn. His booted feet thudded as he ran toward her. Then he bellowed, "You! There are people here! Quit shooting!"

He reached her, crouched above her. His hat had fallen off, she saw distantly.

"Get down!" she told him. "He might—"

"No, no. It was some fool hunting. He heard me and is hurrying home, for sure. Sorry, he'd be, if he'd shot a person, not even noticing how close he was to a farm."

The silence reassured her enough that the tension

gradually drained from her muscles. Even the birds had quit calling. Abby began to breathe again. Of course Onkel Eli would think that. It would never occur to him that someone would shoot at *her*. But she didn't believe for a minute that a misguided hunter had fired from the dim cover of the woods into the sunlit garden. How could the shooter have missed seeing the house and the big barn, the clothes drying on a line, Aenti Nancy's purple dress and apron, Abby's a rich blue? No. And was it coincidence that this was the first time Abby had come out behind the house?

She groaned involuntarily when she moved to sit up. Her uncle helped her, his face creased in worry as he looked her over.

"There's blood on your face!" he exclaimed.

Abby lifted her hand. "It was the bark and bits of the tree trunk. Just scratches." Still sitting, she inspected the tree and saw a fresh groove cut by a high-powered bullet, only inches above where her head had been. "That was no accident," she said slowly. "He was shooting at *me*."

Her uncle's gaze followed hers. He didn't want to believe her, she could tell, but appalled understanding overcame his powerful faith in the goodness of his fellow man.

"God was with you," he said sturdily.

Her eyes returning to the gash in the tree trunk, she murmured, "*Ja.* He must have been."

CALEB WALKED SLOWLY into the dimness beneath the forest canopy, his pauses frequent. He scanned the earth for the glint that would give away a forgotten shell, a cigarette butt or gum wrapper or footprint. Anything to tell him where the shooter had set up—if, indeed, he hadn't been a stupid teenager swinging around to take a potshot at a bird taking flight.

He didn't like admitting that the call from Eli Kemp had shaken him. He'd driven like a crazy man, flashing lights clearing the road ahead of him even if the emergency had come and gone. Abby hadn't been hurt.

The Amish didn't call the local police for something like this, but Eli said, "If you come, then she might be willing to lie down." Either he was making a concession to his worldly niece, or he'd really been frightened.

After he arrived, Caleb had seen Abby immediately. Looking smaller than she was, she sat bent forward in a rocker in the living room. She seemed to be trying to hug herself with folded arms, holding in pain. Shocked by the change, he saw that her usually bright blue eyes were glassy and somehow darkened. Her skin stretched too tight across her cheekbones.

When he asked if she still had pain medication, she'd been slow to answer. "Yes," she said finally. "But they make me—"

"Take one," he'd snapped.

She averted her face but finally gave the tiniest of nods.

Of course she wanted to come out with him. *Cop,* he'd had to remind himself.

Now he hunted for any evidence at all of an intruder with malignant intent. The graze in the trunk of the apple tree had given him a clear direction. The shooter had to have been here, somewhere within a narrow corridor.

At last he let out a long breath, rolled his shoulders and turned back to look toward the garden and house.

There was nothing. Not the smallest sign that anyone had ever stood here, far less planted a tripod or lain down to use a bipod to steady the rifle. He'd looked for any nicks in the trees here in the woods, a broken branch, and found zip.

Yes, somebody had fired a gun, there was no question. Eli and Isaac had heard it, too, as had Nancy in the house. But whether Abby had been a target Caleb couldn't confirm. Or rule out, of course, but he felt increasingly doubtful.

Abby admitted she had no idea where the first bullet had gone. She'd heard the shot, but no thud of the bullet hitting the side of the house or anything else. The second one… It might just have been a wild shot that happened to come scarily close to Abby. If she hadn't dived for cover—and he knew he'd have done the same—the damn shot might not have come anywhere near her.

He leaned toward the stupid-teenager explanation himself, which would reassure the Kemps but make Abby mad. She'd trust him less than she already did, which he couldn't afford.

Walking back toward the house, Caleb wished he'd never agreed to try to worm his way into Abby Baker's confidence. His mixed feelings were only one of the reasons he had hated undercover work. This time… too many of those feelings were inappropriate, given the situation.

He'd long since admitted to himself that physically, she pushed his buttons. He liked his women tall, loved the length of her stride, the curves she probably cursed when she was on the job. Her contradictions drew him. The toughness that kept her chin up even when she hurt enough to have most people whimpering, the bewilderment and sense of betrayal that triggered his protective instincts big time.

If he hadn't known Mike Donahue so long, he'd probably buy into her story. He wanted to. But Donahue was right that her amnesia was damn convenient. The reason her partner was dead while she was alive didn't sit well with Caleb. Neal Walker hadn't been wearing a vest, while she was. Because she was prepared either for him to return fire or because she knew in advance that something was going down? She'd be dead, too, if not for that vest. The shoulder shot was nothing. The bang on the head had likely been accidental.

Yeah, Caleb could think of ways she might have set up the whole thing. Maybe she'd been confident no one would doubt her "sweet" face.

And maybe Donahue had his head up his butt and Abby Baker was everything she seemed to be—a strong and courageous decorated law-enforcement officer. But it was her honesty that struck him every time he saw her.

Once he passed the garden, he took the time to hunt for the bullet, too, looking for torn turf or a fresh scar in tree trunks and the wood clapboards on the house, but wasn't surprised when he didn't find any sign there, either. Bracing himself for Abby's reaction, he went in the back door.

Eli sat at the kitchen table, apparently waiting. "What did you find?"

Caleb shook his head. "Nothing."

The Amishman straightened. "A teenager, then?"

"It's possible," Caleb admitted. "I'd like to have found the bullet, but it would take an intensive search. My budget doesn't justify that when no one was injured."

"*Ja*, I understand." Eli slapped the table with his palms and stood. "I must get back to work. Nancy is with Abby, trying to talk her into lying down."

Hearing Eli's dryness, Caleb smiled crookedly. "*Agasinish*, is she?" The Deitsch word for *stubborn*, *contrary*, seemed fitting.

Eli's face split in a grin that he made vanish when he heard approaching footsteps.

Nancy bustled into the kitchen. "Ach, her head hurts so!"

"Do you think she's up to talking to me before I go?" Caleb asked.

"She would fuss for sure if you didn't."

He went to the living room alone to find that Abby held ice wrapped in a thin kitchen towel to her head. Before she saw him, she sighed and moved it to her chest, which had the effect of pulling the fabric of her dress tight over her breasts.

And he knew damn well he shouldn't be noticing.

She looked up when he walked in front of her to sit on the coffee table, where his knees came close to touching hers.

"How are you?" he asked.

Predictably, she said, "Better." Her mouth crooked. "Aenti Nancy brought my pills and I took one, as ordered." She gestured to the end table, where the prescription bottle sat within reach.

"Good." A frown furrowed his brow as he met her eyes. He wanted to reassure her. Most of all, he wanted to touch her, and he couldn't. "I didn't find a thing," he made himself say. "No shells, footprints...nothing."

"The bullet?"

"Not that, either."

She sat very still, even her facial muscles under impressive control. Her gaze bored into his for longer than was comfortable. Then she said, "Thank you for coming," in obvious dismissal.

He scowled. "That's it? Go away?"

That stubborn chin rose. "You think like my uncle. Nobody would want to hurt *me*. It had to be some foolish teenager. Well, maybe it was, but you'll have to forgive me for not being so credulous, given that I was shot *twice* not three weeks ago. I saw the sun reflect off what had to be a gun sight. Whoever was looking through it couldn't help but see me, and he pulled the trigger anyway."

"Did you hear me disputing that? All I told you is that I can't find shells or a bullet. In fact, I'm thinking the foolish teenager wouldn't have stopped to pick up his shells." And since that was the truth, uneasiness tugged at him. "We need to let Donahue know what happened," he added.

"I feel sure you intend to do that."

Stung by the astringency in her tone even though, yeah, he was on Donahue's side, Caleb turned his head in an exaggerated show of looking for something. "Since I don't see a phone…"

"It doesn't matter." Her sudden resignation bothered him. She looked tired, any light in her eyes dimmed. "We both know what he'll think."

Conscious of an uncomfortable density in his chest, Caleb knew why. This woman was all contradictions: tough one minute, heartbreakingly vulnerable the next.

"Abby," he said, voice rough. "Give me a chance. Talk to me." For the first time, he didn't know whether this was the cop asking, or the man. "Do you believe Sergeant Donahue is out to get you?"

Obviously startled, she echoed, "Out to get me?"

"That's what I'm asking. Before the shooting, did you get the vibe he wanted you out of his unit?"

After the smallest hesitation, she said, "No. Nothing like that. He encouraged me. I thought, I don't know, that he was happy with my job performance. That's why having him turn on me without hesitation came as such a shock."

Caleb braced his elbows on his knees. "You had no doubts about your partner?"

New life—and indignation—sparked in her eyes. "Is this an interrogation?"

He hid a flinch even as he smiled. "Forgot my truncheon."

Abby made a face at him. "No, I never doubted Neal. We'd gotten to be good friends. He and his wife had me over to dinner a lot, and she talked me into trying Pilates and things I'd never done." She spread her fingers. "A mani-pedi, a lingerie party. Stuff like that."

Oh, he could picture her in lacy panties and bra no problem. And he could not afford to let her see him getting aroused. *So keep your mind on business,* he ordered himself.

"Have you talked to her since the incident? What's her name?"

Her breath hitched. "Laura. Laura Walker." Abby swallowed. "I called from the hospital. She hung up on me. Somebody must have convinced her I killed Neal."

If Donahue had, he'd been stupid. If he hadn't… maybe Neal had shared some worries about his partner with his wife.

But Caleb said only, "I'm sorry."

Lips pressed together, Abby nodded slightly. Being careful not to jar her head, he realized.

"Pain pill helping?"

"Some," she said absently, before blinking. "I mean, sure—"

"You're fine. Of course." Without knowing he was going to do it, Caleb took her hand in his. She was so fine boned, her fingers long. Oddly, given how hot it was outside, her hand felt chilly. "Your face is expressive enough to tell me when you're not fine at all."

"I do feel better," she argued. "The ice helped, too."

"Okay." Her lips were so close. All he had to do was lean forward…and her pink cheeks suggested she was thinking the same thing he was. But if he was going to live by any kind of code, he couldn't make that kind of move on her. Besides, what if he found out that she was only playing him and he'd been fool enough to fall for it? Caleb forced himself to squeeze her hand and let go, sitting up straighter to widen the distance between them. Using sexual attraction to gain her trust was a line he wouldn't cross. He said gruffly, "I wish there was something I could do to help."

"You did drive me to that appointment," she said quietly. "And you came right away today. There's nothing else."

Another dismissal…and one he had to accept.

He lingered long enough to watch her climb the staircase as if it were as imposing as Mount Everest. She clung to the handrail the whole way, resting every step or two.

Caleb ached to sweep her up into his arms and carry her to bed, where he could tenderly tuck her in. Frustrated with himself, he waited only until she'd safely reached the hall above without falling before letting himself out the front door.

IT TOOK TWO DAYS before Abby felt strong enough to walk down the long driveway and then a hundred yards or so beside the road to reach the phone shanty that was shared between four families. Of course, in the Amish way, anyone else in need was welcome to use the phone, too.

Her head kept turning. She felt unpleasantly exposed, but needed to speak to her sergeant herself. Anyway, she refused to become housebound. Maybe Onkel Eli was right, and she hadn't been the target of those two shots at all. Even if she was, surely nobody could be watching her night and day. Around here, it was true that strangers were noticed. The woods offered the best cover, and here, she was too far from them. On that thought, her gaze slid uneasily to the cornfield. She'd hid amongst the cornstalks herself as a child. A man with sniper training could ease through the rows, barely causing a ripple.

But why? She didn't remember anything. Only in her dreams did she replay the night in the alley, but the details continued to dissolve the minute she woke up, never holding their shape long enough for her to grab hold.

Once in the three-sided shanty with its slanting roof, she felt protected. No red light blinked on the answering machine today, and no neighbor had left a note saying "Abby Baker, there is a message for you."

She'd brought Sergeant Donahue's cell phone number on a slip of paper, and now she dialed it.

"Donahue," he said brusquely.

"This is Detective Baker. In case your friend the sheriff didn't already tell you, I thought you should know that two shots were fired at me Saturday."

"Doesn't sound like there's any reason to think the shooter was after you."

She stiffened. "Is that what he told you?"

Although she'd been expecting his answer, it still felt like a betrayal.

Gripping the phone tightly, she distracted herself by gazing across the gravel road to a pasture where a team of enormous chestnut-brown draft horses grazed. They could be her canary in the coal mine, she thought—she needn't be alarmed unless the horses saw something unexpected.

"He said he couldn't find any evidence either way," the sergeant said gruffly. "Just who is it you think is going after you, Baker?"

"Whoever shot Neal and me in that alley."

He snorted. "Good one. Someone just strolled up, took your weapon from you and shot your partner while you both stood paralyzed. I gotta go with the odds. Now, if you could *tell* me what happened, I might have something else to go on. But, funny thing, you can't."

"I've been a good cop." Her throat felt tight. "Honest, caring, liked by my fellow officers. I wouldn't have been promoted to detective so quickly if that wasn't true."

"Rot can hide deep, detective." His sneer could be heard. "Haven't you ever bitten into a bright red apple to find brown, wormy flesh?"

Her chest ached, and it wasn't from the cracked bone. The people she'd considered family had abandoned her, except for those who'd made the drive up here to ridicule a kind, gentle people she loved. Everything she'd worked so hard for had ceased to count. From the time her mother was killed, all she had wanted was to become a police officer, her ultimate goal always the homicide squad. She hadn't felt so lost since her father told her that her mother was dead. Gunned down in a convenience-store holdup.

Now her future had become a blank…but going back wasn't even a remote possibility.

"You know," she said, "I thought I always had someone at my back, but I was wrong. I quit. Feel free to let Personnel know. No matter what happens, I won't be back."

"If you think that makes you less of a suspect in the murder of a good man, you're wrong."

His harsh words meant nothing to her.

"Investigate all you like. You'll find nothing to implicate me." She quietly hung up the receiver, cutting off a burst of speech.

Anger and something she might call grief filled her until she wasn't sure there was room for her lungs to draw in the next breath. Even so, she had no doubt she'd done the right thing. He could come up here to interview her as he pleased, but she had no more obligation to report in, and she refused to beg anyone who should have known better to believe in her. A big slice of her memories might have been stolen from her, but Abby knew Neal would never have drawn on her, far less actually shot her…and believed as profoundly that he'd never have given her cause to have to defend herself from him.

She closed her eyes and rested her forehead on the rough plank siding of the shanty. Why couldn't she remember? *Why?*

Chapter Six

A few days after the shooting incident, Caleb stopped by the Kemp farm again. Something was immediately different this time, though. Usually when he arrived, one of the men would appear from the barn or a field, or Nancy would peek out and have the front door open long before he could reach the porch. Today, he didn't see anyone around. At first chilled at seeing the farm deserted, he suddenly realized the Kemps had probably sat down to eat their midday meal. Early, by his standards, but that was because he didn't get up at the crack of dawn.

After he knocked, it was Eli who opened the door and said, "Sheriff, come in."

"I don't want to interrupt your meal."

"No, no, you must join us. We just started."

Caleb hesitated, but chose to follow Abby's uncle. Why kid himself? To see her, he'd make a nuisance of himself. Probably already had been, come to think of it.

Silence reigned in the kitchen. Everyone appeared to be concentrating on their plates. Unless he was imagining things, tension filled the room. Had he interrupted a family argument?

The moment Nancy saw Caleb, she jumped to her

feet, her determination to feed every visitor kicking in. "Joshua, get a chair for the sheriff. *Schnell, schnell!*" She shook her head at Abby, who started to rise, and set a place for him herself.

"I'm sorry," he felt compelled to say. "I didn't mean to invite myself."

He was aware that Abby glanced his way, tension on her face. Or maybe that was irritation. Because she didn't want him involved in whatever was going on?

Lucky he wasn't a sensitive guy.

"There is always plenty," Nancy assured him, but without her beaming smile.

Bowls and plates were immediately handed his way. He dished up, trying not to let greed overcome him. His midday meals tended to be light. As always when he was here, though, the temptation was great, starting with sourdough biscuits fresh from the oven.

Looking up from his full plate, he saw that Abby hadn't done more than pick at her food, while the men were already reaching for seconds.

"You talk to her!" Nancy burst out. "Abby thinks she should leave us."

"What?" Caleb had just split open a biscuit, but didn't pick up his knife to butter it. "You're nowhere near recovered."

"It's not that." She quit even pretending she was eating, setting down her fork. After one glance flicked at him, she focused on her aunt and uncle. "The last thing I wanted was to bring violence with me, to involve other people. If those shots *were* intended for me, the same person will be back. I can't even protect myself, far less my family! What if—" her voice broke "—one of you were hurt? Or Joshua, when he came in late? I couldn't live with myself."

Suspicion was his middle name. Her speech seemed melodramatic harsh, playing on the shots that may or may not have been intended for her.

"Where would you go?" her aunt asked. "Ach, someone to watch over you, you must have."

Caleb jumped in. "I agree. You can't go back to your apartment."

"I can call Dad."

The silence was so conspicuous, Caleb looked around in puzzlement. Why had she come here in the first place if her father was nearby?

It would seem they all knew something he didn't.

"You haven't mentioned your father."

Abby bent her head. "We're not close."

"You mean, he's not from the area?"

"Jefferson City."

The state capital was centrally located, and a fair distance from this corner of Missouri, but not so far from Kansas City.

"What does he do for a living?" Subtext: would the man even be around to take care of her?

"He's a researcher working on pest management for the state Department of Agriculture."

Caleb heard a muttered "Never home" he thought came from Eli.

"Married?"

She shook her head.

"Abby." He waited until she raised her eyes to meet his, her reluctance apparent. "This is a good place for you. *If* somebody is gunning for you—" he made sure she heard where he put the emphasis "—what could be safer than a rural area, where any strangers will stand out? Think about it. If that shooter was after you, where did he leave his car?" He gave her a minute, not positive why he felt an urgent need to stomp on whatever scheme she'd been trying to launch, but going with it anyway. "He'd have had a long walk, and through the woods. If he's from Kansas City, he'd have felt like he'd been plunked down in the Wild West. You think somebody can't find you in Jefferson City? There, you'd be alone all day. Here, you have family surrounding you." More quietly, he said, "You have me." Even if he didn't quite know what he meant by that.

Her lips parted as she prepared to challenge his claim, but instead their gazes locked. It was an oddly naked moment. Her eyes held turbulence, and he feared what she'd see in his. He hadn't had a chance to put up any kind of guard.

After a moment, she dipped her chin in some kind of acquiescence and went back to poking at the food on her plate. Caleb decided to eat while he could.

He and Eli discussed the weather, a perennial topic in farming country, and particularly when forecasters were expressing concern that conditions might be leading to tornadoes. Caleb's attention was only half on what was said, while half remained on Abby, who stood the moment Nancy did to begin clearing the table.

Studying her, he realized the strain on her face when he first walked in might have to do with her purported fear for her family, but also with the headache that wouldn't release its grip on her.

When he thought she'd done enough to help Nancy, he said, "Abby, can we talk for a minute?"

Caleb didn't like seeing her wariness toward him, even if he deserved it.

"Yes," she said after a moment, drying her hands and hanging up a dish towel. "But I only have a few minutes. Joshua is to drive me into town—"

"For your physical-therapy appointment. That's why I stopped by." A small piece of why. "I'll be happy to drive you and save Joshua the trip."

"That's very kind of you," she said stiffly. "Onkel Eli, you heard that?"

"Ja," he agreed. "It is a kindness, and I have work for Joshua."

The kid, obviously crushed but resigned, clapped his hat on his head and went out the back door.

"Why don't we leave now, and I'll buy you an ice-cream cone before your appointment?" he suggested. He wasn't sure he could eat another bite, but given the little food she'd put away, ice cream might be perfect.

She perked up. "At Miller's?"

The general store sold half a dozen flavors of hard ice cream made by an Amish dairy farmer from a freezer behind the counter. Their idea of a scoop was the size of a softball.

He smiled. "Where else?"

CALEB'S SMILES, WHETHER AMUSED, sexy or unnervingly tender, invariably weakened Abby's defenses.

"That sounds good," she admitted. "Thank you."

Within minutes, she was in Caleb's SUV, waiting for the air conditioner to kick in. Fortunately, the wait wasn't long. They were still on the gravel road when she felt the first cool air.

"Let me know if that gets too cold," he said.

The heat and humidity today had sapped Abby's energy and appetite both.

"Are you kidding?" She basked in the chill. "I helped can green beans this morning, and it was *roasting* in the kitchen, even with the doors and windows open. How women did it when stoves were wood burning I can't imagine." She made a face. "I've been spoiled rotten. Air-conditioning in my apartment, my car, the police station…"

The corner of his mouth curled. "Your department vehicle. Grocery stores, banks…" The glance he flicked at her no longer held amusement. "Your head hurts."

"I'm not doing so well hiding it, huh?"

"No. Damn it, Abby. I think you need to see a doctor again."

"It hasn't been that long."

"Memories?"

She'd give a lot to be able to trust him.

Understanding her silence deepened the lines in his forehead. Was he insulted? After a minute, he said quietly, "Would you believe me if I promise not to share anything you've remembered with Donahue?"

"Are you promising?" Abby did believe him, which might be foolish. But it wasn't as if she knew anything meaningful.

"Yeah." He took his right hand from the steering wheel and captured her hand with it.

Electricity ran up her arm.

"Okay." The word sounded scratchy. "I'm having flashes. Some from the days before the shooting. Totally unrelated stuff. Some trivial, like thinking about looking for a new apartment. I won't need to be near the precinct."

"Why not?"

"Sergeant Donahue didn't tell you? I quit."

He nodded. No questions. She saw a muscle flex in his jaw and wondered what that was about.

Abby reverted to the disturbing subject of the fleeting memories that had taken to blindsiding her. "I had this really vivid picture of myself standing in this line at the grocery store, people getting grumpy around me because an old lady was so slow paying. She had a little trouble with figuring out which end of her card to insert, but mostly she just wanted to linger and have someone to talk to. The clerk was being really nice. I wanted to slap the guy in line in front of me and say, *Why don't you tease her? Talk to her nicely, instead of asking if she can't get it right? Offer to carry her grocery bag out for her as soon as your stuff is rung up? Make her day?*" Seeing Caleb's crooked smile, she felt her cheeks heat. "Okay, I have a little Amish in me."

"More than a little, I think." The warmth in his slow, deep voice was reassuring.

"And then…" Her headache intensified, letting her know she was edging into dangerous territory. She kept going nonetheless. "I remember begging Neal to tell me what had him so alarmed. Even scared. It's just this flash, the two of us sitting in our car at the curb, me sure something was really wrong. I already knew he was worried, but this was different. It was as if…" A stab of pain felt like an ice pick. She squeezed her eyes shut.

"Abby?" The SUV swerved and then Caleb braked and brought it to a stop.

On the shoulder of the road, she saw, squinting. When had the sun become so glaring she couldn't bear it?

The next moment, he wrapped his hand around her nape beneath the *kapp* and began to knead, his fingers digging into muscles and too-tight tendons. She stifled a moan.

The SUV rocked slightly and she realized a semi had sped past them. They must be on the shoulder beside the highway.

"Tell me you're okay." He sounded worried. Even scared.

Scared. "I think Neal was scared," she whispered. "Not the for-his-life kind, but as if whatever he thought he knew was huge."

The hand on her neck briefly went still. When the massage resumed, Caleb said dryly, "Terrorist-bomb scared? Mayor-of-the-city-corrupt scared? Or wife-cheating-on-him scared?"

Abby took a deep breath and straightened in her seat, sorry to lose the feel of Caleb's hand on her bare skin. "Not his wife. That's more freaked than scared." Although, what did she know? "And... I'm pretty sure this had to do with our jobs. Even before the period I can't remember, he'd take me along when he went to talk to people. He was investigating *something*. I'd hang back, just there in case he needed me, you know?"

"What kind of people?" His voice sharp, he was suddenly all cop.

"All different. Bartenders, once a biker. Pimps. Oh, and a man who looked like a mob boss. I mean, suit and tie, and he had a semicircle of beefy guys around him, all of whom were carrying. That time we were in front of a warehouse by the river. Nobody else around. It was really creepy. I kind of hovered where I could see Neal, even knowing there wasn't a thing I could do in time if he ticked the guy off."

Caleb swore. "Or to protect yourself. Damn it, he shouldn't have taken you."

"We're partners." She bit her lip. "Were partners." She hadn't quite accepted that Neal really was dead. She didn't remember seeing him go down, if she had, and she hadn't been able to attend the funeral.

Caleb's grunt sounded unhappy. "Partners are honest with each other."

"I think he was trying to protect me." That answer came from her heart. She had no proof. "He was stepping into something that could have gotten him in big trouble, and he wanted to keep me out of it in case he was wrong."

"And yet you were with him. Who'd have believed you didn't know? Whether he meant to or not, he put you at risk."

Abby looked down at her hands, clasped on her lap. Caleb was right, of course, because she had no doubt that whatever Neal had been looking into was the reason he'd been murdered, and she'd been shot. If not for a passerby...

"Did you tell Donahue any of this?"

"Of course I did!" she said indignantly. "He obviously thought I'd made it all up."

A grunt was Caleb's sole response, although she could tell as he got back on the road and drove that he was mulling over what she'd told him. Increasingly, Abby knew if there were to be answers, she'd have to find them herself. Which would mean either moving back to her apartment or collecting her car and some of her working wardrobe so that she could pass unremarked during trips to the city. She was pretty sure she could find some of the places she and Neal had gone. Unfortunately, she could no longer show a badge to compel cooperation. At least, not legitimately.

She'd love to think Caleb could be an ally, but his past friendship with Donahue meant his loyalties were already claimed. How could she even ask?

If there was some way to be sure he hadn't passed what she'd told him on to Donahue, maybe she could trust him that much.

Yes, but how would she ever know?

"Miller's," he said, and she blinked. They'd arrived.

"No, THERE'S BEEN no second attempt on her life, if that's what it was. Don't you trust me?" Irritated, Caleb kept the phone to his ear as he peered into his freezer. A casserole dish labeled Chicken Curry and Rice caught his eye. Tuning out Donahue's rumblings, he grabbed it, studied the sticky note on top with directions for heating and popped it in the microwave. He was grateful to the young Amishwoman who cleaned for him and cooked and froze several meals a week, all while he was on duty. He left her money; she left grocery lists for him.

Caleb replayed what Mike had been saying about expecting results by now: was he too busy setting up speed traps to fund his department, or had he fallen for a pretty face and a flimsy story?

He interrupted. "Why didn't you tell me she'd quit the job?"

"Ah, you know she doesn't mean it. Truth is, I'd be happy to have her back if we can clear her."

Caleb gave an incredulous laugh. "You actually think she'd work for you again?"

"She told me in the interview that Homicide had always been her goal. Somebody she loved was murdered."

Leaning a hip against the counter, Caleb frowned. "Who?"

"Didn't say."

Friend? Sibling? Or the mother who'd left the Amish faith?

"She hasn't admitted to recovering any memories?" Donahue asked. "Real or fake?"

"You set me back by days when you got in her face in front of the clinic," Caleb said. He'd try to avoid straight-out lying. "I'd gotten her talking to me, and then *kaboom*. But I've got to be honest. I don't think she's faking the memory loss, and I don't see her as a killer. If you're not already doing it, you should spread your net."

"She has gotten to you." His onetime partner's disgust came through.

"No." Yes. Hell. "I'm good at judging people, Mike. You know that."

"That's it?" Donahue sounded surly, reminding Caleb that he'd never liked any suggestion he was wrong. "Do you have a speck of evidence to support the conclusion that she's innocent?"

"Ever heard of the concept *Innocent until proven guilty*?"

"I just want to *know*." Frustration boiled in his voice.

Caleb sympathized. He'd feel the same if one of his young deputies had been gunned down. So he said, "I'm still on it. I'll do my best to get that proof, one way or another."

The two men let it go at that. Sitting down to eat

twenty minutes later, Caleb was still brooding. He either should have bowed out—or he should have stamped out every spark of attraction and sympathy he felt. Liking, too. As it was, he hated lying to Abby. And now he was lying to Donahue as well.

He'd hardly made a dent in the chicken curry when he caught himself staring into space while his dinner went cold. No, he realized, backing out on his agreement with Mike Donahue wouldn't happen…because *he* had to know, too. He couldn't so much as touch Abby Baker the way he wanted to until he'd ruled out any possibility that something he couldn't even imagine had driven her to set up that damn scene in the alley.

Maybe it was time he did some quiet investigating of his own.

ABBY SAT IN the shade of the front porch, her feet bare and her sleeves rolled up. Temperatures hadn't relented, even in the waning days of September. Today was particularly hot and sticky, and she'd give a lot to be able to change into shorts and a tank top. At least her feet were bare. There wasn't anything close to a breeze, but she kept hoping for one anyway, wriggling her toes like a child reveling in the freedom of summer. Not that she didn't have a chore to do: Aenti Nancy had her shucking corn. *Lots* of corn. As fast as she worked, Nancy replaced the pile, taking the ears into the house. There, she sliced the kernels off the cobs and bagged them to freeze enough to see them through the year. Most of the crop would be sold; already this morning, Isaac had delivered a wagon full to the produce auction house on the outskirts of town.

Rip. Tearing at the husks had been satisfying when

Abby started, but her hands were getting tired. Picking out the corn silk was finicky.

When she heard a car engine, her head came up. A first spurt of excitement dismayed her, as did the pang of disappointment when she realized she didn't know the engine sound. A produce buyer to see Onkel Eli, perhaps?

But the older blue pickup truck stopped closest to the house, right where Caleb always parked. Of all people, Sam Kirk got out and walked across the lawn to the porch.

Surveying her, he grinned. "You look like you're about ten years old. Ah…" His gaze lowered, then shied from her. "Maybe not that."

Because her figure was definitely not a child's. She made a face at him. "I was just thinking the same. Remember what it felt like when the bell rang at the end of the last day of school?"

He laughed. "Free at last."

Sam Kirk. Who'd think it? And… Sam Kirk in worn chinos, athletic shoes with grass stains and a plain T-shirt?

"I didn't expect to see you," she added, carefully.

He shoved his hands in his pockets, something about his stance making her think he felt awkward. "You've been on my mind since I drove you up here. You looked pretty puny, you know." He shrugged. "I thought you might need someone to talk to."

She'd be touched if she could believe he was genuine. He *looked* sincere, but this might be a well-perfected technique when he was interviewing witnesses and suspects. How could she know?

"I already have a designated cop, ready and willing to hear my deepest secrets," she said dryly.

Sam raised his eyebrows. "Who?"

"The local sheriff. Apparently, he was KCPD for years and worked with Sergeant Donahue along the way."

"Really? I didn't hear about him."

And was perturbed because he hadn't, if she was reading his expression right. And who could blame him? He was supposed to be Donahue's partner on this investigation.

"Why don't you come up here and sit down?" To an Amish man or woman, all visitors were welcome and treated well. Nature or nurture, she felt the same compulsion—except when those visitors insulted her family. Sam had been an exception in that respect. "Would you like a cup of coffee?"

He sat on an Adirondack chair near her seat on a bench. "Not if it's any trouble. I drink more of it than I should."

Predictably, Aenti Nancy popped out. Within minutes, she brought coffee and a plate holding several chocolate whoopie pies with cream-and-vanilla filling. Sam thanked her and took a big bite.

After he finished the first of what was essentially a huge cookie and sipped coffee, he sighed. "I may start visiting regularly."

"You and the sheriff. He's here so much, he's probably had to let out his belt a notch or two by now." At least she sounded humorous instead of cranky.

He smiled. After putting away two of the whoopie pies, Sam groaned and set the plate with the two remaining on the floorboards to one side of his chair. She couldn't help noticing he'd taken only a couple of sips of coffee. In the city, he'd be drinking it iced.

"I hear you resigned," he said.

She grabbed another ear of corn. "In my circumstances, wouldn't you have?" *Rip.*

"Probably." He hesitated. "Do you have any questions about the investigation?"

She did, but how honest would he be?

"Please tell me the witness who saw someone bending over me is being taken seriously."

"I'm confident he saw someone."

"Of course, it might have been some lowlife intending to steal my gun."

"That's...a possibility."

Okay, however reluctant, Sam *had* been honest.

She asked more questions, he answered. Unfortunately, it became apparent that the investigation was going nowhere. They were waiting for her to remember what she'd seen...or were trying to nail down proof that would justify her arrest.

Sam had just asked if she'd remembered anything at all when Abby heard a new arrival. Not answering, she turned her head to see a black sheriff's-department vehicle pull up behind Sam's old pickup.

"Sheriff Tanner," she said simply.

She glanced back at Sam to see an intense flash of anger as he watched Caleb slam his door and start across the grass toward them.

Since they were presumably on the same side—what was *that* about?

Chapter Seven

Caleb didn't once take his eyes from the man sitting so comfortably on the Kemp porch, body language and expression implying he and Abby were best friends. Average height, dark hair, olive complexion, he looked vaguely familiar. Someone from KCPD. Given that she'd been running off her fellow detectives, why the chummy atmosphere with this one?

About the time he reached the foot of the porch steps, she smiled at him, if a bit wryly. "Caleb. Do you know Detective Sam Kirk? Sam, this is Sheriff Caleb Tanner."

Kirk set his coffee cup on the wide arm of the chair and rose to his feet. "Tanner. Abby was just telling me about you."

"All good, I hope," he said easily.

"I explained that you're my designated cop and confidant," she said, tart if you were listening for it, "and that he could have saved himself the trip."

"She's not buying that I came as a friend," Sam said ruefully.

Caleb shot back. "Possibly because you're one of the lead investigators into what happened to her."

Sam opened his mouth, but at the same moment

Nancy pushed open the screen door. "Sheriff! So lucky Abby is, to have two visitors today! I'll bring you coffee."

"Denke," he said, offering her an affectionate smile.

Sam bent and picked up the plate, holding it out. "Plenty of leftovers."

Nancy tut-tutted, snatched the plate and hurried back into the house. Amused, Caleb could read her mind. *Leftovers! Those were for family, not a valued visitor.* Assuming that's how she saw him.

Unfortunately, the tableau remained: Abby holding a half-shucked cob in her hands, Sam rocking back on his heels, his hands in his pockets, smiling, and Caleb feeling like a third wheel. Aggressive, too. He didn't like another man laying a subtle claim to his girl. Yeah, he felt that primitive. He wouldn't be leaving until Kirk did—unless something exceptionally bad occurred in his county, demanding his presence. He willed the radio to stay silent.

Caleb strolled across the porch and sat on the same bench as Abby, leaning back against the house wall and stretching out his legs. *Yep, I'm at home here. Suck eggs.*

In another mood, he'd have laughed at himself.

"So, what's your perspective on the investigation?" he asked.

Kirk talked in circles, which wasn't a surprise. How up-front was he likely to be in front of a suspect? What Caleb couldn't tell was whether the detective agreed with his sergeant or not.

Nancy brought out coffee and a plate of whoopie pies for Caleb. When she offered to refill Sam Kirk's cup, he must have recognized his cue to go.

His voice became gentle when he said his goodbyes to Abby. "I meant my offer—any time you want to take me up on it. I think you've gotten a rough deal, and I don't like it."

She stood and thanked him. They didn't touch. He gave her a nod and strode back to his pickup truck. After doing a U-turn, he waved as he passed the house.

Silence enveloped the two left on the porch.

"Your hands look sore," Caleb said at last, nodding at them.

Abby scrunched up her nose. "I'm not used to doing manual labor, but I'm determined to keep up with Aenti Nancy."

He laughed. "I don't blame you. How about if I help you for a few minutes?"

"Do you mean that?" She plucked at her dress, trying to let air in.

His gaze dropped to her hand, making her realize she'd pulled the fabric over her breasts. When their eyes met, she felt even hotter.

He cleared his throat. "Sure, unless I get called away." He went inside to wash his hands, then returned to join her in shucking corn.

He'd been at it for a few minutes when she said, "You really don't have to do this."

He smiled. "I came out to see you. I can make myself useful at the same time."

"What would the county council members think if they knew they were paying you to do this?"

Caleb grinned at her. "We'll call it my lunch hour." After a minute, he asked, "Why was *he* here?"

Giving him a sharp look, she said, "Do we have a little jurisdictional conflict here?"

"It was just a question." And the conflict didn't have

a thing to do with their respective jurisdictions; it was all about her.

Tiny creases formed in her forehead. "The answer is *I don't know.* He's claimed before that he thinks Sergeant Donahue is wrong to suspect me. Today he offered to answer questions and listen if I wanted to talk."

Caleb heard the undertone. After dropping corn husks atop the pile in the nearly full bin, he said, "You don't believe him."

Abby shrugged. "Hard to."

"And that goes double for me?"

She gave him a wary, sidelong look. "I…don't know. I haven't decided about you yet."

"Huh. I'm encouraged."

The corners of her lips quivered. He loved her mouth, whether it was pursed or smiling or she was nibbling on her lower lip.

Can't touch her.

Conversation strayed as they worked. She told him Joshua yearned from afar for a younger Amish girl. "Too young, thank goodness," Abby said. "Both of them, in my opinion. But she's very pretty. I looked for her Sunday."

He nodded; this had been the church Sunday for all three of the local Amish districts. On alternate Sundays, each district worshipped at the home of one of the members. The following Sunday was for visiting.

"Poor Joshua is not alone in having his eye on her." Abby shook her head, the ribbons dangling from her *kapp* moving over the swell of her generous breasts beneath her blue dress. "I thought she seemed a tiny bit self-satisfied and vain, but I may be wrong."

Caleb laughed. In Deitsch, he said, "Ach, but weren't you the prettiest girl at that age?"

Her smile faded. "I was mostly living with my father then."

"Mostly?"

"I still came summers, and sometimes spring or Christmas breaks."

After the lighter, enjoyable conversation, perhaps he shouldn't ask, but curiosity overcame Caleb. He tried to keep his voice soft, undemanding. "Will you tell me why?"

"My father didn't remarry, and I guess having me home alone every day didn't strike him as a good idea."

"And earlier?"

Her hands had gone still. "He...didn't deal well with my mother's death. He didn't have anything left for me."

The man had a young daughter grieving as much as he was, and he couldn't be bothered with her? It was all Caleb could do to hold back what he really thought.

"You haven't said—"

His radio crackled. "Sheriff?"

A minute later, he was on his feet. "I have to go."

Obviously worried, Abby stood, too, a hand pressed to her chest. "I didn't hear all of that. Did she say a buggy...?"

"Yes." A deputy old enough to know better had gotten so excited about nailing a speeder, he hadn't given a thought to the vulnerability of a portion of their citizenry. Grimly, Caleb said, "I forbid high-speed chases in this county for a good reason. The driver of the car my deputy was after took off when he saw that he was being pursued. Raced over a rise and hit a buggy." He shook his head at her expression. "I know two people were transported to the hospital, but not how badly they're hurt, or who they are."

"Oh, no." Worry—*caring*—were plain to see in her blue eyes. "Can you tell me where it happened?"

"Jenner Road. It probably wasn't anyone in your aunt and uncle's district…"

"But you can't be sure." She reached out as if she couldn't help herself and squeezed his hand. "Can you let us know? That is, if we don't hear in the meantime?"

Despite his tension, he smiled. "Because the Amish grapevine works faster than police radio. I will, Abby."

The impulse to kiss her was so visceral, he felt as if he never parted from her without at least a quick kiss. Fighting the odd feeling, he reluctantly released her hand and then made himself bound down the porch steps and lope across the lawn.

TENSION GRIPPED THE entire household. Abby's uncle had allowed Joshua to stay at the house to help his aunt.

The injured Amish would be acquaintances of the Kemps, at least. Very possibly members of their church district, friends, even first or second or third cousins of Abby's. The Amish men and women in the county all knew each other, if only through business. The injured might be the butcher and his wife, the very fine quilter who owned the fabric store in town, the young couple who only Sunday had shyly let friends know they were expecting their first child. Or Rose and her husband… Surely not them.

Neighbors and friends had heard there was an accident and assumed the Kemps, who had become so friendly with the sheriff, must know more. Visitors came and went. Aenti sent Joshua to the phone shanty twice to check for messages.

Aenti Nancy wouldn't be alone in setting to cooking. The Amish women always saw to it that nobody who was injured or mourning would need to prepare a meal for weeks to come. Levi Graber, the buggy maker, let it be known that he would repair or replace the damaged buggy without recompense. The loss of a buggy horse, many of which were retired harness racers, would be a great loss, all agreed. Everyone prayed that no children had been hurt.

Abby had almost forgotten how intertwined were the lives of the Amish spread across the county, and beyond. How they could truly count on each other. The Leit, as they called themselves—the people—didn't believe in insurance or the government Social Security. Medical bills would be settled by the entire church district, unless they were too great, in which case other groups would contribute as well. Bake sales might be held, or a quilt auction, or farming equipment they could do without might be sold, just as they did to support the local volunteer firefighters, many of whom were Amish.

They all prayed for the driver of the car, too, that he not be badly hurt. They felt sure he was sorry for his mistake; the injured people in the buggy would forgive him, and so should everyone else.

This represented a painful contrast with what Abby had become accustomed to seeing on the job. Drug addiction, alcoholism, poverty and greed brought such tragedy, damaged these very connections.

Three hours later, a buggy rolled up to the barn. Hurrying out, Abby recognized Mary and Lloyd Stoltzfus.

Mary was Nancy's sister, Lloyd a farrier. Before they had their feet on the ground, word had already spread.

Hurt, *ja*, but no one killed. The two in the buggy had been Ernest Wagler and his oldest son, Paul, who belonged to a neighboring church district. The worries were not over. Their bishop was with them, Paul had a broken leg that would keep him from working for a month or two, and Ernest had hit his head and was still unconscious two hours ago, when Mary and Lloyd had been at the hospital to see Lloyd's *daad*, who was in for a heart procedure.

Pain spiked in Abby's head. She knew what Ernest Wagler would experience when—if—he opened his eyes to find himself in such a strange place, with a head that felt like a grenade after someone pulled out the pin. Would he remember everything up to the moment when the buggy splintered into the ditch, or would his brain, like hers, choose to black out some of that time?

"We saw Sheriff Tanner," Mary told a cluster of women. "He asked if we could stop by here so that the Kemps would know what happened. To keep a promise, he said."

Hovering at the back of the group, Abby told herself there wasn't a reason in the world why she should be disappointed instead of pleased that he had done what he'd said he would.

No—she wasn't good at lying to herself, even when the truth was unpalatable. *My father hardly remembers he has a daughter*. That was a truth she had faced a very long time ago.

This truth was different: she'd wanted to see Caleb again. Her heart lifted every time she saw him. She almost trusted him. Worst of all—she felt too much for him, trust and attraction only the beginning.

For the first time in her life, she had met a man she thought she could love. *If* it didn't turn out that she'd deluded herself about who he really was—an entirely realistic possibility.

After hearing everything Mary and Lloyd had to say, Abby returned to the kitchen to share the news and to help her aunt as much as she could. Two more of Eli and Nancy's children, with their spouses and young kids, joined them for dinner that night, crowding the kitchen.

Head throbbing by the time the guests had left, Abby helped put the finishing touches on the kitchen. With the family gathered, Onkel Eli settled in the living room to read passages from the Bible, as he did every night. Abby murmured an apology and slipped outside instead.

Not even seven o'clock and it was already dark. She hadn't paid attention to the passing weeks, but the first of October had to be almost upon them. She'd never expected to stay this long. Vaguely, she'd supposed she would be cleared and back to work by now.

Her cracked sternum still twinged with incautious movements but wouldn't have kept her from studying crime scenes, conducting interviews or spending hours on end on the phone—usually on hold. But even if she had been exonerated, the ever-present headache that worsened without warning would have kept her on leave. Then, of course, there was her lost memory. No matter whether evidence turned up that led Sergeant Donahue and Sam Kirk to make an arrest, how could she do a job when everyone around her, and maybe herself most of all, would doubt the accuracy of all her memories? What if newer ones were slipping into whatever fissure had swallowed the lost week, or jumbling with old ones? Defense attorneys would call open season on her whenever she testified in a courtroom.

Abby chose to sit on the bench where she'd spent a good part of the day shucking corn, partly because it was out of the rectangle of light from the living room. The temperature probably hadn't dropped much yet, but compared to the sweltering kitchen, the air felt cool to her. She closed her eyes and drank in the quiet sounds of the evening.

How can I do the job?

She pulled herself up short. Wrong verb tense. How could she *have* done it was more to the point. She'd already resigned. Or was that a little bit of memory slippage?

No, she couldn't return to work with those same people. She just hadn't let herself think about the future yet, beyond striving to remember what terrible things she'd seen in that alley. Clearing her name.

If she couldn't do that… No, she wouldn't believe that was even a possibility.

But once it happened…would she look for a job in another department? Or consider a different future?

Since absolutely nothing came to mind, she had to accept that she still wasn't ready to think ahead, far less make decisions.

That was the moment she first heard the growl of an approaching vehicle.

CALEB DIDN'T KNOW what he was doing here. He had no doubt that Mary and Lloyd Stoltzfus would have stopped by hours ago—and probably at nearly every other Amish household they'd passed on their way home. At this time of night, he'd be intruding. And yet he parked by the house. He couldn't believe he hungered like this to see one face.

With a sigh, he got out and started toward the front door. He'd keep it brief, say he'd just wanted to be sure they knew about the Waglers.

Something moved in the darkness on the porch, and somehow he knew.

He stopped halfway up the steps. "Abby?"

"Caleb." She sounded both puzzled and glad. The glad part made him feel a little less foolish.

As he crossed the porch to join her, he caught a glimpse through the lighted window of Nancy sitting in a recliner knitting, her head bent over her work. "Are you okay?" he asked.

"Oh…mostly tired. Once we were done freezing a whole lot of corn, we cooked for the Waglers. And people kept stopping by, of course." She added in a rush, "Thank you for making sure we knew what happened."

Mostly tired? That meant her head still ached.

"I didn't know if you'd get a phone message."

"We would have today. Joshua checked the answering machine a couple of times."

Enough soft light came from a window behind him to allow him to see her face. In her old-fashioned garb, wearing the filmy white prayer *kapp*, she made him think of a Renaissance painting, golden light against the dark. Sitting beside her, he reached for her hand and was relieved when she returned the clasp.

"Has he regained consciousness?" she asked. "Ernest?"

Caleb let out a long breath. He wished he could give her a different answer. "No. His wife says he has a hard head and will be fine, although I suspect she's mostly trying to convince herself. Doctors do seem to be optimistic, though. They think it's the swelling around his brain."

"Oh." Her face showed only in profile. "That's what they said about me, too. They drilled a hole in my skull to relieve the swelling. Did you know that?"

His hand tightened on hers. "No."

"I wonder if he'll remember the accident."

"He may not. I told you I've seen other cases like yours."

"I wasn't sure if I believed you."

"It's the truth."

"Then why—" She stopped.

Not even breathing, he waited.

"Why doesn't anybody believe me?"

"You mean why doesn't *Donahue* believe you." Anger roughened his voice.

Abby looked fully at him. "Do you? Really?"

"Yeah." In that instant, he hadn't the smallest doubt. Not about this.

She nodded, just a dip of her head, and looked away again.

After a minute, he broke the quiet between them. "I'm surprised Eli hasn't come out to see who is here."

"I think he must have guessed."

"I'm not offending his sense of what's proper?"

"He might get confused sometimes, but mostly he knows I'm Englisch, a police officer, no *maidal* like his daughters were, that I don't need protecting."

Caleb knew better than to say so, but he wasn't so sure about that. Her strength showed, but he also often sensed vulnerability that he wouldn't expect in a woman who'd made a success of herself in law enforcement. Coming from a background like hers, she must walk an emotional maze every day.

He wanted to ask why there wasn't a man in her life, but he couldn't do that, either, not yet. Today, he hadn't been able to help wondering about Sam Kirk, though.

"Are you and Kirk friends?" he asked gruffly.

"Sam?" she said in surprise. "No, I've never even worked with him before. Although, after I was released from the hospital, he's the one who drove me here. I assumed he was playing good cop to the sergeant's bad. Thinking he could persuade me to open up to him."

"Have you?"

She laughed softly, with a hint of sadness. "No. He may really sympathize with me, I can't be sure, but… it seems unlikely."

Would Donahue have been stupid enough to overkill in sending two different cops to worm their way into her confidence? Caleb speculated. Maybe Sam Kirk did disagree with his sergeant's conclusions. Or maybe—

"Is he married?"

"Sam? I think I heard that he's divorced. Something about how much he hates to work days when he's supposed to have his kids." Abby seemed to mull that over. "You think…? No, it can't be that," she said after a minute. "He'd have asked me out before."

There were reasons he might not have. He was quite a bit older than Abby, and relationships between cops who worked together were discouraged, if not entirely forbidden. The guy may have seen his chance when Abby needed help—and when the possibility was good that she wouldn't be back at KCPD.

Caleb kept quiet.

"It doesn't really matter," she said. "How often is he likely to show up this far from home?"

Caleb knew he ought to leave. He'd indulged himself longer than he should have. He'd be happy to sit here for hours, as long as he was holding Abby's hand.

Sure. Wouldn't want another thing, would you?

He rubbed his free hand over his jaw, feeling the scratch of evening stubble. "I should get going."

"Oh!" Abby snatched her hand back and leapt to her feet. "You must be dying to get home, and I've kept you."

"No." He rose, too, slowly. Somehow, words he hadn't meant to say came out. "I wanted to see you."

This *oh* came out differently. They faced each other, not quite touching, but near enough he could lift a hand to her cheek. In fact, he was doing it without any conscious decision.

Alarm bells went off. He had to use the brains God gave him. *Back away*, he ordered himself. *Say goodnight.*

He did neither. Instead, he cupped her face and bent forward, giving her time to retreat. To his profound relief, she swayed toward him, whispered, "Caleb?"

His lips covered hers.

Chapter Eight

His brief hesitation told Abby he was giving her a chance to slip away. She ought to take it, instead of demonstrating how inept she was at this and thus humiliating herself. What's more, this man could really hurt her. Was almost guaranteed to hurt her.

He was also the only man who'd ever inspired an unfamiliar need to touch him, to press her body against his, to crawl inside his skin if she could.

Maybe there wasn't really a choice at all. She heard herself whisper his name and laid a hand on his chest.

His lips brushed softly over hers, then more firmly when they came back for more. Rapt, she soaked in every tiny sensation. His hard chest rose and fell beneath her splayed hand. At a damp stroke along the seam of her lips, she jerked, the effect like an electrical shock. His tongue…he wanted in. Abby parted her lips and felt the hot slide of his tongue against hers.

From that moment, her thoughts blurred. A moan slipped out. The kiss deepened, became hungry—teeth and lips and tongue. He gathered her in with both arms, and she pushed herself up on tiptoe to meet him. With one hand he kneaded her butt, lifting her, pulling her tighter against his tall, powerful body, into the rigid evidence of his arousal that she ached to feel between her thighs. Her own fingers slid into his hair, thick and cool. She felt shameless, urgent, all longing and need.

He was the one to groan and wrench his mouth away. At first he kissed his way across her cheek, sucked on her ear lobe, nipped her neck. But instead of coming back for more, his arms loosened. She sank back onto her heels, a chill moving through her.

Gripping her upper arms, he stepped back. His eyes were so dark, she couldn't see any color, and yet they glittered. His mouth was softer than she remembered seeing it, swollen. She reached up to touch her own cheek where it burned. From the scrape of his beard stubble, Abby realized in some distant part of her.

"I guess that was good-night." She sounded appropriately sardonic, when she felt like…like a snow globe, just shaken. So much floating inside, no way of knowing how the landscape would look when it all settled.

"Your uncle could come out anytime," Caleb said hoarsely.

She searched his face to see why he pulled back.

She only nodded, backed away herself and crossed her arms, trying desperately to hold herself together.

"It's all right, Caleb. Stick your head in and say hello if you want."

"I can't." He sounded rueful, and she knew why he couldn't let anyone else see him.

Her nod was meaningless.

"I'll be sure you get an update on Ernest."

"Thank you." *Go*, she thought fiercely. *Please go.*

"Damn it, Abby—" Intense frustration infused his voice, but then he shook his own head. "I do need to leave."

Still he kept looking at her. She wasn't sure she so much as took a breath. At last, at last, he backed up a step, then another. Finally, without another word, he departed.

She stood there, unmoving, until the SUV had disappeared down the driveway, until she could no longer hear it. Then she sank onto the bench and bent over, dizzy, her head pounding with each beat of her heart.

She didn't know if she was hurt…or aching for something that wouldn't happen.

WHAT IN *HELL* had he been thinking? Caleb asked himself violently. But he knew—he hadn't been thinking at all. All he'd been able to think about was kissing the woman since the first time he'd laid eyes on her, and tonight, the two of them alone in the warm night, there'd been a compelling sense of intimacy that undermined his resolve.

He clenched his teeth. With her looks, she'd be a natural at playing men, making them see something that didn't go deeper than the surface. God help him; he didn't believe that, but he needed to follow through on the promise he'd made to Mike Donahue.

What he wanted to do was step right smack in the middle of the investigation. Get out there himself, talk to anyone her partner had tracked down, guy with the bodyguards included. Pimps, she'd said. That struck a wrong note, assuming drugs had anything to do with the shooting in the alley. Had Donahue had the sole witness sit down with a police artist? The best of them could pull amazing details from people who thought they hadn't seen anything. Damn it; Caleb wanted to sit down with that witness himself.

Of course, he'd seriously alienate Donahue if he did any of that. Chasing leads on a crime that had happened in another part of the state did not fall in his job description.

His headlights picked out an animal in the middle of the road ahead. Braking, he watched as the possum finally scuttled into the undergrowth.

According to Donahue, Abby had left both her laptop and her phone behind. They'd gotten into her laptop, found nothing work related except notes and drafts of reports that corresponded with assigned investigations. They hadn't been able to break the password for her phone. Caleb presumed she had guessed her apartment would be searched, including the electronic devices she'd left behind.

Which left a logical next step for him, underhanded though it was.

Well, then, don't get caught, he told himself.

HE WAS TOO tied up the next couple of days to make it back out to the Kemp farm. His deputies raided a meth lab hidden in a ramshackle barn and, after a scuffle, made three arrests. Two of the three weren't even twenty-one, and this would already be their second convictions for manufacturing meth. The third guy was a scrawny sixteen-year-old who'd be tried in juvenile court.

All three yelled *police brutality*, although the only person injured in the melee was one of the deputies, who had suffered a broken cheekbone, a giant lump on his head and a heck of a shiner. After taking a two-by-four to the head, he was lucky not to have ended up in a coma like Ernest Wagler had. The good news was that

Ernest's wife was right about how hard his head was; he'd regained consciousness yesterday.

The punks who'd been cooking up meth would be facing charges of assaulting a law-enforcement officer as well as the drug charges. The surprise was that they hadn't had any firearms on the premises.

Gathering information for the county council ate up most of Caleb's time. Then, aggravatingly, he didn't turn out to need most of it during the monthly meeting, during which his biggest challenge was maintaining an alert expression for three interminable hours while not developing twitches.

Thursday afternoon, he drove to the Kemps'. He could pretend to be dismayed when he found out Abby had gone to town for her physical-therapy appointment. Easy for him to forget, right? He took a roundabout way to be sure he didn't pass the Kemps' buggy.

No sign of Eli or Isaac when he parked. He'd half hoped Nancy would be off visiting and no one at all would be in the house, but she opened the door and greeted him with apparent pleasure. "Sheriff! Come in, come in." When he did so, she switched to Deitsch. "You've missed Abby, if that's who you came to see. Joshua drove her to town to see that man."

He gave himself a light rap on the head. "I meant to offer to drive her again. I've just been so busy…"

"Not so busy you can't have coffee and a bite to eat! I just made dried-apple dumplings."

He smiled at her. "I'm never too busy for *schnitz und knepp*."

She chuckled contentedly. "I didn't think so."

After dishing up for him, she bustled around the kitchen, not seemingly doing much. He made conversation for a few minutes, conscious of the clock's ticking, then said, "You must have been in the middle of doing something."

"Ach, working in the garden, nothing that can't wait."

Perfect.

He took a last bite and another swallow of coffee. "You go right ahead, Nancy. I'll finish my coffee and let myself out."

She protested, he insisted and she surrendered, leaving him alone in the kitchen.

Alone in the house.

Caleb dumped the rest of the coffee in the sink and quietly headed for the staircase. Now, all he had to do was figure out which room was Abby's.

THE CAR CAME out of nowhere.

Abby had let herself be lulled into a meditative state by the drone of metal wheel rims on pavement, the clip-clop of hooves, the sway of the buggy. She'd slept even less well since the kiss and had assured Joshua she didn't mind if he listened to his iPod. He had shyly showed it to her the first time he drove her to town. It was an old one, but still working.

"Elam Yoder gave it to me," he'd told her. "You know. After he was baptized."

Abby nodded understanding. Electronic devices like an iPod were strictly forbidden for church members, except for telephones necessary to run a business—and then the bishop had to approve them.

"He says Jacob Mast gave it to *him*." Joshua clearly marveled at that, and she knew why. Jacob Mast was now a bearded man with a pregnant wife and two-year-old son, chosen by God to be a minister besides.

Jacob, listening to who knew what kind of music via an earbud?

Much of the way today, Joshua had steered Sadie Mae, a pretty dark brown mare, along a quiet country road. They could have reached town faster taking the more direct highway as they had Tuesday, but Abby was glad he'd chosen the different route. He and Sadie Mae hadn't seemed to mind the speed with which cars and trucks passed, barely a few feet separating them from the frail buggy, but Abby had jumped each time, her pulse racing until they turned into town.

Now, immersed in her thoughts, she paid no attention to the intersection ahead, not a busy one. Obedient to Joshua, the mare slowed until he clucked and they started across the two-lane road.

The sudden roar of an engine jerked Abby into awareness. A black sedan closed in on them so fast, there was nothing Joshua could do. Even calm Sadie Mae broke her stride. Abby had only an instant to try to brace herself for the impact.

Brakes screeched, but too late. Abby was looking right into the driver's eyes when the crunch came, and the buggy flew sideways. Joshua was yelling something, the horse screamed, but she felt as if time had slowed, as if she was having an out-of-body moment. The steel wheel rims made terrible sounds as they scraped sideways across the pavement. The buggy broke into pieces. Abby realized in a dreamlike way that she lay almost across the shiny hood of the car.

And then they stopped. All of them. The silence was deafening.

The driver's side door opened. She expected to hear

the man panicking, saying, *Are you hurt? I've called 9-1-1!* but maybe she'd lost her hearing.

With difficulty, she turned her head to see what had happened to Joshua. To her astonishment, he remained in his seat, although much of the buggy no longer enclosed him. He sat frozen, his mouth open in an O but no sound emerging.

It's me, she thought, except suddenly she *did* hear a man's voice. More, the hum of wheels, the fast *clop-clop* of an approaching horse and buggy. This voice spoke Deitsch, which her mind momentarily didn't want to interpret, but the alarm was evident.

The car door slammed. She once again saw the driver's face through the windshield, his eyes burning into hers. But the car was moving, backing up, the bumper wrenching free from the wreckage with a horrible sound, and she couldn't find any purchase on the slick metal of the hood. She futilely tried to dig her fingers in, but as the man accelerated in reverse, she slid backward and tumbled off, trying to go limp except for cradling her head as the pavement came at her.

Then the car swerved around them and sped off with a screech and the smell of burning rubber, topping a gentle hill to disappear over it.

"We're so lucky you came along!" Abby exclaimed, for what had to be the third or fourth time.

They were lucky, all around. Neither she nor Joshua were badly hurt, just scraped and bruised. The buggy was history, but Sadie Mae had staggered to her feet and was able to limp slowly up the lane to the nearest farm. The owner, a man named Nick Cobb, wasn't Amish and had appeared with a cell phone in hand. He'd already called the police and was on the phone with a veterinarian by the time Amos King helped Abby and Joshua into the rear seats of his big family buggy to take them home.

Nick Cobb had waved them on. "You don't need to stand around here. The deputy will know where to find you for his report." He'd shaken his head. "Bad enough to hit you, but then to take off."

Hit us on purpose, Abby feared, although anyone else would call her paranoid for thinking so. And… maybe she was. Her throat constricted. Two near misses in a matter of weeks…and this time Joshua could have easily been a casualty as well.

Right now, she hurt all over, and decided she could think about this later. Amos King's buggy rattled and shook its way up the dirt driveway to Eli and Nancy's house, stopping behind a sheriff's-department SUV. Caleb? Why would he be here? Amos secured the reins and came around to help her out. Her knees tried to crumple.

"I think I need to lie down."

"Ja," he agreed, studying her with worry. "I will help you to the house. Joshua, you must wait for me to come back—do you hear me?"

The teenager nodded agreement.

She did lean on Amos's arm until they reached the front door. Inside, she heard someone coming downstairs—Aenti Nancy, Abby thought in relief. The door swung open…but Caleb stood there, looking as shocked as she felt.

HELL. UPSTAIRS WHEN he'd heard voices out front, he'd about had a heart attack. He'd yanked at the duffel zipper, but when it stuck he'd had to abandon it. By the time footsteps sounded on the front porch, he'd made it downstairs in time to swipe the sweat off his forehead with his shirtsleeve. Visitors, he tried to tell himself; he'd have heard a car arriving. But he opened the door to find Abby clutching the arm of a stranger, an Amishman. She'd come so close to catching him red-handed—

He took in what he was seeing. Battered and dirty, *kapp* missing, dress torn and hair wild, she swayed on her feet. "Abby!" He reached for her, looking at the man. "What happened?"

"You are the sheriff, *ja*?"

"Yes."

"There was an accident. I came along just as it happened." His accent was stronger than some. "A car hit the buggy. It was…" He visibly groped for a word. *"Erector."*

"Destroyed."

"Ja."

The images Caleb imagined seemed to tighten a fist around his heart. Abby could have died, he thought, sickened. And he hadn't driven her to her appointment today because he wanted to search her room. "Joshua," he said, remembering suddenly.

The man gestured toward his large buggy. "The Lord was with them," he said simply.

"Did anyone call 9-1-1?"

"Ja, a fellow who lives near. Nick Cobb."

"I know Nick." He bent to sweep Abby up in his arms. "I think you should go to the ER."

Something like panic widened her eyes. "I've had enough of hospitals. I just want to lie down. Please."

Caleb frowned down at her, but finally said, "Okay. For now. I'll carry you up, then find Nancy."

She peered at him as if trying to read his thoughts, but said only, politely, "Thank you." She looked back at the stranger who'd brought her home and thanked him, too, in Pennsylvania Dutch.

"It makes no trouble," the man returned politely.

Caleb ended the exchange by starting up the stairs. He carried her straight to her room, which he already knew was spare as a nun's cell, containing only a twin bed and dresser, and pegs on the wall to hang bonnets and capes. The duffle bag sat atop the dresser, and a box of books beside it. He'd flipped through all those books earlier. Now he pulled aside the covers and gently laid her down. After removing her shoes, he sat on the edge of the bed beside her for a minute, unable to stop himself from smoothing back her hair. He found a lump and inspected the bruise forming on her jaw even as his fingertips tingled pleasantly from the silky feel of her skin.

"You're sure nothing's broken?"

Her lashes rose. "No. Really. Will you go help Joshua?"

"Yeah," he said roughly. "Damn." He pushed himself to his feet. "I'll send Nancy up, then find out what happened."

She opened her mouth as if to say something…then closed it.

Caleb kissed her forehead, stroked the uninjured side of her face and left to do his job.

It wasn't until he descended the stairs to find Nancy fluttering around her youngest son that he realized how badly he'd just screwed up. He shouldn't have known which bedroom was Abby's without asking. He could only hope that, stressed, she hadn't noticed.

After getting the story from Joshua, who appeared less damaged than Abby, Caleb talked to the man who'd brought them home. Amos King. He knew the name, but it took a minute for him to remember why. Amos was a furniture maker who had lost his workshop and house to a tornado last year. But in the way of the Amish, within a couple of weeks a new house had been built, with the barn raising shortly thereafter. Other craftsmen within the community, Amish and Englisch, had donated furniture and pieces of art to be auctioned, the proceeds to replace his tools and household goods. A widower, Amos was a good man from all Caleb had heard.

In telling what he'd seen, Amos echoed something Joshua said.

"The place where the accident happened—it is in a dip, I think you say." With his hand, he shaped a roller-coaster track. "I didn't see the car coming over the hill. It must have," he said in puzzlement, "but..." He shook his head.

When Caleb asked if he'd noticed the license plate, Amos only shook his head again. Approaching from the side, he probably wouldn't have seen it, but being Amish he likely wouldn't have paid attention anyway.

Damn, he should have asked Abby about the license plate. She'd surely have looked for one even amidst chaos.

Caleb drove to the site, hoping Nick Cobb could provide another perspective, but when he rolled to a stop behind a deputy's car and got out, he couldn't do anything but stand stock-still, staring in shock at the wreckage.

The torque from the force of the car striking the buggy had ripped the black fiberglass body to pieces. Both the Plexiglas windshield and the splashboard—the buggy equivalent of a dashboard—had broken in half. The steel tire rims were twisted. Bits of glass littered the pavement, just as they did after a typical car accident. The local bishops all encouraged their church members to have battery-operated lights and turn signals on their buggies, unlike in some more conservative districts. The right front light and turn signal both had been smashed.

Pulling himself together with an effort, Caleb exchanged a few words with the two deputies present, then crouched to study the glass. Was there any chance a headlight or other light on the car had broken, too? Unfortunately, he didn't think there was enough glass for both. They'd go over the panels of the buggy with a magnifying glass in hopes of finding a scraping of paint from the car that had hit it. Paint samples could be compared in online databases and lead them to the car make and model. The fact that it had been black, like the buggy, just made their search a little more difficult.

"It's a miracle they survived," he said flatly. He couldn't figure out how they had.

"Maybe there's something to their faith," the older of the two deputies remarked, shaking his head.

Abby wasn't Amish.

A heavy weight in his chest, he turned his back on the wreckage to return to his vehicle.

ABBY LAY IN BED aching as she waited for the ibuprofen she'd swallowed to take effect. She brooded about whether the accident had been just that and, if so, why the man had stared at her with such fury as he reversed the car before fleeing.

There were people who didn't like the Amish, thought them un-American or cultlike, or at least resented having to watch constantly for their slow-moving buggies. He might blame her and Joshua for the accident, be angry because he could be ticketed for speeding if caught, or see a raise in his insurance rates. Still, remembering the hateful glare, Abby shivered.

Finally, she dragged herself up to find fresh clothing to take with her to the bathroom. A hot bath sounded heavenly. Joshua had already taken one; she'd heard the water draining a few minutes ago. Ruefully, she looked down at the dress. It could be mended enough for her to wear for scrubbing floors or weeding the garden, but not for when she'd be seen by anyone outside the family. Her Amish wardrobe had already been limited, and her own sewing skills were pathetic. Aenti Nancy would probably make her a new dress. Given how much taller Abby was than most Amish women, she couldn't borrow.

It took her a minute of looking around to realize neither her *kapp* nor the black bonnet she'd worn were anywhere to be found. Would somebody think to pick them up out of the wreckage, or would they be beyond repair?

Of course, she could put on some of the clothes she'd brought from her real—or, at least, former—life, although she was reluctant to stand out the way she would then. In case someone *was* watching for her.

Her gaze left the dress hanging from a peg to settle on her duffel bag, which she'd never totally unpacked. About all she'd taken out of it were panties and socks, since Amish women didn't wear bras. She'd swear she had left it zipped shut, and now it gaped open. The clothes, at least semineatly packed, were stirred up. A pale pink bra strap had gotten stuck in the zipper.

Surely Joshua wouldn't have been curious enough to poke around in her things. *Somebody* had been…

How dense could she be?

Idle curiosity had nothing to do with it. Her duffel had been searched, and who'd done it was no mystery. The man who insisted he was on her side, who had promised not to lie to her. The man who'd been in the house, seemingly alone, at a time he knew she wouldn't be there.

She couldn't believe she hadn't wondered earlier what he was doing here, wandering around the house.

Feeling angry and, most of all, betrayed, Abby backed away from the dresser and the evidence of what a creep he really was.

Chapter Nine

The instant she saw him, Caleb knew how much trouble he was in.

He'd come back primarily to ask her about the license plate and for any other details she'd recalled. Okay, and to be sure she really was all right.

She sat out on the porch, hands folded in her lap, as if she'd been waiting for him. Which she probably had been. He had to assume she didn't want to talk to him in front of any of her relatives. As he crossed the yard, Abby's face remained expressionless. This was the cop, not the complex woman he'd been getting to know.

Without a word, he sat down and flipped open his notebook on the wide arm of the Adirondack chair. He had to get this out of the way before he let her take her shots.

"Did you see a license plate?"

"There wasn't one in front."

He frowned. "Two are required."

She gave him a did-you-forget-what-I-do-for-a-living look.

"You're sure."

"The car came straight at me. I lay across the hood, slipped off it when the driver backed up. Yes, I'm positive. And no, I did not see the license plate on the back. I should have made an effort, but had other things going on at the time."

Things that had left her with so many visible bruises and scrapes, he hated to think how many more were covered by her stockings and calf-length dress.

"Could it have been covered?"

"No, just not there. I can picture empty screw holes in the bumper."

"Okay. How many people were in the car?" Joshua had thought only the driver, but Caleb had had the impression that the boy had been paralyzed by fear.

"One that I could see."

She closed her eyes when she described the man to him. Unfortunately, she hadn't seen any distinctive features. He'd worn a baseball-style cap with a tractor logo on it that didn't go with the car, which she described as a full-size sedan. He'd worn sunglasses when he first hit them, but they must have fallen off in the collision.

"He was furious," she said calmly. "If looks could kill."

"You're not suggesting this was anything but an accident." Although he wouldn't be much of a cop if he hadn't already been speculating himself.

"It crossed my mind." Her body language remained placid, her voice willfully calm, her eyes angry. "We should have seen or heard the car coming before we did. I think he was parked on the shoulder in the shade of the grove of trees not that far from the corner. It felt like he was going fast, but if he'd really been at full speed after coming down the hill, I doubt Joshua and I would have survived."

His gut twisted. "The buggy is in pieces."

"I know."

"You didn't recognize the car make?"

"No."

"Anything else you noticed? A bumper sticker, say?"

"No."

After a moment, he closed the notebook and stuck the pen in the spiral-wire top. "Something is on your mind."

"You searched my things."

His jaw hurt, he'd been gritting his teeth so hard. "I...thought it was the one last thing I should do before I told Mike to forget his unlikely scenario."

"I shouldn't be surprised." She stood with a grace that suggested she wasn't feeling any of her pain at the moment. "If we weren't on the porch of my God-fearing aunt and uncle's house, I could tell you what I think of you. As it is, I admit to how gullible I was to believe a single word you ever said."

His chest feeling as though it was being crushed, Caleb rose slowly to his feet. "You can. Abby—"

As if he hadn't spoken, she continued, voice controlled but hard. "This isn't my house, but I'll ask you not to come back, anyway. You have no business with my aunt and uncle, and you have none with me anymore." She walked past him to the door.

"I believe in you," he said to her back.

She kept going. The screen door closed with a slap that stung as if she'd used her hand on his cheek.

"Ach, I need to bake!" Aenti Nancy exclaimed the next morning. "The sheriff is sure to come by—"

"I told him not to," Abby interrupted.

Her aunt turned sharply. "What? Why?"

Feeling hollow, her head dull, she said, "Is Onkel Eli still in the house?" He'd been working on accounts at his antique rolltop desk in the small downstairs office.

"*Ja*, I will get him."

Whether this was right or wrong, Abby didn't know, but she couldn't take any more of her aunt's treating the sheriff as if he was Abby's come-calling friend. He wasn't flirting with her; he was trying to trap her.

Looking worried, her uncle sat down at the kitchen table across from her. Aenti Nancy pulled up the chair beside her. *"Was ist letz?"* he asked.

"You know what happened when I was shot and my partner murdered."

Both nodded. Of course they did.

"I told you that my boss, Sergeant Donahue, believes Neal and I had a falling out and I shot him. I guess the theory is that he got off a couple of shots before he went down."

Nancy began to protest, but her husband silenced her with a glance.

Feeling weary to her bones, Abby continued, "The sheriff already told me that my boss and he had once worked together. That Sergeant Donahue had called and asked him to be friendly to me in hopes I might give something away about whatever awful thing I'd been mixed up in."

"You didn't tell us this, niece." Eli sounded stern.

"I thought—" her voice hitched "—that he had become convinced I was innocent. That he believed me. But yesterday when Amos King brought Joshua and me home, the sheriff was in the house, coming downstairs. I didn't think about it until later, but I found my duffel bag unzipped and everything in it mixed up. When

I accused him, he admitted he'd searched my bag, and probably the rest of the room, too."

She saw shock on her aunt's face. Her uncle looked less surprised because he was more aware of the evil the world held.

"I do believe he's good at his job," she said, "that you can trust him if you have need to call the police in the future. But… I can't. I asked him not to come here again. I thought you ought to know why."

After a long silence, Eli nodded gravely. "Unless something bad happens, we will not call him." He pressed his lips together, shook his head. "I had hoped…"

"Hoped?" Abby prodded.

"That he would help you prove you could never have done that terrible thing."

"I…suppose I hoped that, too." She tried to smile. "But Sergeant Donahue is the sheriff's friend, so it's natural he chose to believe him rather than me."

"I am disappointed," Onkel Eli said heavily, pushing back his hair. "I'm sorry."

"Denke."

When he was gone, Abby squeezed her aunt's hand. "How is Joshua this morning?" Her body stiff, she'd come down late enough to miss breakfast.

"Shaken, but excited, too, I think." Aenti Nancy was clearly dismayed. "He will have something to tell his friends at the singing Sunday."

Abby laughed. "Ah, to be his age again."

Her aunt didn't move. Abby wasn't accustomed to seeing her so still. Even during the evening while Onkel Eli read from the Bible, Nancy knitted or quilted a small piece in a hoop. She was busy from the minute she hustled down the stairs until she went to bed at night. Even given the richness of their diet, Abby couldn't understand how she stayed stout.

"What will you do?" she asked, lines in her face Abby didn't remember seeing before. "Once you are well again. How can you make them believe you?"

"I don't know." The admission made the hollow inside her expand. "They won't find proof to arrest me, but if nobody else is ever arrested, I can't believe any other police department will be willing to hire me."

"We would be glad if you never left." Her aunt patted her hand and finally stood.

"Denke," Abby said again, forcing a smile, even though she knew that the only way she could stay was to join the church and become Amish in truth, and that wasn't something she could ever do.

CALEB HAD TO TRY. He knocked on the Kemps' door the next afternoon but wasn't surprised when Nancy didn't invite him in. She said, "Abby doesn't want to see you," and closed the door in his face.

This wasn't a good moment to realize he'd fallen completely for Abigail Baker. He had zero chance with her now, but he thought the worst part might be that in destroying her trust, he had left her isolated.

As bleak as he felt, he had to do whatever he could to protect her. Since he was out here anyway, he drove from house to house, both on the Kemps' road and on the one that paralleled theirs, sharing the woods as a greenbelt between properties. The folks on this road were all Amish and presumably knew about Abby. Certainly they'd heard about the buggy accident.

He asked each to watch for strangers lurking in the

area, either in cars or in the woods. They weren't in the habit of calling the sheriff's department, but he begged them to make an exception if they saw anything suspicious, especially men they didn't know carrying guns.

Amish landowners were mixed with non-Amish on the next road over. He repeated himself so many times he'd probably mumble the same words in his sleep. Everyone he encountered seemed to be concerned and agreed to watch out for strangers.

To some extent, these rural families would do that anyway. However, since hunting was a way of life for most, the sight of someone passing through with a rifle wouldn't normally occasion any concern. He could only hope that after his warning, they'd be willing to call.

Once back at headquarters, Caleb decided to leave a phone message for Abby, too. Given time to cool off, she might return his call. Knowing his message could well be heard by any of the people who shared the phone kiosk, he had to think about what to say and how to say it.

"Abby Baker, will you sit down with me so I can speak my piece? I want to help, and that's the truth. I can offer resources you need." After a brief hesitation, he added, "Please." That wasn't a word he had intended to use, but he wouldn't have snatched it back if he could.

His phone stayed abnormally silent for the rest of the day. He told himself she probably hadn't gotten the message yet. By lunchtime the following day, he'd given up on that hope.

Midafternoon, a call came in from a local number that he didn't know, which wasn't unusual. His cell phone number did get passed around. He answered, "Sheriff Tanner."

"Sheriff, this is Rudy Yoder. You talked to my son David yesterday." His speech was accented, but clear. "I am calling because you asked. Not an hour ago, my youngest boy and a friend were in the woods behind our place." He paused, as if to be sure Caleb understood what he was saying.

"And what did they see?"

"Two men wearing what looked like military clothing and carrying rifles."

"Camouflage."

"*Ja.*"

Hunters did often wear camo.

"Did the boys talk to them?"

"No, they got frightened. They don't think the men saw them."

"Did you see a car or truck pass by? Or parked?"

"No."

He stifled a sigh. "Thank you for letting me know. I'd recommend you keep the boys out of the woods for now."

"*Ja*, that's certain sure."

Hearing dead air, Caleb set his phone down. Thinking, he went to the detailed county map that hung on a wall in his office. He'd talked to two different sets of Yoders yesterday; the name was common among the Amish in general, and particularly in this area. There was a good reason for that. At a guess, the first Yoders to come here in search of cheap farmland had likely had eight children, now grown up, married and raising their own families. The first Yoder likely moved with siblings or cousins, too, all buying land in the same area.

At one farm, though, he'd talked to a teenager who said when his *daad* came home, he would tell him to watch for men with guns. It took Caleb a minute to re-member where that had been. The picture cleared in his head. The same road as the Kemps, but almost to the end, on the same side.

By the time he got out there, would the men be long gone? The least he could do was hunt for their vehicle.

He drove up and down nearby roads for an hour, fail-ing to find any cars tucked in turnouts or half-covered by shrubbery.

He'd have to trust that Abby was too sore and bruised to do any outdoor work, thus putting herself at risk. Still, he pulled into the Kemps' farmyard. By the time he got out, Eli had appeared from the barn and was walking toward him. Caleb resisted any temptation to look toward the house.

Meeting Eli halfway, he didn't ask if Abby had got-ten his message or whether she might be willing to see him. Instead, he said, "I need you to know that not much over an hour ago, Rudy Yoder reported a couple of men wearing camo and carrying rifles in the woods not far from your property. He may have already let you know—"

"He sent one of his boys down."

"Keep an eye out."

Still expressionless, Eli said, "*Ja*. We will do that for sure."

Caleb nodded and left. In the rearview mirror, he saw that Eli hadn't moved beyond crossing his arms. His hat shaded his face.

In the next day and a half, two more reports came in of a man or men carrying rifles lurking in the woods. One caller's description was, "Sneaking around, they were."

Hunting season for turkey opened today, October 1,

but it would be another month before deer season opened unless you used a bow and arrow. Pheasant and quail couldn't be hunted until November. You could shoot a squirrel, coyote or groundhog anytime you wanted, but Caleb couldn't quite imagine grown men slinking around in the woods wearing camouflage so they could bag a groundhog. Of course, out-of-season hunting happened. Interestingly, nobody who called had actually heard a gunshot.

A non-Amish caller told him about a vacant piece of property half a mile from his own where a man could park out of sight if he wanted to enter the woods unseen. Caleb once again drove out there, and wished he'd known before that this particular farm was untenanted. The ground was too dry right now to hold a tire track, and the only piece of machinery he saw was an ancient tractor in the barn.

His temper was fraying. Getting back behind the wheel of his SUV, he left the door open while he called Mike Donahue.

"Got something for me?" Mike answered.

"A question."

"Shoot."

Not Caleb's favorite choice of words at the moment. "Do you have someone here in my county watching Detective Baker?"

The pause was just a little longer than Caleb liked before Donahue retorted, "I thought I had *you* keeping an eye on her."

Fuse burning, Caleb let the silence ride.

"You accusing me of something?" Mike sounded pissed.

"Wouldn't think of it." He ended the call before he could say something he'd regret.

Of course, his phone rang twenty seconds later. Mike Donahue. Caleb let it go to voice mail. Then he tipped his head back and tried to think coolly.

Was Abby in danger? He lacked enough evidence to believe she was. On the other hand, she'd had two near misses since she came to stay with her aunt and uncle.

Sure, but the shooting was weeks ago, and the car-buggy collision would be a chancy way to kill someone off…and that's assuming it wasn't an accident, which was a lot more likely. Too many drivers forgot about the likelihood of meeting up with the slow-moving horses and buggies. Or they came from a county or state where no buggy had been seen on the roads in the last century. Here they weren't prepared.

He growled an obscenity, snapped on his seat belt and started the engine.

ABBY PEERED OUT the kitchen window at the sullen sky. Yesterday, a tornado had touched down one county south of them. Nobody killed, thank God, but the Amish grapevine reported plenty of damage to property. Englischer and Amish alike had had homes or barns leveled, fences torn out, dairy cattle killed on one farm, alpacas on another.

She didn't like the color of this sky, or the weight of the air when she'd opened the front door earlier. The leaves on the trees didn't stir; even the ones turning autumn colors didn't fall. The whole world felt too still. Waiting.

She rested her forehead on the glass, admitting that she was having an anxiety attack, and it wasn't tornadoes she feared. She'd never known she was claustrophobic, but that was the closest she could come to describing this feeling. That and helpless, which she hated more than just about anything.

She wasn't supposed to leave the house. She'd had to cancel her physical-therapy appointments for the coming week. She couldn't help Aenti Nancy outside, although the sweet potatoes, tomatoes, pumpkin and squash were coming ripe along with broccoli and cabbage and more beans. She couldn't even dash up to the barn to deliver a message, gather eggs or give grain to either of the harness horses when Eli, Isaac and Joshua were busy with other work.

She was condemned to cleaning house, cooking and helping can the onslaught of ripe produce. This, she thought desperately, was the life of an Amishwoman and could never be hers. The life of a modern young woman didn't always feel like a good fit, either, but being a police officer had satisfied her in a way her Amish relatives would never understand. She could forgive much, but never brutal, senseless violence. That could only be punished.

Caleb would understand. The thought slipped in, however hard she'd been willing herself to keep him out.

He would also understand how her inability to do anything to help *herself* chafed. Coming here had been a mistake, she feared. Now she was stuck. No transportation, no chance to quietly follow the trail of clues Neal had left. No chance to try to compel his wife to talk to her.

Alone in the house, she said out loud, "Why can't I *remember*?" It was all she could do not to yell and hammer her fists on the wall. She wanted to punch Caleb Tanner, because if she'd been able to trust him, he could have helped.

But you can't, so live with it, she told herself coldly. Maybe it was time she returned to her apartment, struck out on her own to investigate. If she took a bus or taxi, no one need know she'd returned to Kansas City. If she was careful, she'd have a while before anyone—say, Sergeant Donahue—knew she was back. Maybe, in familiar surroundings—

Without warning, the familiar pain struck, splintering her brain. Images, sounds, smells glanced off shards of broken glass. Someone crouched over—no, no, no! Footsteps, pain beyond bearing in her head, her hair feeling wet. Blood, had to be blood. Grit on her cheek. Empty holster. Boots. "Hey! I called 9-1-1!" Smell of urine. Someone rearing above her, gun pointing—

Moaning, she staggered to a chair. Bending over, she used the heels of both hands to press her temples until she felt as if a vise held her head together.

"No, no, no, no," she whispered.

She couldn't see the glitter of broken memories anymore. No, not true; they were still there, flickers at the corners of her eyes. If she tried to turn her head, they disappeared.

Slowly the pain eased until she could almost think.

The skip in her brain, the emptiness that was really a wall, was meant to protect her. But if she let it keep protecting her, she wouldn't do a single damn thing to help herself. She had to defy this disability, or she would never be able to move forward with her life.

Unconsciously or not, she'd let herself believe that the detectives in her department were out there seeking answers. That they would do the job she hadn't been able to. She could recover, wait it out until they did make the arrest.

Except she'd lost that faith.

She latched on to the memory of Sam Kirk offering to help…but she couldn't trust him, either.

She thought about the phone message Caleb had left the day before yesterday.

I want to help, and that's the truth. I can offer resources you need. Please.

Onkel Eli had written down every word. She wished she could have heard Caleb's voice so she could judge better what he meant and what was merely a slick attempt to fool her.

Now she was being a fool. How many times had he lied to her? The tenderness of his touch, the passion in his kiss, meant nothing.

Gradually she lifted her head, stretched her back and arms. This attack—how else could she think of it?—had passed. It couldn't have taken as long as it felt, or Aenti Nancy would be back with metal buckets full of beans or a woven basket of cabbages. Abby glanced at the clock, surprised to see how far the minute hand had advanced.

Suddenly worried, she rose to her feet and hurried to the back door. Through the glass, she could see only part of the garden. She opened the door and stepped out, calling, "Aenti Nancy? Are you all right?"

The humidity made it hard to breathe, as if she was underwater. Her aunt was getting to an age where she shouldn't have to work so hard, lift the heavy baskets of produce the way she did. With this heat, what if she'd fallen, or even had a heart attack?

Abby slipped out, advancing just far enough to see the full sweep of the garden. Aenti Nancy wouldn't have gone up to the barn, would she? And not to the chicken house—she had Joshua gathering…

Oh, thank goodness! There she was in her violet dress and apron, carrying an overloaded basket. Abby called out to her, and Aenti Nancy waved. "Slow, I am! Now, don't you come out."

Except…she stumbled, astonishment on her face.

Crack.

Bullet! Abby's brain screamed.

Aenti Nancy tipped forward in slow motion, ending sprawled on the grass, cabbages tumbled out around her and her sturdy legs bared for anyone to see.

Operating on instinct, Abby ran full out even as she wished desperately for her gun. She dove to cover her aunt, feeling a sudden burn on her upper arm, as if a swarm of hornets had stung her. Stupid, stupid, stupid, but she'd rather die than let any of her family be killed in her place.

Crack. Crack.

A few feet to the compost bin that would offer some protection. But how to drag Nancy there without exposing them even more?

Where were Eli and the boys? *Safe. Please be safe.*

She wrapped her arms around her aunt's torso, eased her feet under her…and lunged forward.

Chapter Ten

Caleb got there almost as fast as the ambulance, beating the first responding deputy. He slammed to a stop and leaped out, jogging past the pair of medics grabbing their equipment. *Behind the house,* the caller had said. A shaky young voice, according to the dispatcher.

A cluster of people surrounded the women who were down. Amish except for a boy who hovered a few feet back.

Eli turned his head, probably looking for the medics. His hat was missing, his face wild with fear. "Sheriff. They told you."

"Yes." Caleb looked past him to where Nancy lay stomach down in the dirt by a bin built of slats—compost, he realized. Her *kapp* was blood soaked. Damn, if she'd been shot in the head— "Is she conscious?"

"No." Eli ran a shaky hand over his face. "I must trust in God."

Reminding himself, Caleb thought.

The next second, Caleb realized the second woman was Abby, kneeling at her aunt's side holding her hand. His knees weakened and the tight grip on his lungs loosened. He could breathe again. She was all right.

The paramedics shooed everyone back and began a

basic assessment. Nancy didn't even twitch. After scoot-
ing a couple of feet, Abby now sat on the bare ground,
never looking away from her aunt.

Caleb didn't remember moving, but there he was,
squatted at her side, his teeth grinding. "You're injured,
too." The sleeve of her dress was soaked with blood.

"It's nothing."

"Abby." He cupped her chin in his hand and turned
her face to make her look at him. "It's not nothing.
That's a lot of blood. It's dripping off your hand and
smeared on your face. *Where do you hurt?*"

He must have roared the question. One of the medics—a woman—swiveled on her heels, obviously as-
sessing Abby.

"Oh, I…" She blinked a few times. "I think a shot
grazed my arm, that's all."

She'd been shot for a third time, and it was *nothing*?
Caleb couldn't remember ever having been as scared as
he was during the drive. The adrenaline cocktail in his
body would have ignited a fire if he opened up a vein.

"You need to go to the hospital," he said, with the
best semblance of calm he could muster.

For the first time, she looked fully at him. The anguish in her blue eyes did a number on him. "It's nothing compared to—" She gestured helplessly. "If Aenti
Nancy dies, it'll be my fault. I should never have come
here. I should have—" She started struggling to get to
her feet.

Taken off. That's what she wanted to say. "Damn
it, Abby." Caleb rose, too, supporting her with an arm
around her waist.

A deputy had arrived without his noticing and
paused at the back of the ambulance, where the EMTs

were about to load Nancy. Eli hovered beside them, anything he said to the deputy distracted. The woman steered him to the front and held open the passenger door. After a minute he nodded and got in.

Caleb looked back down at Abby. "Can you walk?"

"Of course I can." She tried to shake free of him, then seemed to recognize that he wasn't about to release her.

The same medic jogged to them and handed over dressings to Caleb. "Can you bring her to the hospital?" she asked.

"Yes. Go." She took off at a run. Once she leaped in behind the wheel, the siren shrilled and the ambulance started down the driveway.

Joshua and Isaac stared after it, looking very young and scared.

They wouldn't be alone for long, though, Caleb knew. In fact, he saw two Amish women, undoubtedly neighbors who'd heard sirens, moving to one side of the driveway to let the ambulance by, then hurrying toward the small cluster of remaining people. By then, Deputy Booth was already questioning Joshua and Isaac. Isaac was waving his hands in the air and talking when the two women reached them as well.

Caleb let them fuss over Eli and Nancy's sons. The flurry of questions and reassurances might as well have been the chatter of a bird in the branches of the big maple. His attention was entirely on Abby.

He boosted her into the passenger seat of his SUV, then reached to rip her dress.

She gripped his hand. "I can take out some pins."

She did, dropping straight pins into a cup holder, and gingerly lowered the bodice of the dress to pull her arm out of the blood-soaked sleeve. Her cheeks flamed red even under the circumstances, he was stunned to see.

He tore open the packages and used a splash from a water bottle on the first dressing to wipe her arm enough for him to see where the bullet had torn through her flesh. Then he applied the next dressing firmly and said, "Can you hold this? I'll have to grab some tape."

She nodded and laid her hand over it.

Once he'd opened the first-aid kit he always carried and taped the pad to her arm, he said, "Tell me what happened."

Their faces weren't over a foot apart. The last time they'd been this close, he'd been about to kiss her.

Bad timing for the thought to even cross his mind. Maybe fortunately, his question renewed her anguish.

Her throat worked. "I realized Aenti Nancy had been outside a long time." She described what happened from her perspective in a few short words, ending with, "He wasn't a very good shot."

She was right; the shooter certainly hadn't been sniper trained. But since she hadn't seen him, he must have been nearly a hundred yards away. Caleb would find where the man—or men, if the two the boy had seen two days ago had anything to do with this—had set up.

"How many shots were fired?" he asked.

Her forehead crinkled while she thought. Her fingers twitched one by one, as if she had to count on them. "One that brought down Aenti Nancy, then two more when I ran out." She glanced at her arm. "At least two more while I pulled her behind the compost bin. I think one of them hit the compost. The whole bin kind of jumped. There're at least a couple bullets embedded in the house wall, too."

"Okay." He couldn't help himself. He ran his knuckles over her cheek, along her jaw. Silky, warm, and the way her pupils dilated gave him hope.

But the way she looked at him in perplexity, she might not even have noticed his touch. "I don't understand. Why did they stop shooting?"

He glanced over his shoulder, locating the one person who looked out of place here. "I think we can thank that kid over there. He has to be the one who called 9-1-1. Apparently, he was cutting through the woods and saw and heard enough to get an idea that something bad was happening. He yelled at the shooter to stop, said he had a gun. He fired it once into a tree trunk to show that he meant business, and heard someone crashing away."

"He's not Amish."

"No."

"One of those shots I heard must have been his."

"Maybe." He made himself lower his hand to his side. "I'm going to ask one of my deputies to drive you to the hospital. I need to stay here." However much he hated the idea of letting her out of his sight.

"Okay." She began to squirm forward, but he stopped her with a hand on her shoulder.

"No, we'll just switch vehicles for the moment. You stay put."

Minutes later, he watched as his youngest deputy, a twenty-two-year-old named Caden Vogl, drove away with Abby. Then, as always, he turned to take charge of an investigation that mattered too much to him.

THE MINUTE AN orderly met the police car in front of the ER, Abby blurted, "My aunt, she was just brought in here. Do you know how she is?"

The stocky man raised his brows. "That's a lot of blood. I need you to sit in this wheelchair." Not until she followed his order did he ask, "She came in an ambulance?"

"Yes!"

"I saw them arrive. I don't know any more."

"My uncle must be here—" As the orderly wheeled her into the waiting room, she spotted him. "Onkel Eli!"

He jumped to his feet and hurried to her. Worry had aged his face by a decade. In Deitsch, he said, "Abby, I thought you'd be here sooner. What happened?"

"Nothing. The sheriff sort of patched me up. I'm not hurt badly." Although the pain was starting to make itself felt. "But Aenti Nancy... Have they told you anything?"

"They're moving her to intensive care. Someone is to come and get me. They said the bullet bounced off her head, and they think she will wake up soon, God willing, but she hasn't yet."

She gripped his hand, too close to tears. "I'm sorry. So sorry. This never would have happened if I hadn't come to stay with you, or if I'd left after the first shooting. I should have! I—"

He shook his head. "The person who shot you and Nancy, he must have this on his conscience. Nothing is your fault. What happened today is God's will—you know that, niece."

She couldn't be that accepting. Since her mother had been taken from her, Abby had never lost the burning coal of anger. Mostly, that anger was channeled at the killer, who had escaped justice, but she could not accept that the murder was God's will. She wouldn't have become a cop if she hadn't felt, with a passion her

Amish family would never understand, that police could and did prevent such tragedies. Most of the time, they gave resolution to the survivors. She needed to be part of that, not live her life placidly accepting that brutal deaths and the suffering of crime victims might have a greater purpose.

She declined his offer to come with her, insisting he be available so that he could be at Nancy's side the second they'd allow it.

Once she was established in a cubicle, a nurse came in, winced at the sight of her arm, then winced again when she saw the vividly red scar on the same shoulder. "That looks recent. You're having a run of bad luck."

Abby smiled weakly. "You could say that."

Once she'd been cleaned up, the doctor appeared. After a quick look, she offered to call for a plastic surgeon, but Abby shook her head. "What's one more scar?"

The doctor, a middle-aged woman, eyed her. "Is someone gunning for you?"

"Actually…yes. I'm… I was a detective with the Kansas City Police Department before I had to take time off to recuperate. It would seem my last investigation has followed me."

"Do our local police know?"

"Yes, I've been working with Sheriff Tanner." Now, there was a euphemism. Fighting with him…kissing him…spitting in his face…

"Good." Seeming satisfied, Dr. Henson dressed the wound and gave her instructions as well as prescriptions for antibiotics and painkillers. "Is someone waiting to drive you home?" she asked.

"I don't know." She explained about her aunt and

discovered that Dr. Henson had seen Aenti Nancy initially, too.

"Heads are hard," she said. "I worked in an ER in St. Louis for years, so I can tell you head shots seem like a sure thing on TV but aren't so easy to make. The skull curves. Bullets tend to ricochet off, thank heaven."

That was one of the reasons police officers were taught to shoot for the torso if they had to pull the trigger.

Now if only Aenti Nancy would regain consciousness. *With* her memory intact.

THEY'D DUG BULLETS out of the house walls as well as one that had drilled into the ground after penetrating the rich dark compost. After finding the blind, Caleb had scooped one forgotten shell into an evidence bag. A tech was trying to make a cast of the best of several footprints that weren't very revealing, given that the soil was hard and dry at this time of year. They did know that the shooter wore a men's size ten-and-a-half shoe. If a second man or woman had been there, he or she hadn't left a trace.

Best scenario would be finding a fingerprint on the shell. People did get careless. Caleb would celebrate if that happened. Otherwise, the least damaged bullet might conceivably match up with one used in another crime on the database maintained by the ATF. Unfortunately, most of those matches didn't go anywhere, because no arrest had been made in the previous crime. Still…it would be helpful to know what other crimes the shooter had committed and where they had happened.

Yeah, and Caleb was trying to be cool when *enraged* was closer to the mark.

Having been directed to the ICU in the small hospital, he saw a woman wearing faded green scrubs sitting alone in the waiting room. His brain had to shift gears when he recognized Abby, her bright blond hair caught in a high ponytail instead of covered by a *kapp*. Not Amish. His gaze caught on the thick white gauze wrapping her upper left arm. The reminder didn't do anything to help him regain his equilibrium.

Staring at the double doors leading into the ICU, she didn't so much as turn her head when he approached. Not until he sat down beside her did she blink and look at him.

"How's Nancy?" He sounded rusty.

"She's going to be okay." Her smile might have wobbled, but it was real nonetheless. "The bullet ricocheted. She's concussed—what a surprise—but awake and talking. She even remembers seeing me poking my head out the back door and thinking I'd promised not to do that."

"And she's right."

Abby's smile went away. "I should have just left her lying out there?"

"They shot her to create bait. Which you swallowed, hook, line and sinker."

Her knuckles showed white where she gripped the arms of the chair. "They might have shot her again, just to be sure I got the message. I'd rather have died than let her die."

Now he was flat-out furious. "You think that's what *she'd* want? What Eli would want? What *I* could live with?"

Her eyes narrowed. "What do you have to do with it?"

"Plenty," he said from between bared teeth. He

wasn't about to tell her he'd been falling like a rock for her since they first met, not when they shared a hospital waiting room with half a dozen other people, a couple of whom he knew.

Abby snorted. "Gee, don't tell me. You've actually come around to believing someone is trying to kill me?"

This was a make-or-break moment. "Abby." He waited until she met his eyes. "I never doubted someone tried in that alley. I've known Donahue long enough, I had to give some credence to his suspicions." When her mouth opened, Caleb held up a hand. "Searching your stuff was my last option. I did it so I could call him and say, *You're wrong*. You've taken ten years or so off my life since you got here. You have to know how I feel about you."

Color blossomed on her cheeks. Gazing into her clear blue eyes, he quit thinking. No, not true. The word *beautiful* was in there, as was *shy*. Which threw him back to her serious blushing when she had to expose a little of her body. It made him wonder—

"I...don't," she whispered.

Don't what? Oh. Know how he felt.

He sneaked a glance around, to find that five of the six other people in the waiting room were watching them. Pretty blonde, cop in uniform—of course they were.

Keeping his voice low, he said, "I assume you're not in a relationship."

"No."

"If you'll give me a chance, you are now."

Her head snapped back. The color in her cheeks brightened, became...angry? "I've given you chances. I did trust you, and you stomped on my trust. Ground it into nothing. How can you possibly imagine I'll, what, bat my eyelashes and say, *Oh, you'll protect me*? Or fall into your arms? Really?"

The woman knew how to hit. "Abby," he started, without knowing what he was going to say. He didn't get a chance to say anything.

"Abby!" It was Eli, who had burst through the double doors. "Nancy wants to talk to you, and the nurse says it's fine. Only one of us in there at a time."

She jumped to her feet and threw her good arm around her uncle. "Thank God she wasn't hurt worse."

"*Ja*, thank God," he whispered against that blond hair.

For a moment they stayed that way, an unlikely pair despite the similarity in coloring. Solid Amishman with wheat-colored hair and a long beard, wearing broadfall denim trousers, sturdy work boots and suspenders stretched in a Y over his back, covered by a blue shirt. Englisch woman in green scrub pants that hugged her curvy hips and showcased amazing legs, V-neck scrub top that bared a long line of throat and some pale chest. And yet, despite their differences, nobody could miss the love.

Caleb had the rare experience of feeling his eyes sting.

The two separated, and Abby's gaze glanced off him as if he were a stranger who happened to be sitting nearby. She turned and hurried across the waiting room and pushed through the doors, leaving Eli to slump into the seat beside Caleb.

"So blessed we are," he said after a minute. His eyes were the exact shade of blue as Abby's, Caleb couldn't help noticing.

Normally, Caleb might have said, *Yeah, we got lucky today.* But he didn't waste his breath. Eli would never see it that way, and right this minute, Caleb wasn't so sure he did, either. Every once in a while, he'd have the thought that Abby could so easily have died in that alley. Given her injuries, it was damn near a miracle that she *hadn't* died. He might never have met her.

Never had the crap scared out of him every week or two, he thought ruefully.

"We are blessed," he agreed. Looking toward the double doors, he said, "Although apparently I'm not blessed enough to be forgiven."

"Abby?" Eli sounded surprised.

Who else? "She isn't willing to believe that I'm on her side." He moved his shoulders to release tension. "That I care about her."

"Do you?" Eli's voice was mild, his eyes—Abby's eyes—less so.

"I do." He'd never said those words in quite that way. "I'd do anything for her, but she doesn't want to let me."

Eli patted his forearm, as if he were one of Eli's sons. "Abby understands that God expects us to forgive one another, just as He forgives us our mistakes. *Ja?*"

"*Ja.* Yeah."

"She will remember that you come to help whenever we need you."

Would she? Caleb smiled crookedly at her uncle. "You know she blames herself for Nancy being hurt."

"*Ja*, she did say that. I reminded her that she takes too much on herself."

"Was she convinced?"

Eli chewed that over for a minute, then sighed. "My niece, she is…" He hesitated.

"Agasinish," Caleb reminded him. The Pennsylvania Dutch word nicely summed up his estimation of a significant portion of her personality: contrary, self-willed. Qualities he admired, but ones that were currently working against him.

Eli chuckled. *"Ja*, that is Abby." His expression dimmed. "After losing her mother, she struggled to find a place for herself."

"Why didn't her father give her that?" Caleb asked.

Eli hesitated long enough, Caleb didn't think he was going to answer, but he finally did.

"I think my sister was his framework, like with a good, sturdy barn or house, ain't so? With her killed the way she was, he became…empty. The one blessing was that he often sent Abby here to us."

"Because of you, she knew she was loved."

"I hope that is so," he said, sounding troubled. "With these troubles, she may think she doesn't belong with us. Family should be with you when you need them most, and Abby—" Eli shook his head in sorrow "—she doesn't want to let anyone else carry any of the weight. You see?"

He saw.

Damn, what was he going to do? Caleb didn't see her mood softening in the next couple of hours. She'd feel better once her aunt was home again. He could wait a day or two.

NANCY WAS RELEASED the following day, a Tuesday. From the report Caleb heard, she was in good spirits and thwarting every effort to treat her like an invalid. He imagined her heading straight for her kitchen and starting dinner as if nothing had happened. Of course,

Abby's stubbornness might be a match for her aunt's. Caleb wouldn't have minded being a witness.

He'd decided to give it one more day, though, before he tried to regain at least an inch or two of lost ground with Abby.

Wednesday, shortly after lunch, he sat behind his desk scowling as he flipped through monthly reports, including claims for overtime.

A ring on the internal line interrupted his brood. "Tanner here."

"A Mr. Kemp is here to see you," the receptionist/ dispatcher said. "He says it's important."

Eli, here? "I'll be right down." Caleb moved fast, imagining Abby dead, or having been kidnapped, or—

When he pushed through the doors into the waiting area, he found Eli pacing restlessly, still wearing his summer-weight straw hat.

"Eli?"

The Amishman swung around, his agitation obvious. "It is Abby," he blurted. "She came to town with me. Nancy had a list for me to take to the store. Abby needed clothes. I shouldn't have agreed to bring her, but she rode inside the buggy, where no one could see her. She went into the store with me, but…when I was done, I couldn't find her."

Caleb's hands curled into fists. "Somebody took her?"

"No. She ran away." Eli thrust a crumpled piece of paper at him. "This was on my seat in the buggy."

With dread, Caleb read the brief note.

If I don't leave, bad things will keep happening. I brought my debit card with me so I'd have money, and caught a bus. If you spread the word that I'm gone, that would be good. Thank you for taking me in. I love you both.

Caleb ground his teeth together. She'd drive him insane. Did she really think he'd let her go off on her own with a killer on her heels?

Chapter Eleven

Still dressed as an Amishwoman, Abby had several rows to herself on the swaying bus. That was just chance—for longer journeys, the Amish often took buses, and to locals there'd be nothing remarkable in the sight of her traveling.

Nobody had appeared to be paying attention when she got on outside the Amish Café on the main street, right behind an Englisch woman with two young children. Wearing a black bonnet, Abby had kept her head down and face averted from the few passersby before the bus pulled in. Thank goodness Onkel Eli hadn't come out of Ralph's General Store too soon!

Now she gazed out a grimy window across the westbound lane of the highway at farmland and scattered houses and barns. Those belonging to the Amish were easy to pick out, since no electrical wires connected their homes or workshops to the lines strung between poles on the highway. In the world, but not of it—that was their way. Abby couldn't help feeling an ache in her chest as she saw an Amish farmer plowing under the stubble left from corn, a team of four draft horses pulling willingly. That man, with his broad back and strong arms gripping the plow, could have been her uncle.

Shaking off emotions she couldn't afford, she again studied the bus schedule she'd brought with her. She'd already decided that instead of remaining on this bus as it ambled its way east toward the Mississippi River and the town of Hannibal, she'd hop off in Day's Creek, the upcoming town, and take a different bus that was supposed to stop there twenty minutes later. What she hadn't decided yet was whether, given that twenty minutes, she ought to whisk into a restroom and pull the dress over her head and unroll the jeans she wore beneath it, transforming herself instantly into an Englisch woman, or whether it would be safer to stay Amish for a while. She *would* be noticed if she used an ATM while wearing a dress and bonnet, and her cash would run low soon. No matter which she did, Abby planned to keep switching buses, confusing any tail as much as possible.

She'd considered calling Julie Luong, her friend at the police department, but anyone who knew much about her would expect that, even start keeping an eye on Julie once Abby's disappearance became known. Ditto for Dad, of course. And who else was there?

An annoying, persistent voice whispered a name. She did her best to shut it down. The next-to-last time she'd seen him, he'd been searching her bedroom for information he could turn over to Donahue.

No. Just…*no*.

Several vehicles had passed the bus, drivers frustrated at the turtle's pace that seemed to be its top speed. She'd tried to get a peek at them before leaning forward as if she'd dropped something on the floor. It was paranoid to think anybody would already be after her, but just in case, she'd ensure she wasn't seen until she had get to out at the bus stop.

For a moment, she rested her head back and closed her eyes, taking long, slow breaths in an effort to conquer nausea she blamed on diesel fumes and the swaying, bouncing ride. Something cold to drink would be good. She could take the time to buy a soda, unless the stop wasn't near enough to a store.

Her thoughts flew a hundred ways. She imagined the icy-cold can of soda with droplets of condensation. Caleb's face when she walked away from him in the hospital. What Onkel Eli would do when he found the note. The tenderness in Caleb's touch when she was hurt. Always, she returned to the danger stalking her.

Was someone determined to kill her only because he feared she recognized him as he bent over her in the alley? Or did he know she hadn't seen him and was instead afraid Neal had confided in her, that she would soon remember what her partner had told her? She puzzled at that for a few minutes. Maybe Neal *had* told her in the days leading up to the shooting. If so, that information was locked in the closed vault of her unrecoverable memories.

There must be a way to dynamite that lock, free everything hidden behind the door.

Flick. Her mind took off in a new direction.

Caleb would be mad when he heard that she was gone.

She wanted so much to trust him. Abby couldn't forget the sheer relief of resting against his tall, powerful body. Nobody had held her in such a very long time, and never quite the way he did. She'd never felt even close to the way she had when he kissed her, either.

She steeled herself against the likelihood she'd never see him again. A part of her wanted to believe he'd call her, or even show up on her doorstep, once this was all over. But that was just foolish.

Movement seen in the corner of her eye gave her barely a second to duck below the level of the window. A black SUV—but they were so common here, along with pickup trucks.

Damn it, she had to get over letting *everything* make her think of him.

She made herself envision the can of soda again. The sound when she popped the top, the rush of cold liquid and bubbles and caffeine that would be her first swallow.

The bus was slowing down, the typical small town appearing ahead. Brakes squealed as they lumbered toward an unwieldy stop at the curb in front of a store called E & W Foodstop. No, the bus rolled forward just a little more, and Abby could see into the windows of a diner.

As the front doors flapped open, she gathered her cloth bag and stepped into the aisle. Only two of them getting off here. Hiding beneath the brim of her bonnet, she nodded at the driver as she passed and said a shy, *"Denke."*

Once onto the sidewalk, she moved into the narrow band of shade cast by a roof overhang and waited until the bus lumbered on its way again before starting toward the convenience store.

Because she was a cop, she saw the young man who'd also gotten off the bus hopping into the bed of a beater of a pickup truck with a muffler issue. Not safe, but this wasn't her jurisdiction. On a tiny shock, Abby reminded herself that she didn't *have* a jurisdiction.

Across the street, a woman was outside washing the

plate-glass front windows of a florist. A couple juggling grocery bags emerged from the grocery store and disappeared around the corner of the building into what Abby guessed was a parking lot beyond it.

An old Cadillac that must be a gas hog passed. On her side of the street, a red van approached, slowed, looked like it was either going to turn into the parking lot or pull up to the curb.

She was twenty feet from the door into the store when the van accelerated and slammed to a stop beside her. A side door slid open and a man leaped out. Abby spun, tried to run, but she didn't make two steps before a meaty arm locked around her neck while a hand slapped over her face.

CALEB HAD BEEN hovering in the alcove surrounding the glass doors into the grocery store. Having caught up with the bus and passed it only a mile or so out of town, he'd parked in the store lot, asked the first person he saw where the bus stopped and then found the best place to lurk.

He got some looks, but that wasn't unexpected given that he wore his uniform, as he did most days. A few people smiled when he held open the door for them. He hoped Abby did get off here, because Day's Creek contracted with the sheriff's department for police services. If he had to take Abby Baker into protective custody, at least here he could do it legally.

Once the bus arrived, he weighed whether to get on it as soon as the doors opened and haul her ass out or follow on to the next town. Before he could decide, he saw an Amishwoman rise and start down the aisle. Was this her idea of being tricky?

The approaching van was the kind people bought to ferry a herd of kids to school, activities and friends' houses. A mom van. Caleb watched it, anyway, expecting it to turn into the parking lot. At the same time, he automatically clicked on details that felt wrong. The driver was male, not female, and another man sat in the back. When the van leaped forward, Caleb took off running.

He'd closed half the distance by the time a man dressed in black with a ski mask over his face snatched Abby. Her bonnet wrenched askew, she wouldn't be able to see much of anything. But she fought anyway. Her knee came up to let her stab a foot backward. Her assailant staggered but didn't release her.

And then Caleb reached them. He ripped the bastard off Abby, flung him to the sidewalk. She'd gone to her hands and knees but immediately jumped up. The second guy had gotten out and made it to the sidewalk by then. Instead of wading in to help his partner, he grabbed her.

"Knife!" she yelled, before kneeing this one in the exact right place.

Caleb spun to one side. The sting on his upper arm said he'd reacted barely in time. Facing off with ski-mask guy, he focused on the knife, black from hilt to tip of the blade. KA-BAR, or a knockoff. Behind him, he heard Abby screaming in rage and some clangs off metal.

He'd pulled his Glock often enough to do it in a split second. "Put the knife down."

The creep flung himself toward the van, yelling, "Go! Go!"

Caleb whirled. "Freeze!"

Time shifted into slow motion. The one with his hands on Abby let her go and threw himself in the side door of the van. She fell hard. The other SOB was already behind the wheel. The van burned rubber accelerating away from the curb. Caleb would have shot out the tires, but risked hitting somebody. A couple of dozen people had come out of businesses on both sides of the road to gape. A car approached.

If it hadn't been for Abby, he'd have pursued. But this time, she wasn't getting up, which decided for him.

He dropped to his knees, saw that she was conscious, holstered his gun and yanked out his phone. Since he'd taken in the model and maker of the van as well as the license-plate number, he issued a BOLO on it.

Then he carefully untied the strings under her chin that held the bonnet on her head and pushed it away. The *kapp* went with it.

"You're hurt," he said hoarsely. Hurt again, because he hadn't been fast enough. Because she'd been an idiot. He had no trouble blaming both of them for this fiasco.

"I…don't think so. I landed on my bad shoulder and arm, and… I'm catching my breath, that's all."

He swore and let his head fall forward. "You can't keep doing this to me."

"But you keep doing this for me."

Something in her voice persuaded him to lift his head, to look at her face, where he saw that her lips had curved into an uncertain smile.

She struggled to a sitting position with his help. So far, he'd ignored the crowd of people encircling them.

"What can we do?" asked a middle-aged man in twill cargo pants and heavy-duty work boots.

Caleb rose to his feet. "I'd ask if anybody recognized those men, except, well…"

"Bet they were sweating under those masks," another man commented, nodding toward the bank a half a block down. It showed time and a ninety-seven-degrees-Fahrenheit temperature.

"Safe to say."

"Well, I recognize the van," a woman said indignantly. "Didn't you see the bumper sticker?"

He had. Bright yellow and black, it said HOME-SCHOOL BUS.

Abby started to laugh.

Until the man who'd first spoken said, "Sheriff, you do know you're bleeding."

THE GENERAL PRACTITIONER who was apparently the only doctor in town hustled both Abby and Caleb in, leaving some wide-eyed folks there for appointments waiting in front.

"You're bleeding," the nurse said briskly. "They're not."

Abby had scrapes on her knees, her elbow, the heels of her hands and her jaw. The nurse cleaned them up, applied something that stung and had Abby emitting squeaks, and applied gauze where needed. When she finished, the nurse said, "Now, I know you folks don't carry insurance or probably money with you, so here's what we'll do."

Abby smiled. "I'm actually not Amish. Well, I've been visiting Amish family, which is why—" She gestured at herself. "And even though I do have insurance, I'll just pay."

Belatedly, she wondered if she did still have health

insurance. Something she needed to look into, especially the way things were going lately. She'd pay whatever was necessary to hold on to it until…well, until.

The nurse showed her across the hall to where the doctor was working on Caleb. Abby walked in without thinking. At the sight of his bare torso, she froze and all she could do was stare. It wasn't as if she hadn't seen shirtless men plenty of times, from high school to police locker rooms. But this was Caleb, and he was… beautiful. Perfect. Well-defined muscles rippled under lightly tanned skin and chest hair a shade darker than the sun-streaked bronze on his head. Washboard abs, strong throat when she lifted her gaze…and finally met his eyes, which had a glint that meant he'd been watching her. It took getting a little dizzy for her to realize she'd quit breathing. She sucked in some air and tried to sound nonchalant. "Sorry, I thought you'd be through."

"Almost there," said the doctor cheerfully. He sat on a rolling stool, his bushy white hair a match to the white lab coat. "Had to put in a few stitches."

A *few*? Abby's chest cramped as she studied the line of stitches circling his left bicep.

"Fourteen," the doctor added.

Caleb grimaced. "I've had more."

"So I see."

Abby saw, too: the white line of an old scar crossing his rib cage at an angle. That had to have been a knife, too.

This time, though, it was—

"If you say this is your fault," he growled, "I swear I'll grab that tape and use it to shut your mouth."

The doctor's eyebrows shot up, but Abby found in herself the ability to laugh.

"Well, it *is* my fault, and you can try."

Caleb smiled and held out his right hand. She took the few steps around the exam table to put her hand in his and exchange comfort.

A minute later, Dr. Sanford finished and made a pleased sound, told them the nurse would be in to apply a dressing and give him prescriptions, and whisked out.

"I think I have the same instructions from my last GSW," Abby said. "I could just share them."

Caleb didn't look amused. "Did those instructions mention your suggested activity level? Say, not getting into a fight for your life?"

"Uh, I don't think there was anything that specific." Although she'd been cautioned not to lift heavy weights with that arm, or lift it higher than her shoulder. No wonder it hurt.

Once the nurse had done her part, they went out front to settle their bills and then, after he took a cautious look outside, got into Caleb's department SUV. He put the key in the ignition, then let his hand drop back to his thigh.

"A deputy found the van abandoned half a mile down the highway, within walking distance of where it was stolen."

She nodded acknowledgment, not looking at him. "I can't go back to my aunt and uncle's."

"I have no intention of taking you there."

"Could you drive me somewhere I could safely hop a different bus? They'd never find me."

"Not a chance," he said flatly, finally starting the engine. He released the emergency brake, checked over his shoulder and backed out.

"It makes sense," she argued.

At an angle in the parking lot, he braked hard, then glared at her. "Sense? What are you going to do? Ride buses for the rest of your life? Hole up in the woods somewhere, off the grid? Are you a hunter, Abby? Or, let me think, maybe you intend to settle back at home?"

Home. She had the unsettling sensation of just having gone over a speed bump. Kansas City, her apartment there, wasn't home. Had it ever been? Did she truly have a home?

"I need to retrace Neal's steps." Her fingernails bit into her palms. "I'll never be safe until I know why he had to die."

"And how long do you think you'll live once you stick your nose out there asking questions?"

Oh, he was mad. Well, so was she.

"I've waited way too long for someone else to fix this!" she yelled. "You and your BFF Donahue aren't any use, since you're fixated on me. I can't trust anybody in the department. And what were you doing here today, anyway? Hoping I'd lead you to my coconspirators? And then, heck, they tried to abduct me instead. What a disappointment."

Jaw hard, he said, "Are you done?"

"For the moment." She set her mouth mutinously.

"I followed because I was afraid for you." His voice was quiet. So quiet, she felt shame creep over her. She knew why he'd been here in the nick of time today, and it had nothing to do with suspecting her.

"I know," she mumbled, gazing at her gauze-wrapped palms. He had betrayed her trust in one way, but she'd always known he wouldn't hurt her, or allow anyone else to hurt her.

"You ready to listen to me?"

Her head bobbed.

"We'll give ourselves a day or two, then *we'll* retrace your partner's steps. While being very, very careful."

Humiliated at the burning in her eyes, Abby lifted her head. "What about Donahue?"

"What about him?"

"Will you tell him what we're doing?"

"No."

"Okay," she said after a minute. "I don't think I've said this yet, but thanks. I mean, for following me today."

He bent his head and kissed her, so softly she started to melt. But he straightened before she could lift a hand to that hard cheek. He barely paused before turning out of the clinic lot.

Abby let him drive in silence for at least five minutes before she had to ask, because trust only went so far.

"Where are you taking me?"

Caleb flicked a glance at her. "Home with me."

Stunned, she said inanely, "Your...house?"

He didn't crack a smile. "Yeah."

"But..."

"But what? You'll be safe there. And in case you're wondering, no, you don't have to share my bed."

"I wasn't!" Was she?

"Then what's your objection?"

She came up with a big blank. A whiteboard scrubbed clean. That was the moment when Abby realized there was no place in the world she'd rather go than home with Caleb Tanner.

So she took a deep breath and told him, "I don't have an objection."

"Good." He took one hand off the wheel to take hers in a warm, reassuring clasp that made her too warm and…excited.

didn't/know.

Chapter Twelve

School must have let out for the day, because two teenage boys were shooting baskets in a driveway across the
street, while several younger boys rode bikes over a low
plywood jump on a sidewalk. A toddler girl watched
wistfully from her seat on a plastic big-wheel trike from
a nearby lawn.

Abby let the drape fall back into place, leaving her in
the dimly lit living room. The house was awfully quiet,
and she didn't know what to do with herself. Caleb had
left her because he needed to check in at headquarters
and then take a run out to her aunt and uncle's place to
pick up her duffel bag with another change of clothes
in it as well as her books.

Not that he didn't have books aplenty, as she'd already discovered.

He'd shown her to a guest room upstairs in his home,
a two-story she guessed dated to 1910 or so. It had wonderful woodwork, gleaming oak floors, a carved fireplace mantel that had been restored and a dining room
with built-in glass-fronted buffet. She all but tiptoed
as she explored. She knew he wouldn't mind—the last
thing he'd said was *Make yourself at home*—but there
was a fine line between acting like a guest and being

flat-out nosy. The thing was, she could tell a lot about someone from his living quarters, and Caleb remained too much of an enigma to her. For example, while she had faith that he didn't currently have a girlfriend, had he ever been married? Did he have children? Had he really meant it when he said that he wanted a relationship with her? And what did *that* mean? Just sex, or more?

"Aagh!" She could drive herself nuts. *Was* driving herself nuts. *So go explore.* He'd never know if she didn't touch.

The kitchen was the one room in the house that must have been remodeled from the studs out. The cabinets were oak and fit the age of the house, but she suspected they were new. When she tentatively opened a drawer, it slid like silk. The appliances had to be new, too. An alcove held an antique round oak table, the small-paned windows covered with filmy white curtains.

Tucked in a small room at the back of the house was a businesslike office that included a laptop computer and printer on the desk and old-fashioned oak file cabinets. She barely peeked in there, because poking around on his computer or paperwork *would* have been intruding.

Next to the office was what was euphemistically called a powder room. Upstairs—despite her attempt to step lightly, as several steps creaked underfoot—she already knew there were two full bathrooms: one she'd have to herself, the other presumably attached to Caleb's bedroom. Now she opened doors, finding a linen closet that she guessed had been carved out of the guest bedroom. It was furnished, but Spartan, with cream-colored walls, a queen-size bed, a dresser and a closet that wouldn't have been original in a house of this era.

Opening doors, she found two empty bedrooms. The

door to his stood ajar. His room was plain enough to have pleased an Amishman, with no artwork or wallpaper on the walls. Antique dresser, walk-in closet, door opening into—yes—a bathroom with a claw-footed tub, and a giant bed covered by an Amish quilt, a log-cabin pattern in shades of green.

It was really hard to look away from that bed. Especially now that she knew what he looked like after he pulled off his shirt.

She loved everything about the house, and especially this bedroom. It suited him, she decided. She didn't see a hint that this was a man who missed the big city, nightlife, a risky job.

Abby moaned, went to the guest bedroom and decided to lie down. Not that she'd fall asleep.

Eyes closed, she imagined climbing into his bathtub, filled with hot water. Maybe some bubble bath. She hadn't actually taken a bubble bath since she was a little girl, but this was her fantasy. Besides, she could hide beneath the bubbles if Caleb should happen to open the door and walk in... Floating in her imagined bath, she began to drift.

CALEB HAD BEEN eager to come home in a way he didn't ever remember being. When he walked in the kitchen door to silence, worry took root. Could he have been followed when he drove her here? He'd swear not, but— damn it, she wouldn't have taken off again, would she? He should have been suspicious of her ready agreement to his plan.

"Abby?"

No answer. He took the stairs two at a time, trying not to make too much noise in case she was here and napping. He had to brace himself before he eased her door open enough to see the bed.

The punch of relief when he saw her curled up sound asleep took him aback. She'd had him on a roller coaster, all right, although she was on it, too, a few cars ahead of him. If they could sit in the same car, he'd be a lot happier.

He walked quietly into the room to look down at her. In sleep, she was softer, unable to guard her expressions. He was reminded of how fine-boned she was, and disturbed anew by the gauze wrapping her hands and the raw scrape on her jaw. She'd been repeatedly wounded, although at least this time he'd been there to step in. Not that she hadn't fought viciously, but if it had been two against one, and with her unarmed, Caleb figured they'd have succeeded in stuffing her into the van. She wouldn't have lived long.

It was the *why* of all this that ate at him. If she and her partner had surprised a drug dealer doing business, say, he'd gotten away with murdering one cop and injuring another. How much could she realistically have seen in the dark behind the bar? So what if her memory returned?

And an even bigger question: How did the shooter know she'd lost her memory and therefore hadn't been able to give testimony yet? How did he know where she'd gone after being released from the hospital?

Why was she such a threat?

The answer had been staring him in the face all along, of course. She was a threat because she knew the shooter. Because she would have recognized him.

That could have been because she'd arrested him before, or because he was one of the people she and the partner had talked to in the weeks before the shooting. That left the problem of how this hypothetical bad guy got confidential information from her doctor, or how he'd learned where she had gone after being released.

Caleb had been reluctant to admit even to himself the obvious answer.

She'd been shot by a fellow cop who had also killed Detective Neal Walker. Not just a cop, but one on her squad. He corrected himself immediately. She knew plenty of other officers in the department. This could be a former patrol partner or supervisor. No one would think twice if he—or she—kept following up on Abby's welfare.

Trouble was, Caleb didn't believe that. Odds were against her partner having known the same officers outside their unit well at all. He might not even have recognized them; KCPD had over thirteen hundred officers last he'd known.

From what Abby had said, Neal had been both dismayed and alarmed by whatever it was he'd stumbled across. Unless Donahue wasn't saying, her partner hadn't confided in his commanding officer.

Although it was possible he had, giving the sergeant a reason to jump to the conclusion that she was the bad apple.

Yeah, but then why hadn't he told his good buddy Caleb the real backstory? Because he didn't want to believe some bad stuff had been going on beneath his nose? Yeah, and if he could lay it at Abby's feet, he could relax. None of the detectives he'd worked with for years could possibly have gone over to the dark side. Had to be the newcomer.

Sad to say, Caleb could even sympathize with that

kind of self-deception. Looking at men and women you thought you knew inside and out and realizing one of them was willing to betray his honor and integrity for money?

Yeah, that would be tough.

All the same, somewhere along the line, Caleb had lost his respect for the big, tough Irishman he'd trusted more times than he could count. Donahue had taken the easy out, and in doing so had hurt the woman Caleb loved. Any confusion over who owned his loyalty was long gone.

Unable to resist, he sat on the edge of the bed and gently stroked a lock of blond hair from Abby's face. He felt her stillness, the new tension in her body, just before her eyes opened and fastened onto him. And then she relaxed, smiling. So beautiful in a peaceful moment.

"Caleb," she murmured.

"Sleeping beauty." He planted a hand on the bed and leaned over to kiss her forehead, her cheek, the tip of her nose, and finally her lips. With his body stirring and a groan rumbling in his chest, it was all he could do to pull back, but he made himself. She'd taken a battering today. The last thing she needed was him putting his hands on her.

Although, damn, he did want to.

"Dinner will be ready in about five minutes," he said. "Courtesy of Nancy and my microwave."

Abby's chuckle warmed him deep inside. "And here I expected you to cook for me."

"Oh, I'll do that. But your aunt wouldn't take a *no, thanks* from me."

"Feeding people well is her mission in life." She

swept the room with a glance. "Wow. I didn't think I could fall asleep."

"You needed it." He sounded gruff as he pushed himself to his feet. "We'll eat in the kitchen. Come on down when you're ready." He walked out before he surrendered to his real hunger.

DINING TOGETHER ALONE with Caleb, rather than surrounded by family, felt surprisingly comfortable even as Abby was conscious of all the eddies of underlying emotion. The familiar taste of her aunt's fried chicken and warm potato salad helped. And since she'd missed lunch, she dug in with enthusiasm, as did Caleb.

With the table round, they sat close enough to touch. In fact, his knee brushed hers. He'd produced beautiful china with gilt edges for this casual meal. Abby liked it but finally said, with an effort at lightness, "I expected mismatched plates."

"Plates?" He looked at his as if he'd never seen it. "Oh, Mom gave me ten place settings, including serving dishes." He shrugged, although a small smile played on his mouth. "At least it's plain. Pink roses, I might have had to thank her and hide them at the back of a dark cupboard."

"Would have threatened your masculinity for sure," she teased sarcastically. "Still, these are pretty fancy."

"My mother said she has a couple of sets left even after she gave these to me and another set to my sister. Good God, probably to my brother, too." The thought seemed to amuse him. "Truth is, my mother loves flea markets, yard sales, auctions—you name it. She produced half the furniture in this house. The dresser in your room—how could she *not* buy it, she said, when the price was so ridiculously low?"

Abby laughed, relaxing. "I've never been much for shopping. I guess between not having a mother to show me the way and spending a lot of time in an Amish household, that's no surprise. Because of my *grossmammi* and then Aenti Nancy, I can cook, but everything is calorie laden."

"I'd get fat in a hurry if I ate three meals a day at your aunt's table," he agreed. "I'm competent in the kitchen thanks to my mother, who insisted my brother and I had to learn to cook and wash dishes just like Susan did, but except for my days off, I depend on my microwave more than Mom would like."

"You've never been married?" That just slipped out, but Abby congratulated herself on how casual it sounded.

"Never even came close." He watched her intently. "You know you have to tell me about your mother eventually, right?"

Of course he'd been wondering. In fact, he'd probably already guessed. Still, she took the last bite of food on her plate, a sweet-onion salad, forced herself to swallow, and set down her fork.

"Mom was shot." She made a face. "Like mother, like daughter, huh? Except Mom..." Her shoulders wanted to hunch, but with an effort she relaxed them. "She was gentle and kind and forgiving. She didn't leave the Amish faith out of disbelief. She loved Dad."

Caleb was holding her hand, she realized, which felt right. His dark green eyes stayed on her face.

"She and Dad were coming home from an evening

with some friends, and he stopped at a convenience store for gas. Mom went in to pay."

She could tell he knew what was coming.

"She walked right into the middle of a holdup. I guess she surprised the guy. He shot her, then freaked and shot the clerk, too. He got away with fifty-something dollars."

"I'm so sorry," Caleb said gently.

She forced out a husky, "Yeah, me, too. The guy shot toward Dad, too, but missed. He ran around the side of the store into the alley and disappeared. He'd kept his head ducked so the cops couldn't isolate a good image from the camera over the cash register." Abby had to clear her throat. "Mom died right away, the clerk a day later. Dad haunted the police station for a long time, but no suspect was ever identified. He…never got over it. Even now, I think his body goes through the motions of living, but his mind is not really in there. You know?"

The turbulence in his eyes, Abby recognized. It echoed the bewilderment and hurt and even anger she'd felt then, and to this day, because her father didn't love her enough to stay with her, even to *try* to give her what she'd needed. He'd all but abandoned her, without doing so in a way anyone else but her Amish family would recognize.

Caleb bowed his head for a minute. When he looked back at her, she understood that he'd needed to gain control so he didn't say things that might hurt her.

"Not hard to figure out why you became a cop," he said roughly. "Did your Amish family understand?"

"With their heads, but not their hearts. They kept reminding me that I need to forgive."

"'Vengeance is mine…saith the Lord.'"

"More that we must forgive, as God forgives us. Vengeance isn't the Amish way—you know that."

"I do." His eyes met hers. "Right this minute, vengeance has some real appeal."

"I've asked myself a thousand times what I'd do if I came face-to-face with the guy who shot my mother, a woman who was no threat to him at all. I'm still not sure," she admitted. "I know I wouldn't kill him if I could help it, but I want to see him spend the rest of his life in a prison cell, with no hope of ever walking out. He was…slight. They could tell that much from the camera footage. He might have been a kid. Aenti Nancy would say, *So troubled, so young.*"

"So vicious, so young."

She nodded. "I wonder how many more people he's killed since then."

"He may be in prison by now, you know. If they didn't get fingerprints from that convenience store…"

"He wore gloves."

"Then any later arresting officers would never have tied him to your mother's murder."

"That's true." Abby huffed, not quite a laugh. "Thinking you're right is all the comfort I'll ever get."

"Damn, Abby." He pushed back his chair to stand and pulled her up into his arms.

Abby wrapped hers around his waist and laid her cheek against his shoulder. Caleb didn't say any more, only held her, one hand moving in soothing circles on her back, his breath stirring loose strands of her hair.

THEY STARTED THE next day at the scene of the crime: the alley where she'd been shot. Caleb would have understood if Abby was a little spooked by returning to the otherwise deserted alley and staring down at a rusty stain in the asphalt that was very likely her partner's blood. Instead, she seemed intensely focused in the way of the homicide detective she'd been.

There was a moment he didn't keep it together as well as he should have. She pointed out where she'd fallen, and he studied the corner of the nearest dumpster. His eye caught on a dark streak where her head had likely hit, and his muscles locked. He stared, unable to look away, for longer than was wise. Only her voice broke the spell.

"I thought being here might nudge my memory, but…" She shrugged.

"Let's go into the bar," he said shortly.

The bartender on shift had heard all the talk at the time but hadn't been working that night. The owner came out of his office in back to study them with suspicion even as he grudgingly offered his name, Brad Spooner.

"I've talked to more cops about that episode than I ever wanted to see in my lifetime. No offense," he added. "Who are you two?"

"I'm Detective Baker," Abby said. "My partner and I were shot back there. He died—I didn't."

Spooner professed not to have any idea what went on behind his business. Yeah, she looked familiar, he admitted grudgingly. He guessed she and her partner might have come in here, but if they'd talked to anyone, it must have been one of the bartenders, not him.

Back in Caleb's vehicle, Abby said, "Once he knew who I was, he got squirrelly."

"I noticed." Caleb pulled out into traffic. "And I'm

willing to bet he's on the phone right now telling someone we were there asking questions."

"I'd give a lot to know *who* he called."

"You and me both." Caleb took his eyes off the
rearview mirror, satisfied nobody had followed them.
"Where next?"

Next turned out to be the backside of an enormous
building in the warehouse district near the river. This,
she said, was where Neal had taken her when he met
with what she'd taken as a crime boss surrounded by
thugs.

His reluctance growing by the minute, Caleb contem-
plated several expensive sedans and SUVs, all black,
parked back here. They couldn't have looked more out
of place, given the abandoned feel here and the crum-
bling brick wall of the building punctuated only by a
couple of closed steel doors. Not a single window. Their
arrival wouldn't have gone unnoticed, however. In one
glance, he spotted three cameras.

"I shouldn't do this, but I'm going to give you my
backup piece." He lifted the leg of his trousers and removed the small handgun from the holster.

She palmed it quickly and slipped it into her waist-
band at the small of her back. He'd been glad that morning to see that she wore a linen shirt over a camisole.
Despite the heat, he kept on a long-sleeve khaki shirt
over a T-shirt for the same reason.

"Ready?"

"You bet." No show of nerves.

He'd seen her soft side. Today, he was getting a better look at the gutsy woman who'd been a decorated
cop and made detective at a young age.

He could smell the river but not see it. Heat shimmered around them as they walked across the cracked cement to the nearest door, where he pushed a button that was presumably a doorbell.

A big man with a scar on his neck opened the door within seconds. He took in Abby's more visible bruises and scrapes. "What'ya want?"

"To speak to your boss," she said coolly.

The door closed in their faces.

"He recognized you," Caleb murmured.

"I think he was one of the men there that day," she said as softly.

Not two minutes later, the door swung open again. Mr. Charming snapped, "He'll see you."

A short hall led into a huge open space. Stacked crates lined both sides of the room. The man who waited wore, incongruously, a polo shirt with a discreet label on the chest, chinos with knife-edge creases and athletic shoes. None of that lessened Caleb's impression that this was a man very capable of brutality. The employee who'd shown them in had retreated behind them; three others formed a semicircle with their boss at the center. The small hairs on Caleb's body prickled. They shouldn't have walked into this. His hand wanted to edge for the butt of his gun, but he knew that would be a mistake. A fatal one.

"I've seen you before," the boss said with no particular interest. "You're the woman cop."

"That's right. You spoke to my partner, Neal Walker."

"I heard he was killed."

"He was. That's why I'm here."

"Got nothing to do with us."

"Will you tell me what Neal asked you?"

He blinked a couple of times, the only change of expression he'd so far displayed. "You think it has something to do with the two of you getting shot."

She stayed calm, back straight, looking the man in the eyes. "Yes."

One of the thugs off to the side said, "Twenty minutes."

The boss grunted. "Kid has a soccer game this afternoon."

Well, there was a picture: Daddy in the stands cheering on his daughter. Caleb stayed impassive.

"Guess there's no harm. He thought there was a cop involved with a crime syndicate." His mouth had a small twist, as if he enjoyed putting it that way. "Me, I'm a businessman. There are occasions when I might be willing to pay for a small favor, but what he was talking about—" He shook his head. "I don't know anything about it, and that's the truth."

"You haven't heard rumors?"

"Nah. I told him to look at some of the biker gangs fighting over the city." His gaze flicked from her to Caleb and back. "Now, you'll need to excuse me." Without acknowledging Abby's thanks, he nodded toward the guy behind Caleb.

Without a word, the guy led them back the way they'd come, staying in the open doorway to watch them walk to the SUV. The skin crawled between Caleb's shoulder blades, but by the time he unlocked and got in, the door was closed and they were alone.

The first thing Abby said was, "A youth soccer game."

"If I were that coach, I'd give his kid all the playing time her heart desires."

Abby's laugh was just a little over the top. Caleb grinned at her, relief at making it out of the warehouse, safe, as good as a shot of whiskey.

Chapter Thirteen

Abby strode into the kitchen where Caleb was slicing chicken breasts he intended to stir-fry.

"We're wasting our time," she announced, then swung around and stalked back out. She'd been pacing and venting ever since they got home from their second day exploring the dark side of Kansas City.

Caleb's tension had all gone to his neck today and was refusing to release its grip. The fact that neither of them had any jurisdiction had increasingly nagged at him. On the job was different; as civilians, they'd been at much higher risk going to the places they had, outnumbered by the pimps, bikers, drug dealers and assorted other upstanding citizens of the great state of Missouri they'd sought out for chats.

Cutting meat with a sharp butcher knife was one way to expel some of his frustration and the anxiety balling in his gut. What if they'd ended up in a shoot-out? He'd tried to make her wear the bulletproof vest he carried in the back of his SUV, but she'd refused.

"Anyone we talk to would notice it," Abby had pointed out.

He reminded her that a vest had saved her life not very long ago. When she dug in her heels, he declined to wear the damn thing, either. Maybe she wasn't the only stubborn one in this relationship.

Now, when he heard her returning footsteps, he said, "You're right," and used the knife to slide the chicken strips into a bowl before thoroughly washing both it and the cutting board. "Why would anyone be honest with us?"

"Obviously, they're not being," she retorted sharply.

He reached for a bell pepper. *Whack. Whack.* "We've stirred the pot, which isn't all bad. Whoever is after you knows now that you remember what Neal was doing leading up to the shooting. The scumbag has to be wondering if your memory isn't coming back."

"All the more reason to take me out."

"Which gives me an idea I don't like." A few more *whacks* didn't prevent the muscles in his shoulders and neck from cranking another notch tighter.

She'd stopped pacing, but hadn't sat down, either.

Onion in one hand, Caleb turned to face her.

Her stress showing on her face in a way she hadn't let anyone else see, Abby said, "A trap."

He should have kept his mouth shut, he told himself, but knew she'd have come up with the same plan soon. Truth was, they'd been stumbling around in the dark. He'd gone along with it primarily in hopes either a place or person they encountered would nudge open the floodgates in her mind.

During the drive home from Kansas City this afternoon, he had stolen a few looks at her and wondered if it wasn't doing just that. If those gates weren't quaking even now, her will doing battle with a subconscious part of her brain determined to *keep* them closed.

Last night, the two of them had stopped for dinner on

the way home at the café in town. The chances of being overheard had been good, so they'd set aside the subject of what they'd been up to. He'd talked more than she had, telling stories about his boyhood and pranks he and his friends pulled their senior year of high school. Half a dozen people had stopped by the table to say hello, necessitating introductions. He'd watched her closing herself in. In fact, the minute they'd gotten home, she'd said abruptly, "I need a shower, and then I think I'll read in bed."

When he'd followed her upstairs an hour later, he'd seen a light beneath her door. His feet had stopped right outside it. His awareness acute, he'd wondered if she was holding her breath as she waited to see what he'd do.

Caleb had gritted his teeth and reminded himself, over and over again, that she was working her way around to trusting him. Pushing her now would be the mistake of a lifetime.

He hadn't seen her again until this morning.

Today, her face had become increasingly drawn, as if flesh was melting from her cheeks. She rubbed her temples when she thought he wouldn't notice. During lunch, she slipped a pill in her mouth. Sure as hell, she was feeling those spikes driving into her skull.

Suddenly angry, he said, "You've had a headache for two days. Why are you so determined to hide it?"

Her eyes widened. "How do you know?"

"I'm observant." She fascinated him, which meant his awareness stayed active.

"Oh." As if her knees had given out, she dropped onto a chair in the alcove. "I've...actually felt a little better this afternoon."

"Because you took pain meds."

Studying him warily, she said, "Yes."

"Damn." He set down the onion and went to her, bending to kiss her forehead. "I'm sorry. I shouldn't have gone on the attack."

"No, it's okay." Her smile took an obvious effort. "This was probably a dumb idea from the beginning. I really appreciate you going along with it. We got ourselves into some situations that would have freaked me out if I'd been alone."

He could freak out just thinking of her alone in that warehouse, or at the biker bar that had been part of today's investigative activities.

Fortunately, she didn't seem to notice his reaction and continued talking. "If Neal had learned anything substantive when he was asking questions, I think he'd have told me. He may have caught some hints that worried him, but if so… I didn't yesterday or today."

"They all wanted to steer us in another direction." They should be looking at bikers. A pimp over on Garfield. No, no, back to Independence Avenue. They'd covered a lot of ground today.

"Not hard to see why." She sagged in the chair as if someone had let out the air.

"No." He pulled a chair close to hers so he could hold her hands. She'd acquired a few calluses from her work at the farm, and he moved his thumbs soothingly on her palms while continuing, "I think your partner died because he did the same thing we did, making it plain he was onto something. With him gone, you recovering your memories was the only threat…until now. We've agreed the killer knows what we've been up to. This has to be déjà vu for him."

Alarm widened her eyes. "You're wearing a target now, too."

"Probably not, unless we stumbled too close." And how would they know? They were in the dark as much as they'd been two days ago.

Her hands tightened on his. "Maybe we should call Sergeant Donahue and tell him what we suspect."

"No," Caleb said flatly. "If he hasn't thought of this himself, he's wearing blinders. If he has… I don't like it that he didn't tell me."

"You don't think…"

The suggestion disturbed Caleb on a fundamental level. He shook his head, even as he said, "No, but at this point, we can't rule him out. I don't like that he zeroed in on you so fast."

"It never made sense. If nothing else, Neal wouldn't have taken me along when he talked to people if he'd suspected me at all."

"No." Damn it, he'd known Donahue for a long time, never had even a grain of suspicion that the guy cared enough about money to violate his integrity. A voice inside murmured, *Yeah, but did he ever invite you to his home for a backyard barbecue or to have a few beers and watch a game?* No, he hadn't. In fact, Caleb could only recall meeting Mike's wife a couple of times. Had Donahue kept everyone at a distance?

That was good reason for his current uneasiness. Cops socialized with each other. Their friends were other cops, because their day-to-day experiences separated them from civilians. You couldn't talk about your work with someone who wouldn't understand why you'd drawn on someone that day, or how you'd felt when you arrested an abusive man and then got a good look at a whimpering little girl with pleading eyes and third-degree burns from her daddy dumping boiling water over her as punishment for staying underfoot when he'd told her to get lost.

Caleb's phone rang at that moment, and he wasn't at all surprised to see that the caller was his good friend, Mike Donahue. He was surprised Donahue hadn't called yesterday. He tipped the phone so Abby could see the screen before he answered.

"Mike."

"What the hell have you been up to?" Donahue roared. "You're way out of line poking around in *my* city. Let me tell you—"

Seeing Abby flinch at the bellow, Caleb interrupted without compunction. "I was helping Detective Baker get answers. We're both hoping that revisiting some scenes will help her recover her memory. Isn't that what you want?"

"I want you to leave the damn investigation to us! You're a small-town sheriff now, remember?"

"County." It was a nitpicking thing to quibble over, but Caleb didn't appreciate condescension.

"What?" Suddenly off-stride, Donahue sounded confused.

"County sheriff."

A smile flickered on Abby's lips.

"What the flippin' difference does it make?" Donahue shot back. "Just tell me this. Why didn't you do me the courtesy of letting me know what you planned?"

If Caleb had gone to Kansas City to interview a witness or suspect in a crime that had taken place here in Hearn County, he would have notified KCPD, so Donahue wasn't out of line to ask.

But all Caleb said was a mild "Thought we might stumble across something you haven't."

"You think I'm incompetent? Is that it?"

"What are you complaining about? You wanted me to get close to Abby. I've done that. In my opinion, which I know you don't want to hear, she was a victim at that scene, probably as in the dark about why it happened as you are. But you're hot on her remembering, so we made the decision to push a little, not wait patiently for her memories to return. Which they may never do."

There was a long silence. Donahue had moderated his voice when he said, "I take it your efforts didn't accomplish anything."

Caleb met Abby's eyes. As if she read his mind, she nodded. Time to bait the first hook.

"Not sure. She's getting flashes. Nothing important yet, or I'd have let you know, but I think maybe whatever is blocking her is getting ready to blow."

This pause didn't last quite as long, but Caleb imagined that Donahue was using it for some intensive thinking. So was he.

"Maybe I should try talking to her again," the sergeant said. "She's still with her weird family, right?"

Caleb did not like the casually thrown-out line. Apparently he wasn't the only one fishing. "No, I guess I haven't kept you up to date. A shooter had another go at her. Wounded her aunt, grazed Abby's arm. Not wanting to endanger her family anymore, she took off on her own. I caught up just as two men tried to abduct her. This is serious stuff going on, Mike. Tell me you've been straight with me."

"Of course I have!" Donahue snapped. "What are you implying?"

"That you may think I don't have to know everything."

"You don't."

Having Abby sitting right here listening in, never looking away from him, helped Caleb keep a short rein on his temper. "How did you hear that we'd been in town talking to people?" he asked.

"You two stuck out a little, you know. People tell me things."

"Pimps? Mobsters? Drug dealers?"

"We heard from a couple CIs," he said curtly.

Caleb supposed that it was barely possible he and Abby had spoken to a confidential informant or two.

"I'm making dinner," he said. "Is that all you wanted?"

"I want to know where she is," Donahue said in a hard voice.

"Tonight's temporary. I'll let you know once we find a better place."

"You do that."

Hearing dead air, Caleb dropped his phone on the table. "Guess we're not best friends anymore."

She frowned. "I couldn't hear most of what he said."

"He didn't like us butting in where we don't belong. He wants to keep tabs on you." Caleb shrugged. "I think that's the gist."

"Did you expect different?"

He rubbed the back of his neck. "He should want you to regain your memory."

Still looking perturbed, Abby said, "The thing is, he's already made up his mind about me. Would he believe I'm telling the truth if I did claim to have remembered everything?"

Caleb grimaced. "I don't know." He pushed himself to his feet. "Let me get back to putting dinner together."

She offered to help and was soon slicing bell peppers while he dealt with the onion and garlic. He liked having her here, working alongside him. She teased him a few times about his domestic skill, asked where to find the can of cashew nuts he needed, heated the few remaining sourdough biscuits from Nancy and set the table. Even throwing out ideas for how to set up a situation where she appeared to be alone and vulnerable beat his usual solitary planning.

Having her here was like slotting the last puzzle piece into place, completing the picture. What he had no idea about was whether it felt as right to her as it did to him.

Last night, Abby had been a coward. How else could she explain why she'd fled upstairs at seven in the evening to hide out in her room? Yes, she'd had a headache, but no worse than she had half the time since the shooting.

Being alone with Caleb this way in his home was different than their talks on her aunt and uncle's front porch. Then she'd been as conscious of his body, his every expression, the glint in his eyes when he looked at her, but she'd known nothing could happen. Now... they were living together. Temporarily, but still.

If he kissed her now, he could take her upstairs to his bed. She would know how his hands and mouth felt on her breasts, the texture of his chest hair, whether the sharp tug in her lower belly meant anything. She could find out what sex was all about beyond the sharp pain, fumbling and disappointment that was all she knew.

Last night, she'd been confused about her feelings, frustrated by their day, scared to trust Caleb. This evening might be her only chance. Abby had no idea what would happen once their trap closed. If she survived, she'd have to testify in a trial, or multiple trials, which would take her back to Kansas City. She'd need to look for a job, and obviously she couldn't work for him.

She sipped her coffee, hoping she wasn't blushing just because she was *thinking* about sex. Women her age weren't supposed to be so naive. She had no intention of telling him how inexperienced she was, but he'd probably figure it out at her first attack of shyness.

The timid part of her wanted to forget the whole idea. The woman who'd become a cop and was a good one disagreed.

Suddenly, she realized Caleb had been silent for an awfully long time, too. She raised her gaze to find him watching her, his eyes dark and the hand that lay on the table clenched in a fist. He didn't move at all, which meant…he was waiting for her?

She swallowed. "Caleb?"

"I want you," he said roughly. "If you plan to say no, I'd appreciate it if you'd do it now."

Abby shocked herself by not hesitating. "I won't be saying no."

He surged to his feet, his chair rocking as he pulled her up. And then, well, she didn't have to say anything at all.

His kiss started tender, then became greedy and possessive. She held on tight, arms locked around his neck, and kissed him back. Who cared if their teeth clanked, or if she made odd little sounds? When he lifted his head for a moment, it felt natural to slide her lips along the cords of his neck, taste his skin in the vulnerable hollow at the base of his throat. Her toes curled when he trailed his mouth across her cheek to nibble on her earlobe at the same time as his big hands closed over her hips and pulled her against him. She reveled in his strength, in all those muscles.

"Upstairs," he said, as if his patience had frayed.

A shiver traveled down her spine and she nodded. Fortunately, she seemed to be past any doubts. As her arms dropped, he grabbed her hand and led her through the living room to the foot of the stairs. There, they stopped to kiss until her mind just about shut down. She wanted to climb his body, she wanted—

He groaned, lifted his head and started up the stairs. Abby concentrated on the first step, the next. His enormous bed. Where she would take off her clothes and bare her naked body to his eyes. Where *he'd* strip and she'd get her first good look at a fully aroused man.

She had to be far gone, because her curiosity and eagerness let her ignore the tiny flutters of panic. *He hasn't noticed yet.*

Caleb didn't stop until they reached that bed. Then he swept back the covers…and stalled, doing nothing but looking down at her. "You're beautiful," he said, in a deep, ragged voice. "You know, I found photos of you online before I met you. There's one of you in your uniform looking official."

She bobbed her head. She knew the one he meant.

"I kept staring at it. Told myself not to be a fool. Then the first time I met you, you were sitting on the grass blinking up at me." He sounded…bemused.

She'd never felt her heart hammering so hard. Some

instinct had her lift her hand to his chest, where she felt an echo. "What?" she whispered.

He shook his head. "I was done for." His control seemed to snap. Breathing harshly, he tore her shirt over her head, fumbled with the button at her waist with one hand and the clasp of her bra with the other.

Abby responded by going for his shirt buttons. She *ached*.

Within minutes they'd shed their clothes. She sucked in her breath at the expression on his face, and good thing, too, because the next second he'd claimed her mouth and breathing was the last thing on her mind.

Despite the raw desperation on his face, he laid her gently on his bed, then set about driving her crazy. Abby moaned at the wet heat and suction of his mouth on her breasts, and writhed when his fingers slid between her thighs. Every barrier she had crashed and went down. She gave in to the need to explore his body, too, and if she was clumsy, it hardly seemed to matter. The flex of powerful muscles at her every touch made *her* feel powerful.

He talked, telling her again how beautiful she was, how perfect, groaned when she found sensitive places on his body, murmured, "Yes, like that. Damn." And then, "Are you on birth control?"

"I…" Abby moistened her lips. "No. I didn't think—"

"I have something." He closed his eyes tight. "Just… give me a second."

While she lay still, he pushed himself up and headed into the bathroom. Cupboard doors slammed and he swore creatively. At last he reappeared, packets in his hand. Abby gaped as he walked toward her, confident in his body, although why wouldn't he be? He had that male saunter down, and his erection hadn't subsided.

Abby gulped.

She'd tensed enough that he started over, lavishing attention to her breasts, stroking her until her hips rose and fell and she forgot her worries and just about everything else.

She vaguely heard him tear the packet open. The next thing she knew, he was between her thighs, thrusting into her. Her first thought was that he didn't fit. Her breath caught and she must have stiffened. But he kept pushing until he was seated deep. To her astonishment, it felt good. Really good. She wanted more.

"Please." Abby clutched at his broad back and planted her feet on the mattress to push her hips upward. "Don't stop."

He made a sound she couldn't have described. With his weight on one elbow, he lifted her thigh and kept moving. Almost out, then slow and deep. Abby felt increasingly frantic, needing him to do *something*.

Whatever magical thing it was, he did, because pleasure exploded through her in a way she couldn't have imagined. She heard herself crying out even as Caleb drove hard once more, twice, and she felt throbbing within as he buried his face in the curve of her neck and let himself go.

Abby's hands slipped off the damp expanse of his back, as if she'd lost all ability to move.

THERE WAS ONLY a buzz in his head. He'd never felt anything like this before. Moving ever again didn't seem likely.

The idea that he might be crushing her was his first

coherent thought. Yeah. Had to roll over. It felt like a huge effort when he did.

As his mind cleared, he remembered how exquisitely tight she was.

He pushed up so he could see her face. "You weren't a virgin."

She gazed back with defiance. "Was I supposed to be?"

"I wondered. That's all."

"Because I blush?"

He smiled at her. "Partly that."

"I'm not very experienced." Her lips pinched. "I guess you could tell."

"No."

"Oh." She eyed him. "I had a boyfriend in college. Everyone else was having sex, and I wanted to fit in. To be modern. So..." Her shoulders moved. "It was only a few times, and not that great."

"That's it? A few times?"

"I never really wanted to try again." Her cheeks glowed red.

"So what was this? An experiment?"

Abby gaped at him, then exclaimed, "No!" She shoved him and tried to roll free. He recaptured her effortlessly.

"What, then?"

"It was you! That's what. But you don't have to take this as some...some hearts and flowers thing. It's not. Until now, I didn't want to try this again, okay?"

"This?" That ticked him off. "Make love, you mean."

After a moment, her face softened. "Yes."

"Don't discount me or yourself." He relented enough to kiss her before forcing himself to release her and roll off the bed. He needed to ditch the condom so they could start all over again.

Knowing she couldn't see, Caleb smiled wryly at himself. He liked knowing she'd only had one lover before, and that one not very satisfactory. He'd never felt quite so primitive before. Abby had brought him all kinds of new experiences.

Chapter Fourteen

Abby shaped a sheet of dough over an enormous heap of peeled and sliced apples in a pie pan. From long practice, she deftly united the bottom and top pie crusts, cut a tic-tac-toe design in the top that would vent the heat, and used a fork to flute the edges. Repeat, and she had two pies ready to go in the oven.

Once that was done and she'd set a timer, she began to clean up. Somehow, she'd been consigned to KP duty for herself and her around-the-clock bodyguard, Deputy John Wisniewski. Didn't it figure. His excuse was that he'd never cooked without electrical appliances. The real reason, she quickly figured out, was that his wife waited on him hand and foot.

Since she'd baked bread this morning and chili simmered on the stove, she was done until they'd both eaten. Which they wouldn't do together; one of them needed to be on guard all the time.

Even now, with John prowling this floor of the house, Abby kept Caleb's small backup handgun, a Ruger 9mm, on the table within easy reach. Fortunately, they'd had a chance to drive to a range for her to try the gun out, so it didn't feel completely unfamiliar when she picked it up.

While the pies baked, she supposed she'd go upstairs and peek from the crack between curtains toward the woods behind her cousin Rose's house. No, she'd scan every direction, watch for movement, for anything that didn't belong.

What else was there to do? She couldn't concentrate enough to read, not when her ears were tuned for the tiniest of sounds, not when even John's soft footfall would make her head snap up.

Abby had forgotten the sheer boredom that was a major part of most stakeouts. Somehow, you were supposed to stay alert for mind-numbing hours on end.

The place for her to hole up had been her suggestion. Her cousin Rose was having a hard time carrying twins as her due date drew nearer. Her doctor had ordered restricted activity. Nobody would be surprised that Rose and Matthew had gone to stay with her parents, Rose's pregnancy their excuse. "She is best off with her *mamm* and *daad*," Nancy had insisted to anyone who asked. Abby had expected to resume her Amish garb, but Caleb didn't want her to step a foot outside and had ordered her to keep curtains pulled. In other words, it didn't matter what she wore, since no one but he and the deputy were supposed to see her. She could move more freely without skirts.

"We want them to commit by breaking in," he told her. She had hidden a shudder. Glass shattering as someone came in a window, or the sound of wood splintering when a door was kicked open. An Amish farmhouse wasn't exactly a fortress.

This wouldn't have worked if Matthew had farmed, but the property was small and he worked at a cabinet-making shop in Ruston. At Caleb's suggestion, the

milk cow and small flock of chickens had gone with
Rose and Matthew. That way no one had to take care
of them. Caleb refused to put anyone else in a position
to be used as bait to draw Abby outside.

It had taken twenty-four hours after he and Abby
laid the plans for them to gain permission first from
Abby's family, then from the bishop of their church
district. Given that the Amish wanted nothing to do
with violence, subterfuge or police operations, Abby
was surprised when Samuel Troyer agreed. It helped
that he had known her since she was a girl and been
kept informed of the attempts on her life. That those
men who were determined to kill her had been willing
to shoot Nancy had shocked him deeply.

Within twenty-four hours, Caleb had left her here
with the deputy he said was his most capable. John was
in his midthirties, Abby guessed, a stocky man of about
her own height, seeming dour at first meeting. Given
that the two of them had been alone in the house for
going on three days now, they'd gotten to know each
other. He told her he'd started his career with the St.
Joseph PD but married his high school sweetheart and
decided to come home to Ruston when a job became
available so they'd be near both their families.

She really didn't want him to be hurt or killed because of her. How would she tell his wife, now pregnant
with their second child?

She and John kept watch during the daytime. Mostly
John, because *somebody* had to prepare meals and his
professed ineptness made that her. Once darkness fell,
Caleb would steal across the fields and quietly let himself in the front door. At near-dawn, he'd wake them
before he slipped out. If he was getting any sleep at

all, Abby couldn't figure out how. She wasn't doing all that well herself.

Adrenaline had pumped through her the first day. Hard to forget that *she* was the goat staked out to draw a predator, which made this a tiny bit different than the usual dull police stakeouts she'd done. It also made it next to impossible to snuggle into bed and get a good night's sleep, even if Caleb was downstairs standing guard.

By the second day, anxiety and eagerness mutated into impatience.

By this morning, she'd been flat-out bored.

Maybe this trap wasn't going to work. For all they knew, armed men were still watching her aunt and uncle's farm instead. Caleb had felt sure that any interested party would note that Rose and Matthew had oh-so-conveniently vacated this house. He'd made sure there was talk of it in town at the café, the grocery store, anywhere outsiders might overhear. And of course, he'd let Donahue know where she was, offering him the chance to interview her again.

So far he hadn't accepted the offer, apparently relying on Caleb's reports. They were counting on him having told Sam Kirk, at the least, where she could be found, if not other detectives in the squad.

John interrupted her brooding by entering the kitchen at that moment. "Smells good," he said quietly.

"The chili is ready anytime. I'm going upstairs, if that's okay."

His eyes narrowed on her face. Did he think she was going nuts? If so, he might be right. But all he did was nod. "Must be hot as Hades up there."

It was, she discovered. Today had been uncomfortably hot, the air feeling heavy, the weight almost literal. Trudging up the steps required an effort. Abby was reminded of the day Aenti Nancy had been shot. Whether from nature or man, she had a feeling of impending danger.

The gun in one hand, she shifted the curtain an inch or two so she could peek out the window in the bedroom she was using. Feeling stifled, she'd have given a lot to shove it open. Of course she couldn't do that; the house was supposed to appear unoccupied or as if somebody was trying very hard to make it *appear* vacant. Besides, even the leaves on the trees she could see hung limply. There couldn't be any breeze at all.

The woods and fields were bone-dry; a lightning storm could ignite fires. The sky had a yellowish tinge that made her think about tornadoes, too. Did this house have a storm cellar? She should have asked. Hey, it could have served as a panic room, too.

With a sigh, she let the curtain fall, made her rounds and went back downstairs.

The pies still had twenty minutes to go. John sat down with a bowl of chili while she prowled the downstairs in his place, straining to hear any sounds from outside, even more cautiously stealing looks.

Despite her lack of appetite, she made herself eat a little when her turn came. She wished darkness would fall so Caleb would come. Even though they wouldn't be able to do much more than talk quietly for a few minutes, something in her settled when he was here. He hadn't kissed her when John might see them, so mostly she felt lucky when he brushed his hand over hers, or their eyes met and she saw that his frustration and worry was as great as hers, that he wanted to put his arms around her.

How long could they keep this up? What if no attack happened? Maybe Caleb had a plan B, but if so he hadn't mentioned it, and she surely didn't.

When the timer went off and she removed the pies from the oven, she glanced at the clock. Sunset came at about six forty-five right now, so Caleb should get here in about an hour.

Patience, she counseled herself.

EYE ON THE CLOCK, Caleb gobbled the beef Stroganoff he'd heated in the microwave. Abby seemed to be filling her time doing some baking with ingredients she found in her cousin's pantry or that he brought for her, so he could pretty well count on dessert there. He'd have eaten whatever she put in front of him no matter what, because it seemed to please her to see him enjoying the product of her labor. He guessed some of her aunt's determination to feed everyone had rubbed off on Abby. That, or she was combating the feeling of helplessness that would be natural in her situation.

He felt helpless, too. He didn't like trusting her safety to anyone else, however reliable and experienced. Caleb had seriously considered taking vacation and letting everyone assume he'd gone out of town while he was holed up with Abby, but he had so damn much on his plate these days, he couldn't. He didn't believe the assault would come during the day, anyway. Taking potshots at her from the woods was one thing, but if he were planning a break-in, he'd wait for darkness.

Which was nearly here, he saw with a glance through the window. He cleaned up quickly and put on his vest over his uniform shirt. He'd ordered both Abby and John to wear theirs even when sleeping, however tempting it would be in this hot, humid weather to take them off.

Caleb had just gotten into his SUV when his cell phone rang. Crap—the number belonged to dispatch. "Tanner," he said.

"Sheriff, there was a hit-and-run out on Methany Road."

Caleb braced himself, hearing the stress in the evening dispatcher's voice.

"Three boys riding their bikes. A car sideswiped them all."

"Dead or injured?"

She didn't yet know. Given the address, he paused only long enough to text John Wisniewski. Traffic accident, will be late.

Then he accelerated onto the road, praying none of those boys had died.

By the time he arrived, dusk was cutting down on visibility. He couldn't miss the blinking lights from emergency vehicles, though. Caleb parked behind a sheriff's-department unit, jumped out and strode forward to join the cluster of uniformed personnel looking at the twisted frame of a bike on the right shoulder.

"Sheriff," one of his deputies said in relief. Carson Myrick, only twenty-four years old, but on the job three years now.

"What happened?"

Even as he bent his head to listen, he saw one boy sitting at the edge of the ditch, curled forward in pain or distress. A female EMT crouched next to him, her hand on the boy's arm.

"Jeffrey Groendyke—" the deputy nodded that way "—was in the lead. He had time to throw himself off his bike into the ditch. He swears the driver never braked. He says he and his two friends were riding single file— there was plenty of room to pass them. For some reason, the car drifted."

Caleb knew a Walter Groendyke, a dentist. This had to be his kid. "Teenagers?"

"He doesn't think so. It was a dark-colored sedan, he thinks black, and he saw the driver's head from the back, but no one else."

Caleb drew a deep breath. "The other two boys?"

"Already being transported." Myrick was holding himself together, but now the muscles in his jaw spasmed. "Broken bones, at the least. One of the two, ah, didn't look so good."

"All right," Caleb said. "Let me talk to Jeffrey."

This wouldn't be a quick detour. His gut knotted at the delay, but these kids came first.

ABBY HELD HER BREATH. Holding herself rigidly, she sat in the darkness partway up the staircase, waiting.

Thunder rumbled in the distance. The storm was still too far away for her to have seen the lightning. She let herself breathe again. That's all she'd heard. Thunderstorms came on the heels of oppressively hot days, like this one.

John was downstairs. He'd been displaying some of the same symptoms of growing tension she had. Caleb's text had ratcheted up her uneasiness, and maybe John's, too.

Reason said they were both experienced cops, and armed. On the thought, she wrapped her fingers around the butt of the Ruger that lay on her lap. She hoped and prayed she'd never have to fire it, or the rifle in her bedroom, but tonight, keeping it close was a comfort.

John had positioned her here, where she could retreat upstairs if she heard shots.

"It's you they're after," he'd pointed out. "Once someone is in the house, you need to be ready to fight, too, but the head of the stairs is easier to defend."

Sure, but how would she feel if she had to retreat, knowing he was down, wounded or dead? From here, all she could see was the front door and a slice of the living room. After another roll of thunder, she listened for John's footstep—and for any other sounds.

Gunfire, it had occurred to her, could pass unnoticed in the midst of a thunder storm.

A soft scuff came from below. She strained to make out the figure of a man against the darkness.

"Abby?" he whispered.

"Yes?"

"No more word from Caleb."

The past half hour had crept by. He wasn't all that late. "We're okay," she murmured as much to herself as him, sounding steadier than she felt.

"Sure we are," John agreed, before he merged back into the dark.

CALEB HAD BEEN joined by the deputy he'd promoted to patrol sergeant. A year ago, Raines had completed training from the Missouri State Highway Patrol in accident reconstruction. Caleb had had the initial training himself while he was with KCPD, then taken a more advanced course after he signed on as sheriff. Now, the two of them walked slowly down the two-lane country

road, both carrying powerful flashlights that they swept
to each side in search of any marks laid down by tires
during braking or sharp swerves or turns.

"Damn it," Caleb growled. "The kid's right. He never
even applied the brakes."

"Doesn't look like," Sergeant Raines agreed. "How
could he not see three boys on bikes? The accident happened during full daylight." Raines lifted his flashlight
so the beam spotlighted the torn soil on the road verge
and the damaged remnants of two of the three bicycles.
"You'd swear this creep hit them on purpose."

Caleb stopped where he was. Ice slid through his
blood veins.

This creep hit them on purpose.

What if that's exactly what the driver had done? And
what if his goal had nothing to do with the boys? What
if he had wanted to make sure Caleb was too occu-
pied to reinforce the two people who were otherwise
alone waiting for the killer and his backup to make
their move?

Black sedan—just like the one that had smashed
into the buggy and come so close to killing Abby and
Joshua.

He yanked out his phone. No missed calls or texts.
Good news or bad? He didn't know. He called John…
and heard only rings and then voice mail.

"I have to go," he said. "You're in charge." Then he
ran, not giving a damn that everyone remaining at the
accident site had turned to stare.

A SHOCKING BURST of white light that momentarily
blinded Abby and gave her a jolt was followed no more
than two or three seconds later by a deep roll of thun-

der. The storm had come their way and was almost overhead. She hadn't heard any rain slamming onto the roof. They *needed* that rain.

On the heels of the thunder, a hard slam came from the back of the house. She rose to her feet, straining to hear more. That could have been a tree coming down, but she didn't think so.

The crack of a fired handgun came next. A shout. Another shot. More. How many men had come into the house once they kicked the door open? John had to be firing back. *Please let him be all right.*

Her own gun in firing position, Abby backed slowly up the stairs, feeling with each foot for the next tread. John had had 9-1-1 dialed on his phone, ready for one push of his thumb to send. Did he have time?

A man's voice called out. Another, pitched lower, answered. She went still, listening.

Quiet after that. Which meant John must be down... unless Caleb had arrived and joined him. She shook her head. They'd have called out to her if that was so. No, she had to assume there were intruders in the house, and she was on her own.

She'd have given almost anything to be able to *see*. Another bolt of lightning would be good—except someone looking up the stairs would see *her*.

Run to get the rifle? But that would mean taking her eyes off the staircase. She should have kept it right here.

She felt strange, almost as if she was looking down at herself. She blinked, saw Neal in the diffuse light from a distant streetlamp and the dim bulb over the back door into the bar. Footsteps. A man walking toward them—

This wasn't the time for a flashback! Abby shook her head hard. Thank God, she'd reached the upstairs hall.

All she could hear now was the thud of her heartbeat. She flattened her back against the wall and watched for movement yet saw the alley instead of the green countryside beyond the window. The man strolled casually, not afraid. Better to be cautious. She reached for the butt of her gun, wrapped her fingers around it.

"Where the hell is the light switch?" someone said downstairs.

That voice.

She was in the alley again. It was as if someone was flicking back and forth between television channels, sucking her along for the ride.

We've got to quit meeting like this.

Donahue. Why hadn't Neal talked to him at the station? Why *here*? Or had Neal expected to meet someone else?

The sergeant walked toward her, shaking his head. *You shouldn't be mixed up in this.*

"In what?" She heard her own confusion.

Your partner knows. Sorry, kid. He grabbed her by the upper arms and slammed her backward. Excruciating pain. She was falling.

Flick.

No, she stood in the hall, just out of sight of anyone at the foot of the stairs.

"Abby?" Donahue again, but here and now. "I'm just here to talk, and somebody started shooting at us."

Gee, maybe because you kicked your way in instead of knocking?

"I haven't had time to get up here during the day. Now that I'm here, can we talk?"

She spoke loudly. "Where's John?"

"Who's that? Oh, the guy who tried to kill me? He's down, but okay."

"It was you," she said. "You slammed me into the dumpster then drew my gun and shot Neal. Did you think I'd never remember?"

"Too bad you lived." He sounded genuinely regretful. "It would have been quick and easy."

"You were too stupid to notice I wore a vest."

A faint creak served as warning. She'd learned the sounds of this old house.

"Two more steps, and I'll be able to take your head off," she snapped. "Don't think I won't."

His gun barked, over and over. Chips of plaster from the walls and ceiling flew at her.

For the first time outside a range, she pulled the trigger, heard obscenities. In the ensuing silence, she heard no thuds to suggest he'd beaten a retreat. Like her, he'd probably flattened his back against the wall…or had squatted low, thinking he could creep high enough to leap up and pepper her with bullets.

Abby took a deep breath and waited, the hands gripping the Ruger completely steady.

CALEB PARKED ONE property away. Just as he ducked between boards of a fence, a bolt of lightning lit the sky and left him momentarily blind. He started running anyway, accompanied by thunder. A sheet of rain came out of nowhere, making it harder to see. He didn't hear anything after the thunder and couldn't even see the damn house until he was thirty yards or so away. That's when he saw light moving in the front room. Flashlight, he knew immediately. John or Abby might have had reason to use one, but they'd have to know it would be visible even through curtains.

Fear for Abby had him in its grip, but he still paused long enough to call dispatch and ask for backup.

"Sirens and lights," he ordered.

"Deputy Vogl should be nearest to you."

Damn, the kid.

"Send all available units. Tell deputies to expect to find themselves under fire." Although it would probably all be over before any backup arrived.

Either that or he'd feel foolish when he found John and Abby had turned on a flashlight for a minute to find something one of them had dropped.

He jammed the phone in his pocket, pulled his Glock and broke into a jog. A minute later, he was able to crouch by the porch and hear voices. Two, at least, the rumble too low for him to make out words, but male, both of them.

Caleb made his way around the side of the house, bending over as he passed windows. He was almost to the back door before he saw it swinging open, the wood splintered around the lock.

No mistake, then. The assailants were in the house. Number unknown. *If I'd been here—*

He shook the thought out of his head as he edged up to the door, gently eased it open. No time for that. Despite the lightning, his eyes had adjusted to darkness well enough for him to make out the table and chairs. A shape lay on the floor. A man, but he couldn't let himself stop. If it was John, there was nothing he could do.

One cautious step after another took him into the short hallway. Right now, he was the next thing to invisible. They wouldn't expect him.

Ahead was the foyer at the foot of the stairs, a dining room to the left, living room to the right. Another few feet and his head would show between banisters on the staircase. Instead, he crouched low, gun in firing position, and listened hard.

ONE OF THE men's voices drifted up to Abby. "What are we waiting for? Three of us, we can overwhelm her. If I use the shotgun, I can blast through walls."

"We need to get this done so we can be out of here." Another voice she didn't know.

"Shotgun makes too much noise. Detective Baker doesn't want to shoot anyone." This was Donahue responding. Thinking she'd surrender? Or was he just taunting her?

A part of her had been angry enough to kill someone for a very long time. *For you, Mom. For John.* Abby took a chance, stepped forward and fired down the staircase. Once, twice, three times. The gun jumped in her hands. There was a crash and yelling down below.

She heard a siren, please, please, coming here. Now there was more swearing.

"We've got to get out of here."

"That bitch got me! I'm bleeding!"

"We can't leave her alive."

"She's your problem," one of the men said. "You take care of her."

Rats fleeing the ship.

A hard *thud*. One of them had gone down. Had she killed one of them? Later she might feel bad, but not yet.

Multicolored flashing lights bounced off the walls Abby could see. A bellow came through a bullhorn.

"Come out with your hands up!"

She pinged another bullet deliberately high.

And then she heard Caleb. "Drop the guns! Now! Hands against the wall."

A gun barked, answered by another.

"Last chance!" he yelled. Then, "Abby? Are you all right?"

"Yes. I'm okay." She let her arms sag so that the Ruger pointed at the floor. She took a deep breath and raised her voice. "I'm fine."

Epilogue

Hours later, Caleb was still having trouble believing that Abby was uninjured, that he'd gotten back in time. Yeah, and that his youngest deputy had done exactly the right thing, at the right moment.

One of the men was in a cell in the small jail in town. Another was in surgery at the hospital to remove a bullet from his shoulder. Donahue was dead. He'd opened fire at Caleb, who had shot him. It might give him some nightmares, but he didn't think so. Mostly, he was glad he'd reacted fast enough and that Abby hadn't had to do something that would haunt her.

John had a whopping bruise on his chest and likely cracked ribs, but had been wearing his vest as ordered. When he fell, he'd hit his head and knocked himself out. Lucky thing, too. If he'd so much as twitched, they'd have kept shooting, and he would be dead. Instead, he'd been admitted at the hospital to be under observation because of a concussion.

Abby and Caleb had finally made it home. His house. The minute they walked in the door and he turned the deadbolt, he hauled her into his arms. He opened his mouth to tell her she'd scared him, but kissed her instead. Probably savagely, but before he could even try to ease back, she'd risen on tiptoe, thrown her arms around his neck and kissed him with need as desperate. Words weren't what either of them craved, not yet.

He got her out of what looked like ballet shoes and thin knit pants and skimpy panties. Somewhere along the way, she'd removed her Kevlar vest, but he still wore his. In the end, he unbuckled his belt, unzipped his pants and took her up against the door. The tempest inside the house didn't last long. In the end, he fell to his knees, taking her with him. Both lay on their backs, gasping for air.

When he was able to talk, he rolled his head toward her and said, "Hell of a day."

For a moment, she didn't react. Then she snorted— no, laughed. And tears poured down her cheeks even as she kept laughing.

Caleb wrapped his arms around her, pressed his lips to her head and murmured what he hoped were comforting things.

It was a long time before Abby pulled herself together enough to remember she was naked from the waist down and lying on his hardwood floor. Clutching her pants, she fled upstairs, forgetting he could see her backside. Smiling, Caleb got mostly dressed again and went to the kitchen to put on the coffee. He was so damn tired, he didn't expect it to keep him awake.

By the time it was ready and he had poured two cups, Abby reappeared. He'd heard the shower running but saw that she'd bundled her hair up so it wasn't wet except for some damp tendrils around her face. He leaned back against the counter edge and drank in the sight of her, blush and all.

"It's over," she said. "I can't believe it."

For both of them. He'd called in the Missouri State Highway Patrol Criminal Investigations people, since the crimes spanned counties and he'd shot and killed a fellow law-enforcement officer. They'd learned enough from the first brief interviews with the two men who'd survived to know that Donahue, a man Caleb had respected and even called *friend*, had been involved for years in sheltering a protection racket and prostitution ring operated by a biker gang. Caleb might not regret shooting Donahue, but he'd spend plenty of time wondering how he could have been so blind.

But right now, his life was on the line in a different way. Throat tight, he held out a hand.

Abby came to him still blushing, her gaze shyly lowered, which would have amused him if he hadn't been bone-deep scared. The wild woman who'd held off three gunmen and made frantic love with him against his front door was only one facet of this complex woman.

Closing his hand around hers, he cleared his throat. "I poured you a cup of coffee."

"I saw." She didn't look away from him.

He didn't want to look away from her vivid blue eyes. *Just lay it out there.* "I love you," he said hoarsely.

For too many seconds, she just stared. Then she began to cry again, even as she smiled. She used the hem of her shirt to swipe her tears. "Oh, I'm falling apart! I'm so sorry, I've just been so afraid—" She swallowed. "Falling in love with you scared me so much when I didn't know whether I could trust you. Or…or whether you felt even *close* to the same."

"God." He bent his head. "You'll stay with me?"

"Yes, although Aenti Nancy and Onkel Eli won't approve."

When he raised his head again, he saw that a smile trembled on her mouth. She was teasing—although she was right. Her Amish family wouldn't like Abby cohabiting with him. Neither would the conservative voters he'd need to keep himself in office, come to think of it. But he already knew where the two of them were going.

"You know I want to marry you." He tugged until she leaned on him, thighs to breasts. "I'll give you time, but you need to know."

Expression grave, she searched his face. "You've come running every single time I've needed you. I've seen you mad, and laughing and kind. No." For just an instant, the shyness returned. "Tender. I've seen how your men respect you. Your house tells me about you, too, you know."

"And?"

"I'm twenty-nine, and you're the only man ever I've loved like this. Of course I want to spend the rest of my life with you. How could you think I wouldn't want to marry you?"

Suddenly shaky on his feet, Caleb wasn't sure who was leaning on whom.

"I'll support you whatever you need to do about your career."

Her eyes suddenly had a sheen.

"The rest of our lives," he murmured.

Her arms came around him. "Tonight, I was afraid we wouldn't have that."

"Me, too," he said. "Me, too."

Suddenly, exhilaration burst through him. Who needed coffee? He bent, swept her up in his arms, and carried her upstairs to bed.

* * * * *

STORM
WARNING

MICHELE HAUF

Chapter One

Jason Cash squeezed the throttle on the snowmobile he handled as if a professional racer. The five-hundred-pound sled took to the air for six bliss-filled seconds. Snow sprays kissed Jason's cheeks. Sun glinted in the airborne crystals. The machine landed on the ground, skis gliding smoothly onto the trail. With an irrepressible grin on his face, he raced down an incline toward the outer limits of Frost Falls, the small Minnesota town where he served as chief of police.

Thanks to his helmet's audio feed, a country tune twanged in his ears. His morning ride through the pristine birch forest that cupped the town on the north side had been interrupted by a call from his secretary/dispatcher through that same feed. He couldn't complain about the missed winter thrills when a much-needed mystery waited ahead.

Maneuvering the snowmobile through a choppy field with shifts of his weight, he steered toward a roadside ditch, above which were parked the city patrol car and a white SUV he recognized as a county vehicle. Sighting a thick undisturbed wedge of snow that had drifted from the gravel road to form an inviting ridge, Jason aimed for the sparkling payload, accelerated and pierced the ridge. An exhilarated shout spilled free.

Gunning the engine, he traveled the last fifty feet, then

braked and spun out the back of the machine in a spectacular snow cloud that swirled about him. He parked and
turned off the machine.

Flipping up the visor and peeling off his helmet, he
glanced to the woman and young man who stood twenty
yards away staring at him. At least one jaw dropped open
in awe.

A cocky wink was necessary. Jason would never miss
a chance to stir up the powder. And every day was a good
day when it involved gripping it and ripping it.

Setting his helmet emblazoned with neon-green fire
on the snowmobile seat, he tugged down the thermal face
mask from his nose and mouth to hook under his chin. The
thermostat read a nippy ten degrees. Already ice crystals
formed on the sweat that had collected near his eyebrows.
He did love the brisk, clean air.

It wasn't so brutally cold today as it had been last week
when temps had dipped below zero. But the warm-up forecast a blizzard within forty-eight hours. He looked forward
to snowmobiling through the initial onset, but once the
storm hit full force, he'd hole up and wait for the pristine
powder that would blanket the perimeter of the Boundary
Waters Canoe Area Wilderness, where he liked to blaze
his own trails.

Clapping his gloved hands together, he strode over to
his crack team of homicide investigators. Well, today they
earned that title. It was rare Frost Falls got such interesting work. Rare? The correct term was *nonexistent*. Jason
was pleased to have something more challenging on his
docket than arresting Ole Svendson after a good drunk
had compelled him to strip to his birthday suit and wander down Main Street. A man shouldn't have to see such
things. And so frequently.

He almost hated to share the case with the Bureau of
Criminal Apprehension, but Marjorie had already put in a

call to them. Someone from the BCA would arrive soon. Standard procedure when a homicide occurred within city limits.

"Cash." Alex Larson, who had just graduated from the police academy and headed north from the Twin Cities to find work, with hopes of eventually getting placed on search and rescue, nodded as Jason walked nearer. The tall, gangly man was twenty-four and had an eye for safety and a curiosity for all things female. Unfortunately, most of the women in Frost Falls were over forty. Not many of the younger ones stuck around after high school. Smart move in a dying town. The Red Band iron mine had closed four years ago. That closure had sent the migrant workers—and far too many locals—packing in search of a reliable paycheck.

Alex was the only officer Jason needed in the little town of Frost Falls, population 627.

Though, from the looks of things, the population was now 626.

A middle-aged woman, wearing a black goose-down coat that fell to her knees and bright red cap, scarf and mittens, stood beside Alex. Elaine Hester was a forensic pathologist with the St. Louis County medical examiner's office. She traveled the seven-hundred-square-mile area so often she joked about selling her property in Duluth and getting herself an RV. She gestured toward the snowy ditch that yet sported the dried brown heads of fall's bushy cattails. The forthcoming blizzard would clip that punky crop down to nothing.

"What have you got, Elaine?" Jason asked, even though his dispatcher, Marjorie, had already told him about the body.

Jason led the team toward the ditch and saw the sprawled female body dressed in jeans and a sweater—no coat, gloves or hat—long black hair, lying facedown. The snow might have initially melted due to her body heat, so she was sunk in to her ears, and as death had forfeited her natural heat, the warmed slush had iced up around her and now crusted in the fibers of her red sweater.

"Female, mid-to late-twenties. Time of death could be last evening," Elaine reported in her usual detached manner. She held a camera and had likely already snapped a few shots. "Didn't want to move the body for closer inspection until you arrived, Cash. You call in the BCA?"

"On their way. We can continue processing the crime scene. The BCA will help, if necessary. Last night, eh?"

"I suspect she was dumped here around midnightish."

Jason met Alex's gaze, above which the officer's brow quirked. They both tended to share a silent snicker at Elaine's frequent use of *ish* tacked to the end of words when she couldn't be exact.

"How do you know she was—" Jason drew his gaze from the body and up the slight ditch incline to the gravel road. The marks from a body sliding over the snow were obvious. "Right. Dumped."

Jason studied the ground, noting the footprints, which were obviously from Elaine's and Alex's boots, as they'd remained only on this side of the body. They hadn't contaminated the crime scene. That was Elaine's forte: meticulous forensics.

Jason walked a wide circle around the victim's head and up the ditch to the road. As he did so, Elaine snapped away, documenting every detail of the scene with photographs. Though they were still within city limits, this was not a main road. Rather, it was one of four that left the town and either dead-ended or led deeper north into the Boundary Waters Canoe Area Wilderness, a million-plus-acre natural reserve within the Superior National Forest that hugged the Canadian border. The only people who used this road were two families who both lived about ten miles out of

Frost Falls. The gravel road showed no deep tracks in the mix of snow, ice and pebble, like if a vehicle were to take off quickly after disposing of evidence. But there were boot prints where the gravel segued into dead grass long packed down by snow.

Jason bent and decided they were a woman's boot prints for the narrowness.

"Marjorie said a woman called in the sighting?" Jason asked Alex.

"Yes, sir," Alex offered. "Call came from Susan Olson, who works at The Moose in the, er—ahem—back." If Alex hadn't been wearing a face mask, Jason felt sure he'd see him blush. The back of The Moose offered a low-class strip show on Saturday nights—basically, Susan and a few corny Halloween costumes that had fit her better back in high school. "Miss Olson was driving out to her aunt's place to check in on her when she saw something glint in the ditch."

Jason shuffled down into the ditch, avoiding Elaine as she stepped around the woman's head. "Evidence?" he asked Alex.

"Just the body and the clothing on it. No phone or glasses or personal items that may have fallen out from a pocket. I'll bag the hands and head soon as Elaine gives me the go-ahead. Any tracks up there?"

"They're from the caller, I'm sure. But take pictures of the tracks, will you, Elaine? We'll have to see if Susan's fashion lends to size-eight Sorels, if my guess is correct."

"Of course. Nice thing about snow—it holds a good impression of boot tracks. I hope it's Ryan Bay with the BCA."

Jason cast her a look that didn't disguise his dislike for the guy for reasons he couldn't quite place. He'd only met him twice, but there was something about him.

Elaine noticed his crimped smirk and shrugged. "Guy's a looker. And he's easygoing. I can do what I need to do without him wanting to take charge."

"A looker, eh?"

There it was. She'd nailed his dislike in a word. A looker. What the hell did that mean? Wasn't as if handsome held any weight in this small town. Least not when a man was in the market to hook up. Again, no eligible women as far as a man's eye could see.

"You're still the sexiest police chief in St. Louis County, Cash." Elaine adjusted the lens on her camera. "But if you won't let me fix you up with my niece…"

The niece. She mentioned her every time they had occasion to work together. Blind dates gave Jason the creeps. His brother Joe had once gone on one. That woman had literally stalked him for weeks following. Yikes.

"Didn't you mention she was shortish?" Jason asked with a wink to Alex.

"Short girls need love, too, Jason." The five-foot-two-inch woman laughed. "Don't worry. I know she's not your type."

Jason squatted before the body, thinking that if Elaine actually did know his type— What was he thinking? Of course, she did. Along with everyone else in the county. The gossip in these parts spread as if it had its own high-speed internet service.

Focusing on the body, with a gloved hand he lifted the long black hair that had been covering the woman's face. Her skin was pale and blue. Her lips purple. Closed eyelids harbored frost on the lashes. No visible signs of struggle or blood. She was young. Pretty. He'd not seen her in Frost Falls before. And he had a good mental collection of all the faces in town. A visitor? She could have been murdered anywhere. The assailant may have driven from another town to place her here.

In the distance, the flash of headlights alerted all three at the same time.

"BCA," Elaine said. "We'll review the evidence with them and then bag the body."

"You'll transport the body to Duluth?" Jason asked.

"Yes," she said. "You going to follow me in for the autopsy?"

"You going to process it this morning?" Duluth was about an hour's drive to the east.

Elaine shook her head. "Probably not. But I will get to it after lunch. If you can meet me around oneish, that would work."

"Will do."

The white SUV bearing the BCA logo on the side door pulled up twenty feet from Alex's patrol car and idled. Looked like the driver was talking on the phone. Jason squinted. Couldn't make out who the driver was. A looker, eh? Why did that weird comment bother him?

It didn't. Really. He had a lot on his plate now. And he wasn't the type for jealously or even envy.

He glanced over the body of the unfamiliar woman. Pretty. And so young. It was a shame. "Any ID on her?"

"No, but she's probably Canadian," Elaine said.

Jason raised a brow at that surprising assessment.

Elaine bent and pushed aside the woman's hair with the tip of her penlight to reveal a tiny red tattoo of a maple leaf at the base of the victim's ear.

"Right." Jason frowned. "Are those ligature marks on her neck?"

"Yes." Elaine snapped a few close-up shots of the bruising now revealed on the woman's neck. "There's your signs of struggle right there. Poor thing." She replaced the victim's hair in the exact manner it had been lying and stood. "Looks like you just might have a murder case on your hands."

He'd suspected as much. Even though the weather could

be treacherous and oftentimes deadly in the winter, the evidence screamed foul play.

"We'll get the BCA up to speed here, then I'm heading in to talk to Susan Olson," Jason said.

Jason had seen a lot, and he wasn't going to allow some psychopath to think he could get away with murder. As well, this was his first big case since his humiliating demotion from the CIA. The timing was either laughable or fortuitous, depending on how he looked at it. Because he'd just received notice that the police station had been marked for budget cuts. In all likelihood, it would close in March and Frost Falls would send all their dispatch calls through the county. The tiny town couldn't afford to pay Jason's meager salary anymore. But the notice had also mentioned it wasn't necessary to employ someone who was merely a town babysitter and not involved in real criminal procedures.

That one had cut deep. He was not a babysitter. Sure, he'd taken this job out of desperation. Getting ousted from the CIA was not a man's finest moment. Yet he had made this job his own. And he did have a lot on his plate, what with the domestic abuse calls, the poaching and—the public nudity.

Time to prove he wasn't incompetent to all those who were watching and taking notes. And with any luck? He might earn back his pride and a second chance.

Chapter Two

Nine a.m. on a lazy Sunday. Most of the Frost Falls inhabitants were at church in the neighboring town or sat at The Moose noshing on waffles and bacon. Most, but not all.

Susan Olson yawned and scrubbed a hand over her long, tangled red hair. Her eyes were smeared with dark eye makeup, and one streak veered up toward her temple. She wore a Black Veil Brides T-shirt and bright pink sweatpants. They might have graduated the same year, but Jason had been born and raised in Crooked Creek, a town sixty miles west from here. Susan had lived in Frost Falls all her life.

Another yawn preceded "Really? Do you know what time it is, Chief Cash?"

"I do," Jason reported. He turned his head to block the wind that whipped at the front of the house. "Heard you found something interesting this morning."

"I knew you'd be stopping by. Just thought it would be at a decent hour. Come in."

Jason stepped inside the tiny rambler that might have been built in the '40s. It boasted green shag carpeting in the front living area; the walls were painted pink and—did they have glitter on them? He stayed on the rug before the door. His boot soles were packed with snow.

"Just have a few questions, then you can head back to

bed," he said. "I know Saturdays are your busy night. Hate to bother you, but a woman has been murdered."

"She was murdered?" Susan's eyes opened wider. She clutched her gut and searched the floor. "I thought maybe she just died from, like, frostbite or something. Oh my God. I remember her. I mean, I didn't touch the body, but I did see her face this morning. I always run to check on my aunt Sunday mornings, even though I'm so raging tired after my shift."

"You…" Jason leaned forward, making sure he'd heard correctly. He tugged out the little notebook he always carried from inside his coat. Pen at the ready, he asked, "Remember her? The woman in the ditch?"

"Her and three others. It was Lisa Powell's clique. Must have been someone's birthday. They were loaded and loose last night. But the woman in the ditch didn't look familiar to me. I mean, I don't think she was from around here. It's not difficult to know all the locals."

Jason nodded and wrote down the information.

"She tipped me a ten," Susan said with a curl of a smile. "Doesn't happen often, let me tell you. The people in this town are so stingy."

"She was with Lisa Powell, and—do you know the names of the other two?"

"Hannah Lindsey and, oh, some older woman. Might have been one of their mothers. They are all older than me, don't ya know." She tilted out a hip and fluffed back her hair with a sweep of hand. "Must be in their late thirties, for heaven's sake."

Jason placed Susan at around thirty, same as him.

"Not an issue right now," Jason said. "How long were the women in The Moose? Did they all leave together? Who else was watching your performance?"

Susan yawned. "That's a lot of questions, Cash."

"I know. You got coffee?"

"I do, but I really don't want to wake up that much. I usually sleep until four on Sundays. Do we have to do this now?"

"We do. You'll remember much more detail now as opposed to later. And I have an appointment in Duluth in a few hours I can't miss."

Susan sighed and dropped her shoulders. "Fine. I got one of those fancy coffee machines for Christmas from my boyfriend. I'll make you a cup. Kick off your wet boots before you walk on my carpet, will you, Cash?"

"Will do."

Jason toed off his boots, then followed Susan into the kitchen, where a strange menagerie of pigs wearing sunglasses decorated every surface—all the dishware and even the light fixtures.

YVETTE LASALLE WANDERED down the tight aisles in the small grocery store set smack-dab in the center of Main Street in Frost Falls. The ice on her black hair that had sneaked out from under her knit cap melted and trickled down her neck. If she didn't zip up and wrap her scarf tight when she went outside, that trickle would freeze and— *Dieu.*

Why Minnesota? Of all the places in the world. And to make life less pleasant, it was January. The temperature had not been out of the teens since she had arrived. Sure, they got snow and cold in France. But not so utterly brutal. This place was not meant for human survival. Seriously.

But survive she would. If this was a test, she intended to ace it, as she did with any challenge.

This little store, called Olson's Oasis, sold basic food items, some toiletries, fishing bait and tackle (because crazy people drilled holes on the lake ice and actually fished in this weather), and plenty of cheap beer. A Laundromat was set off behind the freezer section. It boasted two washers and one semiworking dryer. The store was also the hub for deliveries, since the UPS service apparently didn't venture beyond Main Street.

Frost Falls was a virtual no-man's land. The last vestige of civilization before the massive Superior National Forest that capped the state and embraced the land with flora, fauna and so many lakes. This tiny town reminded Yvette of the village where her grandparents had lived in the South of France. Except Frost Falls had more snow. So. Much. Snow.

"Survival," she muttered with determination, but then rolled her eyes. She never would have dreamed a vacation from her job in gorgeous Lyon would require more stamina than that actual job. Mental stamina, that was.

But this wasn't a vacation.

Something called lutefisk sat wrapped in plastic behind the freezer-case glass. Vacillating on whether to try the curious fish, she shook her head. The curing process had something to do with soaking the fish in lye, if she recalled correctly from a conversation with the store's proprietor last week. It was a traditional Nordic dish that the locals apparently devoured slathered in melted butter.

Not for her.

Fresh veggies and fruits were not to be had this time of year, so Yvette subsisted on frozen dinners and prepackaged salads from the refrigerator case.

Her boss at Interpol, Jacques Patron, would call any day now. *Time to come home, Amelie. The coast is clear.* Every day she hoped for that call.

Unless he'd already tried her. She had gotten a strange hang-up call right before entering the store. The number had been blocked, but when she'd answered, the male voice had asked, "Yvette?" She'd automatically answered, "Yes," and then the connection had clicked off.

Wrong numbers generally didn't know the names of

those they were misdialing. And an assumed name, at that. Had it been Jacques? Hadn't sounded like him. But he'd only said her name. Hard to determine identity from one word. Impossible to call back with the unknown number. And would her boss have used her cover name or her real name?

The call was not something to take lightly. But she couldn't simply call up Interpol and ask them for a trace. She was supposed to be dark. She and her boss were the only people aware of her location right now. She'd try her boss's number when she returned to the cabin.

Tossing a bag of frozen peas into her plastic basket, she turned down the aisle and inspected the bread selections. Not a crispy, crusty baguette to be found. But something called Tasty White seemed to be the bestseller. She dropped a limp loaf in her basket. She might be able to disguise the processed taste with the rhubarb jam that she'd found in a welcome gift basket when she'd arrived at the rental cabin.

When the bell above the store's entrance clanged, she peered over the low shelves. A couple of teenage boys dressed in outdoor gear and helmets joked about the rabbit they'd chased with their snowmobiles on the ride into town.

Town? More like a destitute village with a grocery/post office/fish and tackle shop/Laundromat, and a bar/diner/strip joint—yes, The Moose diner offered "pleasure chats" and "sensual dancing" in the far back corner after 10:00 p.m. on Saturday nights. The diner did dish up a hearty meal, though, and Yvette's stomach was growling.

Her gaze averted from the boys and focused beyond the front door and out the frost-glazed window. Had that black SUV been parked before The Moose when she'd arrived? It looked too clean. Not a beat-up rust bucket like most of the locals drove. And it wasn't dusted with a grayish coating of deicing salt that they seemed to sprinkle on their roads more than their meals around here. She couldn't see the license plates to determine if it was a rental.

Yvette was alert for something she felt was imminent but was unable to say exactly what that could be. It reminded her of when she'd worked in the field. A field operative had to stay on her toes and be constantly aware of her surroundings, both physical and auditory. A wise state to embrace, especially in a town not her own.

She'd take a closer look at the SUV after she'd purchased her groceries.

The teenagers paid for energy drinks and left the store in a spill of laughter. Making her way to the checkout, Yvette set her basket on the counter.

"Bonjour, Yvette." Colette, the shop owner, a Canadian expatriate Yvette had bonded with because she spoke fluent French, fussed with the frilled pink polka-dot apron she wore over a slim-fitting black turtleneck and slacks. "Twenty dollars will do it."

Surely the bill was thirty or more.

Yvette nodded, unaccustomed to kindnesses, yet receiving such generosity felt like a warm summer breeze brushing her icy neck. Very much needed lately.

She handed over the money. Colette packed up her provisions and helped Yvette fit it all into the backpack she brought along for such trips. She looked forward to riding the snowmobile into town for twice-weekly grocery trips. And today, despite the single-digit temperature, boasted bright white sunshine. A girl could not ignore fresh air and the beautiful landscape. She always brought along her camera and stopped often to snapshots. It was a good cover for an agent, but photography had also always been a hobby she'd wanted to take to the next level.

"Those wool leggings look *très chic* on you," Colette commented, with a slide of her gaze down Yvette's legs.

"But you really do need to wear snow pants if you're snow-mobiling in this weather."

"I've got on layers." Yvette waggled a leg. The heavy boots she wore were edged with fake fur, and the leggings were spotted with white snowflakes on a blue background. Beneath, she wore thermal long johns, an item of clothing she hadn't been aware existed until she'd arrived here in the tundra. A quilted down coat topped it all.

Fitting the backpack over her shoulders, she paused at the door while Colette walked around the counter and met her with a zip up of her waterproof coat and a tug at her scarf (which happened to match her leggings—score one for fashion).

"You don't have a helmet to keep your ears warm?" Colette asked. She eyed Yvette's knit cap with the bobble of red pom-pom on the top. "You foreigners. I'm surprised your ears don't drop off with frostbite. It's colder than a polar bear's toenails out there. And with the wind chill? *Uff da.*" The woman shuddered.

"Don't you mean *mon Dieu*?" Yvette countered.

Colette laughed. "Minnesota has gotten into my blood, *chère*. It's *uff da* here. Want me to order a helmet for you?" She tapped the pom-pom. "We order directly from the Arctic Cat supplier in Duluth. Takes only a day or two. And some are even electronic so you can turn on the heat and listen to music."

"Sounds perfect. The helmet provided by the cabin is too big for me and tends to twist and block my vision. Thanks, Colette."

"You heading across the street for a bite to eat? I see the chief's snowmobile just pulled up. That is one fancy machine. And I'm not talking about the snowmobile."

"The chief?" Yvette glanced across the way. "You mean a police chief? What's up?"

"Nothing of concern, I'm sure. It's just, have you met Chief Jason Cash?"

"Should I?"

Colette winked. "*Uff da*, girl, he's the hottest catch this side of the Canadian border. Young, handsome and cocky as hell. But none of the local girls can seem to turn his eye."

"I am hungry," Yvette said with a wistful glance across the street. For so many things she'd not had in almost two months. Sunshine. A buttery croissant. Conversation. Sex.

"Good girl. Tell the chief I said hello." Colette pushed the shop door open and virtually shoved Yvette out.

Bracing for the blast of cold, Yvette cursed how easily she had succumbed to the suggestion she hide out overseas until the heat on her blew over. Her boss had chosen this location and given her a cover identity. He hadn't told her exactly what it was that could implicate her, but she knew it had to do with her photographic memory. Thing was, she never really knew what some of the stuff that she worked on meant, as it was generally out of context and merely a list or scramble of information to her brain.

Boots crunching on the packed snow, she crossed the wide double-lane Main Street. A couple of pickup trucks with snow chains hugging the tires were parked before The Moose, as was one of the fanciest, most powerful snowmobiles she had seen. Walking by it, she forgot about the mysterious SUV she'd noticed earlier and instead took in the sleek black snowmobile dashed with neon-green embellishments. The body was like a blade, streamlined for speed.

The owner was handsome, eh? And single?

She wasn't looking for romance, that was for sure. But a woman could not survive on staticky rerun episodes of *Sex and the City* and her vibrator alone. Might as well *give the man a gander*, as she'd heard people say in these parts.

But for the official record, she was just here for the food.

Chapter Three

Jason took in the woman who sat before the diner counter. Two stools separated them. After setting a backpack on the floor, she'd pulled off a knit cap to let loose a spill of long black hair. Unzipping her coat halfway revealed a blue-and-white wool sweater that featured snowflakes and reindeer. Looked like one of Marjorie's knitted projects. Jason had one of those ugly sweaters—it featured a moose and possibly moose tracks (because he could never be sure it wasn't moose scat)—but he wore it proudly because someone had made it especially for him.

The woman at the counter was not a resident of Frost Falls. And today, of all days, he was particularly alert to strangers. This morning had brought a dead stranger onto his radar. Lunch had found him standing over an autopsy of the same woman. When driving back to Main Street, he'd sighted a shiny SUV that did not belong to a local. He'd run a plate check. Belonged to a Duluth resident. No police record or accidents reported. Worked for Perkins. Probably in town visiting friends.

And now Miss America was sitting ever so close.

She ordered mint tea and the club sandwich with extra bacon. The waitress winked and commented that she was glad to finally use up the tea she'd had stashed under the counter for years.

Jason noted the woman's cringe when she heard the date of the tea, and he chuckled.

"Not many tea drinkers in these parts," he said. "I haven't seen you in The Moose. You passing through Frost Falls?"

"In a means, yes," she said with an accent that sounded familiar to Jason.

She was an exotic beauty. Her skin tone was olive, and her features were narrow. Bright blue eyes twinkled beneath delicate curved black brows. She didn't fit the standard profile of the Scandinavians who populated a good portion of Minnesota's frozen tundra. Gorgeous, too, far prettier than most. And she didn't appear to be wearing a lick of makeup. Something about natural red lips...

Jason shook off a bittersweet memory of red lips and sly winks. Weird that he hadn't heard about this beautiful woman from the town's gossip mill. He turned on the stool to face her. "Name's Jason Cash," he offered. "I'm the town's chief of police."

For another few months, at least. If and when he lost this job, what would he have to show for his years of service to both his country and this small town?

Not a hell of a lot.

"Nice to meet you, Chief Cash. I'm Yvette LaSalle. I'm not exactly passing through this cozy town. I've been here a few weeks. For a, um, vacation. Decided to stop in the diner today because I was across the street making a grocery run."

"LaSalle." Must be French Canadian. Nix the Miss America idea, and replace it with...hmm... Her tone didn't seem to possess the rugged edge the Canadian accent offered. Interesting. And come to think of it, he had heard Marjorie mention something about a newcomer sitting in The Moose last week. Why had Marjorie failed to point out how drop-dead beautiful the woman was? Her gossip was usually much more on point. "I'm glad our paths crossed today."

The waitress set Yvette's plate and tea before her.

"Mind if I slide over?" Jason asked. "Then we don't have to yell across the room at one another."

"Go ahead." She pulled a strip of bacon out of the sandwich and munched the crispy slice. "Mmm, meat, how I have missed you."

"You go off meat for some crazy reason?"

"I am a vegetarian," she said, prodding another bacon strip, then eyeing it disdainfully. "Or rather, was." She took a big bite of the sandwich. "*Mon Dieu*, that is so good!"

Miss France, he decided. He'd only been assigned a single two-day Parisian job while serving in the CIA. He knew a handful of French words, but beyond that, his capacity for learning foreign languages was nil.

"You must not order the tea very often, eh?"

She rolled her eyes. "I had a misguided craving. I think this'll be the last time I get tea here."

"Stick with the root beer," Jason said. "Root beer never lets a man down."

"Sounds like a personal issue to me, but to each his own. I like your snowmobile," she said. "The one parked out front, yes? It looks like a racing machine."

"Oh, it is." Jason's back straightened, and he hitched a proud smile in the direction of the powerful machine parked outside. "Could have been a professional racer. I love burning up the track. But I don't have the time. This job keeps me on call 24/7."

"I suppose there is a lot of crime in this sleepy little town." She tried to hide a smirk, but Jason caught it. A fall of dark hair hid half her eye. Oh, so sexy. And every part of him that should react warmed in appreciation.

The last time he'd felt all the right things about a woman had been two years ago in Italy.

And that had ended disastrously.

"Someone has to keep the Peanut Gang in line," he offered.

"The Peanut Gang?"

"Bunch of old farts who think poaching wolves isn't harming the ecosystem. Idiots."

"I'm not afraid of wolves. I think they are beautiful animals."

Jason nodded. "They are. But I'll leave it to my brother, the wolf whisperer, to kneel on the ground and pet them. It's always best to be cautious around wild animals."

Yvette nodded, but then said, "I got a great shot of a moose last week. On film, that is."

"Is that so?"

"I've learned to snowshoe out in the forest behind the cabin. Always take my camera along."

"You should be careful. Those beasts look gawky, but a moose can run fast."

"Tell me about it. I was photographing the snow-laced birch trees and out of nowhere a moose charged through the deep snow. It was beautiful. But I'm cautious to check for big critters now when I venture out."

"You should stick to the trails. Safer."

"Safe is good, hmm?"

Jason almost responded with an immediate *yes*, but he sensed by her tone that she was angling for bigger fish. Were those thick lashes as soft as they looked? And did she prefer not so safe? Now that was his kind of woman.

"Depends," he said. "There's safe and then there's, hmm…wild?"

"*Wild* is not a word I'd ever place to anything in this town."

If that wasn't some wanting, repressed sexual desire in her sigh, Jason couldn't guess otherwise. She had been in Frost Falls a few weeks. Why had he never noticed her before? And could he hope Alex hadn't already hooked up with her?

"You, uh, like wild?" he asked.

"I do." She finished off one triangle of the sandwich, but from his side view Jason noticed her smile did not fade.

Oh, he liked the wild, too. In so many ways.

The waitress set his bill down before him. He did not put it on the station's expense account. He couldn't see asking the town to pay for his meals. And now with the closure notice hanging over his head, he wanted to be as frugal as possible with the city budget. Much as he didn't like sharing the investigation with the BCA—yes, Ryan Bay, the looker, had arrived in town—it was a good thing, considering they had the resources and the finances to serve the investigation properly. As soon as the final autopsy report arrived, Jason intended to meet with Bay at the station house and go over the evidence.

Reaching for her backpack, Yvette shuffled it on over her arms. Ready to head out so quickly? She still had half a sandwich on the plate. He couldn't let her leave. Not until he'd learned more, like where she was staying, and did she have a significant other? And did her hair actually gleam when it spilled across her shoulders?

Briefly, Jason frowned as memories of his early morning stop resurfaced. The deceased had long black hair and a beautiful face.

At that moment, his cell phone buzzed with a text. Elaine had ID'd the victim as Yvette Pearson.

"Yvette," he muttered and wrinkled a brow. That was a weird coincidence.

"Yes?"

He looked up and was met with a wondering blue gaze. He'd once fallen for a pair of blue eyes and a foreign accent—and life had changed drastically for him because of that distraction.

"You said my name?" she prompted.

"Huh? Oh. No. I mean, yes. Not you. It's a text." He quickly typed, Thanks for the info. Forward the final report to me and Ryan Bay. He tucked away the phone and said to the very much alive Yvette, "It's a case. Not you. Sorry. Police business."

She nodded. "Yvette is a common French name."

"You betcha. Lot of French Canadians living up in these parts."

"These parts." With a sigh, she glanced out the front window.

Jason noticed she eyed the black SUV parked across the street. The one that hailed from Duluth.

"Friend of yours?" he asked, with a nod out the window.

"You mean the owner of that SUV?" She shook her head. "Despite my sparkling personality, and a desperate desire for good conversation, I don't have any friends in this town. Other than Colette at the market. She's the only French-speaking person I've run into."

"You speak French? I was wondering about your accent."

"I'm from Lyon."

Lyon, eh? That was a major city in France.

"So, what is there to do in this town that is more interesting than Friday night at the Laundromat slash grocery store?" Yvette asked.

"Let's see…" Jason rubbed his jaw. "A guy could nosh on some of the amazing desserts they have here at The Moose. I have to admit, I'm a big fan of their pie. You want a slice before you rush off?"

"Much as I would love to, I'll have to pass. Wasn't as hungry as I thought I was." She pushed the plate forward to indicate she was finished. "But I won't rule out pie in my future," she said with a teasing tone. "What else you got?"

"Well, there is Netflix and chill," Jason suggested slyly.

"I don't understand."

"It means…uh…" A blush heated Jason's cheeks. Since when had his flirtation skills become so damned rusty? And awkward. Mercy, he was out of practice.

"More coffee, Jason?" the waitress asked.

Saved by the steamy brew. "No, thanks, I should get going. Marjorie is waiting for me back at the office to sign off on some…paperwork."

The last thing he wanted to do was let the cat out of the bag that a body had been found so close to town. On the other hand, he expected when Susan Olson next went on shift at the back of the diner, it wouldn't take long for word to spread.

He pulled out a twenty and laid it on the counter. "That should cover both our bills."

Yvette zipped up her jacket. "Thank you, Chief Cash. I'm going to look up Netflix and chill when I get home."

"You do that," he said. And when she learned it meant watching Netflix together, then making out? "I'm down the street at the redbrick building if you ever need me. Used to be a bustling station house, but now it's just me and dispatch."

"Keeping an eye on the Peanut Gang."

"You betcha."

He walked her to the restaurant door, and she pointed across the street where a snowmobile was parked before Olson's Oasis. It was an older model, similar to the one he'd once torn through ditches on when he was a teenager.

"That's me," she said.

"How far out do you live?" he asked.

"I'm renting. Here for a short stay. It's a cabin about five miles east. Lots of birch trees. Very secluded."

"Everything around here is secluded. You step out of town, you're in no-man's land. That's what I love about this place. And lots of powder."

"Powder?"

"Snow. When I'm not working, I spend my time on the cat, zooming through the powder. Er, *cat* is what some locals call the snowmobile. At least, those of us with an inclination to Arctic Cat sleds and racing."

"Ah, a thrill seeker?"

"You nailed it. You must be staying at the Birch Bower cabin?"

"Yes, that's the one."

Jason nodded. The owners rented the place out in the winter months while they vacationed in their Athens home. Nice place, Greece. Beautiful blue waters. Fascinating local culture. Ouzo in abundance. He'd nearly taken a bullet to the stomach there a few years ago. Good times.

"Thanks again," Yvette called as she walked away.

Feeling as though he wanted to give Yvette his phone number, Jason also suspected that would not be cool. Not yet. They'd only chatted ten minutes. So instead he watched her turn on her snowmobile and head off with a smile and a wave.

Besides, he knew where to find her now if he wanted to.

A glance to the SUV found it was still parked. Exhaust fumes indicated the engine was running. Hmm...

Jason strode across Main Street toward the SUV, boots crunching the snowpack. The vehicle shifted into gear and drove past him. It slowed at the stop sign at the east edge of town. And sat there. Yvette had crossed to the town's edge and taken a packed trail hugged by tall birch trees.

The thunder of Jason's heartbeats would not allow him to dismiss the SUV. It was almost as if the driver had been parked there, watching... Yvette?

He looked at his cell phone. Elaine's message read, Yvette Pearson.

As the very much alive Yvette LaSalle had said, it was a common French name. But two Yvettes in one small town? Both, apparently, visiting. And one of them dead?

Unable to shake the itchy feeling riding his spine, Jason returned to his snowmobile and pulled on his helmet. By the time he'd fired up the engine and headed down Main Street, the SUV had slowly moved toward the birch-lined road heading east. Yvette's direction.

Jason pulled up alongside the SUV, switched on the police flasher lights and signaled the driver to pull over. He did so and rolled down his window. The thirtysomething male wearing a tight gray skullcap and sunglasses tugged up a black turtleneck as the brisk air swept into the truck cab.

"Chief Jason Cash," Jason said as he approached the vehicle. A nine-millimeter Glock hugged his hip, but he didn't sense a need for it. Nor did he ever draw for a routine traffic stop. Not that this was a traffic stop.

"Hello, Officer," the man said with an obvious accent. Texan? A Southern drawl twanged his voice. "Is there a problem?"

"No problem. I've not seen you in Frost Falls before, and it is a small town. Like to introduce myself." He tugged off a glove and offered his hand to the man. The driver twisted and leaned out the window to shake his hand. A calm movement. Warm hand. But Jason couldn't see his eyes behind the mirrored lenses. "Your name?"

"Smith," he said easily. Which was the name Jason had gotten from the plate check. "I'm visiting the Boundary Waters tourist area. Just out for a drive. Beautiful day with the sunshine, yes?"

"You betcha."

Definitely a Texan accent. Fresh out of high school, Jason had served three years in the marines alongside a trio of Texans who had extolled their love for hot sauce whenever they were bored.

"You got some ID and vehicle registration, Smith?"

The man reached down beside him. Jason's hackles

tightened. He placed a hand over his gun handle. Smith produced a driver's license and, opening the glove compartment, shuffled around for a paper. He handed both over.

Hiding his relief that he hadn't had to draw against a dangerous suspect, Jason took the items and looked them over. It was a Minnesota license, not Texas, but people moved all the time. The name and address matched the vehicle registration. It also matched the info he'd gotten earlier. Thirty-seven years old. Brown hair. Brown eyes. Donor. A Duluth address. Hair was longer in the photo, but the man looked like he'd recently had a clipper cut.

"You a recent move to Minnesota?"

"Why do you ask?"

"There's not a lot of *uff da* in your accent."

The man chuckled. "Born and raised in Dallas. But I do enjoy the winters here."

"I gotta agree with you there. You must enjoy outdoor sports."

"Mostly taking in the sights."

"Uh-huh. You got the day off from work?" Jason asked.

"You bet."

"Duluth, eh?" Jason handed back the license. "Where do you work?"

"Perkins. Just off Highway 35 west."

Jason had eaten at that location before. So that checked out, too. In town to take in the scenery?

"Thank you, Mr. Smith. You should turn around here before the road gets too narrow," he said. "It's not for tourism. And it's also not a through road."

"I had no idea, Officer."

"That's part of my job. Making sure everyone stays on the straight and narrow."

The man furrowed his brows. And the fact he'd misnamed the Boundary Waters Canoe Area Wilderness gave

Jason another prickle down his spine. A strange mistake for someone who should be familiar with the area.

"The Moose serves up some tasty meat loaf with buttered carrots," Jason offered. "Stop in before you head out of town."

"Thank you, Officer. I will. Is there anything else?"

"No. You can go ahead and turn around here. Road's still wide enough. But watch the ditch. The snowpack is loose. You'll catch a tire and have a hell of a time getting out. Tow service is kind of sketchy in these parts."

"Sure thing."

The window rolled up, and Jason walked back over to his snowmobile. The SUV sat for a bit, not making any motion to turn around. Clouds of exhaust formed at the muffler.

Jason sat on his cat and swung the driver a friendly wave. If he had been following Yvette, there was no way Jason was going to leave his post. And if the driver had known her, he would have mentioned he was following a friend. Maybe?

When the vehicle finally began to pull ahead, turn, back up, turn some more, then make the arc around to head back the way it had come, Jason again waved.

"Something up with Smith," he muttered.

He could generally spot a fake ID at a glance. The license had been legit. Everything checked out in the police database. But still, his Spidey senses tingled. Sure, Frost Falls got sightseers. The town's namesake, the falls, froze solid in the winter months. It attracted thrill seekers. And idiots.

But the man hadn't mentioned the falls specifically. And if that had been his destination, he should have headed out of town in the opposite direction.

Jason had met three strangers today. And one of them

had been lying dead in a ditch. He wasn't going to let this one sit.

Firing up the cat, he headed back into town to keep an eye on Smith.

Chapter Four

Jason breezed into the station but didn't unzip his coat or stomp his boots. Marjorie had gotten used to his tromping in ice and snow and had laid down a rubber runner mat a year ago. She still complained about the mess, but when he'd given her a budget for a monthly rug cleaning, she'd settled.

That would all change soon enough. He wasn't sure how to tell her the station might be closed in March. He had to tell her. Maybe if he waited, it would never happen?

"There's a message," Marjorie started as he walked by.

"From the BCA?" Jason asked.

"No, Bay's in your office—"

He strode into his office and closed the door behind him. "Bay."

The agent was seated in the extra chair against the wall beneath a sixteen-point deer rack with a laptop open and his focus pinned to the screen. "Cash. Give me a minute."

"Minute's all you get. I'm investigating a murder. Have to get out there. Talk to people. Gather information."

Walking across the room, Jason pushed aside the shades to give him a view of Main Street. He'd seen Smith's SUV heading east toward Highway 35. The man had taken the hint.

On the other hand... He glanced down the street toward the gas station that sat at town's edge.

"They still renting snowcats from the gas station?" Jason called out to Marjorie.

"You betcha. Jason, do you want some krumkake?"

That invite turned his head. He strode back into the next room and eyed the plate of sweet treats Marjorie pointed to on the corner of her desk. Half a dozen delicate rolled sweets sat on a Corelle plate decorated around the circumference with green leaves (just like his mother's set). Krumkake were like crunchy crepes, but so light and delicious.

"You make those?" he asked.

"Of course. I use my grandmother's krumkake iron. They don't make those things anymore, don't ya know."

He grabbed one of the treats and bit into it, catching the inevitable crumbs with his other hand. Two more bites and it was gone. He grabbed another, then tugged out his notebook and tore out a few pages to hand to Marjorie. "Can you type up these notes I took while talking to Susan Olson?"

"Of course. I've already got a case file started. Elaine Hester forwarded the autopsy report for the woman in the ditch. I left a copy on your desk, and Bay's got a copy as well."

"Yeah, she texted me the name Yvette Pearson." Jason wandered back into his office and closed the door behind him.

Ryan Bay stood and set the laptop on Jason's desk. "I've got family info on the victim."

"Lives in a Minneapolis suburb," Jason said. Susan had been sure the women at the club the other night were from the Twin Cities, because one had worn a jacket with a high school logo embroidered on the sleeve. "Blaine?"

"Yes, Blaine. I've already contacted their police department so they can get in touch with the family."

"I've got a list of the deceased's friends I intend to question as soon as I step out of the station. But first, I'm going to head east and check on—"

"That pretty young woman you talked to in The Moose?" Marjorie asked as she entered with the plate of treats in hand.

Marjorie took his silence as the hint she needed it to be and, after handing him the plate, she left the office with a promise to get right to his notes.

Jason closed the office door again and nodded to Bay, who turned his laptop toward him. "Classic homicide. Ligature marks. Struggle bruises on forearms and DNA under fingernails."

"Yep, I was there for the autopsy. It was all very clean. Generally there's much more bruising on the body as the killer struggles to complete the unfamiliar—or unintended—task. Anger and aggression."

Bay shook his head and exhaled heavily. "You said you talked to the woman who found the body?"

"Yes, she gave me the names of the women the victim was last seen with. That's where I'm going next—"

"I thought there was a pretty young woman?" Bay said with a smirk.

"A…" Jason closed his eyes and shook his head. Marjorie really needed to stay out of his personal life. But the worst part of it was that she knew about his personal life before it tended to get personal. "Never mind," he said. "You don't want to question the victim's friends, do you?"

Bay tilted his head, a casual thought process taking place inside his perfectly coiffed head. He wore a suit, for some damn reason, and it looked like his fingernails had been manicured for the glossy shine. Was that what women found attractive? Yikes.

"Go for it," Bay said. "The locals are more likely to be comfortable talking to someone they know. When I consult on a case, I like to guide and keep track, but ultimately, this is your case, Cash. I'm not going to trample on your turf. And I'm starving. I haven't eaten yet today."

"Then The Moose is your next stop." Jason picked up the documents Marjorie had left for him on his desk. "You staying in town?"

"There's no motel. Snow Lake has a halfway decent Best Western and free coffee."

"Not a problem. My office is yours. I'll let you know what I learn." Jason strode out and through the reception area, pleased that Bay was easygoing. Which would give him all the rope he required to control this investigation. He really needed this one. It was an opportunity to show the powers that be that he had what it took to manage real police work, and that the Frost Falls police force, as small as it was, was a necessity.

Instead of the snowmobile, he'd drive the Ford. He could use some warmth. Turning up the car heater to blast, Jason rolled down Main Street, the car tires crunching as if across Styrofoam as they moved over the packed snow. He loved that sound. It was hard to describe to anyone who didn't live on snow six months out of the year. To him it meant home.

From here he could see the small parking lot in front of the gas station. No business name on the broken red-and-white sign above the station. It had been called just "gas station" forever, according to an elder member of the town.

And yet, when Jason cruised closer to the gas station, he saw the black SUV parked around the back side of the white cinder-block building. It was the one licensed to James Smith.

"What the hell?"

He pulled into the station lot. Hopping out of the truck and blowing out a breath that condensed to a fog, Jason quickened his pace into the station.

"Afternoon, Cash," the owner said from his easy chair placed on a dais behind the cash register. Easier to see out the window and watch the town's goings-on from that height.

"You rent out any cats this afternoon, Rusty?"

"I just did, not ten minutes ago. Local fellow."

"Local?"

"Well, you know, he mentioned he was from Duluth. That's local."

It was. The port city that sat on Lake Superior was an hour's drive east and within the St. Louis County lines.

"Gave him directions to the falls and told him to stick to the trails," Rusty said, "but I think he went east. Idiot. Your brother still with the State Patrol?"

"Justin? Yep. He's stationed near the Canadian border right now. Big drug-surveillance op going on."

"Those marijuana farms." Rusty shook his head.

"You betcha. What was the name of the renter?"

Rusty tapped a crinkled piece of paper hanging from a clipboard to the right of the register. "Smith. Sounded foreign. And not Canadian foreign. He was a mite different. Like those duck hunters they got on that television show."

"Thanks, Rusty. Gotta go."

Jason made haste to the truck, and before the door was even closed he pulled out onto the main road and turned to hit the eastbound road that led to the Birch Bower cabin. It was only five miles out, but with each mile the forest thickened and hugged closer on both sides of the narrowing road. It was as desolate as a place could get so close to a small town.

As he drove down the gravel road that the plow only tackled every Monday morning, he noted the snowmobile tracks lain down on the road shoulder. A couple of them. Freshly impressed into the crusted snowpack. One set must belong to Yvette. The other?

"Smith."

In his next thought, Jason wondered if he were getting

worked up over nothing. No. She'd said she didn't know anyone in town. And yet she had looked at the SUV for a while.

Didn't feel right to Jason. And if he'd learned anything over the years, it was to trust his intuition.

ONE OF THE reasons Yvette hadn't minded leaving home for a while was that she'd been questioning her job choice for some time now. She'd never been fooled that being a field operative for an international security agency was glamourous or even 24/7 action-adventure. The job could be tedious at times. Mildly adrenalizing, at best. Most people associated spies with glamour and blockbuster movies. In truth, the average agent spent more time doing boring surveillance than the few minutes of contact with a suspect that might provide that thrill of action.

Yet beyond the intrigue and danger, a surprising moral struggle had presented itself to her when she was faced with pulling the trigger on a human target. She was not a woman prone to crying fits. And yet, the tears had threatened when she'd been standing in the field, gun aimed at a person and—she'd been unable to pull the trigger. Human life meant something to her. Even if the human she had been charged to fire at was a criminal who had committed vile crimes. She'd not expected to only realize such moral leanings until the heat of the moment, but that pause had changed her life irreversibly.

She asked for a change of pace and had, thankfully, been allowed to continue her work in data tech. A job that didn't fulfill her in any tangible manner. It had become an endless stream of data on the computer screen.

Now seclusion in a snow-covered cabin offered an excellent time to consider her future. Did she really want to continue on this career path? Days ago, she'd started a list of pros and cons regarding her current employer.

Yvette tapped the pen beside her temple as she delved deep for another pro. She felt it necessary to write down the good as well as the bad reasons to stay or leave. Solid and tangible. Easy to review. Difficult to deny once inked on paper. Because she'd followed in her parents' footsteps, career-wise. Had thought she was cut out for the gritty hardcore work it required.

Yet to her surprise, the desk job had, strangely, become more dangerous than fieldwork. She had seen something on the computer screen that she was not supposed to see. She just didn't know what that something was, because it had been a list, and perhaps even coded.

Setting aside the pros and cons list and getting up to stretch, she exhaled. She'd been working on the list for an hour while listening to the wind whip against the exterior timber walls. A blizzard was forecast.

"Joy," she muttered mirthlessly and wandered into the kitchen.

No thought cells could operate without a healthy dose of chocolate. Plucking a mug out of the cupboard, she then filled the teapot with water and set that on the stove burner.

She shook the packet of hot chocolate mix into the mug. Right now, she needed a heat injection. Her toes were freezing, even though she wore two layers of socks. And her fingers felt like ice. She'd turned up the heater upon returning from the grocery run, but it didn't want to go any higher than seventy-four degrees.

With the wind scraping across the windows, she felt as if she sat in a wooden icebox. A glance to the fireplace made her sigh. A woodpile sat neatly stacked outside and behind the house. The owners had suggested she carry some in before too much snow fell, but she'd not done that. After she'd fortified her chilled bones with hot chocolate, she'd have to bundle up and bring out the ax to chip the frozen logs apart. The night demanded a toasty fire in the hearth.

The teapot whistled, and she poured the steaming water into the mug. Oh, how she missed the thick, dark chocolate drink served exclusively by the French tea shop Angelina. Unfortunately, the shop hadn't come to Lyon, but she visited Paris often enough and stocked up when there.

Tilting back the oversweet chocolate drink, she sighed and took a moment to savor the heat filling her belly. Who would have thought she could enjoy a moment of warmth so thoroughly? It was a different kind of warmth from the one she'd felt sitting in the diner talking to the chief of police. Colette had been spot on regarding her assessment of the man. He was a handsome one. He'd seemed about her age, too.

A knock on the front door startled her. That was—not weird. The postman knocked every day with her mail in hand. Not that she got personal mail. It was always ads and flyers for retirement homes. But she did appreciate his smile and some chat. He often asked if she was comfy and did she like fruitcake? His wife had extra. Yvette always declined with the knowledge that fruitcake was not a culinary treat.

Yet something stopped her from approaching the door. She still couldn't erase the police chief's question about the mysterious SUV. It had seemed out of place in the small town. And she was no woman to ignore the suspicious.

Grasping a pen from the kitchen counter, Yvette fit the heavy steel object into her curled fingers, then walked cautiously over to the door. She stood there a moment, staring at the unfinished pine wood that formed the solid barrier. There was no peephole.

"Who is it?" she called.

"Delivery," answered back. "Is your name… Yvette?"

"Yes, but…" Yvette frowned. It was her cover name.

She hadn't ordered anything. And she'd only this morning asked Colette to order the helmet.

"It's from The Moose," the man said. "You didn't order anything?"

"No," she called back. "It's food? Who sent it?"

A pause, and then, "Note says it's from a new friend."

A new friend? And The Moose? But she'd just—had the police chief sent her a gift? Of food? They had discussed pie. How nice of him. And if it was a flirtatious move, she was all in.

Yvette opened the door.

The man standing on the snow-dusted front stoop was tall and dressed all in black, including the black face mask he wore that concealed all but his eyes. He growled and lunged for her. He fit his bare hands about her throat, and Yvette stumbled backward.

Chapter Five

Jason ran in through the open doorway and encountered a struggle. In front of the floor-to-ceiling windows that overlooked a snow-frosted copse of maples, he witnessed a man shove a woman—Yvette LaSalle—against the wall. Her painful grunt fired anger in Jason's veins. He dashed over a fallen chair and toward the struggling duo.

Suddenly, Yvette swept her hand forcefully backward, her elbow colliding with the attacker's neck. She twisted and plunged a fist against his head. The man—Smith—yelped and gripped his bleeding scalp.

Jason charged across the room. With a swift right hook, he connected under Smith's jaw and knocked him out cold. The man dropped to his side, sprawling on the floor.

He spun around to find Yvette behind him, clutching a tactical pen in one hand. A fierce, huffing demeanor held her at the ready before him. Her stance declared she was prepared for more fight.

"It's okay," Jason reassured. "He's out."

She nodded, but her defensive pose remained. Impressive. She'd been terrorized. The adrenaline must be coursing through her like a snowmobile around a racetrack.

"That was— You were—incredible." Jason finally found the right words. "You are certainly no damsel."

"No, I'm not." She winced, but lifted her chin. "He was strong. Stronger than…"

Jason sensed the adrenaline was beginning to rapidly drop from the high that had served her the strength to defend herself. Yvette's body began to shake. He rushed over and took her in his arms.

"It's okay." He hugged her firmly, pressing his face against the crown of her head. She smelled like salt and summer. A sweep of soft hair tickled his nose. His thundering heartbeats thudded loudly. But was it from the moment of attack, or from the surprising feeling of holding a trembling woman in his arms? Mercy. She had reacted unexpectedly bravely. And her sudden surge of strength may have saved her life.

"You did good, Yvette. Guy's out like a light." For now. "I need to cuff him. Can I let you go?"

She nodded against his chest, though her fingers clung to his biceps, unwilling to relent. Jason stepped back but bowed to check her gaze. When she offered him a wincing smile, he slowly extracted himself from her grip. She wasn't going to faint. Not this brave woman.

Digging out the cuffs from his jacket, he bent to secure the suspect's hands behind his back.

"You know this guy?" he asked over his shoulder.

"No. Do you?"

"He's the guy from the black SUV."

"I told you I didn't know him when you asked in the diner."

"I know, but he put up my hackles. I pinned him for something more than a guy taking in the scenery. He was following you."

"He was? How did you— Why didn't you stop him before he got here?"

"I thought I had." Jason stood and grabbed the back of a fallen chair and righted it. He lifted a boot, realizing the papers scattered on the floor were wet and torn. No saving them. "I didn't expect him to rent a snowmobile and go after you. Why was he after you?"

"We've been over this, Chief Cash. I've never met him."

"How did he get inside the cabin?"

"I, uh…" She clutched her throat. Her fingers visibly shook. "Opened the door."

Jason stopped an admonishing retort and instead asked carefully, "You always let strangers inside?"

"He said he had a delivery from The Moose. Why did you talk to him in town? What made you wonder about him?"

"He looked suspicious. We've got an active investigation going on and—"

"Investigation? Like what? A man attacking women?"

She was close. Jason never gave out details of an ongoing investigation. Was the man on the floor the one who had murdered the woman he'd found in the ditch this morning? He had been attempting to strangle Yvette. The one in the ditch had died by strangulation. And Jason never subscribed to coincidence.

Yet would a stalker, or even some sort of serial strangler, have allowed a woman to get the upper hand with a weapon so simple as a tactical pen?

As well, how many seemingly innocent women vacationing in a secluded cabin carried a tactical pen on them? It was a self-defense weapon that most did not know about or bother to keep close enough to use.

"That's a handy thing, isn't it?" He gestured to the rugged black steel pen she still held.

She clutched it against her chest and lifted her chin. "I never go anywhere without it. It's something I was trained—"

"You've taken self-defense training?"

When she looked up quickly, as if he'd discovered a secret, a moment of clarity softened her features, then she shrugged. "Like you said, I'm not a damsel."

"I guess not. But didn't the training class teach you never to open the door to a stranger?"

Another shrug. She avoided his gaze, as well. Hmm…

"Are you going to get him out of here?" she asked with a gesture to the fallen attacker.

"I'll give Officer Larson a call." Jason wasn't ready to leave without asking more questions. And he couldn't do that and watch the perp at the same time. "You sure you're okay?"

"Of course I am," she said a little too quickly. Then a sweep of her hand through her hair preceded a hefty sigh. "But if you'll excuse me, I'm going to step into the, uh… little girls' room for a bit."

"Go ahead. I won't leave until this guy is out of your hair." He tugged out his phone and dialed up dispatch. He and Alex alternated shifts, but both were on call 24/7. And he'd rather have him come and assist than the lackadaisical Ryan Bay.

YVETTE CLOSED THE bathroom door behind her and exhaled. Her shoulders hit the door. She caught her head in a palm. Her entire body shook, but she didn't cry. She sank, bending her knees, until she sat on the tiled floor.

That man could have killed her.

She was thankful that the police chief was here and had rescued her in the nick of time. But a retreat to the bathroom had been necessary. She hadn't wanted him to see her break down. And what was this shaking about? She was better than this—trained for such encounters, and well able to defend herself against some of the strongest attackers.

Yet she hadn't panicked when he'd come at her. She had done her best to protect herself from what could have been a terrible outcome. Because the man had had his hands about her neck and his thumbs pressed against her larynx. She'd gasped and had felt her lungs tighten.

It had been over a year since she'd worked as a field agent and had exercised her defense skills. Had she gotten so out of shape and ineffective in such a short time?

"Get it together, Amelie," she whispered. "Why did this happen?"

Because Amelie Desauliniers had been sent out of the country to hide under an assumed identity. But hide from whom or what hadn't been made clear to her. Surely this hadn't been a random attack. And yet she was undercover. Dark. Who had found her?

A quiet knock on the door preceded "Yvette? You okay in there?"

She closed her eyes.

"Yvette?"

"Oh." Despite embracing the name, it just didn't click sometimes. As well, she'd have to form words to reassure the police chief. Inhaling a quiet sniffle, she said, "Sorry. Yes, give me a few minutes. I'm a little shaken."

"Thought you might be. I'll be out in the living room. Another officer is on the way to pick up the perp."

She waited until his boots echoed away down the hall. Amelie stood and walked to the sink. Twisting on the water spigot, she splashed her face but let out a gasp. She would never get used to the fact the water took a good three or four minutes to reach room temperature. But the frigid water did work to shock away her tears.

Pressing a towel over her face to dry it, she then nodded at her reflection. The agent she had once been must be tugged out of retirement. For survival purposes. "I can do this."

But she couldn't ask the sexy police chief for help. Her stay here in Minnesota was classified. And not knowing what she knew had suddenly become a detriment. She had to speak with her boss. And soon.

Returning to the living room, she walked around the prone body on the floor. The attacker was coming to, groaning. Another knock on the door sounded. Amelie jumped. A pair of gentle, warm hands settled onto her shoulder.

"It's Alex, my assistant," Chief Cash reassured her in a deep voice that hinted at the strength she desperately required. "Why don't you sit on the couch." He touched her upper arm, and she winced. "Looks like you got hurt. Your sweater is torn. I'll take a look after I get the perp out of here."

He opened the door, and the waiting police officer nodded and introduced himself to her as Amelie settled onto the couch. He was tall and attractive. Not handsome sexy, more like boy-band cute. The thought summoned her out of the heavy tension that had made her clutch the tactical pen. She set the pen on the coffee table and inspected her sweater.

She'd been hurt? She hadn't noticed while shivering in the bathroom. Yet now that Jason had pointed it out, she felt the sting of pain in her biceps. Her sweater was torn and bloody. And…yes, the pointed tip of the pen was bloodied, so she'd caused her attacker some damage.

The two men picked up the suspect by his upper arms. He growled and struggled against the handcuffs. Both officers had to move him out of the cabin, kicking and gyrating across the threshold. As they exited, the attacker called, "I will be back for you!"

Amelie swore and turned to clasp her arms about her legs, pulling them tight against her chest. Her heart thudded up to her throat.

She knew something dangerous. It was locked away in her brain, and only she possessed the key to dredge out the information.

Chapter Six

Standing on the front stoop, Jason watched Alex back the patrol car out of the double-wide drive. Alex gave him a thumbs-up as he headed toward town. He'd secure the perp behind bars, and Ryan Bay could help book him and start an interrogation.

He leaned back inside the cabin and called, "I'm going to take a look around the cabin and surrounding area. Look for clues. You okay alone for a bit?"

"Of course."

The answer was the right one, but it sounded shaky. To be expected.

"Give me half an hour. I'll stay close. If you need me, just shout out the door."

Wind and snow crystals scoured Jason's face as he rounded the side of the cabin, following the faint traces of boot prints that were neither his nor did they belong to a female. Another hour of wind and the tracks would be gone.

An outjut of stacked pine logs formed a two-sided protection from the wind and elements for the generator. He lifted the blue tarp cover and looked over the machine. Some snow had drifted up about the base, but it all looked in working order. He might turn it on to check it out, but it was windy, and he wanted to beat the storm before it erased all evidence Smith had left behind.

Picking up his pace through a foot of fluffy, dry snow, Jason passed the detached double garage behind the cabin. He sighted sunken boot prints. They did not reveal sole design because the snow and wind had already filled them, but he could see they walked toward the cabin. Scanning ahead, he noticed the line of tracks and veered toward the line of white-paper birches that edged a forest fifty yards ahead. The footprints disappeared for ten feet, but then he could pick up the sunken smooth imprint when he flashed the flashlight beam over it. But he didn't need the tracks when he spied the snowmobile in the woods.

Hastening his steps, he entered the woods, which blocked the wind. Thankful for that reprieve, he huffed out a breath. The cold was something he was accustomed to, but when the wind beat directly at his face, it took a man's breath away.

Tromping over fallen branches and loose snow made footing difficult. The snowmobile still had the keys in the ignition. A rental sticker on the hood told him it had come from the gas station. Smith had likely intended to do the deed and head back to the snowmobile for a quick getaway.

Jason sat on the snow-dusted vinyl seat cushion and flashed the light beam about the sled. The gas station kept its rental machines in tip-top condition, even if they were decades old. This one was fully gassed up. The seat was comfy and not torn. The outer fiberglass hood was not scuffed, save for a small crack where the windshield connected.

The footprints, which now he could plainly see were from cowboy boots, took off from the sled and walked straight on toward the cabin—no pacing about the vehicle, deciding to get up his courage. The man had been focused, set on his task. He'd wanted to get at this second Yvette.

Had it been the same man coming after yet another

Yvette? The implications pointed toward some type of serial stalker. A man obsessed with Yvettes?

He tipped open the cover of the small supply box on the back of the seat cushion. Nothing inside. If the man had intended to use a weapon against Yvette, he would have brought it along with him into the cabin. Jason hadn't removed any weapons from him when cuffing him and patting him down.

Jason flipped the box cover shut. He would check on Yvette, and—hell, she had been bleeding.

BACK INSIDE THE CABIN, Jason kicked off his boots. When he wandered into the living room and sat next to Yvette on the couch, he sensed her shivers before seeing them. She was still frightened. The tactical pen lay on the pine coffee table. He would secure that as evidence.

"You were very brave," he said in his reassuring officer's tone. Something a guy cultivated with experience. "Can I look at your arm?"

She nodded but didn't speak as he carefully pulled away the torn knitted threads from her arm. There was a good amount of blood, but it looked like it might be road rash. Nothing deep. She must have rubbed against something rough when struggling with the perp. All the furniture in this cabin was fashioned from heavy, bare pine logs, so it was feasible she could have fallen against a chair leg or arm.

"I found the snowcat the perp drove out here in the woods. I'll have a tow come get it after the storm threat passes. I think you should come to town with me and have Marjorie, my dispatcher, look at that. Just to be safe. And I do need you to give me an official statement."

"I'm okay."

"Marjorie used to be a nurse," he encouraged.

"It's just a bruise. And I know you have questions— standard police procedure, and all that—"

"I really do need to talk to you while the incident is fresh in your mind. It's just odd. The guy was following you. He sat outside on Main Street, watched you walk across from the grocery store, stayed there while you had a bite to eat and then…" He sighed heavily.

"I've never seen that man before, Chief Cash."

"Then why did you let him inside the cabin?"

"I called out and he said he had a delivery and asked if my name was Yvette."

"A delivery?"

"Said it was from a new friend. I assumed it was from you. We *had* talked about pie."

"You thought I sent you pie?"

"It sounded reasonable at the time. I opened the door, and then he lunged. You arrived a minute or two later. *Merci Dieu.*"

"So he called you by name?"

She nodded.

"Your full name?"

Yvette thought about it a moment. "No, just my first. I did have the clarity to grab the tactical pen before answering the door."

"So you were suspicious."

"I was until he said the—er, my name. Then I believed he was a deliveryman."

"Right. So, he started to choke you immediately? Or did you have a conversation first?"

"No, he immediately went at me. I was able to struggle and move the two of us across the room toward the table, where you see the mess."

"Those papers on the floor…" Jason looked over her shoulder. "Important?"

"Uh, no. Just some journaling stuff. Why? You think he was after something of mine?"

"I don't know. You have to tell me."

"He didn't speak after I'd let him inside. Didn't ask for anything, like where my valuables were. I don't believe he was here to rob me. He wanted to hurt me. Possibly even…"

Jason nodded and tugged out his notebook to make a few notations.

"How many people know you're staying here?" he asked.

"One," she said, then offered him a shrug as if to apologize for that low number.

"No friends? Family?"

She shook her head, keeping her lips tight.

"Sounds kind of odd," he remarked. "Single woman off alone in a country foreign to her, and only one person knows about it? Boyfriend?"

She shook her head again, choosing silence. A silence that niggled at Jason's trust. Why not provide the person's name without his prompting?

"Who knows you're here, Miss LaSalle?"

"Just my boss. This was a retreat," she added quickly. "A photography excursion. A last-minute decision sort of thing, so I didn't announce it to everyone I know. Just… got the time off I needed, and…here I am."

"Here you are. You work as a photographer?"

She nodded.

He wasn't buying it. Wouldn't a photographer have equipment? He hadn't noticed any cameras in the open-layout cabin. "Your boss is a photographer as well?"

She shrugged. "It's a hobby. I'm trying to expand my portfolio."

Jason closed his notebook and stuffed it inside his coat. "Anything else you want to tell me about what happened?"

"No."

"So he was only in the cabin a few minutes before I arrived?"

"Yes. Or it felt that long. I can't be sure, but I'd guess that's about as long as I'd last against someone so strong."

"Fine. I have to head in and help process the suspect." And he'd been on his way to talk with the victim's friends before the detour out here to the cabin.

"I'm going to call you in an hour," he said. "To check in with you. You should be safe now."

She nodded. "Thank you." She glanced to the papers strewn on the floor.

"Will you also promise not to open the door for anyone except the mailman?"

"That's a deal. Write down your number on one of those papers before you leave."

He stood and picked up a paper from the floor. It was a lined notebook page. He read the header. "Pros and cons?"

"Just doing some journaling."

Wanting to read more, but respecting her privacy, he tugged the pen out of his coat and scribbled down his number on the back of the paper.

When he handed her the page, Jason felt her shiver again. "What is it, Yvette? There's something else. I can feel it."

She exhaled heavily. "Did you hear what he said when the other officer took him away?"

Smith had called out that he'd be back for her. The audacity.

Her serious blue eyes searched his. Seeking a comforting reassurance that Jason gave her without asking. It was easy, because he couldn't imagine being alone in this country, with no friends, and having been attacked.

"This town is small, but I take protecting the residents seriously," he said. "Do you want me to stay awhile?"

"No, I'll be fine. And you do need to take care of that man. Lock him up, will you?"

"That's my job. Just call me, okay?"

He headed to the door and pulled on his gloves. As he shoved his feet into his snow boots, he turned to look at her. She still sat on the couch, back to him, gaze focused out the tall windows that overlooked a snow-frosted birch forest not far behind the detached garage.

Was he doing the right thing? Leaving her here alone? The perp had been secured. But he couldn't know whether or not Smith had been acting alone. He'd make a point of checking in with her soon.

Jason couldn't shake the fact that there was a stranger staying in Frost Falls, and for some reason she had attracted danger to the small town. He believed that she didn't know Smith.

But what wasn't she telling him? What woman left for another country and only told her employer? Felt wrong. But he could attribute her nervousness to having just gone through a traumatic event. He'd give her some space.

"An hour," he said as he opened the door. "I want to hear from you!"

PULLING THE TRUCK along the side of the police station, Jason dialed up the radio volume just as the meteorologist announced everyone should head out for groceries. The blizzard was on its way and would be full force by tomorrow afternoon, possibly even the morning. He turned off the engine and got out with a jump. An inhale sucked in icy air. It was too cold for a storm, but the weather was always crazy in the wintertime.

Making a quick stop inside the station's ground level, Jason grabbed another krumkake from the plate on Marjorie's desk, then stepped right back outside. He swung around the building corner and opened the heavy steel back door. Down a short hall and then to the right, he clattered down the stairway that led to the basement cells. He hated this setup, especially when he had a drunk or violent perp to contain. More than a few times, he'd almost tumbled to the bottom with the prisoner in hand. Not the most well-designed police station, that was for sure.

The heater kept the cinder block–walled basement at a passable sixty-eight degrees and each of the three cells even held one of Marjorie's homemade quilts, along with a fluffy pillow. Jason had spent a night in one of the cells a few months earlier after a long night of reading over boring expense reports.

"We have a new guest in the Hotel Frosty?" he asked Alex and Ryan as he joined them before the middle cell.

"Just got him locked up. He's a fighter," Alex said. "Bay had to help me fingerprint him."

Jason noticed the black ink smear on Alex's jaw. "I see that. You get anything out of him, Bay?"

The man's focus was on his laptop again, set on a small table beneath a landline phone that hung on the wall opposite the cells.

"Not yet."

"All he's said," Alex added, "was a whole lot of words that were not favorable toward my mother."

"Is that so?"

Jason stepped up to the cell bars. Inside, the perp leaned against the back wall, one leg bent with his sole flat against the wall. Cowboy boots, not snow boots with traction on the soles. Idiot. The man lifted his chin. A position of challenge that didn't give Jason any more worry than if he'd spat at him.

"You are under arrest for assault," Jason stated. "James Smith, eh? I ran a trace on your plates earlier. You live in Duluth and work at Perkins. What's a line chef doing in Frost Falls strangling women?"

The man mumbled something and ended with two very clear swear words.

"He doesn't like your mother much, either," Alex said.

Jason smirked. "My mother would arm wrestle this skinny guy under the table if she heard him talking like that."

The Cash family—all three of the boys and both mother

and father—was an athletically inclined bunch. Their father had been a marine before purchasing the Crooked Creek land and settling into dairy farming and to raise his family. And their mom, well, she was always trying new martial arts classes and once had flipped the eldest son, Justin, onto his back in an impressive move that had left their brother red-faced and Joe and Jason laughing like hyenas. Jason was never ashamed to admit it had been his mother who taught him some keen defense moves, including the more relaxed tai chi she practiced religiously.

The prisoner lifted his chin haughtily and then flipped them the bird.

"This is going to be a fun afternoon." Jason nodded to Ryan. "Why don't you get the paperwork started and bring down the DNA kit. You get mug shots?"

Alex blew out a breath and offered an unsure shrug. "Bay was taking the shots. Not sure."

"My camera was out of focus," Bay provided on a mumble. "I'm going through the shots right now. Might be one usable image."

"I get it," Jason said. "We'll mark this one down as uncooperative. Wait for fingerprints, then we'll check the CJRS." The Criminal Justice Reporting System was the US database for tracking and identifying criminals and those with police records.

"Will do, boss." Alex started up the stairs.

"And next time you come down, bring some of those krumkakes, will you?"

"If there's any left when I get through with them." Alex's chuckle was muffled by the closing of the upper door.

Jason turned, crossed his arms over his chest and couldn't help a smile. The man giving him the wonky eye might very well be a murderer.

"You interview the dead woman's friends?" Ryan asked as he joined Jason at his side.

"Haven't gotten that far yet."

"Storm's moving in. I hate Minnesota. I put in for a position in an Arizona county office."

"I'm sure they'll be happy to have you," Jason said. Bay was distracted, or probably didn't care much about the situation. Burnout? Maybe. Or it could be the weather. Damn cold was enough to make any man lose focus on what was most important.

And right now, Jason had added a beautiful Frenchwoman to that list.

"I should head out before it gets nasty outside," he said. "Ask this guy about girlfriends named Yvette. Or maybe it's his mom he's trying to strangle? Check the family stats on him."

"Will do," Bay said as Jason left him and headed out.

Chapter Seven

Amelie dialed the international number, and it went straight to her boss's voice mail. It was nearing midnight in France. Jacques needed to know about the attack on her, but, when fleeing France, she'd been instructed to keep any voice messages she left general and vague. He'd warned her not to communicate with him unless the situation were dire.

One man's definition of dire could very well be another man's idea of a challenge. It wasn't dire. She'd survived. Had the attacker intended to kill her? Rubbing her neck where his hands had clasped without mercy, she nodded. He would not have released pressure until she'd ceased breathing. But the police chief had arrived—the American expression was, in the nick of time.

So, not quite dire, but getting there.

Forgoing a message, she almost set down the phone, but then she remembered she'd told Jason she'd check in with him.

She dialed the number the police chief had written down for her. This call also went straight to message. She quickly relayed that she was fine and thanked him for his worry. Then without thinking, she added, "I owe you dinner at The Moose for your timely arrival to fight the bad guy. See you soon."

Dinner? Where had that come from?

She told herself that it made sense to befriend the chief of police—after all, she was alone here. It couldn't hurt to have an extra set of eyes watching out on her behalf, even if those eyes belonged to the most handsome man she'd seen in years.

"I'm just being practical," she said to the empty room.

Hanging up and tossing the phone onto the couch, she added, "Netflix and chill, indeed."

Wandering into the living room, she picked up a stray paper she'd not noticed earlier when cleaning up the mess from the struggle. It had slid partially under the couch. It was the beginning of her pros and cons list. One con read: *no love life.* Because working for an international police organization did tend to put a damper on relationships. Certainly, it was much easier when working in the tech department as opposed to having to go out in the field and never knowing where the job might take her. But still, it wasn't a job she could talk about with civilians. And that made getting close in a relationship difficult.

She set the paper on the desk, and as she did, the lights flickered but did not go out. She suspected the electrical wiring for this old cabin was doing the best it could, given the harsh weather conditions. The rental owners had left instructions on how to use the generator, which sat outside hugging the east wall. As well, candles were in abundance, tucked in drawers, on windowsills, and placed in a box on the fireplace mantel.

Taking the lighter from the hearth, she lit the three fat candles fit into a birch log on the rustic wood coffee table. The ambience was nice, but the flickering flames didn't erase her lingering unease.

She rubbed her palms up and down her arms. She wasn't afraid. Not a damsel. But the question was: Was she safe here? Had someone found her because of what was in her head? What *was* in her head? She'd read a document on the computer. It had only showed up on the screen for ten minutes, and then it had disappeared. She had it all stored in her brain. And someone—her boss—had suspected what she'd seen could be dangerous.

The attack hadn't been random—someone seeking an easy victim in a desolate cabin far from town. He'd known her name. And in further proof, as the officers were dragging him out to the waiting vehicle, the attacker had said something about coming back for her.

An impossible task if he was in jail. But had he acted alone?

It wasn't uncommon for Interpol agents to go dark, especially when they were deep undercover. She wasn't exactly deep undercover, but Jacques had been adamant about keeping her off the grid. She may not have been out on assignment, but the extensive information lodged in her head made her dangerous, whether she liked it or not. She'd always trusted Jacques before. She'd continue to trust him now.

"Another week," she muttered. "That's all I'll give him before I reassess and change tactics."

"You listen to your messages?" Marjorie asked as she popped her head into Jason's office to say goodbye for the evening.

Jason had left Ryan Bay below to interrogate the prisoner, while he was still on his way out to question the other women who had been with Yvette Pearson on Saturday night at The Moose. He hadn't even glanced to his phone yet.

"Will do," he absently replied to Marjorie, his focus on the computer screen. James Smith did not have any known relatives listed.

"Uh-huh." Not convinced at all. "How's the prisoner?"

"Think he's from Texas. But we can't have a decent conversation with him that isn't three-quarters expletives."

"How's Ryan doing with him?"

"Guy's lackadaisical. He feels like one of those mosquitoes that a guy always has to brush away, but the bug never gets too close to bite."

"Annoying?" Marjorie asked.

"That's the word."

"You taking the night shift to keep an eye on him?"

"No, Alex has the night shift. I'll come in early to relieve him. Unless the storm arrives. Then I might have to go for a ride."

"I know you're excited for the fresh snow." Marjorie chuckled. "You need to start racing, Cash."

"I would love to, but can't afford to take time off now. This is a big case."

"That it is. And I trust you'll handle it well."

"You've never seen what I can do with homicide. How can you be so sure, Marjorie?"

"Because you're smart and not about to take crap from anyone. Especially a man behind bars who may have murdered an innocent woman."

"Thanks for the vote of confidence."

"Yes, well, I see how you sometimes doubt yourself, Chief Cash."

He raised an eyebrow at that statement.

"You put yourself out there like the got-it-all-together, cocky police chief. And that's well and fine. You do have it all together. More than most of us do. But I know you were hurt by something right before you came here."

He'd never told Marjorie everything about his reason for taking the job at the station, only that he had come fresh from the CIA.

"You're doing a good job, Cash," she said. "Don't ever forget that."

He nodded, finding it hard to summon a response. He tried his best with what he'd been given. And now he'd been handed a homicide investigation. How he handled this would prove to all watching him that he was capable and trustworthy.

He winked at her. "See you tomorrow, Marjorie," Jason said. "Tell Hank hey from me."

She waved and closed his office door.

Jason returned his attention to the police database. Along with the fingerprints, he entered a description, possible alias of James Smith, nationality and crime. Smith was not his real name. Well, it could be, but a search for "James Smith" brought up far too many hits, none remotely similar in looks to the man sitting below. And none matched the Duluth address from the license, which meant the owner of the license might never have committed a crime and had reason to be booked and have his fingerprints on record.

And that meant that whoever sat in the cell below had stolen the license and the vehicle.

Jason sat back in his chair and flicked the plastic driver's license Alex had taken from the man's wallet. It was easy enough to fake a license, but to take the time to co-ordinate that match with vehicle registration? Had to be stolen. By force?

Tugging open his top drawer, he pulled out a magnifying glass and studied the microprint on the license. The virtual image of the state bird—the loon—appeared to float and then sink on the card's surface as he viewed it from different angles. A rub over the surface felt like all the other licenses he'd held over the years. The card was not flimsy, either. The photo showed a nondescript man in his midthirties with brown hair and eyes who wore a green collared polo shirt. He looked like the man in the cell below, but—well, hell, anything was possible.

The SUV hadn't been listed as stolen when he'd run the

check earlier. But if the original owner had been harmed in some way—or even murdered—the car may not yet have been reported stolen.

He picked up the phone and then called out to Marjorie, "You still here?"

"What do you need?"

Jason smiled. It always took her a bit to gather her things, and shut down the computer, and do a bit of dusting before she felt able to leave the office. "Will you patch me in to the Duluth desk?"

When the call was transferred, he gave the officer the VIN and the license info. There were no reports of theft.

"Will you drive out and check on James Smith?" Jason asked the officer. "I've got a perp here with his license and his vehicle, but I don't think he is who he wants us to believe."

"Will do. Give me an hour."

"Thanks." Jason hung up.

Time to head for Lisa Powell's place. He'd wanted to go sooner, but one of the drawbacks of being on a police force of two was that he had to do almost all of the work himself, from questioning to data search to writing reports. And Bay wasn't as helpful as he needed him to be. Fortunately, Powell lived down the block from him with her husband and a couple of kids. She had to know that Yvette Pearson was dead, but just in case, he'd proceed carefully. Being a Sunday, the whole family would be home. This was not going to be easy, but he did enjoy the interrogative procedure and modulating it for a nonaggressive subject.

Pulling out his phone, he spied the voice mail waiting for him. From Yvette. He hadn't forgotten about asking her to check in with him. She reported she was fine and…

"Dinner?" Jason nodded appreciatively. "Perfect opportunity to figure out who the hell Yvette LaSalle is."

Because in a short time, there had been a murder and then an attack on another woman. Coincidence? He didn't think so.

Chapter Eight

Both Lisa Powell and Hannah Lindsey had been upset to hear about Yvette Pearson's death. Both had known her from Blaine High School, where they'd graduated three years earlier. They, along with Hannah's mother, had been celebrating Lisa's birthday and had far too much to drink. Lisa had been inconsolable, so Jason had left her to her husband. Hannah had been in tears as well, but she'd said that Yvette had left The Moose to head back to the Snow Lake motel where she was staying. When he'd asked why they'd let their drunk friend drive, Hannah had broken out in a bawling fit.

Neither had mentioned a strange man watching them while they'd been partying in the back of The Moose. But would they even remember if they'd been that wasted? Yvette Pearson had gotten a ride to The Moose from Lisa, and yet no one in the Powell family had noticed the maroon Monte Carlo—Yvette's car—still parked out behind their garage in the alleyway until Jason had arrived. Yvette hadn't made the short four-block walk from The Moose to her car. Smith—if he were indeed the murderer—had to have offered her a ride. Very possibly, he'd ended her life somewhere in town.

That would have been an aggressive move on Smith's part. Not taking her to a private place to do the deed. It indicated he'd simply wanted her dead, and quickly. And he hadn't driven far to dispose of the body. Another indication of a rushed job.

Had he known Yvette Pearson? Had anger over something pushed him to take her life? Had she known him from Blaine? Did they work together? They might have known one another and he followed her here and waited until she was alone so he could strike. A crime of passion.

Except that those sorts of crimes were messier, more involved, and didn't involve the perpetrator going after yet another woman with the same name.

Unless, of course, an Yvette had hurt him in some way and he was taking out his anger on any random Yvette he stumbled upon?

Very possible. And the two women did bear a resemblance, both young and beautiful with long dark hair.

Now that Jason had spoken to the friends, he could go back to the office and, along with Bay, figure out a new interrogation strategy. Pearson's family would need to be interviewed, as well as those she worked with.

But really? If Elaine's final report showed Smith's DNA taken from under Pearson's fingernails, then the interrogation wasn't necessary. And the suspect had yet to ask for a lawyer. A good time stall on Jason's part.

He'd had the Monte Carlo towed to the station so Alex could give it a thorough once-over. And Marjorie would type up his audio notes from the interviews with the women in the morning.

Before it got too late, now was a good time to check in on Yvette. And maybe delve deeper into what the hell was happening in Frost Falls.

"Why do I suspect ulterior motives?" Yvette asked as he stepped inside the cabin.

"Just a routine check to ensure you're safe." Jason had

handed her a heat-safe sack of food from The Moose. She *had* suggested dinner. "The meat loaf might need warming," he offered. "It's my favorite."

"I'm not sure I've had loaf of meat before," Yvette teased.

After he'd peeled away all his outer gear layers, Jason settled before the table as Yvette dished up warm meat loaf, mashed potatoes and the soft, buttered dinner rolls The Moose's owner made from scratch. Now this would hit the spot. She bustled about the kitchen while he attacked the meat loaf.

She'd seemed distant since the attack, and instinctively, he wanted to allow her space. But professionally? He could dig for a few relevant clues while engaging in casual conversation.

"I'm surprised a woman who seems prickly about our winter chose to vacation in Minnesota."

Yvette sat across the table from him and tore her bread roll in half. "The trip was a gift," she said. But he knew, from her inability to meet his gaze, that she wasn't being truthful. Not completely. "A friend of a friend knew the owner of this cabin. I thought I'd give it a try. And with the photography opportunities...like I've said."

"Fair enough." Using a quarter of the roll, Jason sopped up the butter melted in the concave top of his mashed potatoes. "I thought you said you trust me, Yvette?"

"I do."

"Then why are you lying to me?"

She pressed her fingers to her chest and gaped at him. Those blue eyes were hard to accuse, so he tried not to look into them for too long. But, man, what about those lush lashes? A guy could get caught in them and never wish to escape.

"You would never in a million years choose to vacation here," he said. "Or maybe it started out as a spur-of-the-moment trip, but I sense things have changed for you. You know why that man was after you, don't you?"

"I honestly don't. Swear to you that I don't. You can even give me a lie detector test if you need to." She bowed her head and poked at the mashed potatoes.

That was an odd defense. Bringing up the lie detector suggestion was something only those who were deeply worried being caught out with their lies would suggest. Was she shaking? Sure, there was a draft sitting here by the window, but he sensed she was not comfortable. And it wasn't because this could be misconstrued as a first date. It wasn't. But he sensed a little of that "get to know you but I'm nervous" vibe about her.

"Can you give me the name of the friend of a friend who suggested you vacation here?" he asked.

Now she looked at him straight on. And he didn't sense any shyness in that gaze. "You're investigating me now?"

"No, just trying to gather as many useful details as I can. You're a stranger to our town, and you've been targeted. I need to put together possible connections."

"I don't have the friend's name. I took the offer as a means to fill out my photography portfolio. I've always wanted to turn nature photography into a career. And I've never taken snowy shots. It was an opportunity, so I grabbed it."

Jason sat back. "Fine. But if I look you up in the international database, what will I learn?"

She shrugged. "That I live in Lyon, France. I have a job, rent an apartment, drive a Mini Cooper and—what else do those things reveal?—I've no police record. I've been hired for a few nature photography assignments for small publications over the last year."

"Kind of vague."

"Chief Cash, I'm not the criminal here. And I'm a bit offended that you're treating me like one."

"I'm offended that you don't want to help my investigation. Anyone with nothing to hide should be happy to help. The man could have killed you, Yvette."

"I know that." She took a sip of water and closed her eyes, looking aside.

Had he pushed too hard? Admittedly, Jason had never ranked high on the compassion stuff. Comforting victims after a crime was always a challenge for him.

Jason placed a hand over hers, and she flinched but then settled and allowed him to keep his hand there. "I've not had a case like this in…" She didn't need to know he was desperate to prove himself. "I've never had a homicide. Small town, you know? I just want to do things right. But if I've offended you, I'm sorry. It's hard for me to keep business separate from other things in this situation."

"Other things?" She lifted a brow.

Hell, he'd gone and said something he probably shouldn't have. And yet, if he couldn't be honest with her, then she had no reason to reciprocate. "I like you, Yvette. I feel protective toward you, and not just because it's my job to keep you safe."

Her nervous smile was too brief. "I like you, too, Jason Cash. I wish we could have met under different circumstances."

"Doesn't mean things can't go how we want them to."

"No, it doesn't." Now the smile returned, more confident.

"But I promise you," he said, making a point of meeting her gaze, "if I ever want you to have pie, it will be delivered in person, and shared."

"Makes sense. Now. It was a stupid thing to open that door. I should have been more suspicious."

Jason lifted his chin. "You have a reason to be suspicious?"

She shrugged. "Shouldn't any woman staying alone in a cabin in the middle of nowhere be cautious?"

He nodded, but again, his Spidey senses tingled. There was something she wasn't telling him.

The phone in Jason's pocket jangled. He reluctantly pulled his hand from Yvette's and checked the message. It was from Ryan Bay. He'd gotten a fingerprint hit on their prisoner. It was not a match to James Smith, line chef at the Duluth Perkins.

"I need to head in to the station," he said to Yvette.

"The investigation?"

"Yes. Sorry." He stood. "I hate to eat and run. And to leave things…well…"

She took his hand and squeezed it. "You know where to find me. Go. Do your job. Text me later if you can."

"That I will."

He almost leaned forward, but then Jason realized it would be for a kiss and—it didn't feel quite right. She'd been angry with him for the way he'd gone about asking her questions—a bit too angry for someone with nothing to hide. And he wasn't even sure what he wanted right now. To interrogate her or to romance her? Best to dial down the need for tasting her lips that he got every time he looked at those lush ruby reds. He had a job to do. He didn't need distractions.

Damn. Why did those blue eyes have to be so stunning? They possessed powers. He could feel them weakening his resolve as well as his legs. If he didn't move now, he'd sit and stay for a while.

Jason moved to the door and got dressed, backing out the front door with a silly wave as he did so. When he stood out on the snowy stoop and the chill clenched in his lungs, only then did he blow out a breath and shake his head.

"What's she doing to your head, man?"

RYAN FLAGGED DOWN Jason as he was driving toward his house. He pulled over and rolled down the truck window.

Ryan leaned out the window of his white SUV. "I'm headed to Marjorie's house for supper. Wasn't sure when you'd be back, but I left the perp's outstanding arrests report on your desk."

"You got a digital file?" Jason asked.

"Sure. I can text it to you now." The man punched a few buttons on his phone, and a minute later Jason's phone rang with a message. "Perp's got some deep stats. Connects him to the Minnesota mafia."

Jason lifted a brow. The Minnesota mafia wasn't an official term; it was what those in the know used because it was easier to say than "the group of half a dozen families who joined with the infamous Duluth gang, the MG12, and were involved all over the state in everything from theft to money laundering, gun running and human trafficking."

And Jason had one of their ilk in his jail?

"I'm going to read up on them after I eat. Apparently Marjorie's husband, Hank, makes a mean roast beef and dumplings," Bay offered, as he was already starting to roll up his window. "It's cold out here! Stay warm, Cash!"

And with that, the man headed south toward the dispatcher's house. Hank did have a talent—Jason never passed up an invite for dumplings.

Now he could only sit there in the idling truck, window still down and cold air gushing in, as he scrolled through the report.

"I'll be," he muttered after he'd read it all. "Mafia. Really?"

The report named their James Smith as one Herve Charley, a Texas native who had no current known residence. Last three reports connected him to the Minnesota mafia. As a hit man. He specialized in close elimination, meaning he preferred to use his hands and not a weapon.

Jason swore. Yvette had managed to avoid harm from a hit man? Possibly the very same hit man who had taken out

Yvette Pearson, a woman who bore a striking resemblance to Yvette LaSalle. What the hell was going on?

The last time he'd been in such proximity to a woman capable of handling her own against a dangerous predator had been in Italy, two years earlier...

Jason lay on the rooftop, peering through the sight of the .338 Lapua sniper rifle. He could hit a target a mile away with ease. Today the target was closer, less than a third of a mile in range. He'd tracked the suspect's movements from the Accademia hotel down the street.

He made a minute adjustment to the rear sight. In forty seconds he would be in position for a kill shot.

It was a windless day, and fluffy off-white clouds dampened the sun. A bird chirped from a nearby tin flue that capped an air vent jutting up from the roof tiles. Perfect conditions to make the shot.

Behind him on the roof he heard Charleze click off on a phone call and say something to him. He ignored her. He was in the zone. No interruptions. She should know better. Thirty-five seconds...

"Jason?"

She had to know he could not chat with her now.

"It's off," she said.

He heard that. He didn't want to hear it. But he processed those two words and grimaced. Twenty-eight seconds...

"Jason Cash, did you hear me? Interpol wants the suspect alive."

Not according to his orders from the CIA. And he didn't answer to anyone but the Central Intelligence Agency. Charleze may have been his liaison here in Verona, Italy, helping him to navigate the ins and outs of this foreign land, but she was not his boss. And she didn't call the shots. Unless they were in bed. And...that had happened, too.

Sixteen seconds. He wouldn't increase pressure on the trigger until the eight-second mark. And he always shot on empty lungs. He began the exhale. The increase in oxygen to his eyes would help his visual acuity.

"Jason." *Her hand slapped over his trigger hand.*

The suspect wobbled out of sight. Jason lost the mark. He reacted, gripping Charleze by the shirt and pulling her down, nose to nose with him. "Do you know what you've done?"

"We want him alive," *she repeated succinctly.*

He squeezed the shirt fabric and shook his head. "We? Who we? The target wasn't yours to have. My orders were to take him out. And now you've spoiled that."

He rolled to his back, knowing he could set up and take another shot, but not without causing a commotion on the ground. He'd chosen the perfect kill shot, a place where the suspect would fall next to a brick building, out of the public's view.

Had she known that all along? Had she been stringing him along? Using him to get to the target?

He hated her for that. Wanted to grip her by the shoulders and force the truth out of her. But he couldn't do that until he got the full story from both his boss and hers.

"You're a sore loser," *Charleze suddenly said. She stood straight, looming over his prone position on the rooftop. The floaty white pants she wore listed against his forearm. The touch was mutinously soft.* "He's one of our own, Cash. The FSB wants him alive to prosecute for crimes in our own country."

"Your own? The FSB is Russian federal security. You're with Interpol."

"Most of the time." *Had red lips ever smiled with such evil relish?* "I do enjoy this vacation in Italy. A breath of *fresh air, if you ask me. Not to mention the sex with an American agent."*

A double agent? Jason blew out a heavy breath. She was a honeypot. "You cost me the hit. He's killed dozens in the US. The CIA had jurisdiction on this case."

"If that's how you want to play it. I've done my job of babysitting you. Ciao!"

She turned on her sexy red heels and strutted across the rooftop to the door, walking inside and closing it behind her.

Babysitting him?

Jason turned to his side and swore.

He'd been played. She'd used him to track the target. She'd probably been relaying his position to her team while he'd been lining up the shot. Idiot! How had he allowed this to happen?

Because he'd slept with her and had let some long blond hair and pouty red lips sway his better judgment.

His boss would have his ass for screwing up this one. Rightfully so. The target had been on a most-wanted list. His death had been imperative.

Now Jason pounded a fist on the steering wheel as he still sat idling on Main Street. He'd never run after Charleze. He'd lain there on the rooftop, stunned, his blood draining from his extremities as he'd processed the shock of it all. He should have gone after her. Should have...

Would have...

Could have...

There hadn't been a thing he could have done to change the outcome after he'd missed the shot. He'd known that then; he knew that now. And he had been punished for that screwup. But he'd always tried not to look at his employment in Frost Falls as punishment but rather, a new opportunity. And it had grown into a job he could be proud of. He loved the people who lived here. Sure, he wished for more real police work. Procedural stuff like the homicide he currently had on his docket. But what else to expect in a small town?

And now they would take that away from him, too.

Chapter Nine

The next morning, Jason hopped out of his truck behind the station house and closed the door. The patrol car, which Alex drove, was parked next to his.

The wind whipped at his face, and he smiled. Despite the ghosts of CIA past that had threatened to haunt him, he'd woken bright and shiny this morning, singing in the shower, and after rereading the report on Charley, happier than a clam that he had him behind bars. He'd nabbed a mafia hit man. That should prove to those who had the inclination to keep an eye on him that he was worthy of a second chance. He seriously wanted to maintain his position as chief of police here in Frost Falls. It was small potatoes, sure, but it was a job he'd made his own.

He'd dressed quickly and headed for the station. The storm had arrived early. He looked forward to it, because in its wake the forecasted two to three feet of snow would invite him to plow through it going well over one hundred on the snowmobile. If he had a clear, open road to race along, he'd push the machine beyond 150 miles per hour. Grippin' it and rippin' it!

His phone jingled with the second reminder tone that played ten minutes after an initial message. Must have missed the first one. Pulling it out from inside his coat, he read the one-word text: Hurry! It was from Alex.

Jason crossed the lot in a race and pulled open the basement door. He called down to the cells, "Alex?"

He descended the stairs quickly. Half a bloody footprint stamped the bottom step. And there before an open cell door lay Alex, sprawled on the floor. His face bled, and he was out cold. His fingers were still wrapped about his cell phone. No sign of the prisoner.

Jason lunged to the floor and shook the officer.

The man roused and groaned, touching what Jason figured was likely a broken nose. It was then Jason noticed the bruise marks about his neck.

Alex coughed and gripped his throat. "Sorry, Cash. I had to open the cell to push in the food. The Moose packaged it up in a box and bag, and I didn't have a plate to slide through the meal slot, so…"

"It's all right, Alex. He tried to choke you?"

Alex nodded. "He was strong. Think I saw my life flash before my eyes. I can't believe I let him get the better of me."

"That's a pattern," Jason said.

"What?"

Jason tapped Alex's throat where the skin was already turning deep purple. "The girl in the ditch. Yvette LaSalle was almost strangled. And now you. They're all connected. Have to be."

"Last night… I asked him how long he'd been in town." Alex gasped and winced, touching his nose tenderly. "You know, trying to tease out more information from him."

"And?"

Alex clutched Jason's sleeve. "He said…since Saturday morning."

"Really?"

"Yes, and then I asked if he'd visited The Moose that night, and he grinned like the Joker. I could feel his evil slide over my skin like some kind of nasty weeds at the bottom of a lake. Creepy."

"He was there," Jason guessed. "I bet he was watching Yvette Pearson, then he followed her."

Wincing and easing his fingers over his neck, Alex asked, "How long have I been out?"

"The text rang through ten minutes ago. I only just noticed it. I gotta get out there now. Pick up his trail. I'll call Marjorie and have her come over to fix you up!"

Dialing Yvette's number while he stomped up the stairs, out around the side of the building and into the station, Jason swore when his call went to messages. He left a quick one: Lock your doors. Don't answer any knocks unless it's me.

He shoved the phone in his pocket, realizing that had been cryptic and would freak out a person. He'd not take more than a few minutes here before heading out to pick up the suspect's trail. He dialed Marjorie and told her he'd found Alex in bad shape. She could be over in less than five minutes, because she was pulling out her laundry at Olson's Oasis.

A few minutes later, Marjorie stomped into the station house and set a laundry basket aside on the floor.

"Marjorie, I need you to put out an APB on the suspect Herve Charley. Using the false name James Smith. Put it out across the Boundary Waters, St. Louis County and the rest of the state. The BCA hasn't reported in yet this morning. Give Bay a call and ring Robert Lane to come in and give us backup."

The county frequently spread their law enforcement employees from town to town when help was needed. Small towns like Frost Falls generally never required more than two at any given time. But Jason had a potential murderer on the loose, and with Alex injured, he couldn't do this himself. Nor would he want to risk screwing up the case because he was too proud to ask for help.

"Check your messages!" Marjorie said as he paced his office.

"Will do. I'm heading out to take a quick run through town, but—" He knew the suspect could only be moving in one direction. "On second thought, I'm headed for the Birch Bower cabin to check on Yvette."

"The dead woman?"

"No, Miss LaSalle. The French chick renting the Birch Bower cabin."

"Oh, right. He attacked her yesterday."

"And he might be going back for a second attempt."

"Take the four-by-four with the snow chains on the wheels," Marjorie offered.

"Nope. The cat will get me there faster, and if the snow drifts, I'll have to dig the truck out. Won't have to do that with the snowmobile."

Marjorie sighed. "Fine. But take one minute to listen to your messages before you leave. There's a weird one on there from Interpol asking about Emily."

"Emily?"

"Something like that. Just listen to it."

Jason eyed the blinking red light on the desk phone, indicating he had a message. She had told him to listen to his messages yesterday, but he'd gotten distracted. A weird one?

He pushed the button on the phone and listened to the male voice, which had a French accent similar to Yvette's.

"I am Jacques Patron, assistant director with Interpol in Lyon, France. This is urgent. My employee Amelie Desauliniers is staying in your town. I've been unable to reach her. She is in danger. You must—"

A crash sounded in the background on the phone line. Jason gripped the edge of the desk.

"Protect her!" shouted over the phone.

The next sound was too familiar to Jason. A gun fired. And then an abrupt shuffle was followed by static.

Had the caller just been shot? Not *just*. This message had been on his phone for over a day. Jason winced. What the hell?

Jason called out, "Marjorie, when you're finished nursing Alex, I need you to trace the call that was on my messages. I think it's recorded another murder."

"*Uff da*, are you serious? I thought it sounded odd. And who is Emily?"

"Amelie. And I don't know."

Jason rubbed his jaw. This new development only added to the mystery. He needed to call Interpol, verify that the caller was indeed who he said he was and then find out if he were dead or alive. He'd asked about Amelie? An employee of his.

He had a foreign spy hiding out in Frost Falls?

And there was a strange Frenchwoman staying out at the Birch Bower cabin who seemed oddly capable of defending herself and yet protective of personal details.

Could Yvette LaSalle be undercover? Using a different name? Or was there another Frenchwoman hiding out in the town?

"I have to get out there." Jason checked the Glock holstered at his hip with a clasp over the solid shape, then zipped up his coat. "Sorry you had to come in when you should be home with Hank preparing to ride out the storm. Call me when you've got a trace on that call. And…have Bay call Interpol and verify a Jacques Patron is assistant director."

"Sure thing, boss." She bent to scribble that information on a piece of paper. "You check in with me once you're out at the Birch Bower place. I don't want to learn you've gotten stuck in a snowbank."

"You know I'm smarter than that!" Jason pulled the door shut behind him. The wind blasted him so fiercely, he took a step back to counter his sudden loss of balance.

Straddling the snowmobile, he fired it up. Pulling on the helmet stopped the pricks of icy snow crystals from lashing at his eyes and face. The storm had picked up. Soon enough, the winds would be vertical. The music blasted inside his helmet, and he turned it off. He wanted to hear when he got a call from dispatch.

Or if he got a plea-for-help call from Yvette.

Pulling up to the gas station, Jason ran out and into the store. He'd had the SUV towed after Alex had given it a once-over, finding no evidence. It was in a Duluth impound lot by now. And of course, it was stolen, belonging to a man he'd yet to learn was safe or even alive.

"Any new rentals this morning, Rusty?"

The old man shook his head. He had a coat on and keys in hand. He stood up straighter at the sight of Jason's urgency. "What's up, Cash?"

"Just following a lead."

"Did that foreigner take off with my rental?"

"If you consider Texas foreign, I suppose so. I found it out near the Birch Bower cabin. It's been impounded as evidence."

"Ah, shoot."

"Don't worry. You'll have it back in a month. You haven't seen that man in the last half hour, have you? Looking for another rental? Walking the streets?"

"Nope, and I pay close attention to what's going on in this little town. You know all I have to do during the day is sit and stare out at everything."

"I do know that. But you're headed home now?"

"No one needs gasoline during a storm."

"And if they do, they can help themselves," Jason said of the station owner's generosity at allowing customers to pay him the next day if they ever needed a fill-up at odd hours. "Give me a ring if you see him on your way home. Deal?"

Rusty nodded. "Sounds like you've got something exciting going on."

"Nothing I can't handle. Talk to you later, Rusty."

Jason got back on his snowmobile and turned on the ignition. Smith, aka Herve Charley, could have fled town. But without killing his target? Didn't sound like a reliable hit man. He must be lying low. That's what Jason would do if he were in the man's shoes.

That message from Jacques Patron bugged the hell out of him. It almost felt…staged. But he'd heard the gunshot. Or had he?

Jason tugged out his cell phone. Bay would have contacts in the FBI. They might be able to get more from Interpol, and quicker, than a simple small-town police chief.

The wind whipped blinding snow through the open cabin door as Amelie welcomed Jason Cash inside. He stomped his boots and slapped his gloved hands together. That was followed by a short jump, which successfully released most of the snow from his head, shoulders and boots to the door mat.

Closing the door behind him, he offered her a rosy-cheeked smile, but concern flickered in his green eyes. "You okay?"

"Yes. Two visits in as many days. A girl could only get so lucky." And maybe she'd been wrong earlier to think he was suspicious of her. "Why did you brave the storm to come out here?"

"Didn't you get my message?"

"No, my phone is dead. Was just going to charge it when you knocked on the door. The electricity keeps flickering on and off. I suspect it'll be a cold, dark day." She noticed his tense jaw. "What's going on, Jason? Now you're frightening me."

"Sorry, didn't mean to. You're safe. That's what matters." He glanced out the window, where only a sheet of white could be seen. "Visibility on the main roads is already less than zero, but if a guy knows where he's headed, he can make it a few miles out here. As for the electricity, you're probably right to suspect it could cut out on you. You should start a fire in the hearth."

"I'd love to, but the wood out back is frozen. I was going to head out with an ax, but it's not that difficult for a girl to talk herself out of hard labor."

He seemed like he had something else to say, but he only clenched his jaw. "I'll bring in some wood," he said after a moment. "Safety precautions first." He slapped his palms together. "I'll head around back and—where's the back door?"

She pointed across the living room.

"I'll bring the wood to that door. Uh…you might want to gather some candles and check if there's a radio as well. With predicted snowfall of twenty-four inches, you're going to get snowed in for sure," he said as he stomped across the living room to the back exit.

He left, slamming the door shut, which whisked in a mist of icy crystals that shivered across Amelie's face. The wind howled and whipped wickedly outside. She could barely make out the man's silhouette as he walked by the back window. His black snow gear was obliterated by the whisks of wind and snow. Kind of him to bring in some wood. And much appreciated.

He had been worried about her? That went beyond nice. That was plain sweet. But also, a policeman doing his job. She'd been attacked. She appreciated having a hearty, handsome man show up when she felt most vulnerable.

Back in the kitchen, Amelie plugged her cell phone in to recharge. With hope, there could be a message on it from Jacques Patron.

Chapter Ten

Amelie met Jason at the back door after he'd made four trips and had deposited some surprisingly dry logs in the iron fire dogs designed to hold half a cord of wood. It was already growing dark outside, and with the visibility so low, the sky was fuggy and gray.

Now he pulled off his outer gear and she hung his hat, gloves and scarf on a hook by the front door. He'd brought in a palpable chill, but it was tinged with his cologne, which was a mix of pine and spice. Maybe it was his natural scent? She could breathe him in all day.

"I've water on the stove for hot chocolate, then I'll start the fire," she said.

"You take care of the treats. I got the fire situation under control. Looks like there's some of those handy fire starters on the mantel." He crossed the room and placed a few logs in the hearth.

Checking that the water wasn't yet boiling, Amelie glanced at her phone, charging on the little stand next to the toaster. "You said you'd left me a message?"

"No need to check it," he called from before the fireplace. He knelt, clicking the lighter until the starter he held took to flame. He nestled it within the logs, holding it there until the wood started to smolder. When satisfied he'd gotten a flame going, he stood. "I called because…"

She wandered over, gesturing he take a seat on the couch while they waited for their respective projects to heat up.

Jason settled onto the old yellow-and-green-checked couch and sighed. "The prisoner escaped. Tried to strangle Alex when he was serving him breakfast and took off. That's why I headed out here. To make sure you were safe. After cruising around town and not finding any trace of him, I suspect the guy has holed up somewhere. That's a good thing. Maybe. He could be inactive until the storm passes."

"He tried to strangle an officer?" Amelie clamped her fingers about her neck. She had faint bruises from the attack, which was why she'd put on a turtleneck this morning. "You think I'm in danger? Again?"

"The man's on the loose, Yvette. You were lucky that I arrived in time yesterday."

She nodded and glanced to the desk where she'd been writing out her pros and cons. Another con? Being pursued by a relentless killer.

A log in the fireplace snapped and took to a glowing yellow blaze. The heat wasn't yet palpable, and the cozy scene didn't settle her nerves. Amelie pulled a blanket folded over the back of the couch about her shoulders.

"If he was intent on harming you, or ending your life, I have to believe he won't leave until the job is done." Jason glanced to her. "Sorry. Shouldn't have said it like that. But I won't lie to you."

"Of course not. I need to know the truth." She tugged the blanket tighter around her shoulders.

"And then there's the phone call from Interpol," Jason said.

She sat upright. She hadn't told him she worked for Interpol. Unless Jason had talked to Jacques Patron? Had the assistant director filled him in? Could she come clean to Jason?

The police chief tilted his head and eyed her fiercely. Amelie felt as though he were trying to read her, to look inside and divine her truth. Truths she had been trained to protect at all costs. He knew something. He must.

"Jacques Patron," he said. "From Interpol." He rubbed his hands together, blew into them, then shot her another delving look. It felt like a blade stabbing at her throat. "Are you a spy?"

"No!" And then she said more quietly, "Yes. I'm not sure. Maybe?"

Did the man have a thing about spies? He wasn't making a point of being open-minded, at least not with his actions. Spies weren't all evil and double-crossing.

"Why would you guess at something like that?" she asked.

"Maybe? Seriously?" He rubbed his jaw with both palms. A sigh had never sounded more exasperated. "How can you not know if you're a spy? It's time you let me ask you some questions."

"What did Jacques tell you, exactly?"

He compressed his lips and nodded. "I get it. Not going to spill the details. Just like a spy."

"I'm not a spy, Jason. I mean…"

"Listen, Yvette—or is it Amelie?—this is serious. And I need your help. Before I met you in The Moose, I'd just come from a crime scene. Dead body of a young woman found in the ditch. Homicide. Ligature marks around her neck. She had long dark hair, and I'd place her at about your age. And…we got an ID on her. Her first name was Yvette."

"That's…"

"Not a crazy coincidence. We have more French Canadians up in our parts than in the lower region of Minnesota. If you're in the business, you know this is all tied together. Or you have to suspect as much."

"But that would mean—" Amelie swallowed. "The

man who attacked me killed an innocent woman because he thought…she was me? What about her family? Oh my goodness."

"I don't normally divulge details of an ongoing investigation to citizens, but it seems like you are involved in some way. And the call from Interpol really threw me for a loop. What is going on? Is your name Yvette or Amelie?"

"I…" Jacques had used her real name. That was the only way the police chief could know such a thing. Unless he'd had her checked out—no. Yvette LaSalle, aspiring photographer, was a hastily created cover that only she and Jacques knew about.

"He specifically asked for Amelie?" she asked carefully.

"Yes. Amelie Des—something or other. He was speaking quickly. Listen, I know something is up with you. You haven't felt right to me since I met you in The Moose. If you're on some kind of a mission—"

"I'm not. I promise."

"Then why do I have a dead body sitting in the Duluth morgue? And an escaped strangler who may or may not be pursuing any woman named Yvette?"

Why, indeed. If someone had truly discovered she had been hiding out here in Minnesota, would they have actually gone after the wrong Yvette? That would make for a very inept hit man.

And yet, someone was after her. She couldn't ignore that fact.

An innocent woman had been murdered. And the killer was now on the loose. She could tell Jason some of her truth. She had to. "I'm no longer a field operative."

He lifted a brow.

"I was a field agent for Interpol for six months."

Jason nodded and clasped his hands before his nose. Thinking. Deciding whether he could trust her? He could. The question was, could she trust him?

"Why didn't Jacques call me?" she asked. "I've been waiting to hear from him."

"The message said he wasn't able to get in touch with you. Amelie. Is that your real name?"

She nodded. "That's strange. The burner phone Jacques gave me—" She stopped before it was too late.

But it already was.

"There's only one reason a person has need for a burner phone, Yvette. Amelie."

"Actually, there are many reasons for any person to want to keep a phone not connected to a network."

He gave her another look of exasperation.

"You're with law enforcement, Jason. You know I can't tell you things."

"If you were on an active case, I might accept that excuse. *Are* you on a case?"

She shook her head.

"But you're not telling me something because…? Do you know why that attacker was after you? Why he wanted you dead? And why would your boss call and beg me to protect you, the call ending in the sound of a gun firing?"

"A gun? What happened? Is Jacques all right? What's going on?"

"You tell me. All I know is the man pleaded with me to protect Amelie, who he said was an employee of his, and then I heard a gunshot and a struggle before the connection went staticky. Marjorie is tracing the call, but I'm going to guess you can give me a direct number."

"He's assistant director at the Lyon office of Interpol. Of course you can get that number. I tried to call Jacques on his personal line earlier, and it went to message. Again."

She caught her forehead against her palm and exhaled. Her world had just tilted. Again. And this time she wasn't sure how to right things herself. She had to tell Jason her story. It was the right thing to do. Especially if she wanted help from law enforcement.

"I am supposed to be dark," she said. "No contact. Wait for Jacques to call me. The last time I spoke to him was on the evening that I hopped a flight to the US. And now such a strange call to you." She stroked her throat and swallowed roughly. "I am in danger, Jason. For something I know."

"Yeah?" He lifted his chin. His gaze was not soft or reassuring. He wasn't willing to give her the benefit of the doubt. She didn't blame him for his caution. Certainly, she would be cautious in this situation. "And what is it you know, Yvette?"

"That's the problem. I have the information in my head, but I don't know what it means."

She exhaled, her shoulders dropping. In the two weeks she had been hiding out here in the States, she'd gone through a list of those people she trusted, who might help her, if she needed to reach out. That list had included only Jacques Patron. She had no close family. And her few friends were all clueless as to her real job.

If she was going to survive, she needed to give Jason as much information as she was able. And then hope that she could trust him.

"It's why I'm here. My boss sent me into hiding after I told him about a strange list I read. I work in information systems and technology. Data tech, for short. We receive coded documents and dossiers all the time. The information is sorted and filed. But the last email I took in was something I'd not seen before. I thought Jacques should know about it. I didn't print it out—there wasn't time to—but I had skimmed it as I was wondering what it was about. I went to his office to tell him."

"And?"

"He asked me to write it out for him, which I did. After he glanced at it, he expressed worry that what I had seen would attract danger to me. He immediately sent me home. Then, in the middle of the night, I got a call from him telling me to be at the airport in two hours. I grabbed my bug-out kit, was given a fake passport for Yvette LaSalle and hopped in a cab, headed to Lyon-Saint Exupéry airport, and…here I am. Still waiting."

Jason swiped a hand over his chin. "You know something but you don't know what it is?"

"Exactly."

"But you just said he asked you to write it out for him. You remembered the whole list you'd read on the computer screen? I don't get it."

"I have a photographic memory for certain instances, like when reading. I never forget a single sentence in any book I read. And documents and lists that I've read? I can recall them perfectly. Coded lists? I may not know what they mean, but I retain all the data like a computer. Even uncoded items may baffle me if I don't know the original context."

Amelie pressed her palms together before her lips and closed her eyes. Her worst nightmare was coming true. "Jason, I've got a list in my head, and someone wants to kill me for it."

Chapter Eleven

Amelie rushed into the kitchen to remove the boiling kettle from the stove. She busied herself with pouring water into mugs to make hot chocolate. But more so, she simply didn't want to face Jason's questions. Because he would have a lot. His gaping expression after she'd confessed what was going on had spoken volumes.

But she couldn't avoid those questions. No smart agent would withhold information that could help to solve a case.

Placing the mugs on a tray, she turned to find Jason standing right behind her. She hadn't heard him approach and was so startled she sucked in a breath. He steadied her hold on the tray as she felt it slip. His warm palm slipped over the back of her hand, and all her focus went to that touch.

"Sorry," he offered. "Didn't mean to pull a sneak on you."

Were his green eyes freckled with brown? Mercy. Why did he have to be such an attractive man?

"So what do I call you now? Amelie or Yvette?"

Just when she was getting used to the cover name... "Amelie is my name. But I wonder if keeping the cover name might be easier when we're around others."

He shook his head. "Woman, you are full of surprises today. Let me get this for you, Yvette." He pronounced it purposefully. "Smells great. I love hot chocolate." He carried the tray over to the couch.

While she pressed a palm over her thundering heart. Chocolate. Handsome man. Sneak charm attacks? A tantalizing touch? Nothing about this day was going to be easy.

Over on the couch, Jason patted the seat beside him. Mug in hand, he put up his feet, clothed in striped wool socks, on the coffee table and sipped.

"I don't know if I can do this with you being Mr. Casual," she blurted out.

He sat upright. "Sorry, thought I was making you comfortable. Making it easier to talk and tell me your deepest, darkest secrets."

"That's a covert tactic."

"You know that from experience?" His tone was still calm, but that question had been edged with a sharp interrogative skill.

"I'm not a spy, Chief Cash. Not anymore."

Amelie sat a few feet away from him on the couch and grabbed the other mug from the tray. It was too sweet, but it was warm, and she needed that right now. The heat from the fireplace didn't quite reach the couch, for the logs were still kindling to flame.

"Please, call me Jason. And I'll stick with Yvette, since I agree that would be wisest. For now."

"I'm good with that."

"And, uh…with the snow blowing like a banshee, I think I'm stuck here for a while, so I hope you don't mind me getting comfy. And asking you the hard questions."

Amelie nodded. "Snowed in with…" She thought, *a sexy cop*, but said "…the local law enforcement. I'm feeling very safe, indeed. As for the hard questions?"

Time to come clean. With hope, she'd gain an ally and not be put on his suspects list.

After a sip to fortify her courage, she started, "Like I

said, I'm a data technician. For Interpol. I sit in an office and type reports and do field research. Of course, my field is bits and bytes. It's something I excelled at in college but had set aside for the excitement and adventure of being a field operative. Until that position no longer fit me. Anyway, I was learning to program and hack all sorts of electronic and digital devices from a distance."

"You a code breaker?"

"Not as accomplished at that skill as I'd like. But with more training, it could happen."

And was that what she wanted to happen? Her pros and cons list was weighted to one side. And no matter how many ways she found to list "using my intellect" and "keeping up with technology" as pros, the heaviest side remained the cons.

Jason cast her a quirk of brow and a gaze that said she wasn't going to get away with any lies. "And does what's up have to do with something related to an Interpol case? You said something about having information but not knowing what that was."

"Exactly. But I don't know if it's an active investigation. Is it covert? Need to know? What's going on in my absence? I haven't been informed beyond 'keep your head down and we'll call you.' I thought the document I viewed was random business details. It looked like an invoice. My boss didn't clarify anything about it."

"So less than twelve hours after you brought it to his attention, he asked you to assume a new identity, leave the country and...you just did?"

"I trust him."

"Why is that?"

Amelie narrowed her gaze on the man. Was he intimating something deeper existed between her and Jacques? There wasn't anything between them. Not that she hadn't had the occasional fantasy. The man wasn't married, but she knew he had a model girlfriend who liked to be treated as if a queen.

"Jacques Patron had been on the same training team as my father decades ago. My dad always had good things to say about Jacques. That he was kind and had the other guy's back. I've known Director Patron over the years, but only from answering phone calls to my parents, and once I met him at a holiday party. After my hire at Interpol, I immediately trusted him, simply knowing how much my father trusted him.

"Jacques was the one I went to when I realized I couldn't cut it in the field. He didn't judge. Instead, he helped to reassign me. And when he learned about my memory, he started using me for special assignments."

"Such as?"

"I can't tell you about them."

"Right. Need to know and all that secure state secrets stuff."

"Exactly. But I can explain how my brain works. My current position sees me sitting before the computer, sometimes mindlessly typing in lists or code, or whatever comes across my desk. I don't process it in the moment, but trust me, it all gets retained here." She tapped her skull. "My ability sounds weird to others, but I've known nothing else since childhood."

"Like a kid who has colorblindness?" Jason asked. "He never knows he sees the world differently until someone points it out to him?"

"Exactly. I retain it all. And yet, not all. It's termed eidetic memory, or photographic memory. The eidetic term refers more to recalling memories like a photograph, and the photographic memory is more related to lists, text and detailed information. What is weird is that sometimes I'll get to the grocery store and realize I've forgotten what I'd gone there for. I don't remember short lists, appointments or even conversations. It's only long lists and random coded data that seem to lodge in my brain. Book text, as well. But if I could ever remember what day my yoga class was scheduled, my instructor would stop giving me the side eye when I wander in on the wrong day."

Jason smirked. "Yoga and covert operations. You're a very interesting woman."

She'd take the compliment, but only because she needed it right now. Anything to make her feel safe and accepted by the one man who could very well make her life miserable. Because if he wanted to, he could turn the tables and investigate her, insist she tell him the things she didn't dare reveal. Or force her.

Jason took another sip of the hot chocolate, then asked, "You've been in Minnesota how long?"

"Two weeks."

"Witness protection?"

"We call it going dark."

"So still working for Interpol, but for all intents you're on an extended vacation."

"Exactly. Let me explain from the beginning. I originally trained as a field operative."

"A spy." He hung his head, and his grimace was obvious.

"Yes, you can call me a spy." Because she did like the term. Something strangely romantic about it. "Former spy, that is. My parents both worked for their respective governments. My father was Interpol and my mother, well…"

Telling him that sad tale wouldn't be easy, and it wasn't necessary to this case. If she were to keep the tears to a minimum, all information about her mother had to stay in the past. Where it belonged.

"The desire to serve my country is in my blood," Amelie continued. "And I've told you about Jacques Patron, and how I grew up trusting him. But after a few months of fieldwork, it grew apparent to me that I would never be able to take another person's life if it became necessary. I couldn't do what I'd been trained to do. Sure, I can use martial arts to defend myself and fend off an attacker. Though I was a bit rusty yesterday. Anyway, I can track and follow, surveil, assess a dangerous situation, but…" Amelie bowed her head and exhaled. "I couldn't bring myself to pull the trigger at a moment when it was necessary to stop a suspect. I choked. Aiming at a human body is a lot different than shooting at targets and ballistic dummies."

"That it is," Jason agreed. "You didn't think, during training, that your job might lead you to life-or-death situations?"

"Of course. But training and real-life experience are vastly different. It's hard to explain. And I'd been surrounded by other recruits eager to prove themselves. I fell into the tough-girl mien. But that has never been me. Or at least, I thought it *could* be me. You know, grow up and take after your parents. Show them you've got the same grit in your blood." She sighed heavily. "I learned differently."

"You handled the attack from Smith like a pro. Make that Herve Charley."

"That's the perp's real name? Where is he from? Did you get a rap sheet on him? Who is he?"

"I'm asking the questions here, remember? What I just told you is what I know so far. And you were telling me how a spy came to sit behind a desk typing in coded lists."

"Sorry, it's natural to want to know everything I can about the guy who tried to kill me."

"I'll grant you that. Go on."

"Fine. After I realized I couldn't pull the trigger, I went to Jacques Patron. They'd spent a lot of money training me. I was disappointed in myself. In an effort to maintain some dignity and save face, I blurted out that I had a photographic memory."

"That didn't come up in training?"

"It really is something innate to me. I don't bring it up because…" She shrugged. "It's my normal. And the skill may have helped with maps and topography and following long, detailed instructions in training, but for the real world, action, think-on-your-feet stuff, it doesn't make much of a difference. But Patron was intrigued at my, as he termed it, 'superpower,' so he put away the dismissal form and assigned me to the tech department. He tested me with a few assignments. I'd receive a classified document that I was to memorize and then later repeat when it was needed. I call it parlor tricks. But Patron was impressed."

"Sounds a little underhanded to me, but go on."

She'd never call it underhanded, but there had been times Amelie had wondered if Jacques was using her for reasons that no one else in Interpol was aware. Sort of his secret data weapon. And she'd not questioned him. In fact, it had made her feel more useful, like a part of the team again.

"One day an unconfirmed email arrived in my box. All incoming documents go through a secure server and are verified with a four-point internal security check. No one can hack into the system. And hacking *out* is even harder. I initially thought it was a regular invoice that got misdirected. I see them once in a while. Agent reports. Expense summaries. Purchase orders. I forward them to Accounts. It didn't give me pause. Until I started reading the data. Dates, dollar amounts, locations. And that mysterious fourth column. I'd never gotten something like that delivered by email. I was going to transfer it to Accounts when I noticed the sender's email was untraceable. That put up an alert. And…for some reason, I read it. Just sat there and read each line. It only took ten minutes."

"You went against protocol?"

"Yes, and no. It hadn't specifically been assigned to me, but Jacques was aware I retain all the information I see. Because it was an odd thing, I knew I had to tell him about it. I called him, and when I was going to transfer the email to him, it blew up."

"Blew up?"

"It was on a timer. It had been set to destruct so many minutes after an open reference was received, and then it did the cyber version of self-destructing. The weird thing was, after I'd written out the list at his request, Jacques merely glanced at it and seemed to know what it was for. I mean, he didn't state that specifically—it was a feeling I got at the time. He suggested I resume work, not worry about it. But he called me twenty minutes later and told me to go home for the day."

"You didn't think that was strange?"

"A little, but he didn't sound upset. And, as I've said, I trust him. I knew whatever I had seen was out of the ordinary."

"The guy must have known it was sensitive information."

"He did, but he didn't tell me what it was. He burned the list I'd written for him."

"So he just burned it? Never to be seen again?"

"He knew that the information could be accessed anytime because it's always in my head, no matter if I write it out or not."

"You must have a crowd in your brain."

She smiled. "I sometimes wonder about that, and then I realize the reason I can't remember to pick up milk along with cereal at the grocery is because my brain is crammed with too much other stuff. Ninety percent of which means nothing to me."

"You sure you don't have some international secrets locked away up there?"

"Well." Amelie set down the mug and tucked her palms between her legs. She faced Jason on the couch. "It is always a possibility."

His lift of brow told her he was intrigued.

"That night," she continued, "Jacques called me at home. It was after midnight. He'd booked a flight for me that left in two hours. He'd also given me a new passport and a new identity. He said the data I had in my head was so sensitive he feared for my safety and that I needed to go into hiding for a few weeks."

Jason whistled. "You gotta love the international spy game. But you've been trained to bug out?"

"Of course. I had a bugout bag packed for such an occasion. It was scary, but at the same time, I've been trained to handle situations like that. I took a cab to the airport. Nine hours later I arrived in Minneapolis, then a car drove me four hours to…this strange land that reminds me half of the tundra and half of a bizarre movie I've seen where the bad guy gets stuffed in a wood chipper."

"I love that movie." Jason cleared his throat. "Ahem. You said you've been here two weeks."

Amelie sighed and nodded. "I'm waiting for the all's clear from my boss."

"The same boss who called me and…" He winced.

She had forgotten about that strange message he'd received. Ending with the sound of a gunshot? Was Jacques okay?

"It baffles me," Jason said, "if a professional was sent after you, that he could make such a stupid mistake. To kill the wrong person?"

"He had to have asked her name." Amelie worked it out. "Might have looked her up. Followed her."

"But then he would have had her last name and should have known she wasn't the right target. And she's from a suburb north of Minneapolis. Was visiting friends here in town. Was in The Moose Saturday night, partying."

"He tracked her from Minneapolis?"

"I don't think so. I'm guessing he knew to look for his

target in Frost Falls and, well—he found the wrong Yvette. That woman was in the right place at the wrong time."

Amelie started to work it out. The only person who knew she'd been staying here as Yvette LaSalle was her boss, and now Jason. So if she had been targeted because of her assumed name…

"Is your boss the only one who knows you're here?" he asked.

She met his pointed gaze with a gape. "But Jacques would never…" No, she trusted him. He'd given her a second chance when he didn't have to. "On the other hand, someone purchased my plane ticket. Made arrangements for the car when I arrived here. Jacques can't be the only one aware of my location, or that I'm hiding under an assumed name. And you know the spy trade. If someone wants to find another, they will."

"True. But there's something I'm missing. If you can help me to understand what it is you know that someone would kill for, that would help."

"That's the thing. The only way I can learn what I have in my head is to write it out. It's how the memory process works. I can't jump into the middle of a list of data. I need to write it from beginning to end."

"You didn't think to write it out when you got here?"

She shrugged. "I've been settling in, adjusting to this cold place, and what good would it have done? I've looked at it before. I didn't know what it was then—why would I know now?"

"I'd like to take a look at it. I'll keep the fire stoked if you will put your pen to paper. Are you willing to give it a go?"

She nodded.

"Sounds like a plan. I'll check in with Marjorie. See if she's gotten a trace on the call from your boss. I'm going to run out and park the snowmobile in your garage. With the way the wind is blowing, if I leave it out, the snow might drift over the top of it."

"Thank you, Chief—er, Jason. I know this is the last thing you want to do on a stormy day."

"Actually, this is what I most want to do. You're in danger? I want to protect you. It's my job. But also..." He winked. "I'd hate to see the prettiest woman in Frost Falls get harassed by a hired killer."

"Harassed?" Amelie laughed at that, only because it was so assuredly not what had happened to her. The man had meant business. She was lucky to be alive.

"I know." He stood. "But I'm trying to not be so direct."

"Please. Be direct. I'm a big girl. I can handle the truth. You want to protect me from someone who has me on his hit list? I'm glad to have you here. I'll even make you soup for supper."

"My night gets better and better."

"Don't get too excited. It's from a can. I just have to heat it up."

"If it's hot, I get excited." He winked and then got up to stoke the fire.

And Amelie felt that fire transfer to her chest, where her heartbeats fluttered. She'd opened herself to him, and he hadn't accused her. She could trust him. And she could drop her brave front and allow a bit of the damsel to emerge. Because, truthfully, it was getting harder to keep up the courageous facade. She was being hunted by a killer.

But now her protector was close.

Chapter Twelve

Jason loved a good blizzard. Snow slashing at his cheeks, eyelids and nose. Veins chilled to the bone. Visibility reduced to zero. Good times. But only when he was out having some fun on the snowmobile. When it arrived while he was in the thick of a homicide investigation, he preferred calmer weather.

He secured his snowmobile in the garage out behind the cabin beside the older Arctic Cat model the owners provided for their guests. With a tug of his scarf to tighten it about his neck, he stepped outside. The wind nearly pushed him over. Or it might have been the ice patch in front of the garage door. Steadying himself, he leaped up two feet onto the snow berm that had formed behind the house. There was already a solid foot of powder on the ground, but the wind would lick it up in dunes that could get as high as his hip if the storm lasted through the night.

Boots crunching over the snow, he wandered around behind the log cabin. The snow glittered like diamonds. The smooth surface hadn't had a chance to take on rabbit tracks. Those critters were too smart to be out on a night like this.

And with hope, so would a killer.

On the other hand, if someone did have it in mind to return and finish the botched hit job, Jason wanted it to happen when he was here. Yvette needed protection. And that was something he could do. Even as his better judgment warned him—another beautiful female spy in his life? The last one had changed his life forever, leaving him humiliated and scrambling to prove himself.

This new woman appealed to him both physically and by prodding his innate need to protect. But could he trust her? Her name wasn't even Yvette. And did she know more than she was letting on? How could she *not* know what she had in her head? He wanted to trust her, but it was never that easy. She had been trained in evasive tactics. A man should never let down his guard.

His cell phone rang, and he stepped around to the side of the cabin where the generator was protected from the wind.

"This is Robert Lane. Your dispatcher wanted me to check in with you."

"Hey, Robert, good to have you in town." Robert had helped out last fall when Alex had been sick for a week. The man preferred to move around St. Louis County, filling in, rather than settling in one station. He was good folk. "I'm currently at the Birch Bower cabin east of town," Jason said. "The renter was the escaped perp's target. I want to stay close. Did Marjorie get a trace on the call?"

"Not yet, but I've been looking over your escaped perp's stats," Randy said. "You've got an interesting one, Cash. Looks like a pro hit man. You say you managed to intercept his attack on a woman?"

"Yes. Actually, the victim held her own until I arrived. Surprises me if his stats are so deep," Jason said. "A hit man right here in Frost Falls. Something's not right with this situation. You talk to Ryan Bay?"

"Yes, and he was in contact with Interpol."

"Did they provide information on Jacques Patron?"

"Gave Bay the runaround. Said the assistant director would contact him soon."

"Seriously?" Jason toed the snowy base of the generator. "So he's alive?"

"Interpol wouldn't say anything more than they'd get back to him. Bay was swearing about it."

"Strange. Well. Okay. I'll, uh…" Think on that one when he was inside and warm.

"I'll hold the fort here in town," Robert offered. "Most of the county roads are closed. I don't think anyone will be cruising around tonight, not even on a snowmobile. I might catch a few z's later in the basement. You still got those cozy blankets down there?"

"You betcha. Thanks, Robert. Call me at any hour."

"Will do."

Jason hung up and leaned against the cabin wall. The flurry of snow whipping about darkened the air.

"A hit man," he muttered.

Yvette's boss had sent her out of the country until the heat blew over. Jacques Patron had then called the local police to warn them that his employee was in danger—and, in the process, he'd been silenced.

Or had he? Interpol said Patron would call them soon. Why hadn't they patched him through to Bay when he'd called?

That weird instinctual creep at the back of his neck wouldn't allow Jason to dismiss the boss as dead. Did Interpol really know where he was? Could the call to the station have been staged? To make it seem as though Patron was out of the picture? Because…he was involved and wanted to erase his tracks?

"I need to know what Yvette knows."

But she didn't know what she knew.

"This is crazy."

As THE WIND pummeled the windows in a fierce symphony, Amelie was happy to be spooning up hearty beef-and-vegetable soup with the sexy police chief. Inside, protected from the bitter chill. She hadn't had company since moving here. And despite the reason for his presence, she found herself enjoying simple conversation about snowshoeing on bright winter days.

"The cabin does keep a good stock of outdoor gear," she said when Jason asked if she had problems getting a good fit on the snowshoes. "The mudroom is filled with things like snowshoes, boots and helmets, fishing poles, and a strange long drill that I can't figure out."

"Sounds like an ice auger. There's a lake eight miles south from here. Great ice fishing. I believe the cabin even puts up an ice house for its renters to use."

"There might have been something about that in the information packet, but I'm sure I breezed over that detail. I'm not much for fishing for my supper. I'll take a breaded, prepackaged hunk of cod any day. As long as it's not been soaked in lye."

"Oh, lutefisk. I love that stuff."

Amelie gaped at him.

Jason chuckled and nabbed another roll from the plate and dunked it in his soup. "It's an acquired taste."

Dark stubble shadowed his jaw and emphasized the dimples in his cheeks that poked in and out as he chewed. And those green eyes. They were as freckled as the spots dotting the bridge of his nose. They appealed to her on a visceral level. Due to lacking sexual satisfaction of late— well, she was thinking about a few things she'd like to do with those freckles. Starting with touching each one. With her tongue.

"I challenge you to come out on the ice with me someday," he said. "I bet I can make you a fan of ice fishing."

"I do love a good challenge."

"A woman fashioned from the same mettle as myself." He winked at her.

Could she get swept off her feet by a mere wink? Most definitely.

His phone buzzed, and he tugged it out of a pocket to look at it. "Got a dossier from Marjorie earlier. It's on the perp. I want to finish reading it and…we heard from Interpol."

"Yes?" She leaned forward. If Interpol were actively involved now, she need no longer worry about remaining undercover and could very likely return home.

"Ryan Bay spoke to them. Sounded like they were unaware there were any issues with Jacques Patron. Said he'd contact us in a few days."

Amelie let out an exhale. "He's still alive?"

"Well." Jason pushed his empty bowl forward on the table and clasped both hands before him. "You say you can't make contact with him?"

"No."

"But you've left messages?"

She nodded.

"Sounds like he's avoiding you. If he is alive. And why make such a strange call to the station, and make it sound as though he'd been shot? And yet Interpol also thinks he's alive. Something does not add up, Yvette. Amelie."

"Just stick with Yvette."

He winced.

Because it was easier for her to have him use her alias. Less personal. On the other hand, she could really use a confidant. Someone to trust.

"Maybe it's time I checked in with Interpol," she offered. "That should clear things up. But I know Jacques was keeping this situation dark. If he didn't tell anyone…"

"And why wouldn't he?" Jason leaned forward. "Unless

the man is hiding something he doesn't want anyone in Interpol to know about?"

Amelie gaped. A niggle of that idea had occurred to her, but she'd pushed it back, unwilling to believe that Jacques could be dirty. He'd worked so closely with her father. They had been good friends. Jacques Patron would never do a thing to harm her or her family.

"I'll let you think about that one." Jason stood. "Thanks for the meal." He wandered into the living area and plopped down on the couch before the crackling fire.

Amelie caught her chin in hand. She didn't want to think about it. But he was right. Something didn't add up.

Gathering the dishes, she set them in the sink and rinsed them. A glance to her cell phone saw it was fully charged. To pick up the phone and try Jacques one more time?

He wouldn't answer. She instinctively knew that. Which meant she had already fallen to the side of distrust for her boss.

It felt wrong. She had always been loyal to him and Interpol.

"You going to write up that list?" Jason called to her.

The list was the one thing that might hold a clue to Jacques Patron's actions. She'd write it out and let Jason take a look at it. If that didn't spark any clues, then she'd go over Patron's head and call the director.

Amelie settled into the easy chair before the fire with a notebook and pen, but it was difficult not to notice the man sitting so close. He smelled like the wild outdoors. And he sent out crazy, distracting vibrations that she felt sure hummed in her very bones.

Jason looked up from his phone and asked, "You know the name Herve Charley?"

Startled out of her straying thoughts, she shook her head. "No. You said that is the name of the man who attacked me?"

"Yes. He showed me a license that identified him as James Smith. The real James Smith—let's see… Marjorie dug up details on him—has been located in the Duluth hospital. He was attacked, nearly strangled. Has been in a coma for days." Jason whistled. "I'll have to call the investigator for that case ASAP. He'll need to know what's going on here. Anyway, our suspect identifies as a known hit man," he read as he scrolled. "No known address in the past five years. But most recent activity has been noted right here in northern Minnesota. I suspect he might be tied to the Minnesota mafia. You ever hear of them?"

"No. Should I have?"

He shrugged. "Interpol knows things."

"Not everything," she replied with a touch of annoyance. He'd grown distant in demeanor since supper. Of course, the man had a lot on his mind. And police work was first and foremost. And yet, she needed to become an active part of this investigation. And the answers could lie in her placing the list onto the paper in her hands.

"Bunch of families in Minnesota all connected," Jason continued as he scanned his phone. "Involved with a gang out of Duluth. We've got a family living nearby at the edge of the Boundary Waters that's into all kinds of criminal endeavors. Poaching is their favorite."

"Is that even a felony here in the States?"

"Misdemeanor. But they're into a lot of stuff, including assault and transporting stolen goods. Charley has a list of crimes half a mile long, but all minor infractions. Never able to pin the big stuff on him. That's how those guys work. Their lawyers are paid the big bucks."

"So he's a legitimate hit man?" Amelie leaned forward on the chair. "But that's so—"

"Big? Serious? You bet it is. The Minnesota mafia is involved with some European big shots. They handle guns, ammunition, sometimes stolen art. That's common for mafia families."

Unable to focus on what Jason was currently musing over, Amelie raked her fingers through her hair. Because to think about it, why would someone send a hit man after her? For an *invoice*.

She tapped the pen on the blank notebook page. The list she had absently read was so much more. Did she want to know what it really was?

Yes.

Jason scrolled up on his phone. "The Minnesota mafia has strongholds in Marseille, Berlin and Amsterdam. There's your French connection." The man whistled and shook his head. Then he looked at her point-blank. "You sure you know everything that's going on with this forced vacation of yours?"

"Apparently, I know very little. Jacques has all the answers."

"Right. Jacques Patron, assistant director of Interpol, Lyon, France. Marjorie also sent a report on him." He scrolled for a few seconds then swore. "Wi-Fi just gave out. Surprised it lasted that long. Can you put in a call to Interpol for me?"

"I intend to. But if the Wi-Fi is out…"

"Should still get cell service."

He leaned over and placed a hand on her knee. "I need you to be smart and help me as much as you can." His intense gaze pulled her up from a swirl of emotion, and she focused on those mesmerizing freckled green eyes. "You are strong and brave, Yvette. I saw that when I arrived to find you fending off the attacker. But now you need to stay strong and keep a clear head. Can you do that?"

She nodded. Gripping his wrists, she gently pulled his palms away from her face and yet didn't let go of him. He was warm, and despite the crackling fire, she had begun to shiver.

"I can do that," she said. "I just… Interpol's lack of concern could mean many things. One, they know exactly what happened to Jacques Patron, but they are unwilling to divulge that information. Or they were not aware of a problem until your dispatch contacted him and they are looking into it."

"I'm going with number one. Because they sure as hell would have noticed if their assistant director went missing a few days ago."

She nodded, knowing that was the likeliest of the two. But that still didn't answer another question: Was Jacques dead or alive? If he was dead, wouldn't Interpol call her back in? Had Patron kept her leave a secret to the organization? If so, then that added another suspicious notch to his tally. "I don't understand any of this, Jason. I'll contact Interpol. We need to sort out the facts."

"Thank you." He waggled his phone. "But calls might not be possible right now. I just lost cell service. Until it comes back, if we can figure out what you know, that might help."

"I've got the list right here." She tapped her temple. "I'm sure I can get it out and onto paper."

"Great. I'll stoke the fire and you do what you need to do. Once you get that list written, I'm going to need you to talk to me about your work and anything you can think of that led up to you being sent to a remote cabin in the Minnesota Boundary Waters to hide. Deal?"

She clasped the hand he held out, wanting to not let go, to use it as an anchor as she felt the world slip beneath her. But instead Amelie sucked in a breath and gave him another affirmative nod. "Deal."

Chapter Thirteen

Jason wandered down the hallway into the bathroom and splashed his face with water. He needed a shower, but he'd survive until morning. Heading out here during the storm, he'd known the options would be few regarding sleeping arrangements. He probably wouldn't sleep much. If anyone who wanted to harm Yvette managed to brave the storm, then he dared them to. He'd like to stand against someone with such moxie.

Smirking, he tossed the towel into a hamper and shook his head. Had he been craving some action so desperately that he'd mentally invited a hit man to come at him?

A smart man would wish for a quiet night and a clear morning. With Bay holed up in a motel until the storm passed, Jason needed to get out there and search for the escapee. He didn't like the unknown. He preferred to know every player's position on the board. He was the knight protecting the queen. And somewhere out there the rook could still be lurking. He had to be. His mission to take out Yvette had failed. What sort of hit man walked away from an assignment after failure?

Jason had never walked away from failure.

Until he'd been forced to walk away or risk endangering so many more. It sucked that he'd left the CIA under such circumstances. And now being around Yvette, despite the fact she wasn't an active field agent, stirred his blood for just such fieldwork. He had loved the job—working undercover, researching, tracking and surveilling, and finally apprehending and making an arrest. On more than a few occasions, his objective had been to eliminate a target. His sharpshooting skills had not been exercised lately, but he was confident with his aim. Always.

Despite the mark against him, he'd served the CIA well. As he currently did as Frost Falls' chief of police. Yet losing the perp could be counted as a failure. He should have been the one to take Herve Charley in for booking, and then stand guard.

Maybe he wasn't cut out for this sort of police work?

He shook his head. Stupid thinking. He was just distracted, that was it. And the distraction—another beautiful spy—was his key either to solving this case or, once again, to ruining his career.

"IT'S FINISHED," AMELIE SAID. "The list." She nodded over a shoulder while wandering into the kitchen to meet Jason at the fridge. She'd left her pen and notebook sitting on the rug beside the easy chair. "You'll have to look at it."

"I will. You got anything to drink in here?"

"Beer and orange juice."

"Beer will work." He opened the fridge. "Now that you've written it out, do you have any idea what the list is for?"

"Like I said, I initially thought it was an invoice. But who kills for an invoice?"

"Not many, I figure." Jason popped open a beer can and leaned against the counter. "You don't know what it means?"

She shrugged. "It can be any number of things. Invoices would normally go directly to Accounts. So I have to believe it was either sent to the wrong email address or, if it was sent to me purposely—"

"It wasn't sent to a wrong address. It freaked the hell out of your boss enough that he sent you out of the country. Someone sent that to you on purpose. Maybe because they knew your connection to Patron and that you would go to him with it."

She rubbed her arms and gave it some consideration. Why would someone want to get to him and do it through her? "Then why not send it directly to Jacques?"

"When involving someone else can twist the screws a little tighter?" he prompted.

The suspicion in his voice troubled her. She hadn't initially thought to suspect Jacques of any wrongdoing. Yet now, all clues pointed to that very real possibility.

"Can I ask what led you to working for Interpol?" Jason asked. "You said something about your parents working for the agency?"

"My dad was with Interpol. That's how he met my mother."

"She worked for them too?"

"No, she was a spy for the Russian FSB. I know, cliché. Not because she chose to, but because she was desperate to protect her family. Her father had been indebted to the Russian government, and he had some black marks against him that the government used to twist the screws. When he grew ill, my mother stepped in and did what she had to do. Which was whatever the FSB told her to do."

"That's tough. But sounds like it ended well? If they met and—she must have gotten away from the Russian government's control?"

"My father helped make that happen. I wish I could tell you my parents lived happily ever after…" Amelie closed her eyes. Memories of that morning flooded back. Her father had been away on assignment. She had been nine.

"What happened to them? If you can tell me. You don't have to tell me," Jason rushed out.

She didn't want to tell him.

She *did* want to tell him. Anyone. Just to release it from her memory. Amelie had thought she was over the grieving—and she was—but it still hurt to think of her mother. And sometimes blurting it out, whether to a stray cat or a cabdriver who didn't speak her language, seemed to alleviate some of the pain.

"My mother was executed," she spilled out.

Instantly, Jason's hand covered hers. His warm fingers curled about hers, and she reactively curled hers around his. "I'm sorry," he said quietly.

"I was nine," she said. "There was a knock at the door. My mother grabbed me and said I should hide. I started to beg for a reason. What was wrong? She said she had done something bad to help good people. I'll never forget that." She met Jason's gentle gaze. "She did something bad to help good people."

He nodded and bowed his head. He understood. It was a spy's lot in life. But a spy's safety was never ensured, even from those he or she worked for.

"I heard a man enter the house," she said quietly. "They exchanged few words." The accent had been French. But her fright and the strain to try to hear the short conversation had kept Amelie from hearing anything more than syllables and sounds instead of actual words.

"My mother cried out. The front door slammed. I knew whoever had come inside the house had left. I waited for my mother to call out again. I waited so long. Then finally I crept out and found her in a pool of blood. It's all a blur after that. I didn't see my father until two days later. He was on a covert mission, and it took that long for Interpol to contact him. I realize now they could have contacted him at any time. They simply wanted him to complete his mission before giving him the terrible news."

Amelie sighed and pulled her hand from Jason's. She wrapped both arms across her chest. No tears. It was what had happened and it couldn't be changed. There had been a formal investigation, but no suspect had ever been found.

"My father died when I was twenty. It was…alcohol poisoning. He drank himself to death. He couldn't handle my mother leaving his life. I almost wished it had been him in her place that day. He was never the same. Doesn't matter now. They are both gone. And I have accepted that."

Jason hugged her, which startled her, but she melted into the warmth of his embrace and managed a smile. She'd never gotten a reassuring hug following either of her parents' deaths. This was a long time coming. She closed her eyes and just let it happen. To feel his heartbeat against hers. To accept that he cared about her. To allow herself to sniff back a tear.

When after a bit he pulled back to look at her, he asked, "You still wanted to work for the government even after all that?"

"I know how things work in the security agencies. Everything is a big secret. Don't tell. Need to know. I signed on for that at a time…let's say I was still reeling from my father's death. But I walked in, knowing what to expect. And that's why I'm here now."

"Gone dark."

"Exactly."

"I'll keep you safe." He squeezed her hand, and his eyes met hers. "Do you trust me?"

"I do. Thank you for listening to my sorry little story."

"It's not sorry. It's tragic. I wish things could have been better for you, Yvette. Amelie." He kissed the crown of her head. He smelled so good. Warm and just so…there.

"I had a great childhood," she offered. "My parents were

the best. And you know, they were always honest with me. Telling me they worked for an organization that saved others, sometimes, as my mom put it, forcing them to do something bad. I always had a sort of knowing that something could happen to them. Didn't make it any easier to accept. But it was almost not a surprise, if that makes any sense."

Jason blew out a breath. "My parents are both still alive. Simple, humble dairy farmers. Well, my dad used to be a marine until he had to muster out with a bad back. They are both retired now. And happy. I'm thankful for that."

"I bet having a son working law enforcement makes them both proud and nervous."

"I know my mom was pleased when I, uh…left the CIA."

"You were in the CIA?"

"Not anymore. And that makes my mother a very happy woman, because I could never tell her what I was doing, and the not knowing part is hardest. Now that I'm watching over Frost Falls, she's decided that at least the one son isn't in as much danger. My other two brothers. Well."

"What do they do?"

"Joe works for the DNR. Department of Natural Resources. He's a nature boy, but I wouldn't mind having his daily patrol out on a lake or tromping through a beautiful forest."

"That does sound like a perk. What about the other?"

"Former State Patrol. Uh, Justin got hurt last year. Crazy woman shot him during a routine traffic stop. Left him with some neurological issues. He's doing good though. But that one certainly tried my mother's heart, let me tell you. Mostly, we don't tell Mom about the serious stuff." He cast her a wink. "How you holding up?"

"Honestly? Since I've been staying here at the cabin, I've had a lot of time to think about my life and the choices I've made. Even made up a list of pros and cons regarding returning to my job."

"Which won? Pros or cons?"

"I'm not finished. No matter what I ultimately choose to do, I don't want to die in this terrible, cold no-man's land."

He smiled at that. "It is terrible in the wintertime, but it's my home. For now, I'm focused on protecting you and solving this case. If there's a killer loose, we'll round him up and bring him in."

Amelie believed him. Even though she knew that if whoever was pulling strings behind whatever was going on wanted her dead, they could make that happen. And she knew Jason knew that, too.

"So you're CIA? Jason, why didn't you tell me that?"

He shrugged. "Haven't known you that long. I'm not much for laying it all out there."

"I can believe that. If I ask nicely, would you tell me about it?"

"Everything you do is nice, Amelie. I like that name. Well, I like them both. But Amelie fits you." He turned and propped his elbows on the counter.

Everything about his physicality fit her just fine. He was so…there. All man, and smelling so good. The sadness over telling him about her parents had slipped away. Hard to stay sad when talking to such a sexy man. Their closeness niggled at her. The idea of tracing his freckles returned, but Amelie pushed it back. He'd revealed he used to work for the CIA. She wanted to know more.

She leaned in beside him. "Tell me what you're willing to divulge."

"That isn't much. You know the drill. I was in the CIA for four years. Circumstances forced me out. That's all I want to say. For now."

He eyed her then, making sure she got his point. She did. Intelligence agencies guarded their secrets. A good agent did the same. Unless she was alone and confused, in a country not her own.

Nodding, she said, "Got it. I didn't tell you my secrets right away. You've a right to yours."

"Thanks for respecting that. You know," Jason said, "all this snow really is a lot of fun. You just haven't done the right things in it yet."

He had dismissed the CIA conversation quickly. She would give him that. For now.

Amelie leaned against the counter, which put her toe to toe with him. "Is that so? Well, according to the instructions left by the owners, I've shoveled, deiced the truck windows and broken icicles from the roof so water doesn't leak in. And I've learned I do like to snowshoe."

"See? That's a lot of fun. You said you take photographs? Or is that just your cover story?"

"Yes and yes. It's my cover, but it's also a hobby I'd like to turn into a career. I'll show you the picture of the moose I told you about." She grabbed her cell phone and tapped into the photographs app. Finding the picture, she turned it toward Jason.

"Wow. That is beautiful. The snow spraying about the moose glitters."

"Magical," she said. "But magic aside, I've dealt with more power outages than a person should have to in their lifetime. And now this blizzard! I guess I'm not seeing the appeal to dressing in layers and learning that sweat freezes on one's eyelashes and upper lip."

Jason laughed. "So does snot. But that's something you learn when you're a kid."

"That's information I will, unfortunately, never lose."

"You remember everything?"

"Most stuff. Not conversations, like this. Mostly data and lists. It's like when you're doing a mindless task and your brain is focused on that one thing? My brain goes into photographic memory mode. I can't turn it off. But if I'm writing a grocery list while I'm running about the house or singing or even chatting with a friend, then no."

"That's cool. What about books and movies? Do you remember them word for word?"

"Sometimes. Again, it depends on my focus and if I'm distracted by friends sitting beside me in the theater. I can absolutely quote every line from the *Italian Job* remake."

"The one with Mark Wahlberg? Wasn't that one the best?" Jason asked. Then he took on a feminine tone, "'My name's Becky, but it's written on my shirt.'"

"'Listen, Becky, I'm gonna need your shirt and your truck.'" She quoted the next line from the popular movie.

The man's laughter was the sexiest thing she'd heard in a long time. Amelie stepped forward, not really thinking, and touched his shirt, dead center over his chest. "Thank you," she said.

"Sure." He clasped his hand over hers. "Just doing my job."

"You're doing more than that. You've given me back the confidence I thought I'd lost since leaving France. You didn't coddle or chastise me after that attack. You said 'good for you.' I need that respect."

"Well earned."

And then she reacted, because it felt right.

The man's mouth was warm, firm and fit against hers as easily as her decision to kiss him had been. She stayed there, inhaling his skin, his breath, his power. One of his hands hooked at her hip and nudged her forward. She pressed her breasts against his chest and then…realized what she was doing.

Amelie pulled away and touched her mouth. "Sorry. I—"

"Please, do not apologize for a kiss," he said. "It'll give me a complex."

"Oh, your kiss was great. Your mouth is so delicious— I mean, kissing you probably wasn't the right thing—"

He stopped her protest with another connection of mouth to mouth. A hot, demanding union that drew up a sigh from the giddy swirl in her core. She settled against him, and when they parted this time, their eyes met. The crackle of the nearby fire mimicked the spark that had ignited in her belly. Everything about her felt melty and relaxed, attuned to his breath, his glance, his subtle nudge of palm against her hip.

Those freckles were like catnip to her purring desires.

Another loud crackle and pop alerted Jason. He looked aside, then pushed her away. "Oh no!" He raced toward the fireplace.

A fire had started on the rug before the hearth. Nothing a glass of water couldn't douse but—her notebook was in flames.

"The sparks must have started it." Amelie grabbed a bowl from the sink and filled it with water.

By the time she made it to Jason's side, he'd stomped out the flames. The rug bore a small black burn in the tight nylon coils. But her notebook was a tattered, ashy mess.

"The list," she said. "It's all gone."

He shot her a direct look. "Forever?"

Chapter Fourteen

The list was a complete loss. Jason had tried to salvage it, but no going. He'd stomped out the fire the spark had started, making sure no hazard remained. Yvette had scrubbed the rug with a towel and tossed the burned notebook. Those old rag rugs made from tightly coiled fabrics always stood up well to stray sparks. They were a northern Minnesota cabin standard.

"The information hasn't been lost forever," Yvette said as she sat on the couch. "But I'll have to start over now."

That was one thing to be thankful for—that she didn't lose the information after downloading it from her brain onto the page.

"I'd appreciate you giving it another go," he said. "It could prove helpful to figure out what the hell is going on."

"Do I have to do it tonight?"

"No." Jason blew out a breath, surprising himself when he felt his muscles stretch wearily across his shoulders. He checked his watch. "It's been a long day. And it's late. It won't matter if you start now or tomorrow."

He sat on the couch beside Yvette. Amelie. He'd better stick with Yvette for the sake of her cover. She'd brought out an extra quilt, and he couldn't avoid the return yawn when he saw hers. Putting up his feet on the coffee table, he settled into the comfortable couch and closed his eyes, pulling the blanket up to his neck.

"I'll sleep here," he said. "I know this cabin has only the one room with two beds."

"You're welcome to one of the beds."

"Thanks, but I like falling asleep before a fire," he said quietly.

"Yes, it is cozy. Do you mind if I sit here awhile longer and take in the ambience?"

"Go ahead."

She sat next to him, and he smiled inwardly. Nice to have the company. And she smelled great. Among so many other things that turned his senses up to ultra-alert. The softness of her skin teased, so close but just out of reach. The accidental nudge of her knee against his. The sweep of her hair across her shoulder.

Outside, the wind had settled some, but Jason expected the drifts to be tall and deep by morning. He didn't mind a good snowing in. Especially when it put him in proximity with a pretty woman. And she had kissed him right before the rug had taken flame. Funny to think, but they had created their own sparks.

He wasn't against making sparks with a beautiful woman. He'd gotten to know her better. She was alone and uncertain. He had known that feeling when first moving to Frost Falls to take on the superfluous job of police chief. But he had made the job his own and was very protective of this town now. Sometimes a guy needed a push in a new direction to restore his energy and positive outlook.

But now that he'd been pushed, he faced the full shove right out of the position he'd grown to love. Damn it, he didn't want to lose this job, as insignificant and quirky as it happened to be.

But he'd be lying if he said he was satisfied living in this small town. Female companionship was hard to come by. He generally dated women from other towns. Not even dates, more just hookups. How to intertwine his job with a happy social life? Marriage was something he looked forward to, but that would never happen if he didn't start playing the field and getting serious.

"About that kiss earlier," he said, eyes closed, content to relax in the warmth.

"I never flirt." She snuggled close against his side. Mm…that contact did not preach relaxation. "I always mean what I say and do."

"Unless you're spying for Interpol."

Her sigh hurt him more than he expected. "I'm not lying to you, Jason. I trust you. *You.* The guy who confessed to being a spy himself."

"Sorry. You're right. I appreciate that you say it like it is. No playing around."

"There's nothing wrong with a little play."

"Gotta agree with that."

When she twisted and leaned in, Jason tilted his head. The kiss was a surprise, but one he surrendered to like a refreshing free-fall dive into a summer spring. With the fire crackling across the room and casting an amber glow through the evening dark, the mood took on a sultry tone. Yvette's mouth was sweet and seeking. Her breasts hugged his arm. He shifted on the couch to hook his hand at her hip.

This was too good to be real. He didn't want to get his hopes up, but it was difficult not to. Yvette was the sort of woman he would like to date, to have in his life long-term while he learned about her hopes, her dreams, her desires. And could he ever share the same with a woman?

The clutch of her hand at his flannel shirt tugged, insistent and wanting. He glided his hand up over her shoulder and tangled his fingers in her hair. As soft as he'd thought it could be.

The kiss almost went deep and delving, but all of a sudden, Yvette pulled back and smiled at him.

"Good night, Cash." She kissed his cheek, then laid her head on his shoulder.

Mercy. Now he would never fall asleep.

BUT HE DID.

Jason awoke from a snore. The room was dark. The fire glimmered with low red embers. His face felt…cold. As did his feet and legs. Sitting up, he noted Yvette had curled up beside him, her head on the arm of the couch and her stockinged feet against his thigh. There along his leg he felt the most indulgent warmth. But she'd stolen the blanket, and—damn, it was cold in the cabin.

And he could make one guess why.

Getting up carefully, so as not to disturb her, he wandered into the kitchen and opened the fridge. The inner light did not blink on. No electricity. The storm must have taken out the power. Not unexpected. But why hadn't the generator kicked in?

He checked his watch. It was 5:00 a.m. Hell of a time to wake. If he went back to sleep, he would fall into a comfortable snooze but be groggy around six when he normally woke, yet if he stayed up he'd be tired later in the day.

A shiver that traced him from neck to toes decided for him. It was too cold to sleep. But did he really have to bundle up and go out to check the generator?

He glanced toward the couch. A warm body lay there, beckoning his return. Only a few steps away. No need to face the brutal weather.

Jason shook his head. He wasn't one to push the easy button. And if he didn't check the generator now, the cabin would only grow colder, and the risk of the water pipes freezing was a real possibility.

Putting on his coat, boots, gloves and scarf, he worked

quietly. Yvette didn't stir on the couch. Yvette, of the luscious mouth. The woman did not tease about flirting. Their make-out session, though too short for him, had stoked a fire within him. He could go there with her. Beyond the kiss and into bared skin and moans. But only as a fling. Because she lived in France and had no intention of staying in Minnesota. And if he started something with her… he didn't want to get his heart broken. It was tough enough being a bachelor in a small town.

Opening the front door and bracing for the cold, he swore silently as his skin tightened. The air hurt his face. Closing the door quietly behind him, he assessed the situation. The snow was not so deep in front of the cabin. Thanks to wind drift, he could still see most of the driveway and up to the gravel road. Here and there, sharp-edged drifts cut across that road. The plow only drove through on Mondays. Which had been yesterday. Though Rusty Nelson, of the gas station, did take his blade through town because The Moose always gave him a free meal in payment. As for the outer, less traveled roads, everybody would have to sit tight. The snowmobile would glide across this fresh powder like a dream.

Walking around the side of the cabin, Jason navigated the dark dawn with ease. He loved the way the darkness could be bright in the wintertime, illuminated by the white landscape. The world was quiet, blanketed to solace with the glittering snow. The stillness amplified his steps, his rubber-soled boots crunching the snowpack.

He bent and scooped up some snow and tried to form a snowball. It held, but not well. Which meant the snow was not too wet. A good thing if he wished to hop on the cat and ride into town.

Keeping his head down and his eyes peeled, he looked for anything out of the ordinary. Tracks, evidence of anything or anyone who may have attempted to broach the cabin during the night. Cut the electrical power. But the snow cover was pristine.

The back of the cabin was hugged by a snowdrift that reached half a foot up and over the window glass. The two walls that shielded the generator had been worthless. The cover was drifted up high; snow completely covered the generator. Jason swore. Somewhere under all that snow sat the key to getting the electricity back on.

He weighed the options. He could get a shovel out of the garage and dig down and try to figure out what was wrong with the generator. The cabin would not be livable if it had no heat. But he didn't have the time to play handyman. The electrician from Ely, a town about thirty minutes east, would be able to get out here, but he couldn't know if it would be today or in a few days.

The other option was to bring Yvette into town with him. There he could do his job and keep her close until they could find the perp.

Nodding, Jason eyed the garage. No drifts before the double door. Thankful he wouldn't have to shovel his way out, he wandered back around to the front of the house.

THE INVITE TO stay at the police chief's house was unexpected, but welcome. Having woken up shivering, Amelie now kept the blanket tight about her shoulders and wandered down the short hallway into the log-walled bedroom. The idea of stripping away her clothing to shower did not seem particularly wise. Instead, she added another sweater over her shirt and then, with the blanket again draped across her shoulders, pulled on another pair of socks and rolled them to cover the hems of her leggings.

"I really hate Minnesota," she muttered.

Though she was never one to hate anything. It wasn't the state—it was this cold. For certain, France did have its chilly moments in the wintertime. However, she'd become accustomed to working in an office building, insulated from the elements. Maybe the summers here were warm and sunny. In this part of the state, surely the nature must be amazing. She'd only read about the Boundary Waters and the forest that hugged the upper part of the state, but for an outdoorsman, it must be a dream.

She did want to venture out with her camera again. And if that meant braving the frigid weather, then so be it. Because it was high time she started facing the facts. That pros and cons list? She'd lied to Jason. It had fallen heavily in favor of the cons. And if she was honest with herself, the idea of returning to her current job did not appeal.

Could she make a living as a photographer? It had started as a cover job for her assignments. A good agent tried to choose a cover she was familiar with, so she could easily blend, and Amelie had always loved photography. Thanks to her father's life insurance policy, she had a healthy savings account that would allow her to quit her paycheck job while seeking something that could satisfy her need for fulfilling work. It was something she needed to seriously consider. And soon.

She wandered back out to the living room. Even if she didn't appreciate the current climes, the male species was something to admire. Case in point? Jason stood before the hearth, ensuring all sparks were completely dampened. Bent over in those blue jeans, he provided a great view of his nice, tight—

"You pack?" he called over a shoulder.

"Uh…" Pack? Oh, right. "A few things." She set down her grocery-run backpack that she'd filled with clothing. "How long do you think it will take to get the electricity working?"

"I'll give Karl a call when we get to town," he said. "Storm dropped a good twenty inches last night. We'll have to take the snowcats into town."

"I'm good with that. For as much as I hate the cold, I actually enjoy dashing through the snow in a horseless open sleigh."

He chuckled. "Good one. You'll learn to like our weather. It's good for the blood."

"It is?"

"Yeah." He slapped his chest, and Yvette could only imagine doing the same, yet gentler, and…under his shirt. "Keeps the blood pumping." His cell phone rang, and he answered as he wandered to the foyer and started pulling on his outerwear. Amelie now realized the Wi-Fi had been available when she'd checked for texts upon rising.

"Yeah?" Jason said to the caller. "You're kidding me? Where?"

Amelie pulled on the snow pants that had been provided by the cabin. They were thermal and designed like over-alls, so they provided a layer of added warmth and protection from the elements.

"I'll be there in…" Jason eyed her, then gave her a forced smile before answering the person on the phone. "Give me half an hour." He hung up and then tossed her the knit cap that was sitting on top of his gloves. "Alex found a body in a running vehicle near the edge of town."

"A body?"

"Yeah. Uh…" He winced as he appeared to consider his words. "It's the perp."

"What?"

"Alex ID'd him as the mafia hit man, Herve Charley."

"How did he die?"

"Carbon-monoxide inhalation? Won't know until I can take a look. The medical examiner is already on her way. The main road has been plowed. I'll have to drop you at my house and run. Hell, maybe I should take you to the station. Be safer there."

Amelie pulled on a pout. "I was looking forward to a

hot shower. Is your place really a target for crime? And you did say the suspect is dead."

"I thought we'd determined we don't really know what the hell is going on."

Amelie swallowed. He was right. She really needed to get smart about this operation. Because it was a mission she needed to participate in.

"Aw, don't give me the pouty face. Fine. You get a shower. And then you're heading to the station where I, or someone, can keep an eye on you."

Amelie bounced on her toes. It was a small victory, but it lifted her spirits. And she needed that.

Chapter Fifteen

The forest green SUV had been pushed into the ditch. Purposely. It hadn't slid off the icy gravel road while traveling. Though, certainly, the roads were treacherous this bright, sunny morning. Ice glinted like a bejeweled crust under the cruel sunshine. Last night's blizzard conditions had kept every smart person inside and safe in their homes. Save this one. But the vehicle couldn't have been in the ditch for long. The tire tracks leading into the ditch were crisp, only lightly covered with a dusting of snow blown by the wind.

Jason stretched his gaze along the road and spied another set of tracks. Faint, but again, snow had drifted slightly to emboss the tire treads. And they were different than those of the ditched vehicle.

"You see that?" he said to Alex, who stood waiting for Jason outside the patrol car.

"Yep. Another vehicle either forced this one in the ditch, or someone stopped to help but left."

"I'm ruling out help," Jason decided. If it had been anyone from the town, they would have called dispatch to alert him to the situation. "You run a plate check?"

"Yes. Vehicle belongs to Carol Bradley. She reported it missing from her garage—door open, keys hanging on the key holder inside the garage—forty-five minutes ago."

"Oh, Carol," Jason muttered. "You were just asking

for that one. So the perp stole a vehicle that was virtually handed to him in the first place."

Stepping carefully on the icy tarmac, Jason inspected the exterior of the vehicle. Grayish-white dust from the salted roads shaded the green paint. Because of the angle the truck sat at, the passenger's side hugging the ditch was buried up to the bottom of the side windows. The engine had been running when Alex had arrived on the scene, and he'd shut it off. And…the back right wheel of the car had sunk into the ditch, allowing snow to cover the exhaust pipe.

"Not good," he muttered. The exhaust had nowhere to go but inside the vehicle.

"Carbon monoxide?" Alex asked from where he was walking to determine that the only footprints were boot marks from him and Jason.

"Looks like it," Jason called.

"Someone could have run him off the road. Guy got knocked out. The other car backed up and drove off. This guy never woke up," Alex conjectured.

"We'll see."

With a lunge, Jason stepped up onto the running board edging the driver's side of the truck. He peered inside and found exactly as expected. The driver, Herve Charley, was immobile, buckled in, his jaw slack. Alex reported that he'd initially opened the door and shaken the man but had quickly realized he was dead, so then he'd stepped back so as not to contaminate the scene.

Jason stepped down and opened the door, having to push it with some strength to fight against the angle at which the vehicle was tilted. Sliding between the door and the car frame, he leaned in and inspected the guy's face. He didn't notice any bruising on the forehead or temple areas where a sudden slam of the brakes might have sent him flying forward into the windshield. And to know if his chest had hit the steering wheel hard would require the medical examiner.

Charley's eyes were closed. His skin was still pink, but his lips were bluing. Carbon-monoxide poisoning did not tend to blue the skin, and, if Jason recalled a few previous experiences with the like, the lips turned bright red. Certainly, the cold could be a factor in the odd skin color. A heater didn't do a person much good when the wind whipped the icy air through and about the steel vehicle.

He wouldn't touch the body without gloves. The medical examiner would chastise him for that. No visible weapons. No pistol, no knife. He couldn't have purposely parked at such a strange angle, and halfway in the ditch. Maybe he had slid a ways and Jason had read the tracks incorrectly. Because why would someone run him into the ditch? Who knew this man was in Frost Falls? Had he started a fight with someone?

Didn't make sense. He'd escaped from jail. Charley should have been lying low or long gone from the town by now.

He scanned the truck's interior. On the passenger seat sat a plastic grocery bag. When Jason lifted the edge, he spied inside a half-full plastic bottle of a bright blue energy drink and an opened pack of salted beef sticks.

Turning the key in the ignition to get power but not spin the engine, Jason listened to the radio station. It was the Duluth top hits channel that played current songs all the way back to the '60s and the '70s. He checked the gas gauge. Half-full. No other warning lights.

Had Charley been staking out Yvette? He was parked a mile out on the east road, which led to the Birch Bower cabin. Nothing else out this way, save the rental cabin. But what had stopped him from proceeding to the cabin? The road, while slick, was not drifted over. Easily drivable at a slow speed. Had he seen Jason head out this way on the snowmobile earlier in the day? Waiting for him to leave? Possible.

But the additional set of tire tracks bothered Jason. They had stopped right behind the SUV. No boot tracks, though. Whoever had driven the other car had not gotten out. Alex's guess about another vehicle pushing this one into the ditch, then taking off, could be right on.

Switching off the ignition, Jason stepped out of the truck as Elaine pulled up in the medical examiner's van. Must be her turn to drive the vehicle. The county shared one van between the four offices in the Boundary Waters area.

"The victim did not get out of the vehicle," Alex reported. With a gesture toward the SUV, he added, "He's wearing those cowboy boots. I checked. No tracks outside to match. Just our boots. Although, with the ice and drifting, even if he had gotten out, those tracks would have been dusted away."

"Thanks, Alex." Jason tugged at his skullcap to cover the tops of his ears. He wandered to the rear of the vehicle and inspected the chrome bumper. Sure enough, a sharp dent crimped the end. "Someone pushed him into the ditch. But I feel like he might have been parked here."

"We got a vigilante going after the bad guy?" Alex asked.

"No one knows about our resident bad guy," Jason said.

Except Yvette. But he'd been with her all night. And while Bay and Marjorie knew to keep a tight lid on police business, he could assume the three women he'd questioned about Yvette Pearson's death had already released that information into the gossip grapevine.

He waved as the medical examiner approached. "Elaine! You made it."

Already snapping on black latex gloves, Elaine executed careful steps over the icy road. "I'm a hardy sort, you know that, Cash. Icy roads don't intimidate me." With a nod to

Alex, she stomped across the snowpack to peek inside the cab. "Sitting here overnight?"

"Alex found him on morning rounds. He always checks on the Enerson couple down the road."

"That couple must be pushing a hundred, the both of them," Elaine said.

"Einer turned a hundred and one last week," Alex called as he wandered back to the patrol car, most likely to retrieve a thermos of coffee.

Jason wished he'd consumed some coffee before coming here. He'd even suffer the bitter, dark stuff Alex tilted down like an addict. He'd pulled up to his house on the snowmobile, Yvette behind him. Handing Yvette the key to the front door, he'd told her to make herself at home. The last time he'd given a woman free rein in his home, she'd put pink pillows on his couch and had suggested he get a juicer. All he could do was shiver at that memory.

Elaine put up a boot on the SUV's side runner, and Jason grabbed her elbow to steady her while also holding the car door open with his shoulder.

"Thanks, Cash. You think it was carbon monoxide?"

"I do. But there's damage to the back bumper and additional tire treads. Someone nudged the vehicle into the ditch."

"Interesting," she muttered out from inside the cab.

While waiting for Elaine's initial inspection of the deceased, Jason watched Alex tilt back the thermos. The one thing Jason never missed was his morning coffee. But this morning had been unusual in that he'd woken snuggled beside a beautiful woman. Both of them fully clothed.

Something wrong with that picture.

On the other hand, he never expected anything from a woman unless they had communicated clear signals to those expectations. It had been sweet to find Yvette's warm body curled up against him this morning. Shared body heat on a stormy winter night. Nothing at all wrong with that.

But what did it mean for their future? Why was he even thinking future about the woman? Was it because she was the first woman he'd met in a long time who hit all his *this feels right* buttons? Or was he desperate and lucky to find a beautiful woman, about his age, in the same vicinity as he was?

No, it wasn't that. She was smart, courageous and in need of his protection. And the courageous part appealed to him. A woman who wasn't afraid to defend herself and could take his garbage? Could he get more, please?

A future would be great. Even if that only entailed the two of them getting to know one another better and doing more than sharing a snuggle. An official date would be a great start.

Elaine jumped down and tugged off her gloves then stuffed them in her left pocket. From her right pocket, she pulled out thermal gloves and slid them on. "No telltale cyanosis. Which means it wasn't carbon monoxide. Though it may have lulled the deceased a bit."

"What's cyanosis?"

"Skin turning blue."

"Right. I noticed that, but, well…" Jason peered inside the cab. The body sure looked as if it had suffered from inhalation of a poisonous substance. He adjusted his stance, pressing back the door with his shoulder, but also fighting the whipping wind that suddenly decided to sweep the snow up and into their faces. "What did you see, Elaine?"

"Did you notice the fine crystal on his collar? And the smell of his breath?"

"I didn't get that cozy with the guy."

She smirked. "That's why I get paid the medium bucks. Cyanide poisoning is my initial assessment. I can only confirm with lab tests. But I don't think he took his own life.

Which may coincide with the dented bumper and extra vehicle tracks. Someone might have wanted to ensure he was dead."

"I'll call Ryan Bay and have him come out to help us process the scene," Jason said. "Things will go much faster. Then we can all get back to a warm office."

"Bay didn't stay in Frost Falls? Didn't you offer him a cell to camp out in?"

"I'm not exactly sure where he stayed last night. He's been cozying up to Marjorie's husband for dumplings a few nights now. Might have earned himself a bed there." Jason tugged out his cell phone.

"Oh, those dumplings." Elaine nodded her head appreciatively.

Jason stepped aside and let the door close with a good push from the wind. He scanned the ground again. His own boot tracks were barely visible for the icy surface, and he followed Elaine's smaller tracks to the back of the vehicle where she stood. The drifting snow covered them quickly.

The BCA agent's phone carried over to messages, so Jason told him where to meet him, then tucked away the phone in a pocket.

He stepped up beside Elaine, who had turned her back to the wind. She looked out over the snow-packed field, which gleamed with sunshine. "So now we've got a hit man's killer running around town?"

"This case is starting to get very interesting," Elaine said. "Mystery. Thrills. Murder. I gotta say it does add some excitement to the usual natural-causes pickups. These parts, the elderly tend to drop like flies. But you see one death because of age or cancer..." She shrugged. "You've seen them all."

"Not sure I should be glad to oblige your need for excitement, Elaine."

She smirked at him. "You love it, too, Cash. I can see that glint in your eye."

He crooked a brow and looked down at her. "My eyes don't glint."

"Yeah? Tell that to your Frenchwoman."

"My French—what?"

She chuckled softly. "Marjorie told me."

Jason shook his head. "The gossip in this town."

"The whole county, Cash. The whole county. When's Bay going to arrive?"

"His phone went to message."

"Could be a while. I'll get the gurney. You guys help me bag and load up the body."

"Will do." Jason headed toward the back of Elaine's vehicle to get out the equipment they'd need.

If the man in the green SUV had been sent to kill Yvette, then why would someone take him out? Had a cleanup been dispatched to take out the inept hit man? Possible. And probable. Anything goes when the mafia was involved. And, very possibly, Interpol.

Uff da. This was getting deeper than the snow.

Chapter Sixteen

Amelie lingered under the hot water. She hadn't had decent water pressure in the weeks she'd been in the country. Washing her hair under the lackluster stream back at the cabin had been a challenge. Now the water blasted her skin and massaged it and—oh. Just. Ohh…

Another bonus? The house had central heating with electricity that worked. Heaven.

After what she determined was half an hour, she decided a good guest would not use all the hot water, so she reluctantly stepped out onto the plush bath mat and wrapped a thick towel about her wet hair and another around her body. Tucking her feet into the slipper-like socks she'd hastily packed, she then wandered down the hallway to the extra bedroom Jason had said she could use.

The room was…some grandmother's creation. It had made her laugh when she'd first walked in to leave her bag. Crocheted pillowcases and bedspread, and the lace curtains were the same off-white as the bed dressings. The furniture was straight out of the '50s with a plain pressboard headboard, and the dresser looked like one of those old-fashioned televisions that, indeed—upon closer inspection—had a record player on one side and the other side fitted with drawers for clothing. So lost-in-the-past yet teasing Twilight Zone. Jason must have inherited the place from a relative. Or so she could hope his idea of decorating style did not include such strange furnishings.

But she wouldn't look a gift horse in the mouth. It was either this or shivering back at the cabin. She did not care to be alone and too far away from the handsome police chief who could provide her protection when she most needed it.

Amelie hated to admit it to herself, but she did like the presence of a strong, confident man. Sure, she'd trained in self-defense. But with the state of her mind and emotions lately, she'd gladly step back and allow him to stand before her if that's what he could do.

Dropping the towels aside and combing out her hair before the full-length mirror on the back of the door, she relished the warmth that did not necessitate she immediately get dressed.

Her cell phone rang, and she picked it up from the bed. No ID, but she recognized the number.

"Settling in?" Jason asked.

"You don't know how much I missed water pressure."

"Did you save some hot water for me?"

"Are you coming home to shower?" Amelie bit her lower lip. That question could be construed as suggestive. But… depending on how he replied, she'd get a bead on his feelings toward her.

"Was that an invitation?"

Score! She turned before the mirror, studying her naked profile. If he came home right now…

"Sorry, I shouldn't be so forward," Jason said. "I, uh, have a lot to do here at the station with this new twist to the investigation. I can't say much more. This is an active investigation. And you're…"

"No longer in danger?"

"Can you come over to the station and we'll talk?" he asked. "I need to wrap my head around as much info as you can provide."

"Can we meet at The Moose? I'm starving."

"I don't know…"

"Sorry. I didn't mean that to sound like a date."

"It's not that, Yvette. I'm just not sure it's safe for you to be wandering around town, putting yourself out there."

"The guy is dead, Jason. What aren't you telling me?" He sighed. "He is."

"What if I walk over to the station right now and pick up something for us to eat along the way? It's a straight shot. You can stand outside and watch me walk there."

"I've got a better idea. I'll meet you there, and we'll walk back to the station together."

"Great. I could go for a big serving of meat and potatoes."

"You've settled into the Scandinavian aesthetic."

"I know. And I fear for my waistline because of it. Give me ten minutes to get dressed and I'll meet you there?"

"You're, uh…not dressed?"

"Just stepped out of the shower."

A heavy exhale sounded on the line, and Amelie smiled. She'd given him something to think about. And she certainly hoped that thought lingered with him for a long time.

"See you soon," he said quickly, then hung up.

JASON PUSHED ASIDE the evidence bag he'd gathered from the ditched SUV and tapped the plastic. Inside he'd collected Herve Charley's cell phone, truck keys, twenty dollars and a fidget spinner, of all things. Not a single weapon. No gun. No garrote or knife. This hit man liked to get up close and personal with his marks.

Ryan Bay had called. He'd made contact with the FBI. Charley was on their list. An agent was headed to Duluth to stand in on the autopsy right now. And likely they'd send an agent to Frost Falls.

All this evidence would be sent to Duluth for forensics

to put it through their tests, and it would be shared with the FBI. Verification that Charley had contact with Yvette Pearson was important to tie the two cases together. Because if not, there could be another killer on the loose. As well, Jason wanted to see what connections, if any, he could find between Herve Charley and Jacques Patron.

It was a hunch. He had no real evidence to link them. But if Patron was the only one who knew Yvette was staying in Minnesota, in a small town with no more than a grocery store and a diner/gas station/strip joint, then that led to one conclusion: Patron had sent the hit after her.

As Jason scanned what little public information he could access on the Interpol assistant director, he remembered Yvette telling him how she'd proven herself to Jacques by reading lists and then later writing them out. A handy skill to have, especially in the spy business. And if the expense for training her for fieldwork had been put out, only to find she wasn't cut out for such harrowing work, then surely the director would want to utilize her unique skill in some form. And he shouldn't be willing to dispose of that same skill for some little infraction.

Whatever she'd read on that list had been confidential and likely hadn't been something Interpol had expected to receive. Someone must have wanted *her* to see it. Could that someone have known of her memory skills? Or was it that they knew she had a connection to Patron? Were they outside Interpol? Or had it come from inside? That made more sense, considering the difficulty of learning about Yvette's skills and then targeting her email specifically. And was the email sender someone dangerous enough to put a hit out on a fellow employee?

This smacked of duplicity. And that grabbed Jason in the gut and twisted. Hard. He knew what it was like to deal with double-crossing spies. And not only his job but his personal reputation had suffered because of it.

Two years ago, in Verona, Italy, he'd trusted the Italian agent who had been assigned as his liaison while he'd been in the city on a critical operation. Despite Jason's trust of his employer at the time, the Central Intelligence Agency, he had never walked into a situation blind. When he'd learned who was to liaise with him, he'd checked her out. Charleze Portello had been with Interpol as a field operative for six years. She spoke five languages, was skilled in various forms of martial arts and had helped take down a billion-dollar counterfeit-antiques operation in Morocco. Impeccable credentials.

He'd never dreamed she'd turn out to be a Russian honeypot sent to learn what he knew and follow him right to the target.

That had not gone down well with the CIA. Which was why Jason currently wore a cloth badge on his coat and sat in a cold office before a computer that should have been bricked a decade earlier.

Leaning back and blowing out a breath, he shook his head. Feeling sorry for himself? That wasn't a Cash condition. His father had taught him better than that. All three Cash brothers were confident and able, and the vein of cockiness infused by their former marine dad ran hot and heavy in them all. Jason had loved working for the CIA. And he would be a liar to say he didn't miss the adventure, action and intensity of the job. But life had decided he was needed in this town at this moment in time. And... he'd accepted that.

But soon enough, that was going to be ripped from his grasp. Was he not meant to settle and be happy? Why did he keep stepping into jobs that weren't meant to last? Was it something he did? He didn't so much love this town as he did the people in it. And while he understood that Frost Falls was small and a police station was no longer a necessity, he'd hate to see it go. It was a town landmark. And who would be there to direct Ole Svendson to put his clothes back on and get off the main drag?

Things had to start looking up. And they were. With forensics reports due from Duluth, Jason might be able to close one case if Charley's DNA could be matched to Yvette Pearson's evidence.

Unless a new hit man had arrived in town.

Chapter Seventeen

To say that every diner in The Moose was watching Amelie standing next to Jason as they waited for their to-go meals was putting it accurately. All eyes were on them, accompanied by smirks, nods and raised eyebrows. Of course, whenever Amelie cast a glance toward the curious onlookers, they all resumed what they had been doing. Even if it meant completely missing the edge of the coffee cup and spilling down the front of that snowflake-patterned red thermal sweater.

Out of the corner of her mouth, she asked Jason, "Are we a local event?"

"Apparently, we are." His freckles were even more pronounced thanks to the bright white sunshine that beamed through the diner windows. Amelie admired those same freckles in his liquid green eyes. A sight she could take in forever. "What are you looking at?"

She leaned in close and whispered, "Your freckles."

"Stupid things."

"Why do you say that?"

"Never liked them. My brother Justin once tried to scrub them off me. With a Brillo pad."

"What's a Brillo pad?"

"It's made from stainless steel and is used for scouring food off dishes."

"That's terrible!"

"Par for the course when you grow up with two brothers. I served him his just desserts. More than a few times. Hey, Hank!" He waved to a gentleman leaving the diner, who returned a wink as he opened the front door.

"Marjorie's husband," he said to Amelie. "My dispatcher."

She loved his self-satisfied smile. It popped in the dimple on his cheek. It was all Amelie could do not to lean forward and touch that indent. But the townsfolk had been served more than enough entertainment for one afternoon. And, weirdly, the place had gotten packed since they'd arrived five minutes earlier. Had all those texts and whispered phone calls brought in the entire town—some having to forge unplowed roads—to watch their very single police chief flirt with a woman? Or even more exciting, to possibly overhear some news about the murder investigation?

Amelie chuckled and turned a blatant smile to the peanut gang along the counter, who all quickly snapped their heads around to pay attention to their cooling meals.

"Here you go, Chief Cash." The waitress set a bag on the counter and took Jason's credit card and slashed it through the charge machine. "Will that be all?"

"You betcha. Thank you very much, Charlotte." Jason tucked away his wallet and grabbed the bag. When they walked to the door, he waved to the audience who followed their exit. "Nothing to see here, folks! Just having a little lunch."

Once outside, Amelie shivered against the brisk cold, but she laughed as their footsteps made them dodge a heap of unplowed snow in their path and they bumped shoulders.

"Am I ruining your reputation?" she asked as they crossed the street and headed toward the station.

"If there was anything left to be ruined, I might be worried. But you gotta give them something to whisper about every now and then, eh?"

"If you say so. But speaking of reputations… I shouldn't ask, but I have to. Tell me why you left the CIA."

"Do I have to?"

"I did tell you my sad tale."

He chuckled. "Fine. I didn't leave, I was fired. But my boss wanted me to suffer even more, so he 'placed' me—" he made air quotes "—in a suitable job that required filling."

"This job you have now? It's such a small town. I'm surprised there is even a police station in it."

A passing station wagon honked, and Jason nodded and gave the driver a wave. "Frost Falls used to be four times the population it is now. Wasn't even three years ago it was booming. Workers from the iron range lived here. Then the Red Band iron mine went bust, and everyone packed up and left. It was a lot of migrant workers, but many locals as well. Since there was already a police station, the chief of police stayed on as he watched the town's numbers dwindle. He died of natural causes two years ago. And when they should have closed the station and left the law enforcement to the county, some smart aleck in the CIA decided he'd send one of his agents here as a means of punishment to watch over the peanut gang."

"Did you have to take the job?"

"No. But it was a job, and it's located within an hour's driving distance of both my brothers and my parents, so… Hell." He stopped at the corner of the redbrick station house and looked straight at her. It was his hefty sigh that told her his truths were valuable. And she would handle them with the care they deserved. "At the time, I wasn't in a mental place where I was willing to stand up and fight the system. I was real down on myself and decided to take my punishment as due."

"Punishment for what?"

"I botched a mission."

"Is that all? But…agents do that all the time. Well, not all the time. But it happens. Backup measures are usually in place—"

"I let a known terrorist walk out of my crosshairs," Jason said firmly. He closed his eyes and swallowed. "Because she got to him first."

"She?" Amelie noticed the muscle in his jaw tighten. "An Interpol agent?"

"How'd you guess?"

"You were not pleased to hear I worked for Interpol. I had no idea at the time, but that explains your reaction."

"She was using me the whole time. I thought she was a liaison provided by the Italian headquarters. Turns out Interpol wanted their hands on the target for their own reasons. And it wasn't to take him out. I want to believe it was some kind of trade to the Russians. Far as I know, the target is walking free. It's not right."

"A lot of what goes on in international and national security agencies isn't always deemed right. But who is the judge of what is right and wrong? There are many situations that can be viewed both ways."

"I know that. One man's freedom fight is another man's misdirected protest. The target had taken out women and children, Yvette. Dozens of them. His weapon of choice was pipe bombs placed at coffee shops in the Washington, DC, area. It was a malicious and vulgar crime. I hate myself for letting him walk."

Amelie knew now wasn't the time for argument or reasoning. It was a challenge dealing with the power an agent wielded. Certainly, she had been faced with many such challenges. And ultimately? She'd not been able to pass the cruelest test. To shoot or not to shoot? She'd not realized which side she fell on until it was almost too late.

Fortunately, she'd been able to step away and still retain her job at Interpol.

Jason had been punished for something that hadn't been his fault. One of her own had tricked him? Likely a honeypot sent in to cozy up to him, earn his trust, learn what he knew, then report back to headquarters. It happened all the time.

"I won't betray you," she said. "Promise."

He nodded but didn't say anything. He didn't need to. Thanks to his training, and his experience in Italy, he couldn't trust her. Not completely. But she was prepared to earn that trust.

"Thanks, Jason. You didn't have to tell me that. I appreciate that you did. It's freezing out here." She managed a face-crunching smile, then ran ahead and grabbed the station door and held it for Jason.

"Jason." A woman with frosted brown hair cut close to her scalp stood from behind a desk. Must be the dispatcher he'd mentioned. "This must be your French—er, uh, Yvette, wasn't it?"

Amelie tugged off a mitten and offered her hand. "Nice to meet you. You must be Marjorie."

"You betcha. You two dining in Jason's office?"

"You know we are," Jason said with a tone that indicated he wasn't about to take any of the woman's sly teasing. "I'm waiting on a call from the FBI," he called as he entered his office and held the door for Amelie. "Patch it through when it comes, Marjorie."

"Will do, boss."

He closed the door, and Amelie took the food bag to set their meals out on his desk. "Do I get the grand tour?" she asked.

"Uh, sure, but this old station house is the least interesting place in the whole town."

"Oh, I don't know. Marjorie's Christmas decorations certainly do brighten up the outer office."

"They stay up until Valentine's Day, and then we have hearts until St. Patrick's and—it's never boring out in reception. Okay, then! Here's the tour. This is my desk. This is my computer. This is me. That's my deer rack collection." He pointed to the two racks, each more than sixteen points, hanging on the far wall. And next to it hung... "And that is the calendar the print shop in the next town makes of local heroes—they donate profits to the Camp Ripley charity."

"Is that man standing beside a real wolf?" Amelie bent to study closely the calendar hung from a bent two-inch roofing nail. It featured a sexy, bare-chested man with dark hair and a six pack that competed with his incredible dimples.

"Yep, that's my brother Joseph. They call him the Wolf Whisperer. I told you he works for the DNR and has an intimate connection to nature, wolves especially."

"I love wolves. They have such a history. Have you heard of the Beast of Gévaudan in France?"

"Can't say that I have."

"It's an eighteenth-century werewolf legend."

Jason chuckled. "Sorry to disappoint, but there are no werewolves here in Minnesota. You like that kind of stuff?"

"What kind of stuff?"

"Werewolves and vampires and all that weird nonsense?"

She cast him a flutter of lash. "I wouldn't chase a sexy vampire out of my bed."

"Yikes. You women and your...weird fascination for all things...weird. I don't understand why having some fang-toothed monster gnawing on your neck is supposed to be romantic."

"Well, I'm not much for being gnawed myself. Are you on a month?" She flipped up a couple pages of the calendar.

"I was in last year's edition."

"Doesn't surprise me."

This time she took him in from head to just there below his belt. Heh. Was the man blushing?

"I'll have to see about finding a copy," she said. "Especially since beefcake is another of my interests."

"I think my mom has ten. Or a hundred. So that's it. My office," he said. "Pretty exciting, eh?"

"I like it all. Quaint, but underneath it all I'm sure there's a vibrant and busy law enforcement team ready and willing to protect its citizens."

"Always." Jason thrust back his shoulders. "Now let's eat and then get to work."

"IS THE FOOD that terrible?"

Jason's voice summoned Amelie from thoughts that were far too deep for what should be a pleasant lunch. Forcing on a smile, she shook her head. "It's too good. I could get used to this home-style cooking. And that's the problem."

"I've never had a problem with a turkey and gravy sandwich."

"I can see why. It's…mmm…so good."

Jason leaned forward and caught his cheek in a palm. "Could a turkey sandwich entice you to stay in Frost Falls longer than you'd planned?"

"My gut answer? Yes." Amelie squeezed her eyes shut. Had she just said that? And the reason it had come out so easily was because there was an excellent incentive for sticking around: freckles and a sexy smile. But. "But I didn't have a planned end date for this stay. And I'm not sure I can survive this place much longer."

"You've been cooped up in that cabin for weeks. Anyone would go loony bin. You should give some consideration to sticking around awhile. Let me show you how to enjoy a Minnesota winter."

She ran her tongue along her upper lip. Not an offer

any sane woman would refuse. "Don't you have a girl-friend, Jason?"

He winked at her. "Does it look like it?"

"No. But that makes me wonder why."

He crimped a brow.

"What's wrong with you?" she said on a teasing tone.

"Not a lot of young, single women here in Frost Falls. Or haven't you noticed?"

"Isn't the Saturday-night stripper single?"

He shook his head and chuckled softly. "What about you? Is there a boyfriend back home in France?"

"There isn't."

"Yeah? So what's wrong with you?"

"I work too much and have no social life. But no cats yet."

"That's a good thing."

"So now—" she leaned in closer over her takeout container "—the burning question."

"Shoot."

"Are you interested in me, Jason?"

"Hell, yes."

"I like a man who knows what he wants." She sat back, pleased with that quick and confident answer.

The intercom buzzed, and Marjorie said, "Ryan Bay is on his way."

"Thanks, Marjorie. Bay is with the Bureau of Criminal Apprehension. He'll want to talk to you," he said to Amelie.

"Sure. Standard procedure."

"Nothing to worry about."

"I'm not worried. I've done nothing wrong."

"Nothing except attract a hit man to Frost Falls."

"Is that an accusation? I'm not sure I care for that."

"Sorry. It's not your fault." He set down his sandwich and leaned forward. "Why would someone take out a hit man?"

"Mafia, right?"

"He was a hired gun. Connected to local mafia. And now he's dead," Jason said.

"You said the vehicle was stuck in the ditch. Was it forced off the road?"

"Yes. There was a dent on the bumper and tire tracks indicating that. But the driver wasn't dead when he hit the ditch. Maybe? I initially assumed carbon-monoxide inhalation. Happens in these parts during the winter months. Car slides off an icy road, gets half-buried in the snow. The driver takes the safe route of not venturing out in a blizzard and doesn't know the safety precautions for staying in a vehicle when trapped in the cold. Gotta remember to check the exhaust pipe if you're letting the engine run to stay warm. Doesn't take long for carbon monoxide to enter the brain and lull the person to sleep. For good."

He pulled off the plastic cover from the coffee cup and sipped. "But the medical examiner spotted signs of poison."

"Poison? Why would someone take out the person who was supposed to kill me?"

"I don't know. That's what I'm asking you."

She detected an accusing tone and didn't like it one bit. Sitting up straight, Amelie took another bite of her sandwich.

"You don't trust me?" she asked.

"I really want to." He challenged her with a steady gaze. Damn, those freckles would be her undoing. "But I know very little."

"I know even less. I'm as confused about all this as you are."

"Every thought I have about this case leads me back to Jacques Patron."

"But he's…" She paused. No confirmation of his death had been given. As far as she knew, he could be AWOL. Could he be a double agent?

"Did you have a chance to write out the list while at my place this morning?" he asked.

"No, I'm sorry, the hot shower seduced me."

She caught his appreciative nod with a subtle lift of brow.

"I intend to get to that as soon as we're done here," she said. "Promise. I want to help you. And if there is someone wandering Frost Falls who is so dangerous as to defeat a hit man, then…" She set down the last corner of the sandwich and tucked her shaking hands between her legs. "I'm a little scared."

"Don't be. I will protect you, Yvette. Amelie."

"I know you will." She stood and gathered her container and plastic utensils and put them in the bag they'd come in.

She turned and wandered toward the window overlooking Main Street, trailing her fingers along the scuffed sill. "I suppose a town this size doesn't see hit men all that often."

"You better believe we don't." He tossed his things in the bag and joined her.

His presence softened her fears. Standing so close to him, she felt lighter, safer.

"Thank you for what you've done for me, Jason." Her gaze met his, and her lips parted softly. "I mean, Chief Cash."

Heartbeats thundered as memories of their kisses resurfaced. She moved closer so their legs touched. "You kissed me yesterday at the cabin. A girl might expect another…"

"Nothing wrong with a kiss. And if I recall correctly, you were the one to initiate the kiss on the—"

She kissed him quickly, pleased at his surprised response as his open arms slowly and assuredly wrapped around her back. He felt right pressed against her.

His fiery kiss quickly melted the ice that had taken up under her skin like permafrost since moving to Frost Falls.

She giggled.

Jason pressed a finger to her mouth. "Quiet. These walls are as thin as paper. Marjorie will hear."

"That's all right!" Marjorie called out from the other room. "I'm happy you finally have someone to kiss, Chief Cash!"

Amelie gaped, then muffled another giggle.

Jason raised a brow as if to silently say, "See?"

Amelie's cell phone rang, then immediately buzzed, indicating the caller sent a text message instead of waiting for her to answer. She stared at the screen ID and blinked. Her heartbeat thundered. She opened her mouth but no sound came out.

"What is it?" Jason asked.

"It's a message."

"Yeah?"

She turned the phone toward Jason. "It's from Jacques Patron."

Chapter Eighteen

"I thought he was dead." Jason took Yvette's phone from her and read the message to himself: You there?

"I should text him back." She reached for the phone, but Jason clasped his fingers about it. "Jason?"

"I'm not sure about this. I know what I heard on that message. It was a gunshot."

"That doesn't mean anyone was harmed or even died."

"True. But the guy hasn't contacted you since you arrived—what—two weeks ago? And now he does only *after* the hit man has failed? This doesn't feel right."

"You think that's a text from someone else? Using Jacques's phone?"

"Not sure. I want to do a trace on this text."

"I thought your dispatch came up with nothing on the first trace to your phone?"

"She did, but it's worth another try. Can I take this with me?"

She was beautiful when she was thinking. Bright blue eyes unfocused and head tilted slightly down.

She nodded. "Okay. I don't have any important information on it. Just a few calls to the grocery store and, of course, to Interpol in Lyon. I'll write down my password." She grabbed a napkin, and Jason pulled a pen out from his inside coat pocket so she could write it down.

He took the napkin and wrapped it once about the phone then slipped that and the pen into his pocket. "Just to be safe. If he's alive, that's good, right?"

"But if he is, don't you think I should return his call soon?"

"Let me answer with a different question. If you don't return his call, will the man think you're dead? And more important—will believing you are dead please him?"

She worried at her lower lip with her teeth. Thinking again. Which was exactly what he needed her to do. Everything about this situation seemed to point the compass toward France, and Yvette's boss.

"I'm not stupid," she said. "It could very well be as you suspect. I'll wait until you can track the origin of the text. If it came from Jacques's phone…"

"Interpol wouldn't confirm Patron's death. If they don't know what Patron is up to, they could have begun an investigation of their own. Which means it's possible they don't know where you are. Patron hasn't told anyone. That doesn't sound like standard procedure when an agent goes dark. At the very least, it's noted and the director would know, yes?"

Yvette nodded. "You're right, I don't know Jacques as well as I think I do. And I have a list I need to get out of my head. Once again."

"It could be key to solving this case," Jason said.

AMELIE SETTLED ONTO the chair behind the police chief's desk with a blank sheet of paper before her.

Jason breezed back in from reception, tucking away his cell phone in a coat pocket. "You going to be okay for half an hour by yourself?" he asked, zipping up his coat. "Alex and I are meeting Bay to go over the medical examination on Charley's body."

He wandered over and stood beside the chair. He smelled

like fresh, clean air. His overwhelming presence lulled her into a swoony smile.

"I will be with Marjorie standing guard out in reception," she teased. "This shouldn't take too long. What will I do when I've finished?"

"If I'm not back, you can..." He looked around the office, then opened the bottom desk drawer to reveal the contents. "I've got provisions. Snacks and Sudoku. Marjorie will talk your head off it you let her, and she's got a lot of work to do this afternoon. Think she's going to head downstairs and do a little cleaning in the cells, too."

"I won't bother her. Sudoku, eh?"

"For stakeouts."

She lifted a brow in wonder.

"Eh." He shrugged. "I might get to use that book someday. There's always hope."

He leaned over, and when Amelie sensed he was going to kiss her on the top of the head, she quickly tilted her head to catch that morsel against her mouth. He didn't hesitate, finding their connection like a pro. The man pushed his fingers up through the back of her hair, holding her gently. He tasted like all the things she needed right now. Safety, connection, intimacy.

Releasing a tiny moan as his kiss deepened in exploration, Amelie twisted and moved up onto her knees. She spread her hands up the front of his coat, wishing it were anything but the thick black waterproof fabric. Like bare, hot skin. Could a girl get a little taste of that?

Sliding down her hands, she felt the hard shape of his gun hugging his ribs, and then, at the bottom of his coat, she pushed her fingers up underneath it. The Kevlar vest he wore was solid, but thin. His flannel shirt hugged the top of his jeans and...oh yes, there.

He smiled against her mouth, then with a glance toward

the closed door, turned and whispered, "You doing some investigation work of your own?"

"I am. And I found what I was looking for." Hot, bare skin. Tight, hard abs. A dangerous tease. "I wish you didn't have to leave."

"You make me wish the same thing." He nuzzled his forehead against hers. "I'd take you along with me, but this is police business and..."

"I get it. I'm not an investigating officer." Amelie took in his scent, his skin, his breath. The moment was so intimate, yet in the background lurked calamity.

With a quick kiss to her mouth, he said, "I'll be back."

"I'll be waiting for you."

"Does that mean what I think it means?" he asked.

"I never flirt."

"You always mean business. I got that about you." He kissed her again, taking the time to make it linger as he swept his tongue against hers and tasted her deeply. Then he swore softly against her mouth, nodded and stood up. "If I don't leave now..."

"I get it. I feel the same. Things are going to happen between us."

"Yes, they are."

"Go," she said. "I'll write out the list. Then we'll...see what happens next."

He strode to the door, pulling a knit cap over his head. "See you soon!"

She waited and waved as he passed before the front window and strode down Main Street. The man couldn't return to her fast enough. Because he had started a fire inside her, and she wouldn't be able to stop thinking about him until all his clothes were stripped away and that investigation practice turned into real-time experience.

Until then, she did have a more pressing task at hand.

Leaning forward on the not-too-comfy chair, Amelie

wrote out the numbers and letters that formed a list she'd viewed weeks earlier in the strange email that she now felt sure had been sent to her with an ulterior purpose. It couldn't have been an accident. Someone had wanted her to take that information to her boss.

And her boss had known exactly what sort of damage that information could do. To him?

More and more, she believed Jacques was involved in something underhanded.

It was slow going this time around because it was difficult to avoid thoughts of Jacques Patron's true intentions. What information was she streaming out onto the paper? It was something worth killing for.

After half an hour, she wrote out the last line. Times, dates, locations and...that mysterious fourth column. Each entry was a jumble of letters and numbers. It had to be code or...maybe a password?

Stretching her arms over her head, she turned and stood, peering out the window. Jason was still gone, and she hadn't heard a peep from Marjorie after she'd called out that she was going downstairs to straighten the cells.

She wasn't about to go out wandering on her own. But she was antsy now, and the office had chilled noticeably. Pulling on her coat, she dallied with the idea of running down the street to Olson's Oasis for something to munch on. No. Jason had snacks in the drawer. And he'd never forgive her for leaving the station.

Picking up her camera, she wandered out into reception. Amelie trailed a finger along Marjorie's pin-neat desk, taking in the photos of Marjorie and a man with blond hair who must be her husband. A bobblehead of a black cat with green rhinestones for eyes sat next to a desk phone. And a cookbook titled *Hot Dishes* that was flagged with colorful Post-its was splayed open, cover facing up.

She stood back and snapped a few shots of the reception

area, being sure to get Jason's office in the background. She'd never been much for interior shots. Nature was most interesting to capture on film. Backing up against the door, she decided a step outside would be worthwhile, because there was a large oak tree that loomed in the back parking lot. And she'd stay close to the station.

Jason's truck was still parked in the back lot, as was a green Honda. Must be Marjorie's. The oak tree's canopy was vast, leafless, and stretched overhead as if an open umbrella.

Tilting back her head, Amelie snapped some shots. Inhaling the crisp winter air, she smiled. Yes, this could become a career that would make her happy.

Chapter Nineteen

"The cyanide killed him," Elaine said over the phone line as Jason scrolled through Herve Charley's cell phone looking for clues. He and Alex stood in the gas station parking lot, where the green SUV had been towed to wait for the Duluth tow to come and take it away. Ryan Bay stood over by his car, on the phone. "I found traces of it in the beef jerky. Clever."

Jason eyed a couple bundled against the day's ten degrees as they passed by, probably on the way to The Moose for some pie. "Whoever followed him must have planted the beef jerky. Probably drove up behind him. Nudged the car into the ditch and waited to see if the driver would react. No reaction. Assumed he was dead, and drove off."

"A fair assessment. The body was clean of any DNA not unique to the deceased."

Jason swore under his breath. They were dealing with professionals. Two of them. One dead. And the other?

"Thanks, Elaine. This may have become an international case. Bay is on the phone with Interpol again, trying to get some real answers about the one suspect that sticks out like a sore thumb."

"Who do you think the perp is this time around?" Elaine conjectured, "A vigilante going after someone who tried to harm another?"

"Why would someone take out a hit man, Elaine?"

"I don't know—"

"Well, I do. It's because the first one has been replaced after a shoddy effort at eliminating the target. Which means Frost Falls has another hit man running loose. The FBI has verified links to the Minnesota mafia right now."

"Which means someone is after your woman."

"She's not my—"

"Where is she?"

"At the station." Jason checked his watch. It had been half an hour since he'd left Yvette. He should check in with her. "I gotta go, Elaine. Thanks for the info."

Dialing Yvette's number, he suddenly jumped when his pocket rang. Alex cast him a wondering look.

"Shoot. Forgot I'd taken her phone as evidence." He patted the pocket and hung up. "I'm heading back to the station. Make sure everyone is all right. Have Bay give me a call as soon as he's off the phone with Interpol."

Jason started walking down the street. For some reason, he quickened his footsteps.

THE SKY WAS white and the sun high. Amelie could even find some good in the cold, because it tingled across her face, making her feel alive. The idea of spending more time in Frost Falls to photograph the scenery, to perhaps even venture into the Boundary Waters Canoe Area Wilderness, was appealing. It would be a great addition to her meager portfolio.

Everything felt normal. Yet a weird feeling of dread prompted her to suddenly twist at the waist and scan the parking lot behind the station. She hadn't heard anything beyond the hum of the heater that puffed out condensation from the rooftop of the station. Narrowing her gaze, she took in the surroundings.

JASON RAN DOWN the street toward the station. His rubber-soled boots took the snow compacted on the tarmac with ease. Four blocks and no one was going to break a sweat in this frigid weather. By the time he reached the parking lot, he cursed when he saw Yvette's figure standing against the hood of his truck.

What was she doing outside?

"Yvette!"

She turned and waved.

Jason spied the flash of red as it glinted across the hood of his truck. "Get down!"

Racing toward the truck, he lunged forward, gripped her by the shoulders and knocked her down to land on the snow-packed tarmac. Their bodies rolled, and he barreled over the top of her. The camera she'd been holding clattered across the snow. Protecting her body with his, Jason looked up and around the front of the vehicle.

"Someone just shot at you," he said. "I was right." He pulled out his gun and switched off the safety. "There's another hit man in town."

Chapter Twenty

"Stay down," Jason demanded to the woman beneath him on the snow.

Yvette nodded. Her eyes were wide, but he detected more common sense than fear in them. She'd been trained for hostile situations.

He scrambled around to the end of the truck bed and crouched low, pulling out his gun. He swept a look around the rear taillight. No movement in the parking lot. Aiming out into the parking lot, he didn't spy the shooter.

Jason's exhale fogged before his face.

The growl of a snowmobile engine firing up alerted him. He sighted a flash of silver that would place the machine in the alleyway behind the antique shop two buildings down.

"I'm going after him!" he called to Yvette. "Get inside the station!" His protective instincts forced him back to the front of the truck where she now crouched. "You got this, yes?"

She nodded. "Go!"

"Tell Marjorie to call Alex here."

His snowmobile was parked ten feet from the back door. Firing it up, he navigated forward out of the parking lot and to the alleyway. He waited until he heard the other snowmobile reach the intersection of Main Street and the corner of the block. The driver was dressed all in black. No cap or earmuffs, and he didn't wear gloves.

"Not a resident," Jason confirmed.

Confident that whoever drove the snowmobile was the one who had shot at Yvette, he gunned the throttle and his sled soared forward just as the other snowmobile took off through the intersection.

Gun tucked in the holster at his hip, he would not fire on the shooter until he could confirm he was indeed the suspect. Worst-case scenario would see him chasing a kid out for a joyride. But his gut told him this was his man.

Picking up speed as he passed through the intersection, Jason saw the suspect turn and spy him. Jason performed a circling motion with his hand, signaling the man to pull over. A press of a button on the handlebar turned on the police flasher lights.

That resulted in the suspect kicking it into overdrive.

Jason had expected as much. He was a hundred yards behind but intended to close the distance before they got too far out of the city. On the other hand, he was an experienced snowmobiler, and even if the suspect had some skill handling a sled, he wasn't dressed for a ten-degree day or a race through the frigid air and newly drifted snowpack.

The road heading north out of town had been plowed by Rusty Nelson early this morning. Jason's machine soared along the hard-packed snow that had formed on the tarmac. Perfect track for racing snowmobiles. In these conditions, he could handle this six-hundred-pound machine like a dream.

He thought momentarily of how close Yvette had come to taking a bullet. Why had she been standing outside? He'd seen her camera on the ground. Taking photos? He should have been more clear about her staying inside.

Was the shooter a replacement for the previous hit man?

Dirty business, that. But all was fair in spies and deception. If that was what was going on.

Jason had been capable of such dirty dealings. Once, he'd been sent in to replace an inept field asset, but termination had not been a requirement. And yet the same could have happened to him after he'd missed the kill shot. He'd been taken in so easily by the female agent. Had truly believed she was on his side. Damn it!

He gripped the handlebars and ripped the throttle, cutting the distance between himself and the shooter.

Had Interpol issued an official agent termination order for Yvette? Because she had read sensitive data? It was possible yet highly unlikely. But if so, her boss was either trying to save her neck or cut her throat.

The suspect veered from the main road and took off across the ditch. Snow sprayed in the sky, glittering against the too-bright sun that proved deceptive in that it wasn't able to warm this frozen tundra.

They headed northeast. That direction would not allow an easy escape.

The falls, the town's namesake, sat half a mile ahead. Frozen this time of year. Always fun to take the cat out on the slick riverbed, but if a person didn't know the area, the falls could prove dangerous. He and Alex put up orange warning flags and stretched a bright orange safety fence before the falls, but it seemed every few years some unfortunate soul crashed his snowmobile or took a flight over the falls, which dropped twenty feet to boulders below.

AFTER JASON LEFT, Amelie squatted near the tire for a while. Back flat against the front quarter panel and palms against her forehead. That had been a close call.

She should have never been out here to give the shooter such opportunity. Taking pictures, of all things.

The glint of something silver caught her eye. She crawled

toward the pushed-up snow that demarcated the edge of the parking lot in front of the truck. Something was wedged into the snow.

She started to touch it, then got smart. Pulling her sweater sleeve down over her fingers, she used that as protection to grip the object and pulled it out.

This was what had been fired at her. A dart with a red tip.

"Not cool," she muttered, because the implications were creepier than if it had been a bullet.

Springing up, yet staying bent and low, she crept over to the building, plucking up her camera along the way, and then around to the front door. She quickly went inside and rushed to Jason's office to close the door. Marjorie must still be downstairs tidying up the cells.

She pulled open Jason's desk drawers and in the second one spied some plastic evidence bags. Dropping the dart into the bag, she then sealed it.

Patting her hip for her phone, she cursed the fact she'd given it to Jason. She looked around the desk for a weapon, but there was only a locked gun case with one rifle in it.

There was another hit man?

Of course, they wouldn't let this rest without eliminating the target. Whatever this was. And whoever they were.

As she settled into Jason's chair, fingers gripping the arms tightly, Amelie asked herself plainly if Jacques Patron were friend or foe.

Her father had valued his friendship with Patron. And her mother—well, she didn't remember her talking about the man. Perhaps she'd even avoided him. Amelie recalled a few times when her mother had bowed out of joining her father over drinks with Patron at a local taproom.

Had Patron gotten into dirty dealings? Was he protecting himself?

And was he dead or alive?

Chapter Twenty-One

The falls loomed ahead. In the summer, it was possible to walk from the creek above, using a jagged rocky trail, to the gorge below where the water fell softly and landed on mossy boulders. There were no nearby trees to block the wind or even provide handholds. It was a tricky descent without snow and ice.

In the wintertime? Only an idiot would try to land at the bottom starting from the top. And more than a few did in search of Instagram-worthy shots of the spectacular frozen falls. The smart ones wore crampons and used rock-climbing gear. The stupid ones? Jason had rescued a handful of injured climbers over the past two years. Couple of broken arms and a head injury from falling ice chunks. The fine was two thousand dollars if he caught the culprits.

But right now he was more concerned about the one idiot who had no idea what waited for him. Snow blanketed the land as far as the eye could see, and the whiteness played tricks with the eye, disguising ridges, valleys and even edges where the land stopped. The suspect would drive his snowmobile right over the falls' edge if Jason didn't intervene. The last thing he needed was another dead hit man on his hands.

Gunning the engine, he pushed the cat to full speed and gained on the suspect. Veering right, he cursed that he only wore a ski cap and no helmet as the snow spraying up from that move spat at his bare cheeks like pins. He paralleled the suspect, who pulled out his gun and fired at him.

The bullet went wide. Jason wasn't worried about being a target—not at this speed. He jerked his machine to the left, forcing the other to veer left. Gauging he had less than fifty feet before the snowy land gave way to a twenty-foot fall, he stood and tilted his body to pull a tight curl. The nose of his sled butted the other snowmobile's nose, and the impact caused the driver to fall off in a soft landing.

Jason gunned the cat and managed to slip ahead of the other snowmobile and clear it before that machine, unmanned, soared over the falls. His own machine skidded up a cloud of snow behind him as he wrestled it to a stop but two feet from the falls' edge.

Muttering an oath worthy of this annoyance, Jason shut off the snowcat and pulled out his gun. He headed toward the man, who struggled in the knee-deep snow. Difficult to find purchase in the fresh-fallen powder. Jason stomped through the crusted surface, wishing for snowshoes.

"Hands up!" he called.

The suspect pulled up an ungloved hand. Sunlight glinted on the gun he held. Jason pressed the trigger but didn't squeeze hard enough to release. He held steady.

The shooter's hands were too cold. Trembles gave way to jerky shudders. The gun dropped out of his frozen fingers. It sank deep into the snow. The suspect's knees bent, his body falling forward. His face landed in the snow as he struggled against the freezing elements and the inability to keep his body warm enough to stand upright.

AMELIE ANSWERED THE landline on the desk the moment Marjorie opened the office door and popped her head in.

"Hello?" Amelie said. She waved at Marjorie to indicate she stay put.

"I've apprehended the suspect," Jason said. "Just wanted to make sure you were safe."

"I am. Marjorie just got in from downstairs. I'll tell her to contact Alex now."

Marjorie signaled with an *okay* shape of her fingers and left for her desk. Amelie heard her say Alex's name.

"I'll be there in half an hour," Jason said.

She nodded. "You should know he wasn't shooting bullets."

"What?"

"It was a tranq dart." Amelie eyed the evidence bag; a few drops of water had melted from the snow on the outside. "He wasn't trying to kill me. It would be a strange weapon to use if death was his objective."

"Interesting. Someone wanted you incapacitated—he had to have been following you. Waiting for…"

"For me to make a mistake and walk outside, giving him a clear target. I'm so sorry, Jason."

"We'll talk when I get in."

"I finished the list," she added quickly.

"Excellent. See you soon."

THE SUSPECT WAS not speaking English. And it wasn't a Texan drawl this time. Jason knew very few French words, but he did recognize the language. Interesting. For about five seconds.

Patience did not come easily today. He was frustrated and yet invigorated at the same time. This was a mystery. Something he'd been wanting since taking the desk here in Frost Falls. If he was going to prove his worth, this was the case to do it. The powers that be wouldn't want to close the station after he'd solved such a big case. This would put Frost Falls on the map. He'd prove he was an asset to the town as well as the county.

Beside him stood Ryan Bay.

"You recording this?" Jason asked.

Bay nodded and pointed his cell phone toward the prisoner. "Go ahead."

Jason turned to the prisoner, who sat on the bed in the cell, head bowed. "You used a tranquilizer dart," he said. The prisoner lifted his head. The man understood him. He had to if he had made his way around the United States to Minnesota from wherever the hell he'd come from. "You didn't want the woman dead?"

The suspect tilted his head subtly, then bowed it again.

"Who do you work for? The Minnesota mafia?"

The prisoner smirked but neither shook his head nor nodded in confirmation.

Then Jason tried a hunch. "Interpol?"

The slightest tensing of the man's jaw told Jason so much. He'd hit on something. He exchanged a raised eyebrow with the BCA agent, who nodded.

Was this hit man really on the same team as Yvette? Jason had to search the Interpol database. With the fingerprints he'd taken upon booking him, he could do that search. But if he was from Interpol, and the previous hit man had not been—what was going on?

Alex wandered down the stairs, and Jason asked, "Did Marjorie run the fingerprints?"

"She's still trying to upload the scan. Sorry, Cash. Won't be much longer."

The station still used the old card-and-ink method of fingerprinting. Which meant they had to upload a scanned image of the fingerprints to run them through the database. What he wouldn't give for the fancy digital scanners all the well-budgeted stations used nowadays.

"I'll check with Interpol," Bay said. "It may cut our time and we won't have to deal with this insolent."

"Good plan," Jason said.

"I get my phone call," the man said from behind the cell bars.

Jason turned at the perfect use of English. The bastard.

"That you do." He took the receiver off the landline attached to the cinder-block wall and handed it through the bars, letting the cord dangle from a horizontal bar. "Alex will assist you with dialing. Good luck getting through though."

He hesitated before walking up the stairs behind Bay. The last time he'd left Alex alone with the prisoner, the man had escaped. Only to be found dead hours later. Jason considered it for a moment. This time the suspect could have his food stuffed through the bars, if it came to that.

He also knew that phone hadn't received any reception since he'd been working here. Maybe a broken wire. Maybe even a frayed cable on the outside phone lines. Too bad it wasn't in the city budget for repairs.

He took the stairs two at a time, following Bay, and stepped out into the frigid air with a brute shout as the brisk chill instantly permeated his flannel shirt. He'd left his coat in the office.

"I'll be right in," Bay said, walking toward his car. "I need to make a few calls."

"You can use my office phone," Jason called, but the man was already rushing toward his vehicle.

Running around to the back door, Jason entered the building, stomping his boots free of snow on the mat.

Marjorie greeted him with a smile.

"You get the fingerprints scanned?"

"Running them right now. The Wi-Fi has been wonky since the storm. But I crossed my fingers and promised my firstborn if it would hold out. The connection is running slower than the old dial-up, but we should have results soon."

Jason swung around Marjorie's desk and eyed the spinning colored ball on the computer screen that indicated it was doing its work. Slowly.

"Miss LaSalle is in your office. I fixed her up with coffee and last year's local calendar. I keep a few copies in my lower drawer. For emergencies."

She ended with a "toodle-loo!" leaving Jason shaking his head. How had Marjorie known Yvette was interested in the calendar?

He knocked his fist against the thin wall as he opened the door to his office. They really needed to insulate these inner walls.

Chapter Twenty-Two

Well, hell. Not like he wasn't proud of the July centerfold that featured him washing the station patrol car shirtless. Heh.

Yvette was seated behind his desk, sipping coffee and grinning widely. Wow. Her eyes actually glinted. Just like Elaine had said his eyes had a glint. Huh. Guess it was possible. And never before had he seen such a bright yet devious smile.

"Hey, I gotta give back to the community somehow, right?" Jason hooked a thigh up on the corner of the desk and leaned over to spy the source of her amusement.

"Marjorie said this was the office copy." She tapped the July spread. "But she already texted me the link to the online version. You definitely go above and beyond with community service."

"I do like to serve the greater good."

"Greater good, indeed." She winked and then covered an even wider smile behind another sip of coffee. "You interrogate the guy who shot at me?"

"He's not overly talkative. Cross your fingers the Wi-Fi stays connected so we get a fingerprint match soon."

Yvette crossed her fingers, then pointed to the plastic evidence bag at the corner of the desk. "It's the dart that

I plucked out of a snowbank. No fingerprint contamination. Promise."

Jason took the item and studied it. "I've seen these in syringe form," he commented. "Used when security professionals are holding down an aggravated target. Firing one out of a gun at a human seems so…"

"Sporting? Like a hunter after his prey?"

"I was going to go with creepy."

He turned the bag to study the dart tip. The only way the shooter could have guaranteed a good placement was to get close to Yvette. Ten to twenty feet maximum. He'd seen the target acquisition red light on Yvette, and yet, he hadn't seen anyone in the area so close. He'd had to have been at least half a block away. Likely, he'd intended to tranq Yvette, toss her over a shoulder—and then what? Take her to crime scene two to finish the job?

"I'll send this to Duluth for forensics to test it. See what this dart contains."

"Jason, I'm so sorry," she rushed out. An exhale preceded a watery look up at him. "I was bored. I'd finished the list. I figured if I stayed right by the station, it would be fine to snap a few shots. I've been so foolish since arriving here. You can see why I would have never made a good field agent."

"Don't give yourself such a hard time. Nobody's hurt. That's what matters."

He noticed Yvette's subtle shiver. Her discomfort gave him the shivers, too.

"They didn't want me dead. At least, not right away," she said. Her voice trembled. "They want what's in my brain first."

He set the dart on the desk and stood, hooking his thumbs at his belt loops as he scanned out the window behind her. He didn't want her to see his concern, but they both knew how desperate this situation had become.

"The perp is behind bars," he offered.

Yvette sighed. "That's what you said the last time."

That statement cut at his pride. He'd screwed up with Herve Charley. No matter that it hadn't been him watching the prisoner at the time of his escape. Jason took responsibility around here. He had to.

Marjorie beeped the intercom.

"Cash, we got a hit on the fingerprints. And the CIA is on the line for you and Bay."

Really? What the hell was the CIA doing nosing in on the scene? Bay had contacted the FBI. They should have matters pertaining to Charley in hand.

"Thanks." He glanced to the desk phone. He'd prefer to take the call in private and not with an Interpol agent in the room. "Be right there."

Yvette stood, but he shook his head, gesturing she sit back down. "You stay in here."

The last thing he needed right now was the CIA sticking their noses in his business. They'd controlled him up until they'd dumped him here in Frost Falls. What next?

"Fine." She sat. "But you know how thin these walls are."

He winced as he opened the door and stepped out into reception. Wasn't much he was going to keep private, and especially not with a conference call.

"The CIA?" He looked to Bay, who was nursing a cup of coffee in a paper cup advertising The Moose logo. "Thought you were connecting us with Interpol?"

"I was, but I got a ping from the CIA looking to conference with us. And…here they are." He nodded to Marjorie, who pushed a button on her phone.

"Jason Cash," the man on the line said. "Marcus Fronde, counterintelligence director for the CIA."

Jason knew the man. Not personally, but more than a few times his name had appeared on a dossier for an overseas job. Counterintelligence? They got involved when a foreign entity was in the mix. They must have gotten wind of Bay's call to Interpol. But from the FBI?

There were too many fingers in the soup for Jason's comfort. And the last agency he wanted to deal with was the CIA.

"You've been busy up there in your frozen little town," Fronde said.

"Yes, sir. That's what they sent me here to do. Keep the peace and enforce the law." He glanced to Bay. Surely he'd been briefed regarding Jason's history. He didn't react, merely crossed his arms high over his chest.

"Not working so well, eh?" Fronde said. "You've got a homicide and a dead shooter with known connections to mafia activity in your area."

Jason swallowed and turned his back to Marjorie, who respectfully penciled something on the calendar splayed open on the desk before her. "Keeping an eye on me?" he asked.

"Always. You've got Agent Bay there?"

"Yes, sir," Bay replied. "We're coordinating with Interpol. Or attempting to. The target in this case is one of their agents."

"You realize when an investigation goes international, the CIA wants in?"

Yes, he did. And no, he did not want a CIA agent charging in and taking over his investigation. He didn't mind sharing with the BCA. Bay was nothing but a handy reference should he need his assistance.

But to step aside and allow a CIA agent to do the job he was supposed to do?

On the other hand, they could probably twist the information he needed out of Interpol merely by cachet alone.

"I've got things under control. And with my experience," Jason said, "I know what to do. Though if you can hook me up with a liaison to Interpol, I'd be appreciative."

"Forget the liaison. I'll be sending out an agent. Should arrive this evening. Tomorrow morning at the latest. They'll relieve you of the case."

Jason opened his mouth to protest, but the call clicked off.

He thrust a fist before him in frustration. The urge to swear, and loudly, was only tamped down by pressing his lips together and compressing his jaw.

"I get your anger," Bay said. "I've read your bio."

Great. Just freakin' great.

"I can handle this," Jason said.

"Another set of eyes and ears isn't going to obstruct the investigation," Bay said calmly. "As you said, they will have more leverage with Interpol. Can't understand why they're giving us the cold shoulder, especially when one of their agents is involved."

"Yeah? Maybe two of their agents are in the thick of this."

"What are you thinking, Cash?"

"Her boss, Jacques Patron. He could be pulling strings on his end, covering things up."

"So he's moved to the top of your suspects list? We don't have confirmation that he's dead or alive."

"Right. And that feels twenty kinds of wrong to me. Admit it, that's suspicious."

"It is. So why not welcome the CIA to assist? Come on, Cash, it's all water under the bridge now. Doesn't matter who works the case so long as we get a good outcome."

Jason nodded. "Just hate to see Frost Falls lose this station. You know they're going to shut us down come March, forward all calls to the county?"

"What?"

Jason tightened his jaw at Marjorie's outburst. Shoot. He'd meant to tell her that at a better time.

"Sorry, Marjorie. I've known about it a few weeks. Was intending to tell you. I thought this case might give us some leeway. Maybe even impress all the right people."

"Uff da." The dispatcher sat back in her chair, shaking her head.

"It's not so much the station you want to save," Bay said, "as your reputation. Admit it, Cash. You were a damn good CIA agent. Your sniping skills were highly commended."

"Can we have this conversation some other time?" Jason said with a glance toward Marjorie, who now looked at him like a deer in headlights. "The case is all we need to discuss."

"Sure. But don't get your hopes up about the station staying open." Bay tossed his empty coffee cup in the garbage can beside the desk. "I'm going back down to see if the prisoner may have changed his mind about talking.

"I'll be close." Jason stepped away and into his office, closing the door behind him. Anything to get away from Marjorie's sad stare. But the escape wasn't exactly what he'd hoped for, because Yvette looked up from her place behind his desk.

"What did the CIA have to say?" she asked quietly.

"Uh, just keeping an eye on me."

"They're stepping in, aren't they?"

She'd heard it all. Damn it.

Jason could but nod. He shouldn't take this so hard, but—damn it, this had been his one chance to prove himself!

"Then we'd better hurry," she said. "And figure this out before that happens." She pulled a piece of paper out of her pocket and handed it to him. "The list."

Chapter Twenty-Three

Jason unfolded the notebook page, which still dangled ragged bits from where Yvette had torn it from the spiral binder. The writing was neat but tiny. She'd said she thought it was an invoice. Dates and locations didn't necessarily imply invoice but could rather denote meetings or pickups or even exchange of goods. Something had occurred at the listed location on the corresponding date. Something associated with a dollar amount. The amounts were even, ranging from two thousand to eighteen thousand euros. Some amounts were listed with a dollar sign, which might indicate a difference in who was giving and who was receiving.

"Could be gunrunning," he mused out loud. The Duluth harbor on Lake Superior was one of the largest US outlets for importers of illegal firearms.

"You think?" Yvette exhaled an exasperated sigh. "I hate firearms dealers. They are the nastiest of the nasty."

"Indeed, they are. But it's a guess. Someone was receiving money for…something. At these dates and locations. And some amounts are listed with a dollar sign so I have to figure it wasn't just euros involved. Interesting."

"Then why would *I* have received that email?"

Jason shrugged. "Someone letting the cat out of the bag? Trying to call attention to it without being the one to do so.

Could be anything. Corporate shills. Assassins. A list of eliminated targets and payouts."

"You really think it came from within?"

He wasn't one hundred percent sure about that. Or anything, at this point. But his Spidey senses were tingling.

"Your boss," Jason said. "Remind me how he acted when you'd told him you had this info stored in your head."

She leaned her elbows onto the edge of the desk. "Jacques has always been a calm, cool man. Hard to get a read on him. His eyes are gray."

"That have significance? Eye color?"

"Soulless," she said. "And his hair is graying, so he was always sort of…not there. Easy to blend in. Which made him a great agent, I'm sure. But as a fellow worker, I could never get a read on him."

"And yet, I initially sensed you had a good rapport with him? That you liked him? You call him by his first name. That indicates something more than a mere business relationship."

"I did. I do. Like I told you, I remember him from when I was a teenager. I've grown up trusting him. So, yes, our relationship is personal, but on a friendly level." Yvette wrinkled up her face. "But after receiving that message, I'm not so sure what that relationship has become. Is he dead or alive? What's going on, Jason?"

Jason took a moment to put himself in the head of a French Interpol director who knew a woman who carried a list in her head—a list he apparently had read quickly, then burned it. Those were not the actions of a man who had nothing to hide.

Had Patron removed Yvette from Lyon to then make her death look like an accident? Why send her all the way to Frost Falls? What was the mafia connection? Was there a connection? Could Herve Charley have been a random hire? No, he'd read about the French connection in the stats.

"No one knows where you are? No family? A girlfriend?"

She shook her head.

He snapped the paper with a forefinger. Had to be sensitive information. Was Jacques Patron protecting someone? Himself?

"Tell me more about Jacques Patron," he said to Yvette.

A knock on the door preceded "Cash?"

It was Ryan Bay.

"Come in."

Jason slid a thigh onto the desk corner and crossed his arms over his chest.

"Talked to Interpol again and sent them the prisoner's fingerprints. They are cooperating with this information. Still couldn't get any info on Patron. Said they're looking into it." Bay handed him a single printed paper. "You won't believe who we've got below."

Jason's eyes dropped to the prisoner's name: Rutger Lund. Thirty-seven years old. A field operative. For Interpol.

He glanced to Yvette. They'd sent one of her own to take her out? Yikes. How was he going to tell her that? Did he need to tell her that? Yes, he did.

"What's up?" she asked.

"Got the prisoner's name," Bay said to her. "Rutger Lund. You know him?"

She shook her head. "Should I?"

"He's an Interpol agent," Jason said.

Yvette's jaw dropped open. And Bay pulled up a chair to sit down.

"You going to do this, or am I?" Bay asked Jason.

Jason pulled his desk chair back and gestured for Yvette to sit down. "I'll do it."

"You guys suspect me now, don't you?" Yvette sat, and

when neither of them answered her, she beamed her big blue gaze up at Jason. "You do."

"Didn't say that," he said.

"Well, I'll say it," Bay tossed out. "We've got an Interpol agent hiding out in Frost Falls under an assumed name…" He handed Jason another sheet of paper from the file folder. "Her real name is Amelie Desauliniers. Has worked at Interpol for two years. Six months in the field and another eighteen—"

"For their tech department. I know," Jason said. "She's told me as much."

Bay stood and leaned his palms onto the desk. This was the first time Jason had seen the fire in him show in his curled fingers and tense jaw.

Jason took an instinctual step toward Yvette. He stood beside her but a step away from touching her. "She was sent here because she had sensitive information in her head that her boss feared could get her killed," Jason said.

"What sort of information?"

Yvette turned the list Jason had set on his desk toward the agent, and he took it and read it. Bay shrugged his shoulders. "What does this mean?"

"Not sure," Jason offered.

"Well, ask her!"

"I don't know what it means," Yvette replied. "It was a strange email that turned up in my inbox. It didn't have an origin, and it self-destructed after a few minutes. But it was enough to put my boss on the alert and want to send me away for a while."

Bay winced. "I'm not following."

"She's got a photographic memory," Jason explained. "She remembers things she reads, like books and lists, but doesn't necessarily know what it is she has seen."

"And you believe her?"

"I'm the one who's been the target," Yvette said firmly.

"I'm not on a case, or running a ploy or—I haven't been a field agent for a long time. I'm just trying to stay alive while we figure this out."

Agent Bay scanned down the list. He tapped his fingers on it. "Three columns of data. Looks like a date column, possibly location and…"

"Time," Jason offered.

"But this fourth column is a mix of numbers and letters. A password? For what?" He shot a steely gaze at Yvette.

But she had no answer. If her boss had wanted this out of everyone's eyesight, including his own…

Over her shoulder, Jason asked, "How do you code operations?"

"That's probably need to know."

He gave her an exasperated look. "I'm not asking for state secrets. I'm trying to keep you alive."

"Right. Uh, usually a three-or four-letter sequence. First few letters of the operation code name. If something were called Blacktail, for instance, the code would be B, L, A, C."

"Gotta be a lot of operations that begin with *black*, don't you think?"

"That's true. Maybe I don't know for sure. You think there are operation code names on that list?"

"I don't know. Let me see that list, Bay."

The agent handed it over, and Jason took a few moments to read it.

"This last column for each entry is eight to twelve characters long. It's gotta be passwords. What makes you so sure your boss, who sent you off to a foreign country and then basically left you here without contact, isn't working for someone else?"

"If he was protecting himself, then why not take me out right away?" she asked. "Fire me or have me eliminated that night I went home. Instead he sends me to Minnesota? For what reason?"

"To get you far away until he figured out what to do with you," Bay offered. "And it would it be cleaner to take you out on foreign soil."

"How so? Taking out a target on home territory would be neater, more contained and something a person could control."

"True, but the evidence would no longer be in Interpol's backyard."

"And if my guess about the mafia connection to France is correct," Jason said, "then perhaps he wanted her in his hire's range. Maybe Jacques is a double agent. Or he's protecting a double who has been taking payouts."

"But agencies employ double agents all the time," Yvette said.

"Don't I know it." Jason shook his head and growled at the same time.

"Oh right," Yvette said. "Her."

Bay and Jason exchanged a look.

Jason scrubbed his brow with the heel of his hand. "That's not what we're discussing. Maybe Jacques wanted this information hidden," he tossed out. "Forever."

"Are you implying he had no intention of ever bringing me back in?"

"I don't know. He is the one man who knew what was on this list. And is he still alive?" He looked to Bay.

"I asked and was told that was need-to-know information," Bay said.

"Don't you think that's a little strange?" Jason asked.

Bay shrugged. "Yes, but they have their secrets just like we have ours. They work much more closely with the CIA. Do you think the prisoner in your jail cell knows what the list is for?" Bay said. "He has to."

"Why does he have to? He's only been sent to take out the target."

"He didn't want me dead," Yvette said. "He wanted me incapacitated."

"Right." Jason had forgotten that detail. "So he could then extract what you know. Maybe he does know. And if he's Interpol…something doesn't add up here. Someone knows something. And I need to find out who and what that is. We need to talk to him again, Bay."

"I agree."

"Come on." Jason headed out of the office but called over his shoulder, "Yvette, or Amelie, look over that final column again. See if it makes any sense to you now."

Chapter Twenty-Four

Jason paced before the cell bars. It was cold down here, but the prisoner had not taken the blanket to wrap about himself. A sturdy man, he was about Jason's height and build and had slick black hair and dark eyes. He sat on the bed, back to the cinder-block wall, knees bent. He faced the bars. Marjorie reported he'd eaten every bit of his food. (And Jason would, too; those meals came directly from The Moose.) He was also fastidious about his personal grooming and had requested a book, any book, to read. One of Marjorie's romance novels sat splayed open on the bed beside him. Jason wouldn't even smirk at that. He'd sneaked a peek at a few pages when Marjorie wasn't looking. Those books were interesting.

And written in English.

The BCA agent stepped up beside Jason and gave him a look. Yes, he was ready.

"Interpol, eh?" Jason said to the prisoner.

The man maintained his gaze but said, "I wasn't able to place a call."

And now he spoke English perfectly well. "I know. Repairman has been called for the faulty wiring." Yes, like a year and a half ago. "By law, I'm supposed to report your whereabouts to Interpol."

"That is not correct."

"How do you know? Are you familiar with Interpol procedure?"

The man looked aside, bowing his head.

"Did Jacques Patron send you here to pick up Amelie Desauliniers?"

The man crossed his arms over his chest and tilted his head back against the wall. No comment.

"You weren't sent to kill her," Jason said. "So I have to figure that means you either came to take Desauliniers home—though, why you'd do it in such a covert manner does puzzle me. And if you're not returning her to Lyon, then the only other option is to extract information."

"Phone. Call."

"Like I said, a repairman has been called. Another storm is headed toward us, though. Makes travel difficult. You'd better hunker down for the wait."

"You have a cell phone in your pocket. Desk phones elsewhere," the prisoner insisted.

"I do, but you are not in a position to access them, are you?"

The man crossed his arms tightly and looked aside.

Jason toed the base of a cell bar. "This is what we've learned from a database search. You are Rutger Lund. An Interpol agent. Home base, Marseille. Seven years in the field. Expertise, black ops. Apparently, covert sniping and operating a snowmobile were not in your training."

"You have no idea what you are sticking your nose into."

Jason propped his forearm against a couple of the cell bars and peered between two of them. "Why don't you enlighten me?"

He didn't mind getting flipped the bird. He hadn't expected the man would engage in a sharing session with him. But he had gotten a roundabout confirmation that he was Interpol. And that only troubled him further.

"I'll let you sit on ice awhile longer." He glanced to the

thermostat on the wall, right next to the phone. "These concrete walls are thick, but they don't insulate against the weather well. Talk to you in the morning."

The man swore in French as Jason and Agent Bay headed up the stairs.

UP IN JASON'S OFFICE, Amelie studied the list. With the CIA headed this way, they had their work cut out for them. She knew the CIA would take over the case, and she also knew that Jason would take that as an affront. He hadn't come right out and told her, but he needed to solve this case. A small-town cop planted in the middle of nowhere who had once traveled the world on covert missions? Hell yes, he probably needed this like a person needed oxygen.

And if she could help him, then she would.

She scoured over the paper. Cash payouts? To whom and what for? Interpol was huge and employed thousands across the globe. If this was a confidential list, it could only have been meant for Patron's eyes. The fact she had received it? Someone wanted to out Patron.

Because if it implicated anyone other than her boss, why wouldn't he have acted on that information immediately and—maybe he had.

No. Then there would have been no reason to send her out of the country.

"I'm missing something."

The final column, Amelie had postulated, could be passwords. But for what? Each was associated with a different date, location and dollar amount. Was it a locker that held the payout, accessible only with the correct password? But the dates were all past. Why include the password if the pickup had already occurred?

She closed her eyes and recalled the day she'd opened the suspicious email. Unless she wrote things down, she wouldn't recall it all exactly, but she could remember the layout of the document on her computer. Two single eight-and-a-half by eleven-inch pages. Four columns. The final column…had those characters been underlined?

She opened her eyes. "Like clickable links?"

The email had disappeared after ten minutes. It hadn't gone to the trash file. Not recoverable. Yet nothing was ever completely lost from a computer's hard drive. Security agencies employed talented individuals who could access even the most buried information on a hard drive. It wasn't in her skill set, but the tech manager was certainly qualified.

The first hit man had to have been ordered by someone who didn't want the information falling into other hands.

But as for the suspect sitting in the jail cell below? He'd wanted her alive. And had very likely taken out the first hit man.

Yet her death was for the ultimate reason of…what? If they'd kept her alive, it had to be for a reason. To extract the information she knew? But it seemed as if Jacques might already know that info, so he couldn't be related to the second shooter.

Amelie leaned back in the uncomfortable office chair. She felt at odds and alone, standing in the middle of a flooding room. She had no allies. Even Jason couldn't be considered one. He was only doing his duty. This investigation had begun with the body of a dead woman. An innocent woman caught in a fouled assassination attempt.

She bit her lip. That poor family.

"How's it coming?"

She stood abruptly with the list in hand. "I didn't hear you walk in."

Jason lifted a brow and cast her a discerning look. Even though the look was meant to be questioning, she still swooned at the sight of that freckled gaze. "You figure out the final column?"

"I think these are passwords," she said. "I recall now, on the original document, the fourth column was underlined."

He lifted a brow.

"Like clickable links," she suggested.

"Good going. How do we access the original document?"

"We don't. Not unless we turn this investigation over to Interpol."

"Not a good idea. I have reason to believe someone is involved in a cover-up," he said. "And I'm beginning to think it was cash payouts."

"Payouts to whom?"

Jason shrugged.

Amelie wrapped her arms over her chest and bowed her head. The sensation of tears niggled at her, but she would not cry in front of him. That was not professional. And she had to look at her exile here as a continuation of her job. For her own sake, she had to stay strong and figure this out.

"What is it?" Jason leaned over her and stroked her hair.

His kind touch tugged at her tears, but she sniffled and shook her head. "I'm sorry. It's all so much. I feel abandoned. Out of place. Feeling sorry for myself, I suppose."

"You have every right. You are alone in a strange country. And a damn cold and inhospitable country at that."

"Why couldn't he have sent me to Florida?" she said with a lighter tone.

"Your boss ever mention friends in Minnesota? Allies? Employees?"

"You think he chose this state for a purpose?"

"The Minnesota mafia does have a connection to France."

Amelie met his gaze. Damn, he was so handsome. Why had she met Jason Cash in such a situation? Any other time, she would have reached to touch those cute freckles on his nose.

He gave her shoulders a reassuring squeeze. "What are you thinking about right now?" he asked.

She set free the smile that was always so close when in his presence. "Your freckles."

He wrinkled his nose. "You spend a lot of time thinking about my freckles."

"They're sexy."

Amelie leaned in and kissed him. She twisted on the chair, and he knelt between her legs. Cupping her head with his hands, he deepened the kiss in an urgent and insistent way. He tasted like coffee. His heat fired within her like no hearth fire ever could.

She gripped his shirt and tugged him closer so she could wrap her legs about his thighs. He bowed his head and kissed down her neck and throat. She almost moaned with pleasure. But she was aware that Marjorie could be in the next room. A few minutes of this pleasure was all she asked.

When his hand brushed her breast, her nipples tightened. And she dared the quietest moan. Jason answered with his own restrained sound of want.

He broke the kiss and pressed his forehead to hers, closing his eyes. He breathed a few times, heavy and wanting, then stepped back and pulled her up to embrace.

"I want you," she said quietly.

He nodded against her head.

"I want this to happen."

"It will," he said in a quiet, low tone that stirred at her humming insides. So sexy to have to be quiet when all they wanted to do was rip each other's clothing off. "Not here."

"'Course not," she said on a breath. "You have an investigation going on."

He gave her another quick kiss. "I do, and it's only just gotten started. Oh, you mean that other investigation? The one regarding the hit man and the French spy?" He smiled.

"I prefer the first, but duty does call. Let's solve this case. Save the girl. And then…"

"And then?"

"And then we'll see what happens next."

Chapter Twenty-Five

Snow whisked across the tarmac, plastering the main road thick white. Jason stomped the flakes from his boots before entering the station. He'd walked Yvette across the street to Olson's Oasis after Colette had waved her down. Said she'd ordered a helmet for her and it was in. The two women had started chatting, so Jason had pleaded off and told Yvette no more than ten minutes. He'd be watching the store out the station window.

The station smelled like roasted turkey, gravy and lots of buttery mashed potatoes. Marjorie did not have a meal on her desk. She handed him a cup of coffee as he entered.

"You already eat? You should go home, Marjorie. Storm's not taking its time today."

"I intend to. Just grabbing a few necessaries in case you need me to make some calls while the station is closed. I've already talked to county dispatch. They are on call. I fed the prisoner again."

"I guess you did. A Thanksgiving dinner?"

"*Uff da*, it's freezing down there and we are not Guantánamo. I gave him back the pillow you removed, too."

"Marjorie."

She lifted an eyebrow, and Jason conceded with a nod. "Fine. He's going to have to sit through the storm down there. I'll turn the heat up a few degrees."

"Already done." Marjorie pulled on her bright red parka. "I left some snacks, too. Cronuts and popcorn. He'll be fine. Isn't the CIA headed our way?"

"You betcha. Just heard from them. On their way from the Minneapolis airport."

"Through the storm?"

Jason shrugged.

"I know you don't want them stealing your case," Marjorie said. "Maybe they'll allow you to work with them?"

"Doubt it. Me and the CIA—it's bad blood, Marjorie. Agent Bay shouldn't have said what he said earlier. But I'm not going to pull a hissy fit. If they want to take over, it's their case. But until they get here—and I'm predicting the storm will hang them up somewhere around Hinckley…"

"Good eats in that town," Marjorie said.

"They'll have to hunker down at Tobie's. Best cinnamon rolls this side of the Twin Cities."

"So speaking of all the things Agent Bay has let slip." Marjorie walked up to him and wrapped a scarf about her neck. "You going to tell me more about the station closing?"

"I don't know much, Marjorie. City budget cuts. They plan to close us in March. I thought I could do something, maybe this case would bring attention to us and they'd reconsider, but…" Jason sighed. "I'm sorry."

"It's not your fault, Cash. This station has been on its last legs since the iron mine closed. Maybe it's time I retired, eh?"

"Uff da," he said.

"Exactly. Bay is down with the prisoner. Not sure what he's up to, but that's where he is. Where's your woman?"

"She's not my woman, Marjorie."

"You want her to be your woman."

"Would you quit calling her my woman? She's… I like her. Okay?"

"There's nothing wrong with kissing a woman you want

to protect. And now that the prisoner is behind bars, what will she do with herself? Oh, there's a handsome policeman willing to keep her warm on a stormy night."

"Marjorie!"

She chuckled and headed toward the door. "It's not very often I get to tease you, Cash. Let me have this one." She waved and left the station.

And Jason smiled to himself. He'd let her have that one. Because he had gotten the pretty one.

"FIVE MINUTES," THE waitress told Amelie, who sat at the counter nursing a cup of coffee. "I need to let the pie thaw a few minutes before I cut it."

Amelie had ordered a couple of slices of pie for herself and Jason. A surprise. The Moose was close enough to the station, and she'd scanned the area. Hadn't felt a sense of unease. She'd be safe by herself for the time it took to finish this cup.

"Pass the sugar."

Amelie startled when the woman next to her at the counter asked for the condiment. She noticed her sitting at the counter when she'd walked in. Her coffee cup was half-full. She was beautiful. Dark black hair was cut choppy just below her ears, and lots of smoky eye shadow drew attention to her gray eyes.

A perfectly groomed eyebrow lifted in question as she silently stared at Amelie.

"Oh, yes, sorry." Amelie slid the sugar shaker toward her. "My mind was elsewhere."

"Probably on the crazy weather, eh?"

She had a definite French accent, Amelie thought. Not unusual in this town, for she'd learned that many passing through came from Canada. French Canadians traveled down to Minnesota to shop because the exchange rate was so good. Add to that, the Boundary Waters Canoe Area Wilderness was a gorgeous vacation site.

"I'm getting accustomed to the weather," Amelie provided. "What about you? New in town?"

"Just passing through. The hubby and I are headed for Canada. Relatives. You know."

"That's the accent I recognize."

"Yours sounds French, as well. But not Canadian. What part of France you from?"

Amelie felt a sudden and distinct twinge in her gut. That instinct alarm that she had been trained never to ignore. Of course, the woman was simply making conversation. While talking to another woman her age, not from the area, sounded like heaven, it was weird that someone would be passing through during a storm. On the other hand, these Minnesotans were a hardy breed, and a few flakes never kept them in one place for long.

"Refill?" The waitress filled the woman's coffee cup and then looked to Amelie.

She shook her head. "I'll be back. I'm headed to the, uh…" She pointed toward the corner that turned into a long hallway leading to the restrooms.

"I'll go check on the pie right now." The waitress walked off.

After a sip of her coffee, the woman with the dark hair beamed a smile at her. Amelie felt that grin on her back all the way down the end of the counter. Even after she rounded the turn, it burned up her neck.

Why was she getting this feeling? Simply because the woman wasn't from around here? Amelie wasn't, either. Still, most travelers would plan ahead in such weather.

With the bag containing the helmet in one hand, she pushed open the bathroom door and paced before the stalls. The strong lavender air freshener gave her a sudden headache.

The same kind of headache she got whenever she thought about Jacques Patron.

Turning to push open the door, Amelie caught it roughly against her palm. She stepped back to allow the new person to enter. With an "excuse me" on her tongue, Amelie stopped speaking at sight of who it was.

"Hey, sweetie." The beautiful woman with the smoky eye shadow grinned at her. Except this time, Amelie didn't need instinct to know that grin was malevolent.

JASON PICKED UP the list that lay on the desk before him and wandered to the window to peer out. Main Street was clear. Back to the list. Jacques Patron was protecting someone who had been taking bribes or kickbacks. That was his conclusion. It made sense. A date, a location for pickup and a dollar amount.

Of course, the list could not be something Patron had made himself. The only reason a person would make such a list—and put it in the hands of an Interpol employee—had to be for blackmail or push. But why involve Yvette?

Jason honestly did not believe she had a clue what she was involved in. She wasn't lying to him. She couldn't be. So that meant someone knew she had a relationship to Patron and that upon seeing the list, she'd go to her boss. And he'd known what it meant as soon as she'd shown him.

He felt sorry for Yvette. All her life she'd known the man only as a kind friend of the family. And now he had betrayed her.

Did it matter who Patron was protecting? He could be protecting himself, for all Jason knew. What did matter was that an innocent woman had gotten trapped in the middle, carrying information she hadn't asked to know in the first place. And now someone wanted her dead.

He tapped the last column on the list. Clickable links? To what? Videos? Of? The person accepting payoffs?

"Makes sense."

The only people who had any clue what was on the list were Yvette and Jacques Patron.

Jason had heard a gunshot at the end of the message Patron had left him. Yet…he hadn't heard a human grunt of pain following. Most people vocalized when shot, even if it was just a moan. Which meant…

"He's still alive." Had to be.

Interpol was generally open with information when asked through the correct channels. And yet, if an investigation into one of their own was underway, they would likely keep that close to the vest. As Jason had done. But if the CIA had already stuck their noses into this, there could be information that Jason wasn't allowed to know.

Time to go with his gut.

"Patron is protecting himself," Jason decided. And he knew it was true.

He checked his watch and frowned. It had been twenty minutes since he'd left Yvette at Olson's Oasis. He glanced down Main Street again. Where was she?

Jason grabbed his coat and soared out of the office. Only to come face-to-face with a smirking man in a black suit, wearing no outerwear. His shoulders crouched forward against the wind.

The CIA had arrived.

Chapter Twenty-Six

Amelie came to with a snap of her head upward. Ouch. She sat upright and blinked. Where was she? She had been in the ladies' restroom at The Moose and—the woman with the gray eyes had walked in and smiled at her so wickedly.

A shiver crept along her arms. She wore no coat, just a sweater, jeans and boots. Taking in her surroundings, she didn't hear anything, but—what was that? Wind whipped wildly against the windows that filtered in hazy light. The storm sounded angry. The concrete floor was littered with dust and debris. She sat on a wood chair with flat side arms, and one of her wrists was bound to that arm. Her other wrist was free, but her arm sat heavily on the chair. She didn't feel tied up, not at the ankles or around her waist or chest. And to test, she slid forward on the chair.

"Not so fast, sweetie. I need you to relax."

Her instincts had been right. The woman had kidnapped her and taken her…somewhere. How much time had passed? How had she gotten her out of The Moose? She must have had help.

Scanning before her, Amelie took in a vast, empty building. Looked like an old garage, the kind used for fixing cars. There were two big doors through which cars could drive in and out, and a small walled-off office toward the front. One window with yellowed glass was frosted over.

But no tools or furniture, save the chair she sat on and a wood table beside her. Actually, the table was a plank of plywood sitting atop two wood sawhorses. A makeshift operation.

"Where am I?"

"I honestly don't know," the woman replied. "Some abandoned garage. This town is overrun with empty houses and buildings."

Her accent no longer carried the Canadian cadence.

"Who do you work for?" Amelie had the clarity to ask. She still hadn't seen the woman. She stood behind the chair.

"None of your business, sweetie."

"I am not your sweetie. Do you work for Jacques Patron?"

The woman laughed and walked around to the side by the table. She set a pistol on the plank and lifted what Amelie now noticed was a syringe. A spill of black hair fell across her left eye and cheek as she studied the clear plastic tube on the device.

"You haven't figured it out yet?" the woman asked.

"If I had, I wouldn't be sitting here right now."

"You do have the list in your head. That's what I've been told."

"I…" She wasn't going to provide information when it wasn't clear what the woman knew. "What's your name?"

"Hey, if you don't want to be friendly, sweetie, then names are off the table. Let's quit with the girlfriend chat. It's cold in here, and I'm sure you'll want to get some warmer clothes on when we're done."

"Does that mean you're not going to kill me?"

"If I kill you, I'll never have access to what you know."

"You don't have access to it now. What's going to change that?"

"This." The woman held the syringe closer to Amelie. "Sodium pentothal. It'll make you tell the truth."

A drug used to obtain information from unwilling subjects. "It might relax me and make me tell you who my secret lover is, but how will it extract information you don't even know about?"

"You tell me."

"About my lover?"

"I'd slap you, but I'm not as cruel as you think. It was a necessary evil bringing you here on the sly. And as for secrets? The whole town knows you're sleeping with the police chief. *Dieu*, he's a handsome one. Now let's get serious. You're going to tell me what was on that list. Line by line."

A snap of a fingernail against the plastic syringe brought Amelie's attention up and to the left. She met the woman's gray irises. She didn't know what the drug would do to her. It was supposed to relax a person's inhibitions and even make them suggestible. But would that also unlock the things she stored in her brain? Things she was normally only able to release by writing them down? A physical action that worked as a sort of dictation machine from brain to hand to page.

"I don't think it'll work," Amelie said as firmly as she could.

By all means, she'd like to stay alive. And if retaining the list in her brain could do that for her, then she would talk her way around it until they were both shivering from the cold.

Where was Jason? Could she hope he'd sense something was wrong and find her? The town was small, but as the woman had said, there were many abandoned buildings and houses. Too many for Jason to go through one by one, and in the storm.

How long had she been out? He must have missed her by now.

"I have to actually write out the information," she tried. "Which means I'll need paper, a pen and probably a whole pot of black coffee."

"That's not the way this is going down." The woman's grip on her arm felt like an ice princess personified.

Amelie struggled. She was basically free, save for her left arm being tied down to the chair arm.

"Sit still or this needle will end up in your eye!"

A male voice alerted them both. "Leslie Cassel."

Both women stopped struggling. Amelie squinted to eye the man who stood near an open door, which let in bright light and snow flurries. He was not Jason. Yet she recognized him immediately.

"She's going to bring you down, Patron," the woman—Leslie—said. "We've been on to you for weeks." She stabbed the needle into Amelie's arm.

"Can't risk Interpol learning about my indiscretions," Jacques said.

A gunshot sounded. Leslie screamed. And Amelie grabbed for the syringe, still in her arm.

Chapter Twenty-Seven

Blood spattered Amelie's cheek. Leslie had been hit, and she'd dropped to the floor behind her. Had it been a kill shot? She did not groan, nor did Amelie hear her moving. But she wasn't in position to turn and assess with Jacques Patron standing thirty feet away with a pistol aimed at her.

She glanced at the syringe she'd dropped on the floor. The plunger had not been depressed. *Merci Dieu.*

"What the hell is going on?" she asked, more out of anger than fear, or even a desperation to make conversation and delay the man's likely goal of shooting her. Out the corner of her eye, she spied Leslie's pistol that lay two feet away on the wood plank.

"Doesn't matter, does it?" Jacques had a calm manner to his speech when he spoke French. An affectation that had once reassured her. Now it made the hairs on the back of her neck stand upright. "I hired an idiot to do a job I should have taken care of in Lyon."

Jason had been right. Jacques had been protecting himself all along. Amelie's stomach performed a squeeze, and her heart dropped. Why Jacques was hesitating was beyond her. He was a skilled operative who had never paused to pull the trigger when called for.

"You don't want to kill me," she said calmly. "If you

did, you would have done so, as you've said, right away in Lyon. Is it because you don't have the list?"

"Oh, I know what's on that list. I thought I could make it go away by sending you away. After all, you are Vincent's daughter. We were friends. But then I got smart."

"I still don't know what's going on, Jacques. And if you think about it, that means you are the only one with all the facts. You can trust me. Let me walk away from this."

"You may not know." He redirected his aim toward the floor near her feet. "But they do." He fired again.

Behind her on the floor, Leslie yelped and cursed.

In the commotion, Amelie grabbed the gun from the table. She stood. Her left wrist was still bound to the chair, but she could take aim and defend herself.

She heard Leslie's body shift on the concrete floor, as if she were dragging herself.

Jacques laughed and splayed his hands up near his shoulders, the gun barrel pointing toward the ceiling. "Go ahead, Desauliniers! Take your best shot!"

Never had mockery cut her so deeply. Because he knew…

"Tell me why you did this," she insisted. Her aim targeted the man's heart. "What do I know?"

"He's been taking hush money from the mafia…" Leslie said from the floor. "They're running guns through the Superior Lakes. Patron is their French connection. You're our only proof… Amelie…" Leslie gasped. Coughed. "What's…in your…head. A list with links to security videos showing Jacques accepting payoffs."

How did she know so much? And she knew her real name. And Jacques. Apparently, she was investigating him. And had tracked his connection to Yvette here to Minnesota…

"She's with…" Amelie quickly did the math. Jason had mentioned the man they had behind bars was an Interpol agent. He must have had a partner. "Interpol. Because you know her," she said to Jacques. "You called her by name. And she didn't kill me because they need me to—" Jacques took aim at the floor again. "No!"

Another bullet fired. With a hard bite on her lower lip, Amelie realized she hadn't fired the gun she still held in defense. Not even to protect Leslie.

No sounds from behind her this time. Had he killed her?

Amelie stretched out her arm, willing herself to pull the trigger. Yet a tear threatened at the corner of her eye. He'd killed Leslie. The man had lied to her. Had used her. And had sent a hit man after her. The same killer who had murdered an innocent woman. And now Jacques was here to finish the botched job.

Her fingers clutched the weapon surely. Why couldn't she pull the trigger?

Images of her mother flashed before her. She hadn't told Jason the entire truth. Scared and wanting to know if her mother was all right, Amelie had sneaked out and into the living room, crawling behind the sofa. The man who had entered hadn't noticed her. And she'd seen her mother. Kneeling on the floor, head up and pleading with the stranger who Amelie could never see or reconstruct in her memories.

Amelie's life had never been the same because someone had pulled the trigger and ended her mother's life.

She never wanted another daughter or son to know the loss of a parent. No matter their crimes.

Jacques's chuckle was unnerving. The man was unhinged. If he had been taking bribes and had sent a hit man after her, then he deserved to die. And yet, Amelie wanted him to pay for his crimes. Most importantly, for the innocent woman who had died by mistake, and for killing the woman lying on the floor behind her.

"I'm waiting," Jacques cajoled with a tormenting tease

to his tone. "You can't do it. You father would be very disappointed in you, Amelie. You couldn't cut it as a field agent because you couldn't pull the trigger. What makes you think you can do it now?"

She didn't want him to be right. But—what was wrong with her? All she had to do was pull the trigger. She had been an ace aim in training. She didn't have to kill him. She could aim for his shoulder so he'd drop his weapon, and then send another bullet into his thigh to incapacitate him.

Yes, she could do that. Maybe?

Jacques shook his head and tutted as if she was a child. "Just like your mother. On her knees and unable to defend herself when the stakes were at their highest."

"My mother was assassinated," Amelie yelled in English. She didn't want to play nice with the man anymore. "Wait. How could you know she was on her knees?"

Jacques's smirk curdled Amelie's blood.

"No," she said with a gasp. "You?"

He shrugged and nodded, before saying in English, "She was a liability to your father's work."

"You bastard!" The gun suddenly felt three times heavier. It slipped in her grasp.

And Jacques chuckled. "You can't pull the trigger!"

"She doesn't need to," called out another male voice. "Because I can."

Chapter Twenty-Eight

The target turned toward Jason.

Jason had heard him talking to Yvette. It was Jacques Patron. Very much alive. And that man intended to kill his own agent. He wasn't sure if the woman on the floor was dead. Or what had gone down in the conversation that had all been in French, save the last few lines. But it all stopped now.

He'd panicked when Yvette had not returned to the station. He'd raced to Olson's Oasis, and Colette had said she'd seen her stop in at The Moose. There, the waitress had told him about the unfamiliar woman with the great hairstyle and how she'd followed Yvette into the bathroom. It had been easy enough to follow the trail of a woman's boot prints—deeper in the fresh-fallen snow because she'd been carrying a load—and to the tracks that had led toward the south end of Frost Falls, where a string of abandoned shops and businesses had sat empty for years.

As Patron raised his arm to fire off a shot, Jason squeezed the trigger. No waiting. No pausing to allow the villain his "this is why I did it" speech. Just take him out, efficiently and quickly. No foreign double agents to redirect his focus. But Patron was damn well going to live to answer for the crimes he had committed against his agency and Yvette.

Jacques yelped and clutched his thigh with his gun hand. Not a direct hit on the femoral artery. Jason didn't want him to bleed out. But a painful strike that should lodge in bone.

Another shot landed in Patron's shoulder. The bullet entering muscle and bone brought him to his knees. Still, he held the gun. And managed to fire. The shot went high, pinging a steel ceiling rafter.

This time, Jason aimed, breathed in—and on his out breath he squeezed the trigger. The bullet pinged Patron's gun, sending it flying from his grasp to land spinning on the floor six feet away.

With the hostile disarmed, Jason ran forward and kicked the gun he'd wielded toward the wall. Out of his peripheral vision, he saw Yvette struggle with the leather strap binding her wrist.

He rushed to help her. "Are you okay?"

She nodded. "Check Leslie. The woman on the floor. You didn't kill him."

"Didn't need to. Don't want to." Jason tugged out his cell phone and hit a speed-dial number. "Alex."

"Yes, Cash?"

"You locate Bay?"

"You betcha. We're waiting for orders. The CIA agent is wondering where you've gotten to."

Jason had told the agent he had to run out to his truck for something and to make himself at home in his office. He could have used him for backup, but—hell, he'd needed to move, and fast.

"I found the perp, Alex. Come to the old Reynolds Repair garage south of town."

"Will do, Cash."

Seeing the strap about Yvette's wrist was actually a thin leather belt, Jason helped her get out of the clasp. She gripped his forearms as if to steady herself.

"You sit," he said. "Take the gun." He nodded toward

the pistol on the plank. "Keep an eye on Patron. Can you do that?"

She nodded. She was flustered, but he had confidence she could hold a gun on her boss. Another bullet wasn't required to subdue him. Yvette could maintain her innate need to not harm another human being. No matter what the man had done to her.

Jason bent to inspect the woman on the floor. A bullet had nicked the side of her neck, and she was bleeding profusely. Her eyelids fluttered.

"She's alive." He tugged out his phone again and dialed. "Alex, get an ambulance on the road as well. Call Ely. Bob Hagar drives the ambulance. He can navigate this storm like Rudolph through a whiteout."

"On it, Cash."

The woman had taken a bullet to her shin as well as the thigh. With some field triage, Jason could keep her stable. Shedding his coat, he unbuttoned his flannel shirt and pulled it off. He needed to put pressure on her neck so she didn't bleed out.

The woman's eyes fluttered. Briefly focusing on his bare skin, she said, "Nice."

With a smirk and a shiver now that his bared chest had taken on the chill, Jason pressed the shirt against her neck.

Over his shoulder, he saw Patron topple in a faint.

Yvette took that cue to join Jason's side. "Is she going to be okay? Her name is Leslie Cassel."

"Should be. Did she kidnap you?"

"Yes, but she's on my side. Interpol has been following Jacques for weeks. They needed the information in my brain to implicate him for taking bribes from a gunrunning operation moving through Lake Superior."

"Figured it was something like payouts," he said to Yvette. "Might have been his reason for sending you here. He had contacts in the area. Minnesota mafia."

"It makes too much sense now. And Interpol didn't call me in because they must have had no idea where to find me until recently. Jacques kept my location a secret."

She blew out a breath, and her body tilted against his. She was exhausted and probably didn't realize she'd leaned on him. Jason hugged her about the waist and bowed his head to hers. The moment was bittersweet, but he intended to remember only the sweetness of her body against his. "I couldn't pull the trigger, Jason."

"Because you're a good person, Amelie. Don't feel bad for that."

"But it's my job."

"It was your job. Now your job is to make sure Jacques Patron pays for his crimes."

"I can do that. I will do that. Now tell me how to help. Unless it involves getting half-naked?"

He chuckled and pulled on his coat and zipped it up. "That was a good shirt," he said. He switched positions with her, leaving her to triage. "Watch her. I'm going to take care of Patron."

He cuffed the man, who struggled, despite what had to be painful injuries.

"Got 'em," Jason said, feeling satisfaction for a job well done. "And without the CIA's interference."

They would assume control of the case from here. And take credit for it all.

Didn't matter. Jason had gotten to Amelie before Patron could harm her. He wished he could have found her sooner, so he could have protected Leslie. This case had gotten him scrambling, and all had ended well.

With the suspect in hand.

"You saved me," she said from across the room. "I knew you would."

Jason caught her smile. It made the stormy day feel like springtime.

Epilogue

Days later...

Jason and Amelie stood beside the hospital bed where Leslie Cassel lay, recovering from the gunshot wounds. The damage had landed within centimeters of her artery, but fortune had not wanted her to die. She was eager to return to France and her job as soon as she could.

"I apologize for jumping the gun," she said to Amelie.

"I don't understand." Amelie moved closer while Jason clasped her hand. He'd taken to holding her hand lately. A lot. And she loved every single clasp.

"I won't apologize for kidnapping you. That was part of the job." Leslie smirked. "You know how we need to be covert for the integrity of an operation. But I should have waited. Lund was in jail..." She gave Jason a sharp glance.

Jason put up his hands. "I had no idea the guy was Interpol until a few hours before you took off with Yvette. Amelie." He gave her a wink. "I suspected he was another inept hit man. And really, for a trained agent, he should have known how to handle a snowmobile much better. I saved him from a plunge over a frozen falls."

"He told me that." Leslie smiled. Rutger Lund had been released immediately after Interpol had verified their agents had been sent to Frost Falls to extract the information from

Amelie so they could make the case on Patron. He'd stopped in to visit Leslie before flying out of the country. "But I panicked. It was supposed to be a two-man operation. Pick up Amelie Desauliniers. Extract the information from her head. Send her to a safe house. We couldn't let you know we were from Interpol, Amelie, because we weren't sure if you were colluding with Patron."

"How did you finally decide I was not?"

"I didn't know for sure until the moment he faced you down in the repair shop."

"Nothing like coming down to the wire," Jason said. "Patron has been arrested."

"Yes, that's good," Leslie said. "But we never did get the information. And I'm sorry, Amelie, that things could have gone so wrong in that garage when Patron showed up. I thought I could handle it myself, but I needed backup."

"Apology accepted," Amelie said. "I know what it's like in the field and second-guessing your own judgment." She dug into her pocket and pulled out a piece of notebook paper to hand to Leslie. "Here's the list you wanted. But don't worry. I've already sent copies to the director at Interpol. Enough damning evidence to prove Jacques Patron was taking bribes from a gunrunner connected to the Minnesota mafia. And we've recovered the links from the original email, which lead to CCTV videos showing the handoffs in various major European cities."

Leslie folded the paper and closed her eyes. Pale winter sunlight beamed across her face. "Thank you. Are you going to be all right?"

Amelie nodded noncommittally. "I've already spoken to the director about the incident and have been debriefed. It's been suggested I remain in data tech, but I'm not so sure anymore."

"Don't let this scare you away," Leslie said. "You joined this organization for a purpose, yes?"

"I did. But that purpose may have been misdirected. It might have been more of a fearful reaction to a past event that made me follow in my father's footsteps. I'm going to give returning to Interpol some thought." Amelie looked to Jason, who squeezed her hand.

And Leslie also looked to Jason before smiling at Amelie. "I get it. This weather sucks. But the scenery..." She shook her head appreciatively. "I hear there's a calendar a girl should look at?"

"I think I know where to find you a copy," Amelie said. "We'll leave you to rest."

The twosome left as health services wheeled in a savory-smelling lunch. As they entered the chill outside air and walked toward Jason's truck, Amelie felt that what she'd told Leslie was the truth. She did need time to think about the job she'd always thought was the right fit for her. But it wasn't anymore. She had a misbalanced pros and cons list to prove that.

She'd been granted another week's leave before she was expected to report for duty. And she'd take it.

Jason opened the passenger door for her and helped her up inside his truck. Once seated, she reached for the door, but instead, Jason stepped up onto the side runner and leaned inside the cab to kiss her.

Even with the wind brisking her cheeks and bare hands with an icy chill, the heat they generated when their lips touched warmed her whole body. Amelie pulled him closer, and he leaned inside, reaching to embrace her about the waist as he deepened the kiss.

Leaving this man would be a challenge. But who said it had to happen right away? Or even... Dare she consider it?

When he broke the kiss, Jason bowed his forehead to hers, and for a while they simply shared the intense silence. Finally, he said, "Amelie. I love that name. I'll never forget that name."

Her heart did a flip-flop.

"I know you don't belong here," he said. "But maybe you could stay awhile longer?"

He wanted her to stay? Yes! "I do have a week leave. What if I extended my vacation here?"

"You'd do that?"

"I've been changed by my service with Interpol, Jason. I need to think of what it is I really want. Am I doing it because my parents were in it? Was it a fearful reaction to watching my mother get killed?"

He kissed her forehead. "Questions that only you can answer."

"What about you? Is the station still closing?"

"Probably. The CIA tossed me a freebie, though, and didn't step in on the case as I suspected they would. I got the credit for this one. And the sheriff's department called me this morning to offer me a position in Ely. I'm considering it."

"Is Ely another small town like this one?"

"A bit bigger." Seeing her frown, he added encouragingly, "They've got tourist attractions. And the wolf center."

"Wow. Exciting times abound here. But still cold, right?"

"Still cold." He leaned in, nuzzling a kiss at the base of her ear, then whispered, "If you stay awhile longer, I'll keep you warm."

"That's an offer I won't refuse."

* * * * *

COMING SOON!

We really hope you enjoyed reading this book. If you're looking for more romance, be sure to head to the shops when new books are available on

Thursday 7th March

To see which titles are coming soon, please visit

millsandboon.co.uk/nextmonth

a name," Ray said to her. "Zuger